WELCOME TO THE LEGEND OF THE FIVE RINGS!

You are about to enter Rokugan, a land of honorable samurai, mighty dragons, powerful magics, arcane monks, cunning ninja, and twisted demons from the Shadowlands. Based on the mythic tales of Japan, China, and Korea, Rokugan is a vast empire, a unique world of fantastic adventure.

Enjoy your stay in Rokugan, a place where heroes walk with gods, where a daimyo's mighty army can be thwarted by a simple word whispered into the right ear, and where honor truly is more powerful than steel.

Legend of the Five Rings

Books

THE SCORPION
Stephen D. Sullivan

THE UNICORN
A. L. Lassieur

THE CRANE
Ree Soesbee

THE PHOENIX
Stephen D. Sullivan

THE CRAB
Stan Brown

THE DRAGON
Ree Soesbee

THE LION
Stephen D. Sullivan

Legend of the Five Rings

THE LION

STEPHEN D. SULLIVAN

Clan War
Seventh Scroll

THE LION
©2001 Wizards of the Coast, Inc.

All characters in this book are fictitious. Any resemblance to actual persons, living or dead, is purely coincidental.

This book is protected under the copyright laws of the United States of America. Any reproduction or unauthorized use of the material or artwork contained herein is prohibited without the express written permission of Wizards of the Coast, Inc.

Distributed in the United States by Holtzbrinck Publishing, Inc. Distributed in Canada by Fenn Ltd.

Distributed to the hobby, toy, and comic trade in the United States and Canada by regional distributors.

Distributed worldwide by Wizards of the Coast, Inc., and regional distributors.

The Wizards of the Coast logo is a registered trademark owned by Wizards of the Coast, Inc., a subsidiary of Hasbro, Inc. LEGEND OF THE FIVE RINGS is a trademark owned by Wizards of the Coast, Inc.

All Wizards of the Coast characters, character names, and the distinctive likenesses thereof are trademarks owned by Wizards of the Coast, Inc.

Made in the U.S.A.

The sale of this book without its cover has not been authorized by the publisher. If you purchased this book without a cover, you should be aware that neither the author nor the publisher has received payment for this "stripped book."

Cover art by r. k. post.
Map by Dennis Kauth.
First Printing: November 2001
Library of Congress Catalog Card Number: 00-191038

9 8 7 6 5 4 3 2 1

ISBN: 0-7869-1904-3
620-T21904

U.S., CANADA,
ASIA PACIFIC & LATIN AMERICA
Wizards of the Coast, Inc.
P.O. Box 707
Renton, WA 98057-0707
+1-800-324-6496

EUROPEAN HEADQUARTERS
Wizards of the Coast, Belgium
P.B. 2031
2600 Berchem
Belgium
+32-70-23-32-77

Visit our web site at **www.wizards.com/fiverings**

*To my wife, Kifflie Helen Scott,
for over twenty years of love and support.
I'm a better man, father, and author
because of you. Thank you, darling.*

Acknowledgments

Thanks to the many fans who have enjoyed and supported my work on this project. Your kind wishes have meant a lot to me. Thanks also to the L5R crew—Ree, Steve, Luke, Ed, et al.—for your help and enthusiasm.

Special thanks, again, to Ed Henderson for being my resource on all matters oriental. As always, anything I've gotten wrong is my fault, not his.

Finally, my deepest and most sincere thanks to J. Robert King for his help and guidance during this entire series. An author could not wish for a better editor.

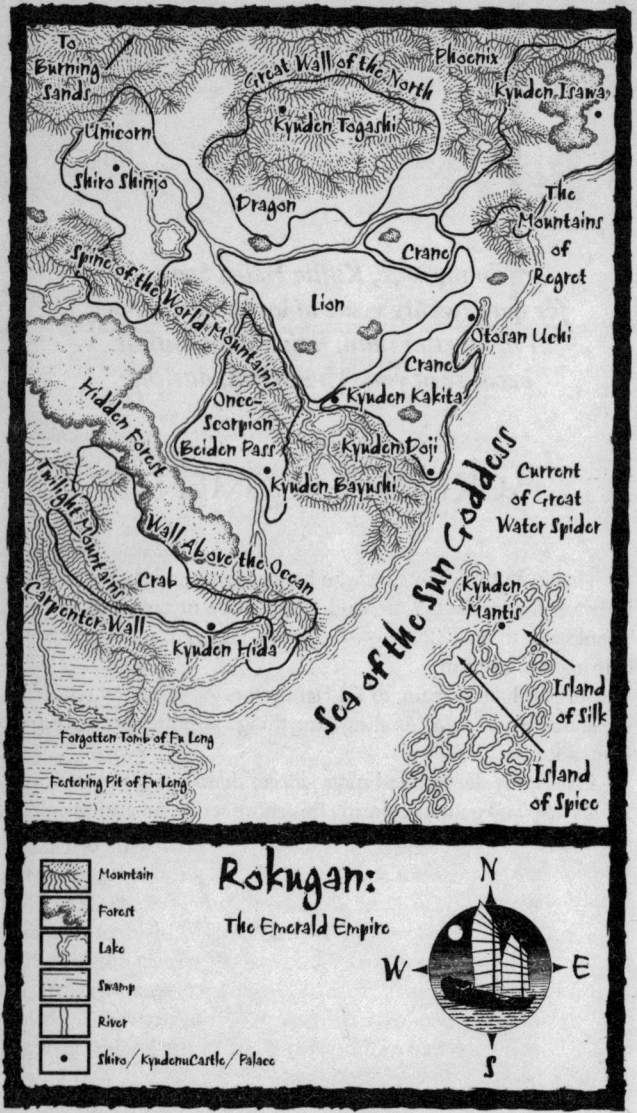

PROLOGUE: THE LION'S ANGER

Matsu Tsuko removed her diademlike helmet and shook her pale golden hair free from the headpiece. The last light of the setting sun caught the samurai maiden's armored form and painted her outline a fiery red. "See that I'm not disturbed," she growled, her dark eyes holding her commander, Matsu Yojo, in their icy grip. "If Shiba Tsukune or Toturi himself comes riding into camp, let me know. Otherwise . . ." She let the threat hang in the air like a keen-bladed tanto.

Yojo, a clean-shaven man with black hair and a red-maned helmet, nodded and bowed respectfully to his daimyo. "What about Doji Hoturi?" he asked. "He and his demon-spawn troops won't like what we've been doing to their Crane cousins." Tsuko's commander cast his eyes over the rutted, corpse-strewn field below the foothills. Not many of the bodies belonged to the Lion Clan.

"At last report, Hoturi was headed for the

Crane capital," Tsuko replied, pulling off her bloodstained arm guards and tossing them to the ground. "That makes him Matsu Agetoki's problem. However, my spies inform me that Tsukune is lurking around here somewhere. I'll find that Phoenix witch and kill her." The Lion daimyo's brown eyes narrowed, and she spat to show her contempt for Tsukune, Tsukune's Phoenix troops, and their Crane allies. "If Tsukune's *not* nearby, my informants will be looking for their heads next time I see them."

Yojo nodded, acknowledging his daimyo's blood feud against Tsukune; as a samurai, he was bound to follow her, no matter where she led. "Can Agetoki-san handle both the Crane daimyo and the Doji castle's defenders?" he asked.

Tsuko smiled fiercely at her young charge. "Agetoki's a *Lion*. Of course he can handle the Crane. Hoturi's not even a cub compared to my general. If Agetoki needs help, he'll send word. But to kill a few more Crane . . . ? Ha!" She scanned the gore-spattered plains at the base of the ridge and smiled. After she and her troops passed the Crane frontier, the Daidoji hadn't put up much of a fight—at least not by Lion standards. "Have the eta clean this place up while I'm gone," she commanded, waving her crimson-stained hand at the field.

Yojo nodded. "Hai, Tsuko-sama."

"And remember, anyone who disturbs me will be meeting his ancestors before morning." She turned her back on Matsu Yojo and hiked up the ridge, stripping off her blood-covered armor as she went.

Yojo bowed curtly and turned quickly away. Tsuko was an attractive woman, but to let his eyes linger upon her would have meant his death. He hurried back downhill toward the rest of the Lion encampment, lying just beyond the battlefield.

Tsuko walked over the top of the hill, unfastening the knots and hasps that held her elaborate armor together. She cast aside first her sode shoulder guards and then her golden throat protector and breastplate. Her metal kusazuri skirt and suneate shin guards followed. She would pick them all up later, of course, but for now she just wanted to breathe and exercise her cramped muscles.

Holding a sheathed sword in each hand, the Lion daimyo stretched wide her arms and reached toward the snow-topped mountains in the distance. The Spine of the World, they were fittingly called. Tsuko envied their strength and serenity.

"I am Matsu Tsuko!" she cried to the stony, ancient range. "Today I slaughtered my enemies in honorable battle, neither giving quarter nor expecting any." The remote peaks echoed their approval. Tsuko smiled.

Before her, atop the ridge, lay a wide, indigo pool ringed by low cryptomeria trees and scrub pines. A hoary willow sprawled beside the water, its fat roots drinking deeply of the shadowy liquid. The willow's leaves had long since departed, though the fronds still dangled from the branches like the hair of a wrinkled crone. A subtle breeze caught the thin trailers and whispered through them. The short reeds at the water's edge had gone brown with autumn and limp with the ravages of the weather. They, too, murmured in the wind.

By the water's edge, Tsuko carefully set down her daisho, the paired swords of a samurai. She sat and stripped off her golden-brown kimono. The silk was damp with her sweat and stiff where the blood of her enemies had seeped through the joints in her armor. She took a few moments to wash out the stains and then hung the robe on a denuded mulberry bush to dry, careful not to tear the fabric on the leafless branches.

The late fall air was cool and raised goose bumps on her tanned flesh. Tsuko stood and stretched again, yawning like a great cat. She gazed down her lean, well-muscled body. The many scars on her tanned skin traced a map of her life, telling of a battle-filled journey. The drying blood of her freshly killed enemies accentuated the tale, boasting of her victories along life's road.

Nude, Matsu Tsuko waded slowly into the pond, savoring the chill touch on her skin. She dipped her hands into the cold water and began to scrub away the sweat and dust of battle. Blood streamed down the Lion's muscular arms and washed off her hands in long crimson rivulets. Tsuko watched the gore dissipate into the clear, dark liquid, feeling the tension slip out of her knotted limbs at the same time.

She dived under the surface, letting the icy waters embrace her. It was the only kind of embrace that she'd allowed herself since the death of her fiancé, Akodo Arasou—many years ago, now. Arasou had been her equal in skill and temperament. He was the only one worthy to be her mate. The Crane had killed Arasou—taken him from her, and she would make them pay. Even the Crane blood she and her armies had spilled in recent months wasn't enough to wash the memory away. Not nearly enough.

Tsuko surfaced and shook her head. Fine droplets of water flew from her long, pale golden mane and danced in the twilight air. She took a deep breath; the cold squeezed tiny needles into her chest. She savored the pain and scrubbed her face with the chill water.

From somewhere far away, she scented the smoke of war. The aroma sent a thrilling shiver down her spine and made the downy hairs on the backs of her arms stand up. Perhaps it was the smell of Agetoki burning the Doji capital.

Arasou, we still fight for you, Tsuko thought. We will *always* fight for you.

The memory of her dead love stuck in Tsuko's mind like cold steel, bringing with it images of Arasou's brother, Akodo Toturi. Toturi. The Black Lion, they called him now. He'd been called other things previously: monk, daimyo, traitor, and—for a short time—emperor. No matter what they called him, though, he was still ronin, a mercenary sell-sword without clan or honor. His acts had stripped all the Akodo of their name—even Tsuko's late fiancé. The house of Akodo no longer existed in the Lion Clan, and it was Toturi's fault. All his fault. Tsuko would hate him forever for that, even if there were nothing else to despise him for. Toturi's sins, however, were legion: shirking his duties as the empire's general, consorting with geisha, failing to protect Hantei the 38th from assassination, assuming the sundered throne just to satisfy his own ego....

Tsuko snarled and spat out her rage. She dipped her hands into the icy water and scrubbed her face again but couldn't wash the memories away.

Turning, she dived into the water once more. The cold

darkness surrounded her, pressing in, threatening to engulf her. Tsuko kicked through the chill, swimming with long, powerful strokes, diving deeper into the inky pool.

Something brushed her leg.

At first, the Lion daimyo thought it only a weed, or perhaps a decaying tree branch. The second time it touched her, though, she felt the rough scales of a body as cold as the water itself. The thing sought out her warmth, wrapping itself around first her right ankle, then her calf.

Tsuko turned, but saw nothing in the darkness. Still, the clinging menace wound up her naked body. The samurai maiden shot for the surface, fighting both the icy water and her unseen foe. Her head bobbed up, and she gasped in sweet air. She tried to swim toward shore, but the coiling, scaly thing wrapped around her other ankle as well, hobbling her.

She paddled forward, sputtering, her head dipping underwater with every stroke. She didn't dare to glance back but, instead, set her eyes on the shore. It was farther away than she had hoped. She focused her will on it and paddled determinedly with her arms while simultaneously trying to kick her legs free of the cold grasp.

Slowly, the shoreline drew closer. As it did, the tightness around Tsuko's legs increased. Now, both limbs were held nearly immobile. Almost to the shore, she stole a look back.

Behind her, the surface of the pool roiled in the gathering darkness. The silhouettes of the mountains jutted upward, jagged teeth in the shadowy maw of night. Her foe remained hidden beneath the black water. Could this be some sorcerous trap laid by the Phoenix?

With a sudden lash, the creature pulled her under.

The Lion daimyo struggled for air but couldn't get her face above water. Her feet touched the muddy bottom of the pond as the serpentine thing wound farther up her body, past her hips to her waist, squeezing all the while. Tsuko kicked out, pushing with her feet and launching herself out of the water and back toward the shore.

She splashed down hard onto her stomach. The water was

shallow but rose to her belly and back. In the dim light of the rising moon, she finally glimpsed her foe.

It was a monstrous black serpent, its ugly head crowned with thorny spikes. The thing's murderous red eyes gleamed in the darkness, sparking with evil sorcery. Magic. Yes. The work of Tsukune's people. The Phoenix had left behind this trap for her. The snake wound its ebony coils around the Lion and tried to pull her back into the deep water. Tsuko's body jerked, and her head went under again.

Fortunately, Tsuko's arms hadn't been caught yet. As the monster tried to squeeze the life out of her, she used her hands to push off the bottom and thrust herself to the surface once more. The water was only hip deep here, but the serpent could drown her in it, nonetheless. Tsuko struggled to regain her feet. She seized the snake's body in her steely grip and loosened its hold on her legs.

With a final titanic effort, Tsuko stood. She rose shivering, the pond still covering her from the hips down. Long rivulets of water dripped from her pale hair and tanned body. Her lungs ached and heaved in the chilly air.

The black serpent constricted, and the Lion daimyo nearly tumbled back into the dark waters. She looked to the shore, scant paces away. Withered reeds grew nearby, but she doubted any were strong enough to help her clamber out of the snake's grasp. Her ivory-handled swords lay well out of reach. The cold, scaly body wound around her like a monstrous noose. She had to fight hard just to stay erect.

Suddenly, the serpent's head rose from the shallows and struck at her. Tsuko ducked. The acid spray of the monster's breath burned across her naked shoulder. The snake tried to recoil on her and strike again, but she seized it behind the eyes and pushed its head back under the water.

The snake's body squeezed tighter. Tsuko's muscles and bones screamed with pain. Spots of light flashed before her eyes as her breath rushed out. She staggered, dropping to her knees in the icy liquid. The snake wriggled free of her grasp, and its head broke water again, this time coming straight for the Lion's face.

Tsuko's reflexes saved her. Instinctively, she brought up her hands and grabbed the monster's neck. The creature's powerful jaws snapped shut a finger's width from the Lion daimyo's face. Serrated teeth clashed in the wicked mouth, and caustic spittle sprayed on her cheek. The serpent squeezed its mighty coils.

Narrowing her eyes, Tsuko squeezed back. She tightened the iron thews of her fingers around the monster's throat. The muscles in her body burned as the snake bruised them. Tsuko's senses swam, but she merely squeezed harder.

Just when she feared she would black out, the Lion daimyo felt something pop behind the serpent's skull. The monster's airway collapsed. Tsuko dug her ragged fingernails into its neck. Black blood oozed out of the hideous snake's eyes and nose and dripped down the samurai's fingers. Tsuko's lips pulled back in a grim smile.

The coils loosened, and Tsuko staggered out of the water. Only when she reached the shore did she relax her iron grip. The snake's limp, scaly body fell onto the withered grass. Tsuko looked at it and then at the black blood on her hands. She frowned.

She had been mistaken; the snake wasn't the work of her Phoenix enemy. The dim light of the moon revealed the Shadowlands taint running through the creature's scales. The disease shone with a sickly green light. Tsukune and her Phoenix didn't use such vile enchantments. The monster belonged to an army that menaced all the world; it was a minion of the undead god Fu Leng.

Tsuko had heard reports of such monsters here, close to the heart of Rokugan, but this was the first time she'd seen one herself. Its presence didn't bode well for the empire's battle against the darkness. The Lion ground her teeth at the thought that she'd mistaken one enemy for another. She couldn't afford such lapses.

"Damn all sorcerers anyway, alive and undead!" Tsuko hissed. She gazed around the pool, her brown eyes plumbing the twilit depths—but she saw no more foes. She knelt on the shore, dipped her hands into the cold water, and washed the blood off. She'd done the same many times during her career as a samurai. The hand washing was a familiar ritual to the Lion daimyo, perhaps more familiar than the tea ceremony.

Tsuko frowned again. In the dim light, the blood and the indigo water looked the same.

1 FORTUNES OF WAR

Cursing, Tsuko rose and donned her kimono once more. The silk was still damp from washing. It clung to her muscular form, and made goose bumps rise on her tanned flesh. Tsuko ignored the chill. She'd faced worse in battle many times. She retrieved her ivory-handled swords and tucked them into her obi. Making her way back downhill, she picked up her armor as she walked.

The fires of the Lion encampment burned warmly below her. A rising moon silhouetted dark tents and pavilions in the foothills. Matsu Tsuko smiled. Combat was thrilling, and victory its own reward, but the life of a true warrior was often a lonely one. It would feel good to join her comrades and celebrate victory. Tsuko looked forward to sitting by the fire and drinking sake. Her samurai would recount tales of today's battle against the Crane. Then she'd tell them of her struggle alone against the Shadowlands monster in the pond. As she walked, she donned her headdress and adjusted her hair into a pleasing fall.

Noticing what she had done, she silently upbraided herself. She was not some maiden trying to look her best for suitors; she was daimyo of the Lion—supreme commander of the strongest armies in Rokugan. She shook her head to ruffle her mane and smiled grimly when the action had the desired effect.

She stepped into the camp; several sentries bowed low as she passed. No one spoke to her. Her samurai knew enough to leave their mistress alone if she didn't speak to them first. Tsuko's temper was legendary among her troops, and more than one warrior's head had rolled for an impertinent remark to the daimyo. Tsuko stopped and motioned to two nearby samurai-ko. The women came and quickly helped their ruler don the rest of her armor. Adjusting the final straps herself, the Lion dismissed them and returned to her walk.

Her keen eyes sought out Matsu Yojo and found him sitting by the largest fire. Yojo and the other samurai with him rose to bow as Tsuko arrived. A young samurai-ko rolled a wide log to the fireside to serve as the daimyo's chair, and Tsuko seated herself on it. The Lion daimyo nodded at the girl; the samurai-ko bowed and scurried off into the darkness.

Yojo handed his mistress a cup of sochu. When Tsuko downed the strong sake in one gulp, he handed her the jug. She put it to her lips, took a long drink, and smiled. "Good battle today," she said, her brown eyes wandering over the rough faces of the samurai gathered around the fire.

The others grunted their assent and chuckled. "The Daidoji run like rabbits," one man said.

"And they fight about as well," added another.

"And they die just as bravely," said a third.

The samurai around the fire laughed, as did Tsuko. She took another drink of sochu.

Matsu Gohei emerged into the firelight. Gohei was a square-faced man with a pointed mustache and narrow eyes. His chestnut-colored armor looked red in the firelight. Its gold decorations glimmered in the darkness. He carried a yari, a straight spear slightly longer than he was tall. Once, the Lion general had been a mere bushi—a simple country warrior. During those times, he wielded a pitchfork as a weapon. Despite his lofty position, Gohei still preferred the yari to the traditional katana of the samurai. Most of the time, Gohei's daisho swords remained tucked securely into his belt.

Gohei bowed, laid down his weapon, and knelt before Matsu Tsuko. "Tsuko-sama," he said, "our sentries report that Matsu Agetoki has ridden into camp."

"What?" Tsuko asked, rising to her feet in disbelief. Anger danced across her firelit face.

Gohei nodded. "Hai. It's true. Our scouts say that his army is crossing the plains to our position, not far behind their general."

Tsuko stalked circles around the fire. "How can this be?" she growled. "If he took the Doji castle, he should still be there. If he didn't, he should either be waiting near the castle for my orders, or be dead." The Lion daimyo stopped pacing, turned to Gohei, and said, "Bring him to my pavilion immediately."

Gohei bowed, rose, and hurried off into the night.

Tsuko turned and strode purposefully to her tent. She couldn't imagine any reason why Agetoki would be here. For the Lion to desert a battlefield—even after a devastating loss—was nearly unthinkable. In either defeat or victory, he should have sent a messenger to Tsuko, not come himself. Could his courage have failed him? Could Doji Hoturi have broken the Lion's siege of the castle and driven her troops from the field? Tsuko could hardly conceive of it.

She poured herself a drink from a jar of sochu in a chest near her tent's doorway. She had hardly touched the drink to her lips when Matsu Gohei entered through the flaps.

He bowed. "Matsu Agetoki," Gohei said, and stepped aside.

Agetoki, a huge, burly man dressed in red armor emblazoned with the Lion Clan mon, strode proudly into the tent. He bowed respectfully to Tsuko and knelt before her on the floor.

Tsuko seated herself on a low stool on the far side of the tent.

"Tsuko-sama," Agetoki said, his gruff voice booming. He bowed again.

"Agetoki," Tsuko said, "why are you here? Why have you brought your army? Why are you not slaying the Crane at Kyuden Doji?"

Agetoki frowned, wrinkles of displeasure creasing his wide face and making his black mustache droop at the corners. "I have been ordered from the field."

"What?" Tsuko asked, rising to her feet. "I gave no such orders."

Agetoki nodded gravely. "I know, my daimyo," he said. "You would never give such a command. But the emperor . . ."

Tsuko's cold eyes narrowed. "Are you saying that the emperor ordered you to leave before the Crane castle fell?"

"Yes, my lady," Agetoki said.

"Are you telling me that our enemies still sit in their high towers, laughing at us?"

Agetoki shook his head. "No, my lady. Though the emperor ordered your army to leave the field, I doubt very much that the Crane are laughing."

"What do you mean?" Tsuko asked, arching one pale eyebrow. Anger and confusion warred in her. "Did we destroy Kyuden Doji or not?"

"We did not destroy the castle, Mistress—Doji Hoturi did."

"What? Explain yourself."

"Doji Hoturi rode into the battle with his army of undead and other abominations." Agetoki almost shuddered. "We thought they came to battle us and save the castle. Instead, they turned on Hoturi's own people. Just before the two forces met, we received an order from the emperor to stand aside and not interfere in the conflict. It burned my heart to do so."

"Did the emperor give these orders, or did Kachiko?" Tsuko scowled, thinking of the boy emperor's scheming wife. Kachiko had been a Scorpion before her new husband disbanded that clan of spies and assassins. Rumors insisted that she, and not the emperor, now held the true power of the Emerald Throne.

"I don't know, my daimyo," Agetoki said. He reached beneath his armor and withdrew a small scroll. Handing it to her, he said, "Here are the orders."

Tsuko took the silk and examined it. Nothing on its golden surface showed whether the order might come from the emperor or his conniving bride. Cursing, Tsuko cast the scroll into a corner of the tent.

Agetoki had brought her bad news before. It was he who told her of her friend Kitsu Koji's death at the hands of Shiba Tsukune. The recollection of that elusive Phoenix further nettled Tsuko. She kicked aside her stool and roared, stalking around the tent.

Agetoki knelt, impassive, before her.

To be defeated in fair combat as Koji had been was bad enough. To be ordered not to fight was a grave insult to Lion honor and pride. Still, with the emperor's seal on the scroll, what else could be done? Tsuko was the emperor's sword; she could never disobey him. Her honor in such matters was spotless. Impotent rage welled up in Tsuko's heart.

"A curse on the Scorpion and their schemes!" she spat.

Agetoki nodded. "I know, Mistress. It burns in my belly as well. But what else could I do?"

"Nothing," she said angrily. "The Lion fight for the emperor . . . always." Tsuko cursed silently for not having been at the battle. She upbraided herself for following a trail of petty revenge when she could have been assaulting the Crane capital personally. The Phoenix had merely slain her friend, while the Crane . . . ! The Crane had killed her fiancé and altered the course of the Lion's destiny.

Because of Arasou's death, Akodo Toturi had risen to become daimyo. Because Toturi was unworthy, he betrayed the office and besmirched the Lion's reputation. Because Toturi was lazy, Emperor Hantei the 38th had been slain and a boy now sat upon the throne. Because Toturi had tried to hold the throne for himself, the Akodo family had been stripped of their name.

Arasou, the only man Tsuko had ever loved, didn't even have a name anymore—all because of the Crane and Toturi. Tsuko hated them both with all her soul. The boy emperor should have killed Toturi rather than merely casting him out and making him ronin. Someday, Tsuko hoped to correct that error and slay the Black Lion herself.

She turned on Agetoki so suddenly that the burly general nearly jumped. "From now on," she said angrily, "*I* will be at the center of all Lion battles."

Agetoki shifted uncomfortably where he knelt. It looked for a moment as though he might say something. Instead, he merely bowed low, almost touching his head to the floor.

"You've done well enough, Agetoki," Tsuko said, realizing that she might have offended his honor, "and I thank you for your faithfulness. No man could have done more."

Agetoki sat up once more. "Had it not been the emperor," he said, "I would have died rather than leave the field."

She nodded grimly and folded her arms over her chest. "I know. Even I could have done no more."

"Perhaps it's not too late, my lady," Agetoki said. "We were ordered not to interfere, it's true, but once the battle is over . . ."

"Yes," Tsuko said quietly. "Once the battle is over, there will still be Crane left to fight."

"And they will be weaker now, Daimyo," he said.

"Yes," she replied. "And perhaps Shiba Tsukune will be among them."

"If Hoturi has not killed her," Agetoki said.

"If she's dead," Tsuko said thoughtfully, "there's still a Crane castle to take, and beyond that, a whole province."

"What about Hoturi?" Agetoki asked. "He's mad, and his legion of undead may be even more dangerous than the Crane."

"Doji Hoturi can burn his own cities to the ground for all I care. He's a Crane. There's no understanding him anyway. If he gets in my way, though, I'll kill him just as quickly as I'd kill any of our other enemies."

Agetoki smiled and nodded. "Yosh," he grunted.

"Gohei!" Tsuko bellowed. The yari-carrying general appeared in the doorway of the tent. "Take your samurai and help Ikoma Tsanuri's forces on the western frontier."

Gohei bowed. "Hai, Tsuko-sama."

The Lion daimyo continued. "Agetoki and I are returning to Kyuden Doji," she said. "We'll cut through whatever's left of these Crane like a sickle through dry wheat." A satisfied smile tugged at the corners of her lips.

The flickering light from a paper lantern in one corner of the tent caught Tsuko's face and, for a moment, the Lion daimyo's eyes burned red.

2 THE BLACK LION

"If a big tree falls in the forest, and there is no one around to hear it, who *cares* if it makes any sound?" asked Toku.

Toturi smiled at the young man riding beside him. Toku was hardly more than a boy—awkward, gangly-limbed, and lacking experience in both battle and the ways of the world. Yet, he made up for his inexperience with enthusiasm and nearly boundless energy. The ragtag armor the teen wore could hardly contain Toku's vitality. The young samurai spurred his shaggy mare to keep up with the ronin general's great warhorse.

Toturi, clad in black samurai mail from head to foot, reigned in slightly so that Toku could keep up. They rode at the head of a huge column of samurai. The army wound through the foothills of the Spine of the World Mountains, searching for enemies. Late autumn dappled the countryside in shades of orange, red, and brown.

Toturi's ebony armor shone in the midday

sun, and the chill wind tossed his long black mane into the air. Once, his hair had been golden, but that was before he lost his clan and his honor. Toturi was tall and lean, confident in his posture and gait. He had a handsome face, sparkling eyes, and a strong jaw.

Behind the proud body lurked a mind even more keen. No one in Rokugan could match Toturi in strategy and tactics. Perhaps the traitor Bayushi Shoju could have, but Shoju was dead, and Toturi had killed him. In the end, the Scorpion had been no match for Toturi in either wits or strength.

The Black Lion gazed down at his young friend. Toturi liked Toku and enjoyed his company. The boy was a fresh wind amid the world of stodgy, stoic samurai. He was even impertinent at times, but the ronin general seldom minded. Toturi envied the youth his freedom.

Once, I was like him, the Black Lion thought.

Indeed, had his brother not been killed, Toturi might have lived like Toku—wild and free in the natural world. Raised in a monastery, Toturi's temperament was suited to a simple life. But Akodo Arasou's death had thrust Toturi first into the ruling seat of the Lion and then into the bloody arena of Rokugani politics. His mistakes there had made him traitor, then emperor, then madman, then ronin . . . and finally lord of a great army of outcast samurai. Toturi had tasted the pinnacle of achievement and the depths of dishonor. Through it all, he remained determined to save the world from the Dark Lord Fu Leng, or die trying. The Black Lion's long-tarnished honor mattered little. His goal endured. He could not fight for the emperor, but he could still fight for the empire.

Toturi glanced at Toku and at the wild, hilly landscape surrounding them. He took a deep breath of the cold autumn air. "It's not a question of who cares," he said patiently. "The answer lies in seeking the truth. Is the world, Shinsei was asking, only real when we experience it—or does it go on without us?"

"I think it probably does," Toku said, "though I have no way of knowing for sure. Once I was away from a town for a year and discovered my favorite teahouse gone when I returned. I suppose the kami could have just stolen the teahouse in the middle of the night and taken it to heaven. Probably, though, somebody knocked it down. It was a pretty shabby place, really. But the tea was good."

Toturi chuckled, a rich, deep sound that echoed off of the surrounding hills. The ascetic's mantra ran through his head: Chop wood, carry water; live in the present; take one step at a time. "Shinsei suggests that we can never know, and so we should concentrate on where we are right now."

"I wish I had some of that tea right now," Toku said. "It's pretty cold up here."

"Winter's nearly upon us," Toturi replied. "Often it brings cold weather," he added, smiling.

Behind the two of them, the vast ronin army wound through the hills like a gigantic snake. Outriders and ashigaru foot soldiers beat the brush and forests on either side of the road, searching for Crab stragglers and other less savory foes. The Crab and their Shadowlands allies had been defeated at the Battle of Beiden Pass. Usually, defeated samurai would be left to roam the countryside, but Toturi was loath to abandon such marauders to their depredations.

As the Black Lion chatted amiably with his charge, General Ikoma Bentai rode up to join them at the front of the long line of troops. Bentai was a wily old samurai, having worked his way up through the Lion ranks to become one of Toturi's most trusted advisors. Shiny black armor with gold and silver trim adorned the aging general's stocky frame. Bentai dyed his thinning hair golden, refusing to give up the long-held Lion tradition, though following Toturi had made him ronin as well.

Bentai spurred his horse and caught up with Toturi. The Black Lion looked resplendent on the back of his great warhorse. The old general gazed with admiration at his friend and leader.

"Hida Yakamo and his people will have a hard time getting past these mountains," Bentai said as he reined his horse in beside Toturi. "Those scum won't be menacing the empire again anytime soon."

"I hope not," Toturi replied. "The Crab are wily, though, as well as proud and strong. I doubt we've seen the last of them."

Just then, a scuffle broke out in the woods to the right of the column. Black-clad samurai ashigaru struggled for a few moments with a hidden foe. Then the fighting settled down. Bentai turned his horse and addressed the Black Lion's men. "Ho, there, what's going on?"

A scraggly-bearded samurai lumbered out of the woods, followed by a group of fellow ronin holding a struggling prisoner. Toturi remembered the lead man as Bo, a rough-hewn foot soldier, sometimes overenthusiastic about his duties.

"A Crab straggler," Bo said, rubbing his gnarled beard, "trying to spy on us or cause trouble, no doubt." He eyed the prisoner angrily.

Bo's compatriots pushed forward a battered samurai-ko in red and blue Crab armor.

Toturi, Toku, and Bentai rode back to take a look at her. A long cut traced down the woman's left cheek, and the shoulders of her kimono had been torn and pulled down, revealing the pale skin beneath. Her hakama trousers were little more than tatters, barely covering her bruised and scarred legs and hips. Despite her battered appearance, the woman's eyes still held fire.

"Who tore her clothes?" Toturi asked sternly.

"*We* did," said Bo.

"We were looking for Shadowlands taint," added one of his compatriots. The group around Bo nodded and grunted their agreement.

Bentai leaned toward the Black Lion and said quietly, "You can hardly blame them, Lord. Many of the Crab have been touched with Fu Leng's evil."

"Would you rob a samurai of her dignity, then?" Toturi asked them all. Turning to the captive he said, "What's your name, woman?"

"I am Hida Misae, ronin lord," she said defiantly. "I am not tainted by the Evil One. Either kill me, or set me on my way home."

Toturi frowned at the woman. "Are you through fighting then, Misae?"

"Through fighting for a cause I don't understand and a lord I no longer respect," Misae said. "Perhaps it makes me ronin—like you—to say it, but Crabs should be manning the Carpenter's Wall, battling Shadowlands monsters, not fighting Unicorns over some barren mountain pass. I say it again, Toturi the Black: either kill me, or send me home."

"She seems bewitched," Bentai whispered. "Shall I fetch a shugenja, Lord, or perhaps some jade to test her with? The minions of the Evil One cannot stand the touch of jade."

The Black Lion shook his head. "No, Bentai, she's not bewitched, just disillusioned. And, as to whether she is evil . . ." He nodded at the men holding Misae. "Bring her forward."

Misae resisted their attempts to drag her and, instead, stepped forward on her own. Bo looked as though he might clout her on the head, but a glance from Toturi stopped him. Bo and his men bowed courteously and stepped back into the ranks.

Toturi's deep brown eyes gazed at Misae. At first, it seemed she might turn away, but she couldn't resist looking at him. "Who is your lord, Misae?" Toturi asked in a quiet, sonorous voice. "Is it Fu Leng or Amaterasu?"

"Amaterasu, the sun goddess," Misae answered, her eyes unwavering.

The ronin lord nodded. "Misae," he said, "you may end your battles and make your way home to the land of the Crab. We will not stop you—though we will take your katana and your armor, lest you cause mischief in the lands between here and there."

Misae nodded grimly. "The armor's almost useless anyway," she said. "Leave me my wakizashi, though, Lord. It has been in my family for a long time." The short sword, the second half of the daisho, represented a samurai's honor.

"Hai. I will," Toturi said. "That and a supply of food and water. *If* you want to go." His gaze remained fixed on her as they spoke.

"*If* . . . ? Are there other alternatives, besides honorable suicide or death?" she asked.

"Hai," Toturi repeated. "You can join me and fight the Shadowlands here, in the heart of Rokugan."

The bitter anger slowly slipped from Misae's face. Moisture

appeared at the corner of her right eye, but she blinked it back. "You would take me?" she asked quietly. "I who have only recently fought against your people? I who have cursed your name and the day you were born?"

"It is never too late to change, Misae," Toturi said. "Join me. Join my cause. Help free Rokugan from the disease of Fu Leng."

Bentai looked skeptically from Toturi to Misae. "We may have to fight more Crab stragglers along our way."

Toturi never took his eyes from the woman. "She knows that."

"I will not fight my brothers," Misae said firmly, "but I will go with you. If you fight the Shadowlands, even here, so far from the Kaiu Kabe, my swords are yours."

Bo stepped forward and cut her bonds while another samurai brought her daisho forward.

Misae knelt and offered them to the Black Lion.

"Domo arigato, Misae-san," Toturi said. He turned to Toku, who had waited silently at the ronin lord's side all this time. "Toku, take Misae to Tetsuo. He's recently joined us and should be a good choice for guiding her in our ways."

"But he's from the nameless clan," the boy protested.

"We are all nameless here," said Toturi. "Only by banishing the Evil One and his minions from Rokugan can we regain our honor and station."

"I still don't trust anyone who was ever a Scorpion," Toku said sheepishly.

Misae glanced from Toku to Toturi and then back. In her eyes, Toturi saw contempt for the fallen clan.

"Don't worry," the Black Lion said jovially, "Tetsuo's a pleasant enough fellow."

"All Scorpions are pleasant on the outside," Misae said flatly.

Toturi smiled. "Some people distrust the Crab because of their appearance," he said. "Shinsei teaches us to find the value of people *inside* their shells."

Misae laughed, picked up her swords, and tucked them into her frayed belt. "Very well," she said, bowing once again.

The ronin chief glanced from Misae back to Toku. "Find her some new clothes as well," he said. "We may be a ragtag band of ronin, but there's no sense scaring our allies any more than we have to."

Toku laughed, and Misae did, too. So did the other samurai nearby. They turned away and returned to their tasks as Toku dismounted and walked with their new recruit toward the rear of the column.

When they were out of earshot, Bentai asked, "Do you think it's wise to pick up every stray we find, Toturi-san?"

"Only those worth saving," Toturi replied. He turned and rode back to the front of the army. Bentai went with him.

▲▲▲▲▲▲▲▲

That night, they bedded down in the foothills on the western side of the Spine of the World. Toturi's mind wandered over the range, to the lands of his former people, the Lion. Wistfully, he remembered riding among his old clan's holdings—the green hills, the clear streams, the snowcapped peaks, the towering pine forests.

Had the grip of the plague been broken there, or did they still suffer as the people here did? Toturi knew the answer. Fu Leng's evil could not be banished from the land by any force the Lion mustered. Only by driving the Evil One's influence from Rokugan could the plague be stopped. For a moment, Toturi wondered if the people of the Emerald Empire were up to the task.

As he sat on a log at the edge of the wooded foothills, Ikoma Bentai strode up and seated himself beside the ronin lord.

"The Lion have attacked the Crane," Bentai said. "Kyuden Doji has fallen, and the Kakita cities are burning. I just got word from one of our scouts. You were right about these former Scorpions. They do have their uses. Assuming they can be trusted."

"I trust every man and woman with me," Toturi said, "but you and Toku most of all."

Bentai nodded. "Thank you, Lord. What shall we do about this?"

Toturi stood. "We'll have to put a stop to it."

"What about mopping up the rest of the Crab stragglers?"

"It will have to wait," Toturi replied. "We can't let the great houses destroy each other. We'll need the strength of every clan to defeat Fu Leng."

"Do you think so, Lord?" Bentai asked. "What about the Crab? Surely they've been corrupted beyond redemption. Other houses have been tainted as well. Perhaps we should let the clans fight each other. Maybe it's best if the ranks of evil are thinned before the final battle—whenever it comes."

The Black Lion shook his head and his dark eyes gleamed with the light of distant campfires. "Are you so sure that only the evil will be killed? Are you so certain that good will win that you think we don't need to aid our friends?"

"No, Lord. But are *you* so sure that, if we cross the mountains, we'll be able to tell friend from foe?"

"Nothing is ever sure, Bentai. Nevertheless, we must try."

Ikoma Bentai nodded. "Hai, Lord. You are right." He smiled grimly. "As always."

A faraway look glazed Toturi's eyes. "Not always."

Together, they charted a course back through the foothills to Beiden Pass, and from there into the lands of the Crane beyond.

In the morning, Toturi's army broke camp and marched north. They encountered other Crab stragglers along the way. Those who did not fight them to the death, Toturi offered the same choice that he had given to Misae: to join his forces, or to return to their homelands with only one sword and some provisions. Most chose to return to their people, but some few bolstered Toturi's ranks. Two committed seppuku. Toturi had Bentai stand as second during the ceremonies to honor both samurai's bravery.

By the time the mighty army reached the craggy entrance of Roka Beiden, Misae and the other new recruits fit right in with Toturi's irregulars. They marched up the trail solemnly, until snow capped the rocks and the trees fell away on either side. The path they traveled was well worn, the main route from the southwestern portion of Rokugan to the capital and lands beyond in the northeast.

Despite this, the road was all but deserted. War and Fu Leng's plague had taken their toll on the prosperous land, and few people ventured far from their homes anymore. The crimson stains of battle still covered the canyon walls of the pass. The rain and snow of winter had not yet washed the rocks clean.

Toturi gazed at the remnants of carnage not long past. Every drop of blood tells a story, he thought. It pained him to think of the sadness of those tales.

As they neared the pass itself, Toturi spotted a large contingent of Unicorn holding the broad defile. The horse lords had constructed a barricade and gate to protect the road. Toturi smiled. Roka Beiden was in good hands. The Unicorn Clan was loyal to the land of Rokugan and the people who lived there.

Toturi, Toku, Bentai, and several of the Black Lion's bodyguards approached the sentries at the head of the pass.

The Unicorn guards milled about as the ronin contingent rode up. One Unicorn left and soon returned with a high-ranking samurai. Toturi recognized the man as Shinjo Yasamura.

Yasamura was a serious-faced warrior with a mustache and a small triangle of a beard tucked below his lower lip. The Unicorn commander rode a tall, white stallion—clearly one of the best animals from a superior line of Unicorn steeds. Yasamura nodded gravely at Toturi as the Black Lion rode up to the barricade.

"Kon-nichiwa, Yasamura-san," Toturi said.

"Kon-nichiwa, Toturi-san," Yasamura replied, bowing slightly. "What business do you have, bringing your army here?"

The tone of his question startled Toturi, but the ronin lord ignored its disrespect. He answered politely, "I have business in the east, fighting the enemies of the empire. We would be honored if you, or some of your samurai, would join us in our mission."

"I have few enough to hold this pass in dark times like these, Toturi-san," Yasamura said.

Toturi nodded. "I understand. Then open the gates, and we'll be on our way."

"I cannot do that, Toturi-san."

The Black Lion felt the blood rising within his body. "*Cannot?*" he asked, holding his voice under tight rein.

"Cannot," Yasamura repeated.

"I fought beside Utaku Kamoko to free Beiden Pass from the

claws of the tainted Crab. How is it that you deny me access to that very route now? I am sure that neither Kamoko nor your daimyo would approve."

"My lords have no say in the matter, Toturi-san," Yasamura said, shifting uncomfortably on his ornate saddle. "This order comes from the emperor himself."

Toturi raised his black eyebrows. "The emperor?"

"No army is to pass through Roka Beiden," Yasamura said.

"Then the order is not directed toward me *personally*," Toturi said good-naturedly.

Yasamura kept his face impassive. "I couldn't say, Toturi-san."

Toturi smiled. "Yasamura, we've met before. We share many friends. You know me and aren't fool enough to believe the things said about me. You know I fight for the empire. Do not hinder this fight. Join me or, failing that, at least let me pass."

Though the Unicorn's jaw remained set, his eyes sparkled with temptation at the thought. Then he mastered himself. "No, Toturi-sama. I cannot. I am bound to my daimyo and the emperor. You of all people should know that."

The Black Lion nodded. "Hai, I understand." He turned his horse and rode back toward his army. Toku, Bentai, and Toturi's yojimbo did the same.

"But, Master," Toku said when they were out of earshot of the Unicorn, "we could have overwhelmed them easily."

"The evil in Rokugan is growing. The clans must come together rather than battling endlessly," Toturi said firmly. "I won't fight my friends. Not when there's another way."

"Another way?" asked Bentai.

"Yes," Toturi replied. "When I was young, I learned of a secret pass—known only to the Lion—through the mountains. It is difficult and dangerous." He paused and smiled. "But no more so than fighting against a well-entrenched Unicorn force with a fine commander."

Bentai nodded and grunted his assent. "Where is this hidden path?"

"North, a good journey from here. And, when we're through, it debouches in Lion lands. Let's hope that we don't meet Matsu Tsuko on the other side."

"Hai," said Bentai. "Let's hope."

"I've always wanted to meet Tsuko," piped Toku. "I hear she's one of the bravest samurai in all the land."

Toturi and Bentai glanced at each other and laughed. Seeing the puzzled look on Toku's face, Toturi added, "She's brave, all right. She's certainly not afraid of me—nor are her troops. And they'd be happy to prove it by cutting us to pieces if we meet."

"But wasn't she engaged to your brother?" Toku asked.

Bentai looked at his master, as if fearing that Toku's tongue might cost the lad his head. Toturi, though, merely grew distant. "Hai," the Black Lion said. "But that was a long time ago."

"She blames Toturi for her lover's death," Bentai put in, "though our lord had nothing to do with it."

"Indeed," Toturi added. "I'd have given anything to avoid becoming daimyo of the Lion."

"You would have?" said Toku. "I thought everyone wanted to be a daimyo."

Toturi shook his head. "Not I. I had much simpler dreams . . . then."

"What about now?" Toku asked.

"Now I have duties that can't be ignored," said the Black Lion. "We should get going." He spurred his horse and rode through the ranks, conveying his new plan to the troops.

"Think they'll go for it?" Toku whispered to Bentai.

Bentai shot the young samurai a rough look. "Of course. They are samurai. And he is their lord."

"I'd begun to think the master could persuade anyone to our cause," Toku said, "but that Unicorn resisted him easily enough."

"Some minds are forever closed to the truth," Bentai replied. "Our master is no shugenja, winning people through spells and trickery. He relies on the power of his words for persuasion." The old general rubbed the stubble on his chin thoughtfully. "What I want to know, though, is how the emperor knew we were coming."

3 ECHOES OF THUNDER

Mifune stumbled, and the other Shintao monks ran downhill past him, trying to reach the small abandoned fort at the bottom of the defile. As he splashed face-first into a cold mud puddle in the middle of the path, Mifune doubted that he'd live to discover whether the ramshackle stronghold's defenses were adequate.

It was not his nature to rail against his luck, but Mifune certainly had enough to curse about in the last few years. His lord Bayushi Shoju had been killed; that was bad enough. To also lose the young Scorpion heir at the same time was almost unbearable. Bayushi Dairu had been a good young man: strong, loyal, and well-loved by his mother, the current Empress Kachiko. Mifune had even participated as the priest in Dairu's gempuku ritual. Such a terrible loss!

Hundreds of other Scorpions had been killed as well. Many of whom Mifune had known all their lives. Those that survived saw their clan stripped of its name, lands, and honor. The Scorpion were no more. All that were left were outcasts, ronin. Even monks of Scorpion heritage—like himself—were looked upon with suspicion. As he lay in the puddle amid his running brethren, Mifune wondered if the dead had been luckier than he.

He heard the roar of the Shadowlands horde attacking the small band of Shinseists and thought, just for a moment, that it might be better to lie in the mud and surrender to cruel fate. As the thought crossed his mind, though, strong hands lifted him from the ground.

"No time to rest, Brother," said a deep, melodious voice, "or Fu-Leng will flay your skin into parchment."

Mifune scrambled to his feet and looked at his savior. The man wore a red and black kimono with a green traveling cloak pulled up over his head. In his hands, he carried a long wooden walking staff, the upper end of which had been carved into a flute. The stranger had joined the monks on their journey several days ago, well after Mifune and his brethren had escaped Yogo Junzo's purge of their temple.

The priest didn't know much about the hooded man, though Mifune had noticed that the storyteller carried the daisho swords of a samurai beneath his weathered cloak. What really mattered, though, was that the stranger pulled his own weight during the journey, and even supplied the priests with foraged greens upon occasion. For this, and his thoughtful conversations around the campfire at night, the sojourner had earned the respect of his fellow travelers.

The wanderer spun to face a ravenous boghound thundering toward them. The dog leapt, its phosphorescent jaws slavering for human flesh.

The samurai-philosopher stepped aside and deftly smashed the center of his staff into the creature's neck.

The boghound's spine snapped under the blow. The animal's body slumped into the mud, where it lay quivering for several long seconds. Then, it gave up the ghost.

Mifune smiled. This man was no mere storyteller, as he and the other priests had supposed.

"Well?" the Hooded Ronin asked. "What are you waiting for, priest? Run!"

Mifune nodded a quick bow, and then shambled down the slope after his fellows. The samurai wanderer turned back to face their awful pursuers.

As Mifune reached his comrades, though, he found another contingent of undead creatures waiting at the bottom of the hill. Skeletal faces leered over the earthen parapets that the Shinseists had hoped would shelter them. With a piercing scream, the abominations threw open the fort's bamboo gates and streamed out.

"Back uphill!" the highest-ranking monk called. His fellows turned and ran, but the rotting horde caught the abbot and pulled him down. "Keep going! Don't . . . let . . . them catch . . . you!" the monk gasped as the fell warriors disemboweled him.

Mifune turned from the awful sight and scrambled back up the path as quickly as he could.

"Fools! Do you seek your own deaths?" the Hooded Ronin called. His staff smashed the head of a zombie. Then he used the rod's other end to parry the sword of an undead samurai.

"We're surrounded!" Mifune shouted.

The ronin cursed. "Then fight like samurai or die where you stand!" he said.

Seeing they had no choice but combat or death, the monks cinched up their saffron robes and leapt into battle, using their bare hands and feet as weapons.

▲▲▲▲▲▲▲▲

The Hooded Ronin smiled. He had feared that the brethren might not be suited to combat, but clearly martial discipline had been part of their training. Even so, the odds against the group were terrible. They were outnumbered nearly two to one—and the ronin knew that he couldn't tip the balance the other way by himself.

"For the glory of Amaterasu!" he cried.

An undead horseman bore down on him, swinging a two-handed

no-dachi. The great sword hummed and sparked red with fell magic as it cut through the air.

For a moment, the Hooded Ronin considered ducking out of the horseman's way. The rider was clumsy, if powerful, and his mount lacked the maneuverability of a living horse. If the ronin did that, though, the horseman and his enchanted blade would surely make quick work of the monks.

Steeling himself, the ronin pressed a hidden stud on his staff. A metal spear point popped out of the bottom end. The wanderer swung the blade up to meet his undead foe.

The rotting samurai saw the danger and tried to chop off the spear point. The Hooded Ronin reacted quickly, dipping his weapon out of the way and then thrusting up as the sword past.

The spear punctured the dead samurai's armor and breastbone. A look of surprise washed over the decaying face as the ronin lifted the monster off the back of the horse and up into the air. The wanderer spun, catapulting the undead horseman headfirst into the rocky cliff-face behind him. The creature's skull shattered, and its body slid down the rocks, leaving a long trail of gore.

The bony horse reared and clouted the wanderer on the head with its front hooves.

The Hooded Ronin dropped his staff and staggered back, dazed, as the undead steed came at him. He drew his katana, barely in time.

Iron hooves struck down toward the ronin's skull. He ducked to the side and chopped hard with his sword. Steel bit deep into the undead horse's neck, shattering vertebrae; the rotting head flopped to one side.

Though nearly headless, the monster continued trying to trample its foe. Black blood spurted from the monster's gaping neck wound. The foul ichor hissed and smoked as it hit the ground.

The Hooded Ronin swung his sword once more. He sliced cleanly through the remaining neck muscle, and the horse's head splashed into the mud. The mangy body toppled and moved no more.

With his sleeve, the ronin wiped sweat from his eyes. Sadly, his hard-won victory had not turned the tide of battle at all. Undead samurai and skeletons plodded inexorably among the unarmed priests, inflicting terrible wounds. Several monks already lay dead in the cold mud.

A sound from uphill caught the ronin's attention. He turned and saw more undead creatures, including a rotting ogre, shambling toward the melee.

"Against the cliffs, Brothers!" the ronin cried. "Keep your backs to the stone and defend each other!" He ran to the monks and cut down the two zombies nearest him.

The remaining monsters swarmed around the humans, encircling them, pressing them back against the cliff. The rock face was as tall as three men and too steep to climb. Anyone attempting to do so would be instantly cut down by the swarming undead.

"Though we die, make our enemies pay!" Mifune called. "Damnation take these monsters and their evil masters!" He lashed out with a powerful kick and crushed a skeleton's ribs.

Undead reinforcements arrived. A decaying ogre woman picked up a large rock and tossed it into the midst of the beleaguered humans. The stone crushed the head of the monk nearest the Hooded Ronin, splashing the wanderer's cloak with brains. The ronin wished he had taken the time to retrieve his spear.

"That monster can pick us off one by one!" Mifune hissed.

The ronin nodded grimly, his labored breath puffing out in great, white clouds. He stabbed at the zombie nearest him, but it stumbled back out of the way, content to hem the humans in and let the ogre dispose of them at her leisure. The Hooded Ronin raised his katana high, preparing to charge the horde one final time. Perhaps he could cut his way through and buy the monks an escape. At the least, he would make the enemy pay dearly. He looked for the weakest link in the enemy line.

Suddenly, a rain of red-fletched arrows fell among the undead. Four pierced unliving eyes, smashing skulls and splattering black brains. Two more shattered skeletal breastbones and the rib cages attached to them.

The undead troops wheeled around, confused by the sudden attack.

The cold air resounded with an echoing, "Banzai!"

A shadow leapt out of the woods atop the cliff and arced behind the ogre woman. A fiery blade flashed in the afternoon sunlight. The head of the monster fell from its shoulders, and the giant body toppled into the mud.

The priests' rescuer landed lightly on his feet where, moments before, the ogre had stood. A smile creased his handsome face, and his orange and gold kimono sparkled in the afternoon sunlight. Fiery birds fluttered on the kimono's silk. Shiba Ujimitsu, the Phoenix Champion, stepped forward and felled two more zombies before they had a chance to move.

"For Rokugan!" the Hooded Ronin cried. He decapitated the undead samurai nearest him and kicked the body into a skeleton. The monster shattered into fragments of bone.

The monks roared their approval and, with renewed fury, dived into the mass of undead.

Ujimitsu moved like a living whirlwind, seeming to be everywhere at once. Where his sword flashed, undead fell like rice before a sickle.

The Hooded Ronin augmented the Phoenix Champion's work, breaking holes in the undead battle lines and attacking their most vulnerable spots. The two of them soon had the battle well in hand.

Before Amaterasu sank behind the western mountains, the defile ran black with Shadowlands' blood. In the end, a dozen monks lay dead, but none of the zombies and their fell allies remained. The Shinseists quickly set to tending their wounded.

The Hooded Ronin retrieved his walking staff, sheathed its spear point, and leaned heavily against the dark wood. He nodded approvingly at the Phoenix Champion. "Your arrival was most timely," he said. "You appeared exactly when we needed you."

"I'm told I have a gift for that," Ujimitsu said, smiling. Though sweaty, he looked completely unruffled by the battle.

"You are Shiba Ujimitsu, if I'm not mistaken."

"You're not. Are you the man who calls himself the Hooded Ronin?"

"I do not call myself anything, but that is what others call me," the ronin said, bowing. "How is it you happened this way, Ujimitsu-san?"

"I go where I'm needed," the Phoenix Champion replied.

The ronin nodded. "I understand," he said. "I travel such roads frequently myself."

"Which is how you came to be with these monks?" Ujimitsu asked.

"Hai," the ronin replied. "Fu Leng's minions seek to erase temples, monks, and all other traces of Shinsei from Rokugan." He smiled slyly. "They're none too fond of me, either, so I'm happy to thwart them whenever I can. The monks were lucky our fates took the same path."

"Do you think you can finish the rest of the trip on your own?" the Phoenix asked. His eyes glossed over, acquiring a distant, detached quality.

"I think we can manage," the Hooded Ronin said. "You have business elsewhere?"

"Yes, though there's one thing I must do before I go," the Phoenix said.

Walking beside the body of the undead horseman, Ujimitsu gazed to where the no-dachi had fallen. The blade's steel was dark, and it shimmered with a red haze. Ujimitsu picked it up.

Sparks flew where the sword's pommel met the Phoenix's flesh, and Ujimitsu's hands burned with red fire. His dark eyes narrowed and he swung the sword hard into the cliff face, chanting a prayer to Shinsei as he did so.

The evil blade shattered into a thousand tiny pieces and dissolved in red smoke. The screams of an angry demon filled the afternoon air before fading into nothingness.

The Phoenix Champion took a deep breath and clenched his fists.

"Are you all right?" the ronin asked.

"The sword's voice was dark and powerful, but there was only one spirit within the blade," Ujimitsu said gravely. "The champions of a thousand years fill my soul to overflowing. The sword was no match for them."

The Hooded Ronin nodded. "Well done."

"Thank you."

"These are evil times," the ronin said.

"Hai. Some say it portends the end of the world."

"It does."

Ujimitsu cocked an eyebrow. "Can you be so sure?" he asked.

"I can," said the ronin. "Your voices tell you of the past. Those that speak to me tell of the future. The end time is nearly upon us. Soon, the Thunders will gather once more." He turned and gazed down the valley, to where the monks sat tending their wounds. "We both have much to do before the end comes."

"Hai," Ujimitsu replied, "and I must be about my work."

"Amaterasu's blessing upon you, then. Domo arigato gozaimasu." The cloaked samurai bowed low, though his eyes strayed from Ujimitsu to the battered monks. Their journey was nearly over; his had barely begun.

Ujimitsu bowed in return. "The Sun Goddess be with you as well," the Phoenix said, his voice fading in the afternoon air.

When the ronin turned to look for him, Ujimitsu had vanished. The wanderer sighed and leaned against his bloodied staff.

Mifune plodded up from where the rest of the monks had gathered below. Despite several cuts and bruises, the former Scorpion looked little the worse for wear. "We want to thank both of you," he said, rubbing his shaved head. "But where has your friend gone?"

"Even the Phoenix Champion cannot be everywhere at once," the ronin explained.

"Hai," Mifune said. "There must be a lot of work for one such as he."

The Hooded Ronin nodded, a grim smile creasing his handsome face.

"There is," he said. "More than enough for one samurai. More than enough for seven."

4 RUINS

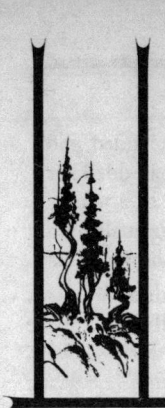

The once-proud towers of Kyuden Doji thrust up from the blasted landscape like broken teeth from bloodied gums. The ruins stood above a steel-gray winter sea. Surf hissed like a slumbering serpent. The city's craggy perch had protected it from the waves, but not from its true enemy—the Shadowlands forces of Doji Hoturi.

Matsu Tsuko steered her warhorse through the toppled buildings and burnt-out temples of the Crane capital, leading her troops from the destroyed city and into the surrounding countryside. The Lion daimyo's cheeks ached with smiling.

Her people controlled the land as far as the eye could see in every direction. The Crane's civil war had left them ill-suited to fend off the strong Lion armies. Tsuko's conquest of the Crane province had been almost too easy. The lack of strong opposition made the Lion feel somewhat cheated in her victory. Still, she couldn't help grinning.

A crow banked down from the soot-smudged sky, landed, and pecked the eyes out of a fallen Crane samurai. Tsuko nodded her approval. Nearby, wild dogs fought over the corpse of a temple priestess. The Lion rode up and killed the mangy animals with her lance. Cranes could be left to rot, but a sister of Shinsei—that was another matter. For the first time in days, Tsuko frowned.

The Lion daimyo wondered why the Crane had done it. What had made Doji Hoturi turn on his own people and become the head of an undead army? Could it be true what the priests whispered, that Fu Leng had already returned to Rokugan, that they—all of them—were living in the end days?

Casting her gaze across the burnt landscape and the slaughtered people, Tsuko could almost believe it. Then she shook her head. No. This was the work of the Fortunes, surely. Why would the Evil One want to exact such a toll on Tsuko's enemies? Why would the master of the undead leave the Lion armies all but untouched by his dark hand? Why would he give the Lion their long-awaited victory? Tsuko and her people were no servants of Fu Leng.

The resistance against Tsuko's armies had been pitiful at best. Her troops had joined up quickly and swept across the barren landscape, felling all who stood before them.

Matsu Agetoki, Kitsu Motso, and Matsu Yojo rode nearby, laughing and joking with their samurai. They drank sake and sang loudly of the Lion victory and Crane cowardice.

Tsuko heard the voice of her dead love in their songs: Akodo Arasou sang proudly of glorious battles. How she wished he could be here to enjoy this! Capturing the province nearly made up for his death and that of her friend Kitsu Koji. Never more would the Crane and their allies cut down the flower of Lion youth.

The thought turned Tsuko's mind to Shiba Tsukune once more. The thing that galled the Lion most in this whole victory was Tsukune. Where was she? How did the Phoenix witch escape their patrols?

The Lion daimyo cursed the Phoenix's luck and their skill with magic. Still, she felt confident her scouts would find Tsukune again. Then Tsuko would finally settle accounts.

Finally.

A noise from her left caught Tsuko's attention. Kitsu Motso and some of his people had rousted a band of Crane stragglers from a copse of unburned pines. The enemy samurai shouted, waved their swords ineffectively, and tried to run. Motso's people quickly hemmed the group in.

One samurai-ko, the only woman among the Crane band, ran forward brandishing a long naginata. She aimed the polearm's curved blade at Motso's horse, but the lion commander deftly reined the beast out of the way. He turned and thrust his bronze-tipped spear at the woman's breast. She died bravely on the point of Motso's lance, neither crying nor begging for mercy. Her compatriots perished like dogs, groveling in the dusty earth.

Tsuko nodded and smiled. Motso waved a salute to his daimyo and bowed. She laughed and breathed deeply of the cold, winter air.

As the sun set like a ball of red fire over the barren Spine of the World Mountains, Matsu Yojo rode to Tsuko's side. In his fist, he carried a weatherworn scroll. "News from our troops in the mountains," he said, a broad smile creasing his handsome face.

"Out with it," Tsuko said.

He nodded a curt bow. "Our troops have encountered the ronin Toturi and are preventing his army from crossing out of the mountains and into the eastern plains."

"Have they . . . *killed* him?" Tsuko asked, arching one pale golden eyebrow.

Yojo shook his head. "Not as of this report. Shall I send them a message to slay him at any cost? It would be our honor to lay the Black Lion's head at your feet."

"No," Tsuko replied, a slight smile creeping over her stern face. "There's plenty of time to deal with Toturi. I look forward to slaying him myself."

The young commander nodded. "Hai, Tsuko-sama." He turned and gazed across the corpse-strewn fields of the Crane. "We have won a great victory against our enemies," he said. He blinked back the dust blowing across the plain, and for a moment, his eyes appeared troubled. "The Crane's foolish civil war has cost them dearly. It would have been better for them if Hoturi had never been born."

"Lucky for us that he was," Tsuko said. Her breast swelled with the pride of victory. *Nearly everything I desire is within my reach,* she thought. The idea, though, triggered memories of Akodo Arasou. *The emptiness in her heart would never be filled.* The mountains cast long, purple shadows over the desolate battlefield.

Tsuko turned back to Yojo and said, "Time to make camp. There's an unburned village just over the ridge. They should have some provisions for us. March the troops there and see to it. Then join me in my tent for a drink. Tell the others to come, too, when their duties permit."

Yojo bowed in the saddle. "Hai, my lady." He rode off shouting orders.

Tsuko's samurai mounted up and moved quickly to the outskirts of the village—a congregation of two dozen mud-brick houses with thatched roofs.

Quickly, a small city of tents sprang up outside the town. Samurai laughed and sang and took what supplies the army needed from the frightened villagers. Clouds rolled in just after sunset, and snow flurries began to fall.

Within her pavilion, Tsuko shivered and cursed the weather. She walked to the woodpile and cast another small log on the big iron brazier in her tent. White smoke drifted up from the fire through the opening in the apex of the silk. A few stray snowflakes found their way down through the smoke hole and evaporated over the brazier's heat. *Why did the night have to be so cold? A victory this great called for bright sunlight and colorful blossoms blowing on the wind like butterflies.*

Matsu Yojo entered through the tent flaps, patting snow off his shoulders and shaking himself to relieve the cold. The Lion daimyo nearly laughed at the sight. Yojo noticed her gaze, bowed, and turned slightly red. "My apologies for getting snow on your silks."

She waved off the nicety. "Seat yourself near the fire and pour yourself a drink," she commanded.

He nodded and did as she bade, seating himself on the floor and fetching a jar of good sake from where several jugs warmed beside the brazier. Tsuko sat down opposite him. Yojo poured her a cup and then filled one himself. They downed their first drink in silence. Yojo refilled their cups.

"To victory," he said, holding his drink in the air. She nodded and did the same. The wind outside the tent howled like a lost soul.

After more long moments of silence, she asked, "Where are Motso and Agetoki?"

"Attending to some issues with the village peasants," Yojo said. "They'll be here shortly. Motso is worried about something, I think, though."

Tsuko frowned. "What could worry him? This province is all but pacified. The fat Crane storerooms will make this an easy winter for our clan. All our enemies will be dead by spring."

The door to the large tent flapped open once more, revealing Agetoki and Motso standing outside in the blowing snow. They paused at the threshold for a moment, silently vying with each other over who should enter first. After nearly a minute of feigned, intense politeness, Tsuko said testily, "Come in before the snow smothers our fire."

Both men bowed to her and tried to enter at the same time. Finally, Agetoki, who was larger, shouldered his way past Kitsu Motso. The hefty general kneeled and bowed to his daimyo; the thinner man did the same.

Tsuko waved her hand impatiently at them. "Sit down and stop this nonsense. Just because you're in Crane lands doesn't mean you have to act like them."

Agetoki roared with laughter, and Motso, who looked annoyed at first, soon joined him. They laid aside their weapons and sat by the fire. With Tsuko's permission Agetoki poured more sake, and all four of them drank.

After a polite interval of drinking, Motso cleared his throat. He was a square-jawed man with an angry countenance that made him look less handsome than he really was. He wore bronze samurai armor with long, silk locks like a lion's mane around the headpiece. The armor shone red in the firelight.

He nodded a curt bow and said, "Tsuko-sama, I think it might be well to move the camp."

"Tonight? In this weather?" Tsuko asked, incredulous. She reached to refill her cup.

Agetoki chuckled.

Motso shot him an angry glance. "Yes, tonight. My lady, there is plague in this village."

A chill shot down Tsuko's spine, but she kept her nerve steady as she poured.

"There's plague everywhere," Agetoki rumbled. "This whole damn province is full of it."

"Even our own lands are not immune," added Yojo.

Motso looked from one commander to the other, clearly annoyed. Finally he nodded. "Hai, but there's no sense exposing the troops to more plague than necessary. We already have this place under our heel. Better we should take what we need and move on quickly."

"The way Motso talks," Agetoki said, "you'd think he didn't *like* the Crane lands."

Tsuko downed her sake in one gulp and said, "Plenty of time to move in the morning. No sense in stirring up our people now—not in this weather. Now stop worrying and drink."

She held out the still-warm jar to her commander.

He took it, nodding his thanks, and drank directly from the container.

Agetoki laughed. "Does that change your view, Motso-san?" he asked jovially.

Kitsu Motso wiped his lips with the sleeve of his kimono. "Not yet," he said, "but it will." With a smile that looked almost like a scowl, he put the jar to his lips again.

They drank long into the night, laughing and joking. However, as the hours wore on and the wind howled more loudly, this cold victory began to prey upon Tsuko's mind.

Even with these proud, strong Lions surrounding her, she still missed her long-dead love. As, one by one, her generals succumbed to the drink and the darkness, Tsuko's heart ached with a void that none of them could even begin to fill.

What do you really have to be proud of? asked a nagging voice in the back of her mind. Your demolition of pitiful Crane irregulars? Your seizing of blasted, ruined, and plague-tainted lands? Where is the honor in all this? Better you should ride home to your high-walled fortresses and wait for a more worthy foe.

Tsuko pushed the dark thoughts aside and gradually slipped off into sleep. Her dreams, though, were troubled with images of fire and death and plague. No matter how many enemies she killed, more arose to take their place. No matter how full the mass graves became, nothing could fill her empty heart.

She woke sweating, though the tent around her was cold. Agetoki, Motso, and Yojo slept by the nearly dead fire. Agetoki snored like a wounded bear. These were *her* men, her samurai. Each one was willing to lay down his life at her command. Each had made sacrifices at her behest—which was only right. Every samurai in the clan—even Tsuko herself—worked for the greater honor of the Lion.

What had that sacrifice bought her, though?

The pale light of dawn crept in through a crack in the silken door. Tsuko rose silently and made her way to the exit. She had never removed her armor the previous evening; Lions frequently slept in their armor on the battlefield. Now, though, the small rings of metal mail felt cloying and terribly cold.

Stepping outside, Tsuko shook herself to warm her limbs. Beyond her pavilion lay a vast armada of Lion tents, floating like ships on a foamy sea. Snow painted the landscape white, hiding the scars from numerous battles beneath a blanket of pristine ivory. The sky was clear and blue, fading to indigo above the mountains in the west.

In a small valley below the encampment lay the conquered village. Smoke from scattered hearth fires smudged the early morning air. The entire world looked serene and beautiful. Tsuko took a deep breath and exhaled it slowly. Small clouds, like dragon's breath, formed near her mouth and nostrils. She watched as they drifted up toward heaven.

A sound behind her caused her to spin, her hand flying for the hilt of her sword. It was only Matsu Yojo. He stumbled out of his daimyo's tent, rubbing the sleep from his eyes. Tsuko smiled at the bleary look on his handsome face.

"Morning," he said, slurring the words slightly, and then added, "Tsuko-sama."

"Good morning," she replied.

"The plague doesn't look so bad from here," he said, gazing toward the village. "Maybe Motso was worrying for nothing."

Tsuko peered back toward the village. Now that she looked harder, the snow didn't seem to cover up the land's scars quite so well. The leafless trees of the valley told not of winter, but of fire and destruction. The great waterwheel of the village mill lay sideways, broken, in the dirty-looking stream that meandered through the center of town.

Every building in the settlement showed signs of war: burn marks, broken walls, gutted outbuildings. Despite this, life went on for the villagers. Even now, they scurried around below the Lion encampment, going about their daily routines.

Chop wood, carry water, Tsuko thought. Even the mighty must go about their duties, just as the peasants do. She shook her head and cursed herself for thinking like a mendicant priest. What's wrong with me? she wondered. Where is my Lion's heart?

As she watched, several of the villagers made their way slowly up the hill toward the Lion encampment.

"What do you suppose they want?" Yojo asked.

Tsuko shook her head.

"I'll go see," he said.

"I'll go with you," Tsuko replied. The heart of the sleeping camp seemed suddenly even colder to her. She longed for contact with fellow human beings. Even such scum as these villagers would provide a momentary distraction.

The small band of peasants hiked up the hill, dragging a cart filled with trade goods: blankets, bags of millet and rice, jugs of sake. They trudged solemnly up the snowy path. An older man leaning on a gnarled walking stick led them. Three other men and a doughty, unattractive woman followed behind.

Yojo and Tsuko met them at the edge of the camp, just past the sentry outposts.

"What do you want?" Yojo asked, sternly surveying their goods.

"We've come to offer tribute to our conquerors," said the old man with the stick.

"That's most . . . generous of you," Yojo said stiffly, trying to ignore the filthy condition of the petitioners.

The villagers were dressed in little more than rags, and their faces were dark with soot and grime. The woman in the group smiled at the handsome commander, proudly displaying her few teeth.

"Not at all," the old man said pragmatically. "We know you'll take what you want anyway, so we figure we may as well give it to you and save everyone a lot of trouble."

Tsuko snorted derisively. "A wise decision."

"Thank you, Lion-sama," the old man said, bowing his bald head low. "We know that you're far more powerful than we. It is our honor to serve."

"Yes, yes," Tsuko said impatiently, eyeing the blanket-covered cart. These peasants were filthy, but their goods seemed clean enough. "What is it you've brought us?" the Lion daimyo asked.

The old man looked around, as if about to convey a message that he didn't want anyone else to hear. He leaned toward Yojo and whispered, "We've brought you . . . plague!"

At the final word, the old man lashed out with his stick, tripping the startled Yojo and sending the young commander stumbling into the bamboo cart. The other villagers fell on Yojo and dragged him down to the muddy, snow-covered ground.

The old man sprinted forward with surprising speed. The cold morning breeze tugged open the front of his ratty kimono, revealing his scabrous, green-veined skin.

Startled, Tsuko stepped back and nearly lost her footing in the soft snow. The man raised his stick high, as if to crush her skull with it.

The Lion daimyo's hand flew to her katana. She drew her sword and, before the man could take another step, cut him from breastbone to hip.

He wheeled, a look of surprise in his yellow eyes, and toppled backward into the snow. A white cloud of vapor rose up where his spilled guts warmed the morning air. His blackish blood stained the snow a deep crimson.

"You!" he hissed at Tsuko. "You are responsible for all this. You and your kind brought this plague to our land! Your petty clan feuds have poisoned our soil with blood!" The breath rattled out of him, and he died.

By this time, Matsu Yojo had freed himself from the scabrous peasants. Three lay dead around his feet, and before Tsuko could come to his aid, he lopped off the head of the last. The woman's grinning, nearly toothless face rolled back down the hill toward the village.

Yojo grimaced in disgust and shook the blood from his blade in the ancient shiburi movement. Giving the corpses a wide berth, he scrambled quickly back up the hill to where Tsuko stood.

"I'm sorry, Mistress," he panted. "I should never have let this scum get by my guard. I would die rather than let such as these touch you. I offer my life in recompense."

"It's my fault," Tsuko said, eyeing the still-steaming body of the old man. "I never should have left the camp's perimeter. Only a cub would make that kind of error. Do you think I'd let one of my best samurai kill himself for a mistake that was my own?"

Yojo shook his head. "What shall we do now?" he asked, suspiciously eyeing the village below.

"Burn the town while we pull up camp," Tsuko said. "Motso was right. We should have moved last night."

"Should I try to salvage anything? Supplies?"

"No, nothing," she said, shaking her head angrily. "Burn this plague-infested hole to the ground. Take nothing. Leave no one alive."

Yojo bowed. "Hai, Tsuko-sama."

▲▲▲▲▲▲▲▲

Before the last fires had died down, thick gray clouds rolled in, turning the Crane province into an endless wasteland of featureless sky and bleak snow. Tsuko's army pulled up camp quickly and set a course up the coast, away from the Doji's plague-infested capital and its outlying towns.

As they moved north, the Lion ran across more diseased villages. On the fourth day, Tsuko looked back down the path they'd taken. Behind the army, smoke from the Lions' cleansing fires danced like black ghosts in the winter wind. The bleak, diseased landscape stretched endlessly before them.

Sitting astride her steed, Tsuko felt a knot tightening in her guts. There is no joy in this victory, she thought. Is this what Jigoku is like for the damned? Gray landscape and sky, the smell of burning bodies and towns, the call of crows echoing in the air, dead trees and poisoned rivers? She could hardly think of anything worse, but she kept riding, kept her troops moving.

They passed through more murdered towns and wasted fields. None of it was Lion work, and the brutality of it disgusted even Tsuko. Hoturi the Mad had done this to his own people. Tsuko felt queasy at the thought that she and her people were profiting from such dark deeds.

She longed to see the mountains and fields of her homeland, though they, too, would be snow-covered now. As the midwinter sun set red behind the Spine of the World, Tsuko considered marching from the Crane lands back to her own provinces. Her mind was black with destruction and death.

Caught in her own thoughts, she almost didn't notice when Matsu Yojo rode up to her. With him came Akodo Kage, the wise Lion Clan teacher—the only man in Rokugan to retain the Akodo name. The sensei's long white hair and pale golden robes danced in the winter wind. He rode a dappled horse with mud-caked legs. The animal whinnied as it approached Tsuko's proud steed.

Inwardly, Tsuko frowned. Kage had not been traveling with any of her armies. During the wars he remained, as always, in the Lion homeland. What, she wondered, could bring him out in the middle of winter? Despite her trepidation, she greeted the venerable teacher with the warmth and honor due his position.

"Sensei," she said, bowing slightly in her saddle. "To what do we owe the honor of your visit?"

Kage returned the bow. His weathered face remained grim. "I bring news of the Crab. Through means of my own, I have learned that a Crab fleet is massing. They intend to sail to Otosan Uchi and take the capital—probably by force of arms."

Matsu Yojo's mouth dropped open. "Surely Hida Kisada could not be so foolish!"

"The Great Bear's ambition has overwhelmed his good sense," Kage said. "I fear that he may succeed in his plan, unless we stop him."

"Of course we'll stop him," Tsuko replied.

Burning pride gripped her heart. Here was a challenge worthy of the Lion. To protect the emperor was their highest duty, their greatest honor. This would be far better than riding through the blasted plains, counting the bodies of their Crane enemies. The thought scorched away the black depression that had settled on Tsuko's mind. Here was a battle against a *real* enemy, not an endless fight against shadows and plague.

She bowed again to Kage. "Thank you, Sensei," she said. "Your warning brings honor to our clan and a chance for glory as well. Yojo, gather our troops. We march to Otosan Uchi to protect the emperor."

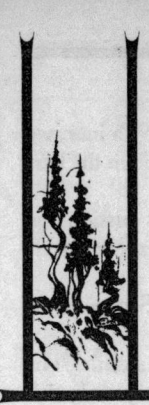

5 THE ENEMY WITHIN

Ikoma Bentai frowned at the Black Lion. "I know you're determined to do this, Toturi-sama. I'm not foolish enough to try to talk you out of something once you've made up your mind."

"Wisdom comes with age, I'm told," Toturi said, a slight smile playing across his lips. He crossed to the paper lantern on the other side of his tent and blew out the candle inside.

The sole remaining lantern, near the doorway, cast warm, flickering light on Bentai's battle-worn face. A winter breeze rippled the tent flaps and caused the flame inside the paper shade to dance and flicker.

Bentai crossed his gnarled arms over his chest. "I want to tell you, though, that I think this mission is a mistake."

"It's chancy, I'll admit, but it may be the only way to discover who our foe is," Toturi said. "I didn't cross the mountains only to be hemmed in by my former clan. They've kept one step ahead of us for weeks now. I won't wait any longer, and this is the best way to deal with them. With luck, we won't even have to kill anyone. I know this area well. I'm the best man for the job."

"Hai," said Bentai, "I'll agree with that. But with a mission this dangerous, I can't imagine why you're taking . . . *Scorpions* with you."

"I need stealth," Toturi said. "Who better than Scorpions to help me?"

"You killed their traitorous master," Bentai said sternly. "I'm sure some of them would be happy to stick a tanto in your back."

"Then I'll be sure to give them a good target," Toturi replied with a grim smile.

"I'm serious."

"As am I," Toturi said. "Every ronin here, including you, has joined his or her fortunes to mine in hope that, together, we may regain our lost honor and save the world from Fu Leng. The Scorpion have the most to regain. They didn't lose just name or position, as I did—they lost the right to exist as a clan. In my own way, I played a part in their loss. It is only right that they should redeem themselves with me."

"They got what they deserved," Bentai said. "Bayushi Shoju needed killing."

Toturi took a deep breath. An image of the dead Scorpion lord formed in his mind. Shoju stalked the throne room, graceful, cat-like, taunting Toturi for his weakness. Toturi knew he should have died then, but Shoju had spared him.

In the end, the Scorpion had seen something that Toturi did not; he had recognized his own flaws and repented them. That repentance had allowed Toturi to kill the Scorpion Emperor. Perhaps, in dying, Shoju had sought to regain the honor he lost in assassinating Hantei the 38th.

And if Bayushi Shoju, the proud, the terrible, could attempt to make up for his mistakes, if he could pay for those mistakes with his life, surely Toturi could do no less. By leading an army to free Rokugan from Fu Leng's evil grip, Toturi not only atoned for his own selfish errors, he also redeemed the Scorpion's sacrifice.

Some Scorpions—like Tetsuo, the usurper's nephew—understood this, even if Bentai did not. Thus, the Black Lion felt at home among the scoundrels and assassins in his troops. Like them, he sought redemption.

"Indeed," Toturi said softy. "He did need killing. And, as a true samurai, he willingly paid the price for his actions."

Bentai looked as though he might spit, but then he remembered where he was and swallowed instead; it wouldn't do to spit in his lord's tent.

"Now, perhaps, Shoju's people can make up for his mistakes."

"I doubt it," Bentai said. "Not if they worked for a thousand years. Rokugan will never recover from what that usurper did."

"Be that as it may, I will let them try. They *will* come with me on this mission."

Bentai gritted his teeth and breathed out through his nose. "Well, then, let me go with you, as well."

"No. I need you to stay with the troops. They know I trust you, and they'll obey your orders without question. Someone has to be in charge while I'm gone."

Bentai growled softly. "If you won't take me, take the boy. I know I can count on him to look out for your best interests—even amid a pack of Scorpions."

"Toku? Out of the question. He's too brash for this kind of work. Don't worry, old friend. We'll sneak across the river, raid the Lion encampment, kidnap their commander, and be back before you know it. Lions fight battles in a straightforward way; such a plot would never occur to them. Therefore they won't be prepared to defend against it."

When Bentai looked skeptical, Toturi added, "And I'll choose my companions carefully—for your peace of mind." He extinguished the lamp by the doorway and exited the tent.

Bentai held the flaps as his master went. Only after the ronin lord had gone did the old general shake his head in disapproval.

▲▲▲▲▲▲▲▲

Toturi slipped silently through the icebound woods at the base of the Spine of the World Mountains. Midwinter had long passed, but spring seemed no nearer than it had a month ago. A wan moon lit the snow-covered hills, its light barely scratching the deep shadows in the forest. The seven samurai with Toturi had been chosen for their stealth. Tetsuo, Shoju's nephew, kept close to the Black Lion's side. Three other Scorpions went with them. Toturi never gave them a second glance.

The tall pine forests at the mountains' edge embraced the ronin general. In his youth, he had spent many days alone in the wilderness, walking and thinking, contemplating life. He felt more at home with nature than he ever had in the Lion's palaces. Those moments served him in good stead now. He paused and peered into the darkness, but saw nothing out of the ordinary: tall cryptomeria pines; frigid, rushing waters; wet, ice-slick stones.

The Black Lion knew that his former clanmates were camped somewhere beyond the river. They'd dogged his troops for weeks, but he'd held back, not wanting to slay them. That time was over now. Soon, he would be able to march past these annoying Lions, cross their lands, and aid his friend Doji Hoturi.

He'd heard disturbing tales of the Crane daimyo lately. Vagabond storytellers said that Hoturi had gone mad and was killing his own people. Toturi felt confident he'd soon know the truth of the matter. All that stood between the ronin and his goal was a small but persistent Lion army. Toturi intended to behead that army tonight.

At the Black Lion's signal, he and the other spies sneaked across the ice-clogged river. They made it to the far bank without incident; not one samurai slipped into the frigid waters. Toturi smiled; he had chosen his companions well.

They crept up through the pines to the ridgeline above the river. As they neared the top, they heard the sound of armor clanging in the small defile beyond the ridge. Poking their heads above the snow-topped ground, they saw a man in Lion armor walking below, struggling with a large sack. The sack rattled and quaked with every move the man made as he walked away from the river.

Tetsuo edged close to Toturi. "Shall I deal with him?" he whispered, his hand on the pommel of his katana.

Toturi shook his head at the former Scorpion. "No. We don't want to kill anyone if we can help it. Besides, this straggler might provide us with information about the Lion troops."

Tetsuo nodded. "I understand. Two of us should be able to subdue him easily. Pick someone to go with me."

Toturi smiled. "I choose myself. Let's go."

Together, they sneaked down the defile toward the straggler. The man shambled on up the slope, seeming unconcerned with the amount of noise he was making.

"The Lion camp must be very near for this fellow to be so bold," Tetsuo whispered.

Toturi nodded his agreement. They crept to a boulder overhanging the game trail the man was following, and when he passed below, they pounced.

The samurai fought furiously. He swung his heavy sack at Toturi, catching the Black Lion in the midsection. Toturi sprawled back onto the snow-covered ground, the air rushing out of his lungs. He sprang up quickly as the man elbowed Tetsuo in the face.

Blood leaked from the former Scorpion's nose. Tetsuo's visage contorted in anger, and he reached for his sword. A solemn glance from Toturi kept him from drawing it. Instead, he threw himself at the man's legs as the straggler swung at Toturi once more.

All three of them collapsed in a heap. Two more of Toturi's spies leapt from their concealment as the Black Lion, Tetsuo, and their quarry rolled downhill toward the riverbank. When the three wrestlers landed in a pile on the shore, the two spies grabbed the Lion by the shoulders and pulled him to his feet.

One of the men raised a staff to clout the man on the head, but Toturi hissed, "Stop!"

Everyone froze, even the Lion.

Toturi chuckled. In the dim moonlight, the Lion samurai was nearly impossible to recognize. Toturi knew him, though. It was Toku.

The young samurai looked around at his captors. "Hello," he said. "I was coming to give you a hand, but it looks like you found me first."

"What are you doing here?" Toturi asked calmly.

A broad smile broke over Toku's boyish face. "I know you didn't choose me for this mission, but I figured I could lend a hand anyway. I brought you a present."

He opened the sack he'd been carrying, and two more sets of Lion armor fell out.

Tetsuo bent down to examine the treasure. "Where did you get these?" he asked.

"I found some scouts that weren't being too careful about their duties," Toku said. "I persuaded them that they should lend me the armor if I got it back to them by daybreak." He smiled again.

"Did you kill them?" Toturi asked.

"No," Toku replied. "I left them tied up and gagged on our side of the river. I hung them up in a tree, so they'd be hard to spot. We can cut them loose in the morning, if you like."

"When you were having this fun, I don't suppose you asked directions to their camp."

"Funny thing," Toku said, rubbing a nasty bruise on the side of his face, "we didn't do much talking."

"This armor makes our job easier," Toturi said. "Tetsuo, find two of our men to wear it. We'll replace the Lion sentries with some of our own."

Tetsuo hefted the sack. "What about you, Toturi-sama?"

"I'd rather have a secure way past the perimeter and take my chances being spotted within the camp," Toturi said. "Besides, a black lion is hard to see in the dark."

"Hai, Toturi-sama," Tetsuo said, smiling. He gathered the other spies and soon had two of them outfitted as Lions.

As the samurai dressed, Toturi scouted ahead. Toku wanted to go with him, but the ronin lord thought the young samurai would make too much noise. Toturi quickly discovered the Lion encampment and returned to his spies.

He led them stealthily over three intervening hills to the perimeter of the Lions' defense. There, they subdued two sentries and replaced the guards with their own Lion-dressed samurai.

Leaving most of the spies in the woods beyond the camp, Toturi and Toku stole out among the Lion tents. The encampment was dark; the Lion eschewed watch fires, to avoid giving their position away to Toturi's troops. The darkness made Toturi's mission easier.

He discovered the Lion general's tent with little trouble; it sat in the usual position and was unguarded—testimony to the leader's bravery. Toturi posted Toku outside to warn of stray Lions, and then crept through the tent flaps.

Toturi held his breath as he gazed into the dimness. A thin futon covered with warm quilts rested on the far side of the tent. Under the blankets lay a young woman, asleep and breathing deeply. Small white clouds of vapor hung like halos above her head. Toturi recognized her.

Her name was Ikoma Tsanuri. Before his disgrace, she had been his greatest pupil. Tsanuri was nearly his equal, both in martial prowess and in strategy. No wonder he hadn't been able to give these Lions the slip.

Toturi frowned. Though he made no sound, Tsanuri suddenly woke. She sprang to her feet and drew her katana from where it lay near her head. Facing him across the narrow tent, she recognized her old teacher. A smile creased her pretty face, and her deep brown eyes sparkled in the darkness.

"Hello," she said quietly. "I didn't expect to see you here."

"I didn't expect to see you, either."

"Did you come to kill me?" she asked.

"No," he replied.

"What then?"

"The empire is crumbling from within," Toturi said. "I intend to stop it if I can."

"You've come to discuss philosophy?" She smiled darkly. "I'm afraid you have me outclassed, there. Sorry I didn't study to be a priestess."

"You know the empire's troubles as well as I," the Black Lion said. "We don't need to debate them."

"What *do* you need, then?"

Toturi's eyes blazed warmly in the cold darkness. "I need you to step aside. I need you to let me pass through the Lion lands so that I can fight the darkness beyond."

Tsanuri shook her head and flexed the iron muscles of her supple limbs. "You know I can't do that."

"The clans are slaughtering each other to no end," Toturi said firmly. "It is our duty—as citizens of the empire—to prevent that from happening."

"I know my duty," Tsanuri said testily. "I have given my vows to Matsu Tsuko, and she to the emperor himself. My duty to the empire is clear: You will not pass these borders—not without my blood on your sword." She assumed a defensive stance, her sword raised parallel to her face.

"I don't want to fight you," Toturi said.

"You can't avoid it," she replied. "I am bound by my honor to oppose you."

"Tsanuri," he said gently, "we are friends. You were my best pupil. . . ."

"That is why I will *not* let you pass, Toturi-san. If you were me, you'd do the same."

"I would have, once. But I've grown up since then."

His words stung her. Her mouth drew into a thin line, and her eyes narrowed. "Kill me, if you're so sure you're right."

Toturi felt his padded armor hanging heavily upon his well-muscled frame. Tsanuri stood before him wearing only a heavy kimono. She was strong and fast, but Toturi knew he could best her. He knew, also, that to beat her he would have to kill her.

Slowly, the Black Lion backed toward the tent flaps. "If you follow too quickly or rouse the guards," he said, "I *will* have to kill you. For now, though, I prefer to hope that someday we will be allies once again." He turned quickly and exited Tsanuri's tent.

"Where's our captive?" Toku whispered as Toturi came out.

"A complication arose that I hadn't anticipated," Toturi said, striding toward the edge of the enemy camp. "We can't go through Lion lands. We'll have to skirt the mountains and go south, even if it means marching all the way to the sea."

"But that will take *forever*," Toku said.

Toturi nodded. "Longer than I'd like," he said. "Let's hope it's not more time than we have."

They gathered Tetsuo and the others and made their way to the sentries they'd replaced. As the group of spies reached the edge of the encampment, though, a young Lion guardsman stumbled out of his tent for a breath of fresh air.

Spotting the unfamiliar band, he shouted, "Alarm! Enemies in the camp! Everyone to arms!"

A shuriken appeared in Tetsuo's hand, but Toturi kept him from throwing it. "No!" the Black Lion hissed. "Now, we run!" He turned and dashed downhill toward the river. The others quickly followed.

Watch fires sprang up around the Lion encampment. Tsanuri emerged from her tent, dressed in full armor. She scowled, watching the fugitives retreat down the hill. Matsu Gohei appeared at her side, bow in hand.

He drew the string to his ear and took aim at Toturi's back.

Tsanuri looked at him and said firmly, "No."

Gohei did not relax his aim. "Mistress," he said, "they will escape. I think that might be the Black Lion himself. Let me fire."

"No," she repeated. "I won't spill his blood unless I have to."

"I doubt he'd have the same compunction about you," Gohei said.

"He visited my tent," Tsanuri replied. "He could have killed me, but he didn't. Now we are even."

Gohei nodded and let his bow fall to his side. "I understand."

"Find out which of our guards let Toturi slip into camp," Tsanuri said. "If the guard lives, have him or her flayed."

Gohei bowed. "Hai, Tsanuri-san."

▲▲▲▲▲▲▲▲

The Black Lion and his companions splashed back across the river, not caring now who heard them. They scrambled up the hill on the far side, cut down Toku's tree-bound prisoners, and quickly made their way back to camp.

Toku and Tetsuo seemed disappointed that they'd returned from the mission without a captive, but they said nothing.

Toturi went about his purpose grimly, saying only, "I've found out what I needed to know. To do more would have been a waste of blood."

The others nodded, accepting their leader's decision without question.

As they reached the edge of the ronin lord's camp, Ikoma Bentai sprinted up to them. He looked around and, seeing no prisoners, frowned. Spotting Toku, he said, "Well, you picked up a stray cub even if you didn't beard the Lion."

Toturi and the other men laughed; Toku scowled.

"Tsanuri is leading their troops," Toturi said.

Bentai nodded. "That explains a lot."

"Yes," said Toturi. "It would be foolish to engage them any longer. We'll go south until we can either outflank or outrun them."

"Hai," Bentai said, stroking the stubble on his chin. "There's something you should know before we move though: Doji Hoturi is in the camp."

"What?" Toturi asked, surprised. Many of the samurai with him put their hands on their swords.

"That madman, here?" Tetsuo said. Toturi silenced the young Scorpion with a glance.

"Hai," Bentai said, "though he's not as mad as reports would make. In fact, he says that the man leading the undead troops is an imposter. He says he wants our help to regain his birthright."

Toturi frowned. "Do you believe him?"

"It's not my place to believe him or not, Toturi-sama," Bentai said. "However, he does look as though he's been to Jigoku and back."

"Take me to him," Toturi said.

6 THE SCORPION

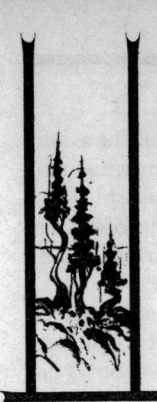

Empress Kachiko walked quickly through the cold, dark corridors of the palace at Otosan Uchi. The immense white walls of the castle had gone gray with soot, and the interior stank of mold and decay. Outside, late winter held the once-proud city in an icy grip, and plague ran rampant through the broad streets.

Kachiko felt nervous, which was even more disturbing to her than it would have been to most people. The Mother of Scorpions was used to being in control at all times, just as her late husband—Bayushi Shoju—had been. Her mind was filled to overflowing with plots and schemes and a million tiny details; very little escaped her notice.

Still, lately, events were slipping out of her grasp. Someone had freed the true Doji Hoturi from the dungeons below the castle, showing up his demon-double to be a fraud. Kachiko didn't know who had perpetrated this deed, a fact that annoyed her even more than Hoturi's escape.

The Crane daimyo's return home, she knew, would be a difficult and painful one—and he deserved every excruciating moment. Once her lover, Hoturi had killed her son, Bayushi Dairu, during the final hours of the Scorpion Coup. The horrible irony was that Dairu was Hoturi's blood son, the result of a long-ago affair with the Scorpion Lady.

No matter how much Hoturi suffered, it would never be enough for Kachiko. Never. Her black eyes blazed at the thought even now. Still, the Crane would fall within her grasp again, Kachiko felt sure. "It is not over between us!"

Bayushi Aramoro, the empress' yojimbo and Scorpion brother-in-law, gazed at Kachiko as he walked beside her. His eyes held reverence and devotion, both things that Kachiko valued highly. She trusted him implicitly.

Kachiko turned to Aramoro and asked, "Any word on our fugitive?"

Aramoro shook his head. He was a handsome man with a strong jaw and serious features. As a Scorpion, he had worn the traditional face-covering mask. With the clan outlawed, he looked similar to any other courtier at Otosan Uchi, though the color schemes of his kimonos tended toward crimson and black—Scorpion favorites.

In all of Rokugan, only Kachiko openly maintained the tradition of mask wearing. Even the persuasive powers of the emperor couldn't convince her to give up the delicate silken lace that decorated her lovely face. Her clothing, though, spoke of the imperial line, not her Scorpion heritage. She wore a vast multilayered robe of ivory silk, decorated with patterns of the sun, the moon, clouds, and stars. The fabric rustled around her like a flock of birds as she walked.

"Hoturi seems to have vanished," Aramoro told her. "Probably he's made his way home." He smiled grimly. "I'm sure Hoturi's kinsman have prepared a warm welcome for him."

Kachiko nodded, the sea-green flecks in her black eyes sparkling. "If his twin has left any of them alive." She walked to a wood-paneled wall, opened a secret passageway, and stepped inside. The Mistress of Scorpions knew more of the palace's secrets than anyone.

Aramoro followed her into the seldom-used corridor. Cleverly placed mirrors in other parts of the castle reflected dim light into the passage. Kachiko and her bodyguard walked silently over the smooth wooden floors toward a panel at the other end.

"What about Toturi?" she asked. "Any word of him?"

"Thanks to information we supplied to the Lion, their armies have him hemmed in against the Spine of the World. If he's planning to help the Crane, he'd better think again."

"Good," Kachiko said. Her heart burned for the chance to murder her husband's killer, but she knew she would have to wait. Eventually, Toturi would come to her.

"And our people have gotten word to Matsu Tsuko of the Crab's planned trip to the capital," Aramoro said. "Her armies are on the way here. They should be enough to stop any Crab assault."

Kachiko nodded, a bit of the nervousness seeping out of her body. Despite some setbacks, her plans for revenge against the men who murdered her son and husband were proceeding apace. All she needed to do was wait, and Scorpions could be very patient indeed.

A slight sneer wrinkled her red lips. "I'm glad that the empire's most 'valiant' defenders will be on hand to fight for us," she said. "Even though we did summon them, we wouldn't want the Crab to think they have run of the capital. The Great Bear must be held to his agreement with us, after all. As it is, the Lion and Crab should balance each other out nicely."

"Hida Kisada is wily and shouldn't be underestimated," Aramoro said.

"I don't underestimate him," Kachiko replied. "That is why I sent for the Lion. But Kisada is a fool, nonetheless. He thinks only with his muscles and could never become a true emperor—even if he were to slay the Hantei."

"Still, he could cause a lot of trouble," Aramoro said. "I've prepared a plan in case you need to leave the city."

"Leave the city?" Kachiko said, raising her delicate eyebrows. "Why should I leave *my* city? I have everything under control."

"Including the emperor?"

She nodded gravely. "Including my young husband."

"He worries me, Kachiko-sama," Aramoro said. "There's something not right about him."

Standing near the exit on the far end of the corridor, Kachiko rolled her head languidly. Her long hair fell over her shoulders like a black waterfall, and the pale flesh of her neck looked like silk in the semidarkness.

"I have the emperor well in hand," she said. From a fold in her kimono, she removed a small vial of poison. "This will make sure that he doesn't slip out of my control. Which reminds me, it's about time for his evening 'feeding.'"

Aramoro bowed. "Is there anything further I can do, my empress?"

"Continue searching for Hoturi," she said, holding her jaw muscles tight. "I don't want him popping up in the wrong place at the wrong time."

Aramoro bowed again. "I will attend to it, my mistress."

"And see if you can find your nephew, Bayushi Tetsuo," Kachiko added. "It's been too long since we've heard from him."

"He was one of Shoju's favorites," Aramoro said.

"Hai," Kachiko replied, a note of sadness in her musical voice. "I hope he survives this madness."

"As do I, my lady."

Kachiko turned and opened the panel. "Return when you have news."

Aramoro bowed a final time, turned, and hurried back the way they'd come.

The Mother of Scorpions stepped through the exit and into the corridor beyond. Her foot fell softly on the dark wooden planking of the lofty hallway. Great timbers supported the plastered ceiling high overhead. Despite the corridor's white walls, the light filtering in through the high, paper-paned windows seemed dim and confused.

Kachiko wondered if another storm was brewing outside. They'd had far too many storms this winter.

She set off down the corridor toward the imperial bedchambers. Until recently, she'd held the young Hantei cloistered within the bowels of the castle. Last week, though, as sick as he was, the young emperor had insisted on moving his quarters closer to the throne room.

Kachiko had argued that he was too ill to make such a move, but her husband would have none of it. Now he reposed in a chamber on the southern side of the main keep, a room with a view of both the sea and the far-off Spine of the World Mountains.

The Mother of Scorpions didn't like the room. It was too vulnerable, too accessible to other parts of the castle. She wanted to keep the young emperor as far away from his servants as possible, lest one of them should discover her plot against him.

She checked the poison again, making sure that she had plenty for tonight's dose. She wouldn't kill the boy—not yet—but her ministrations did make him easier to deal with. With Hantei incapacitated, no one in all of Rokugan could question Kachiko's orders. She replaced the poison in her kimono and smiled. The Mother of Scorpions stepped toward the painted fusuma panel covering the doorway of the royal bedchamber.

Voices came from within—two voices.

A chill ran down Kachiko's spine, and apprehension spun in her belly. No one was admitted to this part of the castle. Even the royal yojimbo stood guard several corridors away. Only she and the emperor were allowed here.

Yet, two voices echoed out of the paper-paned walls and into the tall corridor beyond. One voice belonged to the young Hantei emperor. The other—the voice that should not have been there—was eerily familiar as well.

Kachiko stepped silently to the panel and was pleased to find it slightly ajar. She put her eye to the crack, and her blood froze.

The boy emperor stood in the center of the room, before a burning brazier of coals resting on the floor. He wore a pale kimono, decorated with jagged mountains and storm clouds. His skin looked wan and sweaty. His black hair hung over his forehead in long points. His dark eyes reflected the fire before him.

The coals in the iron cauldron burned red in the waning light of late afternoon, and their heat cast rippling waves into the cool air. Her husband wasn't warming himself by the fire, though. He was talking to someone. Someone Kachiko knew very well. Someone she'd hoped never to see again this side of Jigoku.

The corrupt image of Junzo, the former Scorpion master shugenja, hung above the brazier. Junzo's skin looked leathery and cracked. His hair hung from his head in long white clumps. The sorcerer's parched lips smiled evilly as he spoke to the emperor.

Kachiko put her ear to the crack, trying to make out the words.

". . . him within our grasp," Junzo rasped. "But it could all fall apart if we don't act soon."

"Don't worry," Hantei the 39th said languidly. "I'll make sure that everything goes according to plan." Then his boyish face grew stern. "Just be sure that you do your part. Death and destruction can be diverting, I know, but they are only a means to our end. Never forget that."

Junzo's disembodied head nodded. "Never fear," he said. "I'll find the descendant of Shinsei if I have to burn every temple in Rokugan to do it."

A sickly smile parted Hantei's lips. "I'm sure you will."

The evil shugenja's head bowed and then dissipated into wisps of black smoke. Hantei chuckled and turned toward the doorway.

Kachiko jerked back, away from the crack, unsure if her husband had seen her. Her head wheeled with the scene she'd witnessed. Hantei, the boy emperor, talking to the most evil man in all the empire? What did it mean? Her mind swam with possibilities, and her stomach threatened to turn over. She looked toward the secret passage, thinking to leave before she could be discovered. She needed time to think and clear her head.

The fusuma door to the room slid open, and Hantei looked at her with his dark eyes.

"Kachiko, my wife," he said, "what are you doing here?" His tone was placid enough, but his eyes burned with a fire Kachiko had never seen before.

"I heard voices," she said, "and I was worried for you."

He crossed the distance between them in one long step and

grasped her shoulders roughly with his bony hands. "What did you hear?" he hissed.

"N-nothing, Otennoo-sama," she said. His ragged fingernails pinched her kimono and dug into her soft shoulders. "Only voices. I thought perhaps you were talking in your sleep."

Hantei looked at her, and she saw in his face that he wasn't sure whether to believe her lie.

"I hoped to comfort you," she said, subtly flexing her shoulders so that the front of her kimono slipped open. "Perhaps we should lie together awhile. You could tell me what troubled your slumber."

"Yes," the boy emperor said finally, the word hissing out from between his pale lips. "I was talking in my sleep. I had some bad dreams, but they've gone, now." He let her shoulders go, stood back, and gazed at her.

Kachiko took a deep breath and smiled lovingly at him as his eyes wandered over her splendid figure. She made no attempt to adjust the open front of her robe. "Shall we lie together, my husband?"

Hantei shook his head and looked away from her. "No. No, I . . ." He stumbled, and Kachiko caught him. She supported his thin frame against her elegant body and helped him back into the room and over to his bedroll. His flesh felt hot.

How can anyone live with such fire inside? Kachiko wondered.

"I think I should just rest awhile," the emperor finished.

She nodded understandingly. "If you need me," Kachiko said, holding her voice under tight control, "simply call." She eased him down onto the futon and lowered his head gently to the pillow.

He seemed little more than a boy now, very different from the iron-thewed man who had accosted her moments earlier. She smiled sweetly at him.

"I'm feeling better every day," he said, his dark eyes flickering closed. "Better every day."

As Kachiko stood, he fell into a deep slumber. She paused at the doorway, wondering if she had time to poison his water jug. She decided not to chance it; he might only be faking. After what she had seen and heard, the Mistress of Scorpions felt she could take no further risks.

She stepped quietly from the room and into the deserted corridor beyond. Only when she had slid the fusuma shut behind her did she dare to breathe once more. She wiped her sweat-slick hands on the hem of her kimono. Her heart pounded in her breast until she felt like it would burst out. She closed the front of her kimono and pulled it tight around her body.

Quickly, the Mother of Scorpions moved back to the secret panel. She opened it and hurried to the other end of the corridor. Stepping through the far panel, she felt somewhat safer, but only somewhat. She wished Aramoro were at her side: strong, confident Aramoro. Just his presence would make her feel better.

She brushed a sweaty lock of hair from her forehead and closed the passageway behind her.

"Not all secrets are so easily dealt with," said a voice.

Kachiko spun, her thoughts flashing to the daggers concealed in her hairpins. She didn't pull them, though, not yet.

In an alcove nearby stood a man in a green traveling cloak. He carried a long staff and wore the daisho swords of a samurai. The shadows in the corridor hid his face from her.

"How did you get here?" the Mother of Scorpions asked coldly, as though she might slay the intruder with her piercing gaze.

"I have friends in high places," he said, "just as you have friends in low ones."

Kachiko's eyes narrowed. She drew herself up to her full, regal height. "Who are you?"

"My name isn't important," he said, "what I've come to tell you *is*, though."

Kachiko almost laughed. "You're a messenger?"

"Among other things," the Hooded Ronin said. "You're frightened, I know."

"I'm *not* frightened."

"Your desires have made you overreach your considerable abilities, I think," the ronin said. "Ambition caused your husband's downfall. See that it does not cause yours as well."

"I could have you executed for speaking to me like this," Kachiko said icily. "I could have you killed just for being here."

"Then you'd never hear what I have to say."

The Mother of Scorpions frowned. "Speak, then."

"Though you are frightened now, it is nothing compared to what will come," the ronin said gently. "Soon, your bravery will be tested as it never has been before. When that time comes, you must be the woman your late husband thought you were. You must be the Scorpion."

Kachiko snorted derisively. "What else could I be, fool?"

"You could be the ambitious, frightened, hateful woman I see before me now," the cloaked man said calmly.

A wave of anger passed over Kachiko's beautiful face. Her mind flashed to her concealed daggers once more. Her right hand stole toward her hairpins.

At that moment, a balding middle-aged man rounded the corner at the far end of the hallway. Kachiko turned toward him like a tiger ready to spring but saw that it was only Seppun Bake.

The ronin moved quickly. His cloak swirled wide, hiding the alcove in which he stood. Kachiko turned back, but by the time she did, the Hooded Ronin was gone. His empty cloak rested on the floor.

The empress stepped into the alcove, knelt, and picked up the edge of the ronin's green hood. *He must know the secret passages here nearly as well as I do,* she thought. *But, how?* The distant sound of a flute wafted to Kachiko's ears.

Seppun Bake shuffled quickly down the hall to her side.

"Is there anything wrong, Highness?" he asked in his grating, high-pitched voice.

The empress rose, straightened her kimono, and adjusted the dagger hairpins holding her raven tresses. "No," she said. "Nothing wrong. Someone left a cloak here. The servants have been remiss in their cleaning."

"I'll see that the proper person is flogged," said Bake, bowing low.

Kachiko nodded, turned, and walked regally down the corridor away from him. "See that you do."

She didn't stop until she reached her private chambers. There, she sat in a dark corner, alone and silent, until she fell asleep.

7 THE LION'S DUTY

Waves crashed against the sandy shores outside the great capital of Otosan Uchi. The tall, white breakers still carried the sting of winter on their crests, but the southerly breeze held a hint of approaching spring.

The city itself ran uphill from the bay, cresting in the towering cliff-top palace. The imperial castle shone white in the rising sun—reflecting the dreams and the glory of the kami of Rokugan. The great waterfall, Fudotaki, crashed down from the cliffs, sending rainbow sprays high into the morning air. Even in the grip of the plague, even in the waning of winter, the castle and the Forbidden City spoke of the grandeur of the sun goddess, Amaterasu.

Soon, Matsu Tsuko thought, *the plague will wash away and spring will blossom within Otosan Uchi. The emperor will leave the white walls of his palace and shine upon the people like his mother the sun goddess. We will defeat the Crab and send them scurrying back to their* holes along the Kaiu Kabe. Then the Lion can cast out the weak-kneed Crane and the sycophant Seppun and take their place in the councils of the emperor. The empire will be strong once more.

Sitting atop her proud steed, Tsuko gazed out over the waves. In the distance, tall white shapes bobbed to and fro. These ghostly silhouettes were not whitecaps, Tsuko knew, but the sails of the Crab armada. Soon, they would storm ashore and try to take the palace. Perhaps they would do as the traitor Shoju had done and overthrow the emperor.

Tsuko smiled. The Crab could not yet guess that the Lion were waiting for them. They'd know soon enough, though, and then the proud Crab would also know fear.

The Lion daimyo had prepared carefully for the coming battle. She'd arrayed her troops along the shoreline, protecting the most vulnerable spots, all the while leaving a few strategic beaches open for a Crab landing. Those beaches were traps, designed to lure the headstrong Crab into the Lion's jaws.

Tsuko looked forward to clashing swords with Hida Kisada, the Great Bear himself. Kisada's battle prowess was renowned, and he had led the powerful Crab armies for many long years. Tsuko knew, though, that those years were beginning to tell on the Crab daimyo.

Part of her wished she could face Kisada in his prime. Another part rejoiced in anticipation of the Lion's victory—*her* victory.

The defeat of the Crab would quiet the tongues of doubters and make them forget about Toturi—supposedly the greatest general in the history of Rokugan. Tsuko snorted at the thought and spat into the coarse sand.

The Lion daimyo's heart thundered. For the first time in many months, she felt happy. This was where she belonged. This was the duty she was born to. None could doubt that her honor was spotless in this matter. None could serve the emperor better than she.

Kisada and Toturi had forgotten their honor. They had forsaken the oaths that bound their ancestors to those of the Hantei. Honor and oaths were things that Tsuko could never cast aside. That was why she would crush first the Crab and then the Black Lion himself.

Her samurai marched down the long strand of beach between Tsuko's massed troops and Otosan Uchi's wharves. Occasionally, a patrol would root out a Shadowlands straggler or a Crab sympathizer. The guards quickly put these traitors to the sword. They stuck the bodies on long poles as a warning to the Crabs coming to invade the capital.

Tsuko smiled and charted the arc of the sun overhead—watching time pass, anticipating the victory. Soon, now. Very soon. Her generals had their orders. All waited in perfect readiness.

She returned to her tent and pored over her battle maps one last time, just to be sure. The plans were perfect—deadly and flexible. Following them, she would lead the Lion to complete victory.

I'd like to see Toturi do better! Tsuko thought. She carefully rolled the plans into their cases.

As she did, a young samurai-ko named Mei opened the flaps of the tent and bowed low. "A thousand pardons, Tsuko-sama," she said. "A messenger has come from the capital."

"Show him in," Tsuko said.

Mei bowed aside, and a bald-pated man stepped into the tent. The two yojimbo accompanying him lingered just outside the tent flaps. Black hair sprung up below the man's crown and hung in long strands over his narrow shoulders. He wore a carefully arranged kimono festooned with flower designs. His smile seemed cloying and insincere.

Tsuko recognized him as Seppun Bake, one of the emperor's yes-men. Bake held no opinions of his own, preferring instead to reflect those of more powerful samurai. The Lion daimyo frowned. It was not unusual for the emperor to send written wishes for success in battle before a war. It was strange, however, that he should chose this sycophant to deliver the missive.

Bake looked around nervously and withdrew an ornate scroll case from his robes. He bowed and handed the silk to Tsuko. "Our glorious emperor sends his regard to the most loyal of his daimyo," Bake said. "As a servant of the Shining Prince, we are sure that you will understand his glorious instructions." Bowing again, he retreated quickly from the tent.

Tsuko scratched her head as she heard Bake and his bodyguards ride out of camp. Her eyes fell to the scroll in her hand. Something about the decorated silk made the fine hairs on the back of Tsuko's neck stand up. She pulled the scroll from the case and carefully unrolled it.

The characters painted on the scroll's silk burned into Tsuko's eyes and made her brain go numb. Tsuko knew now why the emperor had sent his best toady to deliver the message. No one with more honor could be trusted to relay such a missive.

The Lion daimyo let the scroll slip from her fingers. It dropped onto a low table and nearly slid over the edge. Tsuko wandered the tent in a daze, rubbing her head and trying to comprehend what she'd read.

> By the grace of Amaterasu, we command our most loyal Matsu Tsuko to ride away from Otosan Uchi upon the opening of this scroll. She must leave the field of battle and not return. She is to appoint no one to command in her stead. By the will of the Fortunes, the Lion must fight this battle alone.
>
> Do this without hesitation as you love your emperor and Rokugan.
>
> —Emperor Hantei the 39th, the Shining Prince

Tsuko's head swam. Cold sweat broke out upon her brow.

Could this be one of the Scorpion empress's tricks? No. Tsuko felt sure of it. Why would the Scorpion want the Lion to be leaderless? Why would she want the troops protecting the city to be slaughtered? Why would she want the Crab to enter the great city?

But why would Emperor Hantei want such things either? It made no sense! Tsuko gazed once more at the emperor's hanko signature and imperial seal. The chilling reality of the parchment made her head spin. These orders came from the emperor himself; they could not be disobeyed, or even questioned.

Anger churned in Tsuko's breast. She stalked around the tent, kicking over her low dresser. Her carefully chosen victory wardrobe flew into the air and floated to the ground in a jumble.

She roared her defiance, seized the pavilion's brazier and overturned it, spilling the contents onto the tent's sole rug. Charcoal sparked and ashes covered the silk's brilliant designs, turning them as dark as Tsuko's soul. Still the remains of the embers glowed, and the fire in the Lion's heart was not quenched.

In her mind's eye she saw the battle turning. What might have been a glorious Lion victory now degenerated into a vision of ignominious defeat. The blood of her troops would stain the sand and sea.

"I am sworn to obey the emperor in all things," she hissed quietly. "My pledge is my honor. My honor is my life." She put her hands to her temples and held on tight, feeling her head might explode.

Sparks and bright stars danced before her vision. Embers from the brazier caused the silk rug to smolder; the smoke stung her eyes and made her nostrils flare. She stumbled and leaned against the tent's central timber.

For a few long moments, she could do nothing but cling to the pole as she struggled with her emotions. Finally, the Lion daimyo mastered herself.

She had no options. There was only one thing she could do.

Tsuko threw back the flaps and exited the tent. Her dark eyes gazed past the battlefield and over the sea. The Crab loomed close now, very close. Heavily armored samurai stood on the gunwales of the boats, and Crab archers readied a volley to "soften up" the beachhead.

Turning from the ocean, she saw her samurai waiting patiently on the shores near the great capital. They needed only her command to crush the invaders. Tsuko clamped her teeth shut and willed her lips to stop quivering. She blinked back the moisture at the edges of her eyes. Many of these brave samurai would die today—and she could do nothing about it.

"Bring my horse," Tsuko barked to a guard standing near the doorway. The man bowed and quickly returned with her proud mount.

As she took her reins in hand, Matsu Yojo rode up, his handsome face smiling. "All is in readiness, Tsuko-sama," he reported. "This shall be a glorious day for the Lion." Still grinning, he bowed to her.

Tsuko glanced at him, her eyes filled with pride, anger, and sorrow. She turned away without a word and mounted her tall steed. She spurred her horse uphill, away from the battlefield.

As she rode out, a great cheer rose from her troops. They thumped their spears against their armor and called her name. Matsu Tsuko bit her lip and kept riding, not daring to look back.

The cheers built to a crescendo as she crested the hill above the city. The afternoon sun blazed in her eyes, scalding her sight. Her horse whinnied a question. "Don't stop," she whispered desperately. "Don't stop."

The horse trotted on. Tsuko heard the cheers turn to bewilderment as she dropped out of sight behind the hill. Cries of "Fire! The daimyo's tent is burning!" echoed to her. The roaring of the Crab-filled sea thundered in her ears. She heard the pulling of the oars, the creaking of the ships' timbers, the murmured anticipation of the Crab samurai.

On shore, her samurai cried out in confusion. Each voice was a dagger into Tsuko's heart.

Suddenly, a new sound: hoofbeats. She glanced back to see Matsu Yojo riding hard behind her. He reined up beside Tsuko.

"Mistress," he said in a perplexed voice, "where are you going? The battle is about to begin. Your samurai cry out for your leadership."

"I've been ordered from the battlefield by the emperor," Tsuko said, the words almost freezing on her lips.

"Ordered not to fight?" Yojo asked, shocked. "B-but that's the gravest insult!"

"Do you think I don't know that?" Tsuko roared, spinning on him. Her eyes blazed with anger. "There's nothing more I can do." She spurred her horse onward.

"But, who shall command our troops?" Yojo called plaintively.

"There's *nothing* more I can do," Tsuko called back, not daring to face her commander lest he see the tears in her eyes.

Yojo turned and galloped back toward the battlefield. Tsuko crested the next hill and looked back. She saw Yojo's Lion banner, the one attached to his armor, flapping in the breeze as he disappeared beyond the ridge.

The Crab boats rolled ashore, just as Tsuko had anticipated, but there was no one there to lead her people—no one to close the trap.

Her heart froze as the war cries of the two clans shook the hills. Time slowed to a crawl as the terrible tableau unfolded. Crab archers rained red-fletched death among the Lion troops. Brave samurai charged forward, only to be cut down in the surf before the Crab boats.

Some of her commanders, Yojo among them, tried to rally the troops and organize them, but it was no use. The Crab struck quickly, swarming ashore and attacking with terrible brutality. The Lions fell back. Severed limbs littered the beaches like driftwood; the sea ran red with blood.

The invaders pushed forward, scattering the great city's defenders before them like kindling. Fires sprang up among Lion's tents. Horses neighed in fear and pain. Oni strode among the Crab forces. The demons killed everyone they encountered.

Tsuko gripped her reins tightly, knuckles white with exertion. She longed to ride down, to strike out, to slay the demons and to avenge her people. Yet, her oath held her fast.

With every Lion that toppled, a heavy blow fell upon her heart. She felt her spirit shatter into a million black fragments. All her years of impeccable service, all her vaunted Matsu honor—it all came down to this.

Lion blood stained the land dark and ran in crimson rivers down to the sea. More blood than the oceans. Her people's blood. Her blood. Endlessly.

Tsuko couldn't rip her eyes away from the carnage. Unfelt tears streamed down her face. No amount of tears could wash this blood from her soul, though. There wasn't enough water in all the world to erase this stain.

When the sun finally set behind the distant mountains, Matsu Tsuko thanked the gods for the darkness.

8 THE UNICORN

Utaku Kamoko spurred her stallion over the hedge and forded the muddy stream beyond. Several armored Battle Maidens rode beside her, taking the stream as easily as their daimyo. A cry of joy escaped Kamoko's throat. The noise pierced the crisp, early spring air and shook flurries of snow from the withered branches of the awakening forest. The wind whipped Kamoko's long black hair behind her and tugged at the purple silk of her kimono. Her bejeweled armor rattled softly as she rode, music to the Utaku daimyo's battle-bred ears.

The bandits the Unicorn pursued broke into several smaller groups and scattered toward the snowy pine forest. The robbers were on foot but had a big head start on the mounted samurai.

"Split up," Kamoko called to her friends. "We'll teach them the price of their actions!"

"Hai, Kamoko-sama," Tetsuko called back.

Kamoko turned to the young woman and

smiled. Not too long ago, Tetsuko had been little more than a child. Now, though, she was a tested veteran, worthy of her own command. Tetsuko's armor shimmered in the early morning light. Her topknot blew behind her, echoing the mane and tail of her proud steed.

"Keep yourself out of trouble, colt," Kamoko said playfully.

"Trouble, ha!" Tetsuko replied. "It's our enemies who should be worried about that."

"I'm sure they are," Kamoko said. She spurred her horse and split away from the main group, chasing the bandit leader. Tetsuko waved to her and veered away as well.

Pride and joy lit the Utaku daimyo's smile. Perhaps her clan could not overthrow the Shadowlands forces oppressing Rokugan, but—by Shinjo—they could fight the darkness wherever they found it. The other clans may have chosen to ignore the suffering of peasants, but that was something the Unicorn would *never* do.

The bandit she chased was Shibooichi, the Fat One—an infamous local bully. Since the Scorpion Coup, he had lorded over the farm villages on the south side of the Drowned Merchant River. Shiboo thought that the position of these settlements, between the provinces of the Unicorn, Dragon, and Lion, kept him safe from reprisals. The emperor's Emerald Magistrates were generally too busy to take notice of one such as he.

The Unicorn had noticed, though, and Kamoko had taken it upon herself to bring the bandit to account.

Before her, Shiboo bounded like a fat deer, fleeing into the trees. He was surprisingly quick for a man his size, a head taller than the Unicorn commander and three times her girth. Evidently, he had some brains, too. Unicorn horses would be at a disadvantage in the snow-dappled forest, and the way the fat man maneuvered among the trees, it was clear he knew the woods well. Perhaps Shiboo and his men thought they could evade Kamoko and her samurai. If so, the bandits had another think coming.

Kamoko spurred her steed into the pine forest. Shiboo disappeared into the underbrush well ahead of her. Her horse's hooves slid slightly on the melting snow, but the animal's years of experience helped him recover. He bore his mistress quickly through the tall timbers, deftly avoiding the low-hanging branches that might have unseated Kamoko.

The Unicorn commander clucked encouragement to her steed and patted his neck. She kept her eyes fastened on Shiboo's retreating footprints. He can't be far ahead now, she told herself. A man that fat can't run forever.

Shiboo's marks took a sharp right turn, between some small boulders and up a heavily wooded hill. Kamoko tugged on the reins and shot after him. Ahead, she saw the bandit's corpulent form laboring through the wet snow. Kamoko smiled.

A tall sapling suddenly snapped before her, showering her face with snowflakes. Kamoko's steed reared. He stumbled, tripped over the bent tree, and almost went down. Kamoko held tight to the reins, trying to keep her seat.

Bandits sprang from the rocks on either side of the trail. Strong hands seized Kamoko's armor and pulled her from the saddle. The Unicorn commander fell to the ground and hit her skull on a rock. Only her helmet kept the blow from being fatal.

Kamoko's head swam, and strange music whistled in her ears. More by instinct than intent, she drew her katana. She cut blindly and felt gratified when the sword hit flesh. A man squealed, and the crowd around her parted.

The Utaku daimyo's sight cleared, and she saw about ten scraggly ronin surrounding her. One man held the remains of his arm and screamed; the limb had been lopped off below the elbow. The severed hand lay in the snow near her feet.

Shiboo advanced downhill toward her. Beside him lay her steed, whether unconscious or dead Kamoko couldn't tell.

"You didn't count on my having friends in these woods," the fat man said, his rumbling voice filled with malice. He nodded at Kamoko and said, "Kill her."

The ronin bandits swarmed around her.

Kamoko lashed out with her sword and took a bandit down. A second she smashed in the face with her elbow. Two men tried to gut her with rusty spears, but she chopped the hafts off as they jabbed at her.

Shiboo picked up a rotting tree trunk and bore in, swinging the log like a club.

Kamoko darted out of the way and tried to slice open the bandit leader's belly. Shiboo tripped one of his men so that the unlucky fellow landed on Kamoko's sword. The katana stuck in the dead man's rusting armor.

Shiboo's club smashed down on Kamoko's left shoulder, barely missing her head.

The Unicorn reeled back, hearing the strange, piping music, closer now. If the bandits heard it, they paid no attention. They kept bearing in, trying to kill her. She ducked and dodged, kicking one and punching another. They fell back. She put her foot on the dead man and wrenched her blade out of his gut.

The Fat One swung again, clipping her chin. Spots flashed before Kamoko's eyes.

The Unicorn fell back against a boulder, slashing with her sword, cutting another man in two. Blood gurgled out of his mouth as he died. She ducked away from Shiboo's next blow. The rock at Kamoko's back shook with the impact. Her head throbbed, and her arm ached. Flashing spots danced before her eyes.

She swung again and sliced a deep gash in Shiboo's thigh.

"Bitch!" Shiboo bellowed. "I'll kill you for that!"

Kamoko almost smiled. "You were going to kill me anyway," she said, tasting her own blood in her mouth. She kicked one of the fat man's cohorts in the stomach; the bandit tumbled back into his leader.

The Battle Maiden saw her chance. She darted between two of the bandits and back down the trail the way she'd come. Luck wasn't with her, though. Her sandal caught on a rock, and she tumbled face-first into the slush.

She rolled over quickly, but as she did, a bandit thrust his broken spear through the kimono under her left arm, pinning her to the ground.

"Arr! Missed!" the man said, spit flying from his chapped lips.

Kamoko thrust her sword at him, but he backed out of the way. Another spear jabbed at her. She batted it aside and, on the return stroke, beheaded its wielder. The rest of the bandits kept their distance after that, and for a moment, Kamoko thought she might be able to pull the spear out and escape.

Then a stone struck her temple, just under her helm. Light exploded behind her eyes. Before she could gasp a breath, Shiboo's club smashed into her stomach. Other blows rained on her body—not swords, but rocks, long sticks, anything that could keep the wielder out of range of her deadly sword.

Finally, Shiboo struck the katana from her hand. Kamoko heard it land on the snow downhill.

The eerie music welled up in her mind once more.

The bandits crowded in, surrounding her. Shiboo and his half-dozen cronies leered down at her, like hyenas moving in for the kill. The chapped-lips man drew a rusty tanto from his belt. He leaned down to cut Kamoko's throat, but Shiboo stopped him.

"No," the Fat One said. "Plenty of time to kill her later. We'll take her back to our lair first—find out how well she screams."

The others chuckled violently.

Kamoko's head felt as though it were filled with caterpillar silk. Her stomach rolled slowly. She tried to stand, to cry out, to do anything, but her body wouldn't obey. The music in her ears suddenly stopped, and she feared she might pass out.

"Drag her to the hideout," Shiboo commanded, pointing uphill with one beefy arm.

The order had barely left his lips when a stout staff came crashing down on his head. Shiboo fell like a sack of millet, landing on his face and leaving a huge dent in the snow.

The chapped-lip man whirled and got a spear point through the eye for his trouble.

A lithe figure leapt over Kamoko's body and laid into the remaining bandits. The man's green cloak obscured the Unicorn's vision, and she heard the sounds of combat.

Bandit voices cried out and then quickly died away. Soon, silence filled the snowy forest.

The ronin warrior leaned over Kamoko and looked into her eyes. "You shouldn't go charging off alone like that," he said gently. "One day, it may get you killed."

"Wh-who are you?" Kamoko managed to gasp. Her world still looked blurry around the edges.

"Just a friend," the ronin said. The shadow from his hood made his face impossible to see, but his smiling teeth shone in the gloom. "I need you to remember something."

Kamoko nodded weakly.

"The time is near. You must come when called. Do you understand?"

Kamoko nodded again.

"Good," said the Hooded Ronin. He stood up, lifting his staff. One end was carved into a flute, and the other featured a spear point. He pressed a hidden stud, and the blade slid back into the staff. "You'll be all right," he said, his voice deep and sonorous. "It's a good thing your friends are nearby, though. Remember what you learned today."

Kamoko tried to say that she would, but no sounds came out.

The ronin nodded. "Good-bye, then. I'll see you again when the time comes." He stepped out of her sight, and the world went dark.

A warm, damp cloth pressed against Kamoko's face, and she heard the sounds of horsemen nearby. She tried to brush the cloth away, but it came back persistently. Annoyed, the Utaku daimyo snatched out. She caught not a cloth, but a tongue—the tongue of her faithful stallion. Kamoko smiled, and her heart filled with joy that her steed had not been killed by the bandits.

The bandits!

Kamoko sat up so quickly that her head throbbed. She looked around frantically. The broken spear that had pinned her was lying on the ground by her side. Next to it rested her katana.

The criminals she had been chasing lay in a rough circle around her. Most of them were dead, but some few—including Shiboo—lived. None would be waking anytime soon.

As the Unicorn leader's wits returned, she heard horses galloping uphill toward her. Tetsuko reigned in beside her commander and jumped from the saddle.

"Kamoko-sama," the young Battle Maiden said, "are you all right?" Tetsuko knelt down beside her commander. Concern flashed in the young Battle Maiden's eyes.

"Where's the man who saved me?" the Utaku daimyo asked.

Tetsuko stood and scanned the forest. "I don't see anyone else around. Are you sure you saw someone? That's a pretty big dent in your helmet."

Kamoko took off her helm and looked at it. Sure enough, it was a *very* big dent. "You think I killed all these men by myself, then?"

Tetsuko shrugged. "You could have. I've heard of wounded Battle Maidens killing a dozen men to save their own lives—or the lives of their loved ones. Some didn't remember anything afterward."

"Hai. I've heard those tales, too. That's not what happened this time, though. A hooded man saved my life."

"If you say so, Kamoko-sama."

Kamoko looked at her young charge and frowned. "He had a message for me. He said that the time was near and that I must come when called."

"Perhaps it was a holy vision," Tetsuko offered.

The Unicorn commander tried to stand, but faltered. Tetsuko put her hand under Kamoko's elbow and helped her up.

"A holy vision," Kamoko said thoughtfully. "I suppose it could have been. I've dreamed of the Great Dragon lately, but this man seemed far more . . . worldly. " She stretched her stiff, bruised limbs. "If he was a vision, I'm glad he carried a big stick."

Tetsuko prodded the unconscious form of Shiboo with her toe. "What should we do with this sack of dung?"

"We'll take him back to town and leave him for the local Emerald Magistrate to administer justice," Kamoko replied. As she leaned against her horse, her head began to clear.

"And these others? A few of them are still alive."

"Arrange for someone to drag them into town when we get back to camp," the Unicorn said sternly. "Have them build some litters. These scum aren't worth sullying our horses with."

Working together, the Battle Maidens soon slung Shibooichi over the back of Tetsuko's steed. Then both of them mounted their horses and rode with their captive back toward the Unicorn encampment.

"And to think," Tetsuko said playfully, "it was you who told *me* to be careful."

"Hai," Kamoko replied, rubbing her head. "I guess I'll have to take my own advice from now on."

9 THE CRANE

Doji Hoturi strode purposefully through the blasted landscape, his clear brown eyes taking in every detail. Before him stretched the ruins of Kyuden Doji. The scorched timbers from its high towers lay scattered on the rocky ground like kindling. All that remained of its stone walls were piles of rubble. The smell of death hung in the spring air like an invisible fog. The odor seeped into his lungs and clouded his brain.

Beside the Crane daimyo, the Black Lion rode into the ruins. Toturi kept his face impassive, but his heart ached for his friend's loss. Even Toku, riding with his master, kept silent; this was neither the time nor the place for jests. On the far side of them rode the Phoenix general, Shiba Tsukune. The samurai-ko's black hair drifted gently in the evening breeze; the golden birds on her kimono winked and sparkled in the waning light.

The false Hoturi had been overthrown.

Order had been restored to the Crane provinces. Together with Toturi's ronin troops and Shiba Tsukune's army, Hoturi and his people had achieved a great victory over their Shadowlands oppressors. The imposter Hoturi was dead; the clan was free once more. The cost, though, had been terrible. It would take years to rebuild the Crane homeland.

"I'm sorry I did not come here sooner," Toturi said.

Tsukune looked at the ronin lord and nodded grimly. Many of her people had died waiting for reinforcements.

"Don't blame yourself," Hoturi said to the Black Lion. "If this is anyone's fault, it's mine."

"How could it be your fault?" blurted Toku. "You couldn't know that an evil double would take your place and run amok in your homeland."

"The boy is right," said Toturi. "No one could foresee this."

Hoturi nodded, but in his heart he knew they were wrong.

He had coveted Bayushi Kachiko, the Scorpion's wife. That mad love had cost him everything: his marriage, his honor, his homeland—and even the son he never knew, Bayushi Dairu. Hoturi had slain the boy, thinking to strike at the Scorpion, not suspecting the child was his own flesh.

Dairu's death had set the destruction of the Crane in motion. Kachiko had used Hoturi's lust to trap him and replace him with an evil double. Now his land was as dead as his son. Hoturi could not blame anyone for the destruction but himself. Hoturi had taken everything from Kachiko; now she did the same to him.

The damnable thing was that part of him still loved her. Oh, he no longer burned for her as a boy does for a maiden, but he could not deny his lingering feelings. Hoturi loved Kachiko; he would always love her, even if all she felt for him was hate. Even if their love could bring only tragedy.

The Crane daimyo silently cursed his own weakness.

Toturi's strong voice broke Hoturi's reverie. "I hate to say this," the Black Lion said, "but I must move on. There are other places, other people, who need my sword."

Hoturi nodded. "I understand."

"We'll meet again soon, I'm sure," Toku said cheerfully.

He scratched the back of his shaggy head and yawned.

"Sooner than any of us would like, I fear," Toturi added.

"Hai," Hoturi said. He gazed out over the palace ruins toward the sea. On the horizon, a spring thunderstorm roiled and brewed. Soon, it would come ashore. He turned back to his friend. "Ride safely. May Amaterasu guide your steps."

"And yours," Toturi replied. He spurred his horse to the northwest, away from the shattered city. Toturi's troops fell behind him in neat ranks.

"Bye," Toku said. "Good luck, Hoturi-san." He waved at the Crane daimyo, and then turned and followed his master.

A slight smile tugged at Hoturi's lips. Shiba Tsukune reined her horse in beside the Crane daimyo. She looked at her friend, her brown eyes sparkling. "I see great things for that one, some day," she said.

"Toku?" Hoturi asked skeptically. "He's just a boy pretending to be a samurai."

"Boys grow into men," Tsukune said. "At least, most of them do." She caught Hoturi's eyes, and both of them chuckled. The daimyo and the Shiba general had been friends—and occasional lovers—since their teens. Hoturi felt glad to have her at his side, if only briefly.

"I should be going, too," she said, gazing off into the distance. "Ujimitsu said things were amiss in our homeland, and I fear what I may find when I return home."

Hoturi nodded. "Will you stay for tea?"

"If I stopped for tea, I'd stay for more," she said jovially. "I really must be going."

"I understand," Hoturi said. He meant it, but his heart felt lonelier at the prospect.

"When this is over, perhaps we can get together," she said.

"*If* this is ever over," Hoturi replied.

"It will be," Tsukune said. The setting sun caught her black hair and made it shine golden. "Winter may be clinging past its time, but it's loosing its grip even now. Amaterasu won't allow cold and darkness to dominate her world forever. That's why Fu Leng can't win in the end—even though he has a toehold on

Rokugan. Don't worry, Hoturi. It has been a long winter, but spring is coming. Things will be better when it arrives."

"Looking at you, I can almost believe it," Hoturi said. He bowed curtly. "Farewell, Tsukune-san."

"And you, too, Hoturi-san," she said. "I'll see about sending some of our Phoenix artisans to help you rebuild."

"Their aid would be most welcome."

She turned and clicked gently to her warhorse. The animal galloped off toward where the Phoenix army waited. They formed up quickly and marched off to the north.

Hoturi watched his friend's troops as long as he could, but the looming darkness soon swallowed them.

After a while, Hoturi's yojimbo, who had kept their distance during the conversation, stepped toward their lord. "Shall we escort you back to camp, Hoturi-sama?" the lead bodyguard asked.

The Crane daimyo shook his head. "No. Leave me. I have some thinking to do."

The guards took a few discreet steps away from their master. Hoturi scowled. "No. I mean *really* leave. I want to be alone."

"But the city is in ruins," the foremost man said. "It may be dangerous, Hoturi-sama."

The Crane waved his hand dismissively at them. "Go."

The guards bowed and scurried away.

When they had gone, Hoturi closed his eyes and took a deep breath. The distant sounds of the surf filled his ears. Beyond rumbled an approaching thunderstorm. In his mind's eye, Hoturi imagined Kyuden Doji as it had been: green gardens, proud towers, well-ordered streets, lively shops.

Even with his eyes shut, Hoturi could not deny the truth of the matter. He smelled the odors of burnt wood, charred flesh, and decay. He heard the scrabbling of rats and, drifting to him from somewhere nearby, weeping. Someday, the Crane capital would be as it had been; that day was a long way off.

As Hoturi opened his eyes, an old man loped into view from behind a ruined battlement wall. The man was short and hunched over. Rags draped his bony frame, and his gray hair hung in long strings down his round shoulders. When he saw

Hoturi, he grinned a toothless grin and shambled forward to greet the daimyo.

"You think you've won," the old man said pleasantly. "You think this is a day of great victory over Fu Leng for the Crane."

Hoturi shook his head. "Great? How could it be? Look around you, old man. This victory is not great, though it is far better than defeat."

The old man's dark eyes sparkled. "A storm is coming, you know. This is not over yet."

"I know," Hoturi said. "I pray to the Fortunes that I will be ready for the trials to come."

"Better you should pray to someone who will aid you," the old man said. He now stood only an arm's length from the Crane daimyo. Hoturi noticed that the man smelled of fresh earth. Clearly, he had not bathed lately.

"You think I should pray to Amaterasu then," Hoturi said. He nodded and looked out to sea once more. "Hai. Perhaps. Her light would be welcome in these times of darkness."

"No," the man said, his toothless mouth grinning wide, "you should pray to Fu Leng."

Hoturi turned, an angry question on his lips. The creature that faced him, however, was no longer an old man. The thing's limbs had grown longer, and even more bony. Its eyes were large and yellow, with small red pupils. Its mouth gaped like that of a yawning wolf.

"Pray to the master!" the creature hissed. "Join us and regain your former glory! Rokugan's true lord welcomes men like you. That's why I stayed behind when the other's fled. That's why I waited for you. Look how much you've achieved already in the master's cause. Think how much you could accomplish toiling at his side. You *belong* with us!"

A noiseless snarl creased the Crane daimyo's lips. He reached for his sword, but a long, purple tongue shot out of the creature's mouth and wrapped around Hoturi's wrist. The tongue twisted suddenly and flipped the katana out of the Crane's grip. The sword sailed through the air and skidded under a pile of rubble ten paces away.

Before Hoturi could react, the monster leapt on him. It kept the Crane's arm wrapped in its sticky tongue and lashed out at him with its long claws. The daimyo fended off the attack with a martial arts block, but the talons shredded the left arm of his kimono.

Hoturi fell backward under the creature's weight, landing hard on the bare earth. The air rushed out of his lungs as the monster sat on his chest. The daimyo struggled to free his arm from the tongue, but couldn't.

"Never! I'll never join you!" Hoturi gasped.

The thing raked with its claws once more. Hoturi twisted aside, but the blow still bloodied his left shoulder. The wound burned like fire, and sweat broke out on the Crane's forehead.

He seized a handful of dirt and flung it into the creature's eyes. The thing shrieked, blinked, and rubbed its eyes, trying to clear the dust. Its tongue slackened momentarily.

That was all the chance Hoturi needed. He pulled his wakizashi from its scabbard and chopped the tongue in half. The monster wailed. It lashed at the daimyo with its claws.

Hoturi ducked beneath them and plunged the short sword deep into the creature's belly.

The monster hissed, and its mouth fell open. Yellow eyes rolled back into its bony head, and the corpse flopped onto Hoturi's chest.

The Crane daimyo pushed the carcass off and scrambled to his feet. He beheaded the monster, just to make sure it was dead. Then he shook the blood from his sword and went to fetch his katana.

As he probed under the stony pile of rubble, a deep, pleasant voice said, "Well done."

Hoturi jumped up, scraping his hand on the rocks.

Before him stood a ronin wearing a green cloak. The cloak was pulled low over the man's eyes, but from what Hoturi could see, the stranger had a strong, handsome face.

"Who are you?" the daimyo snarled, quickly drawing his short sword once more.

"I've been called many things," the man said, "though most know me as the Hooded Ronin."

Hoturi nodded. "I've heard of you. They say you fight the forces of the Evil One. I could have used some help here."

"If you had truly needed help," the ronin said, "I would have offered it." He leaned on his tall wooden staff and peered out from beneath his hood.

Hoturi scowled. "I could use less mysticism and more practical advice right now. I expect such riddles from Dragons, not nomadic ronin. Why are you here?"

"The oni you fought said the battles were not yet over," replied the wanderer. "It was right. The war has barely begun. You will be called to fight again before the end comes. You have much to answer for, Doji Hoturi."

The Crane daimyo nodded thoughtfully. "Hai, I know."

"I'm here to tell you that you will have a chance to make amends for what you've done."

Hoturi brightened at the prospect. "I would do anything."

The ronin nodded. "Yosh. The end time is nearly upon us. We will meet again on the Day of Thunder."

"When will that be?"

"When the time comes, you will know," the Hooded Ronin said.

Hoturi sighed. "You talk like Shinsei himself: all riddles and warnings, few answers."

The Hooded Ronin smiled. "Perhaps I do. Is that such a bad thing, though?"

"No," replied Hoturi. "The world could use Shinsei right now, but he's as dead and gone as the Seven Thunders you speak of."

"Is he gone?" the ronin asked. "Or does he merely live in our hearts, waiting for us to call him forth once more?"

Hoturi looked at him skeptically. "You weren't raised by priests, were you? My friend Toturi talks like that sometimes."

"Toturi is a wise man. Though he, too, has much to make amends for."

"Hai," said Hoturi. He stuck his thumbs in the waistband of his obi and felt something soft. Pulling it out, he discovered a lock of hair from Doji Ameiko—the wife he had betrayed. She was long gone, now. Sadness filled Hoturi's heart. "I have more to make up for than Toturi, though, I think."

"Perhaps," said the ronin. "Then you must be prepared to sacrifice even more to make amends."

Hoturi nodded. "I will do whatever it takes. I will pay any price."

The Hooded Ronin nodded in reply. "Good."

The Crane daimyo took in a deep breath and exhaled it slowly. His demeanor brightened. "Dinner awaits in my pavilion. I'm certain your travels don't permit much time for a relaxing meal. Why not take a moment now? I would welcome the company."

"You're correct," the ronin said, "I have little time for such things." He sighed. "Even now, I have few moments for luxuries. So I fear I must decline."

"As you wish," Hoturi said. "Perhaps some other time, when all this is over—after we've rebuilt Kyuden Doji."

"Perhaps," the ronin said. "Domo Arigato, Hoturi-sama." He bowed, and then straightened and took his staff in both hands. Hoturi noticed that the top end of the traveler's walking stick had been carved into a flute.

"Fare you well, Hoturi," the ronin said. He put the flute to his lips and walked quickly over the blasted ruins, playing a haunting melody. "We'll meet again soon."

"Hai," Doji Hoturi said quietly. "Far too soon, I suspect."

The ocean thunderheads had crept very close to shore now. The Crane daimyo turned and walked back to camp, seeking shelter from the impending storm.

10 JUNZO

The man who had once been Yogo Junzo smiled. The black fires of Fu Leng had long ago burned away his soul. Now the skeletal creature in the blood-red robes was merely Junzo, master sorcerer and warlord of Fu Leng.

Junzo cast his desiccated eyes over the landscape and saw victory there. The temple before him burned. In the distance behind it—flames leapt up from the local village. A tall pile of corpses lay in the temple courtyard. The samurai shugenja enjoyed the looks of terror on the faces of the dead. Soon, the feasting would begin.

Junzo's parchmentlike lips pulled back from his yellowed teeth, and pestilent breath hissed out. "Bring me the abbot first."

Yakushi, a skeletal man with oil-black armor and an ashen face, bowed to his lord and walked to where a small group of Shinseist clergy lay facedown on the flagstones. A half dozen skeletons armed with no-dachi long swords guarded the shivering priests and priestesses.

The dark lieutenant seized a chubby, bald-headed man in a saffron robe and lifted him to his feet. "Walk, or die," Yakushi said, his coarse voice rattling in his desiccated throat.

The head priest looked calmly at the corrupt samurai, as if to say that he did not fear death. Nonetheless, he walked to where Junzo sat atop his onikage. The demon horse champed and snorted steam at the abbot's approach.

"You lead these people?" Junzo asked.

"Amaterasu leads; Shinsei teaches; I am but a humble servant," the abbot said.

"Where is the descendant of Shinsei?" Junzo snarled, green spittle spraying from his lips.

"If you think I would answer, even if I knew," the priest said calmly, "then Fu Leng has rotted your mind as well as your soul."

Junzo leaned forward in his saddle, so that his face nearly touched the abbot's. "Do you not fear me, little priest?"

"You have no power over me, fallen one," the abbot replied.

Junzo plunged his fingers into the man's eyes and drank his death.

As the abbot's corpse tumbled backward, Junzo said, "Then it is *your* brain that has rotted, monk. You will join the other deluded meat on the table of my great lord." He turned to Yakushi and said, "The head priestess, next."

The black-garbed samurai walked to the line of Shinseists, their number now reduced to four—two men and two women. He grabbed the long black hair of the younger woman and dragged her before his master.

The woman stood and brushed the dirt from her black kimono. Clenching her fists at her sides, she lifted her chin and forced her lower lip to stop quivering.

"Tell me where to find Shinsei's descendant," Junzo said, his hollow eyes blazing.

"Cut out my tongue, evil one," the priestess said, "for I will not tell you what you want to know."

"I'll do far worse than that," Junzo hissed. He reached for the woman, abominable green energy playing over his bony fingertips.

The priestess held her head high. "This body is but a shell and life an illusion," she said. Her brown eyes were clear and determined.

Junzo snarled and whirled his skeletal demon-horse in a circle. The monster snapped at the priestess's face, but she held strong. "Stand the others up," Junzo ordered Yakushi.

Yakushi and the skeletal guards pulled the other woman and the two men with her to their feet. These initiates were not so practiced as their masters; fear shone on their gentle faces. Their bodies shook and sweated.

"Be brave," the priestess said. "Amaterasu watches over you."

"The sun goddess may have them, then," Junzo said. The evil shugenja reached out and twisted his fingers. Crimson energy coursed from his hand and struck one of the men—a tall, thin fellow—in the chest. The man gasped, and his eyes went wide. His sternum shattered, and his heart ripped from his chest.

Still beating, the organ sailed through the air into Junzo's outstretched hand. The monk had only a moment to register the shock as Junzo squeezed his heart into red pulp. The man fell to the cold earth.

"Would you see them all meet your precious goddess, Mother?" Junzo asked the priestess. "Would you watch them all die?"

"To save the world, I would," she said. "And they would die gladly to deny you and your dark lord victory."

The remaining man, a short, middle-aged fellow, suddenly bolted for the temple gate. Junzo spoke a word of power and gestured. Iron-fanged serpents sprang up from the soil in front of the frightened monk. The snakes surrounded the man, twisted around his body, and crushed him. Their razor-sharp teeth tore the flesh from his face. He screamed horribly as he died.

The remaining novice shrieked, her eyes wide with terror.

"Silence!" the priestess said sternly. "Would you threaten your soul to save your body?"

The novice clamped her mouth shut and stood whimpering softly, tears streaming down her round face.

Junzo looked at his lieutenant and pointed to the frightened woman.

Yakushi nodded his understanding. He walked to a burning building and stuck his glove into the blaze. The dark samurai grinned as the hand caught fire. He strolled slowly back to the trembling novice and held the burning limb before her face.

"Beg your mistress for your life," Junzo said to the novice. "A simple word from her can save you."

The novice looked from Junzo to the priestess. Her superior's calm gaze told her that no compromise was possible. The novice bit her lip and clenched her fists at her side.

"Burn her!" Junzo said.

Yakushi put his burning hand into the woman's hair. His touch was as gentle as a caress, but the hair caught fire nonetheless. The woman screamed and tried to pat out the blaze. When she brought her hand up to her face, her kimono ignited as well. Soon her whole body was ablaze. She wailed until the hellish fire consumed her lungs and her charred corpse fell to the flagstones. Yakushi smiled.

"See my power," Junzo said to the priestess. He rubbed his skeletal hands together in satisfaction.

"Your power is nothing but illusion," she said.

Junzo's pale, paper-thin skin crackled with rage. "Tell me where to find Shinsei's heir. My wrath is terrible, but my grace can be just as marvelous. Tell me and my master will grant you any boon you desire."

"I would not tell you, even if you swore to destroy every last Black Scroll," the clear-eyed priestess said.

"The scrolls have given me more power than your gods, bitch!" Junzo shrieked, spitting the words at the defiant woman. "Yakushi, show her the embrace of Fu Leng."

Yakushi nodded. He touched his still-burning hand to his own face. His flesh caught fire. Quickly, the inferno spread over his body, until every part of him blazed with evil flames. He walked to where the priestess stood and held out his arms to her.

The woman leaned away from the blazing man, though she knew she could not escape. She did not cry out as he encircled her with his blazing arms and kissed her. Her long hair became a sizzling torch. Her flesh melted, and her eyeballs burst. In moments, she was as dead as the other Shinseists.

"Fool," Junzo hissed. "Run her up. I want to speak to our master."

Yakushi bowed slightly and took the burning corpse in his fiery arms. Several skeletal samurai brought iron chains and threw them over the great torii—one of few structures in the temple compound that had not been destroyed by the blaze.

The burning samurai fastened the chains around the dead priestess' wrists, and the skeletons hoisted her into the air under the sacred wooden gate. Yakushi chained the woman's ankles as well, and the skeletons pulled the bonds tight. Ashen flakes of skin fell from her body as the woman dangled beneath the torii.

Junzo smiled and chanted evil-sounding words of power. The woman's body shook, and her head jerked back. Her charred lips opened and spoke words that were not her own.

"I hear you, my servant," the deep, pleasant voice said. "Have you found my nemesis yet?"

"The descendant of Shinsei remains at large, my lord," Junzo replied. "Though he can't evade us much longer. Soon, there will be no more temples for him to cower in."

"Do not be so sure that he is cowering," the master said. "Soon, he will assemble Seven Thunders to face me, just as he did long ago."

"I will kill him before he has the chance," Junzo said.

"You cannot kill what you cannot find," Fu Leng said. "Beware. My patience grows thin."

"Perhaps in the Phoenix lands I shall find the answers we seek," Junzo said. His fingers twitched nervously, and he ran them through his stringy white hair. "The Phoenix are nothing now. They have destroyed themselves with their arrogance and lust for power. I will burn their great library and rip the knowledge from their rotten minds."

"Yes," the voice hissed. "Though their soul is ours, they are strong of will. Perhaps the Phoenix still hide our enemy."

"I will speak to our ally within their ranks. We will root out the chosen one and slaughter him and his followers. The Thunders will never assemble, and you will stride the land unfettered once more."

"I chose well when I called you to my service, Junzo," Fu Leng said. "Go now, and do my will."

Junzo bowed, his crimson robes rustling in the draft from the fire.

The burning priestess' dead lips ceased moving. Her head lolled limply to one side, snapping her charred neck. Her skull fell to the flagstones and rolled to Yakushi's feet, leaving a long trail of blackened skin. The flaming samurai picked up the grizzly object and kissed it on the teeth.

Junzo surveyed the destroyed temple. Though he had not obtained the information he desired, the carnage pleased him. He gazed from the tall pile of bodies nearby to the temple gate. Then, turning to Yakushi, he said, "We ride at midnight."

The black-clad samurai bowed, flames already dying out on his body. "I'll make sure your troops are ready, Junzo-sama. Shall I have the temple searched again? Perhaps there is something we missed."

"I smell no one left alive," Junzo said, "but do so anyway. Our prey is clever, but he can't hide forever."

Yakushi nodded. "I look forward to showing him Fu Leng's embrace."

Junzo laughed. "I think we may have something better than that planned for Shinsei's damnable spawn."

"As you wish, Master," the dark lieutenant said. "Searching the temple will not take long, though. What are we to do between then and midnight?"

"Until midnight," Junzo replied, his yellow teeth glistening, "we feast."

11 THE LION'S DECISION

Matsu Tsuko tumbled off her horse as it fell, lifeless, to the snow-dappled ground. Rattled, she staggered to her feet. A goblin had killed her steed. She jabbed her katana through its green eye. The creature gasped, its breath forming a hot cloud in the cool evening air. It fell backward into the mud. Tsuko withdrew the sword and turned to face her next enemy.

Maddened goblins swarmed up the hillside, banging their weapons together and working up the courage to attack the warrior maiden. Eight or so creatures surrounded her. They shouted obscenities and babbled incessantly, spittle flying from their ragged-toothed mouths. They jeered and stuck their green tongues out at the Lion daimyo.

Their din matched the din in Tsuko's mind. She should have been able to slay these goblins, and speedily, but ever since she had left the field at Otosan Uchi, her will and mind lay in pieces around her.

"Come on," she whispered, sending small clouds into the cool air, "who wants to see Jigoku next?"

Even as she swung her katana, her shattered mind flashed images from the Lion council, weeks before.

After their terrible defeat at Otosan Uchi, Tsuko's armies had retreated to Shiro No Yojin to lick their wounds. The castle was the stronghold of Tsuko's family. Years ago, it had been won from the Crane in a border dispute, and the Lion were determined never to give it back. Shiro No Yojin had become the seat of the Lion Assembly. Nearly all of the Lion forces gathered there following the massacre at the imperial capital. Clearly, explanations needed to be given, grievances aired, and clan strategies clarified. Tsuko was loath to initiate this council. She had spent much of the journey home brooding about her army's failure—*her* failure. She sat in the great council chamber, ignoring both her surroundings and the arguments being made. It was all just noise to her, noise similar to the racket the goblins were making now.

Tsuko charged forward and cut off the head of a tall, lanky goblin. The other Shadowlands troops fell back before the ferocity of her assault, retreating into the rocky foothills. They were cowards, these creatures.

Tsuko stalked after them. In search of solitude, she had ridden away from her camp near the Spine of the World Mountains. She couldn't stand having the eyes of everyone gazing at her constantly. Now, even the goblins were staring, but she'd have her solitude—if only by the sword.

Her belly felt as though it were full of broken glass.

Her commanders understood what had happened at Otosan Uchi. The emperor's order could not be disobeyed, could not be questioned. Still, they were angry at their daimyo and uncomfortable with that anger. Lashing out was a Lion's first defense.

Tsuko aimed a cut at the hindquarters of a retreating goblin. The greenish creature yelped as the Lion severed its hamstrings. It made no sound whatever when she cut off its head. She stepped over the body and continued chasing the others. Darting among the foothill's boulders, she soon lost sight of her horse's steaming body.

What am I doing? Tsuko asked herself. She knew she should probably go back to camp for reinforcements rather than chasing the enemy by herself. She knew that, horseless and alone, the odds were against her. Yet, her anger drove her. Here was an enemy she could fight, unlike the enemies in the assembly. There, she had been just as surrounded as she was here, in the wilderness.

The assembly had quickly broken into two factions. Ikoma Tsanuri led the imperial loyalists. The Ikoma general favored honor, and the oath to the emperor. To her, Tsuko's decision was the only proper one, despite lost Lion lives.

"Our oath is our soul," Tsanuri said, her eyes narrow with concern. "Are we Crab or Scorpion, to take whatever means necessary to achieve our ends? Remember what that ideology has cost both those clans. The Scorpion do not even exist anymore. If we break our oath to the Hantei, we lose the essence of our being."

"We are fools to follow the oath if it means the end of the empire," Kitsu Motso countered. The clean-shaven man scowled across the wide, wooden floor at the Ikoma partisans. His strong voice echoed off of the chamber's high-beamed ceiling. "The emperor is corrupt. His treatment of Tsuko-sama and our armies shows that beyond any doubt. We are not Go pieces to be used and then cast aside. Our loyalty has been repaid with unjust death. The emperor is no longer worthy of that loyalty. Our duty is to all of the empire, indeed, to Rokugan itself. That obligation is greater than words given to any man, even the emperor."

Murmurs of assent echoed around the chamber, clashing with equally loud grumbles of disagreement.

Matsu Yojo and many others sat in the middle of the argument. The looks on their faces said they felt as torn as the Lion daimyo did. Fortunately, they would not be deciding the fate of the Lion; unfortunately, *she* would.

Tsuko ducked barely in time. A huge rock sailed over her head and crashed into a boulder only two paces behind her. At the top of the rise stood a huge shutendoji. The creature was half again as tall as the Lion and had huge fangs protruding from its wide mouth. The oni picked up another small boulder to hurl at the Lion daimyo.

Apparently, the goblins' retreat had been a trap. Tsuko chided herself for being led into it. Her breast burned at the idea of being penned in. Was there nowhere she could escape such tricks?

Matsu Tsuko sat in the back of the Lion assembly, her head in her hands, her elbows resting on her knees. The smooth wood floor felt cold beneath her, even though she sat on a thick tatami mat. The dagger in her stomach twisted; her ears rang with the sound of breaking glass.

Around her, her clanmates jabbered gruffly. Even when arguing they sat stiff, their legs folded under their bodies, their swords laid by their right hands. So proud. So honorable. The hard decision to come was not theirs, though, but Tsuko's.

As daimyo, her word was law within the clan, just as the emperor's word was law to her. If the Lion were to break their oath with the Hantei, it would be upon her head.

Tsuko's head pounded with the surge of her own blood. The arguments around her swirled into a whirlpool of noise. Voices crashed like the surf on the shores outside Otosan Uchi. Mingled with them, Tsuko heard the cries of her dying men in the battle before the imperial gates—a battle she had been powerless to affect.

How could she choose?

Either way, her clan would be damned. The blood would be on her hands. Always.

The oni's attack emboldened the goblins. They charged screaming from behind their rocks. The first died quickly as Tsuko slashed her blade across the goblin's greenish throat. Blood sprayed out, staining Tsuko's sword arm up to the elbow and splattering droplets on her face.

Always blood on her hands and darkness in her soul.

Another goblin died when it got in the way of a boulder thrown by the shutendoji. The monster cackled with delight.

Matsu Tsuko had let the wave of her clan's words wash over her. In her mind, she saw the blood of her people staining the tide red. She heard the roar of the surf, the roar of battle, the roar of the assembly. At Otosan Uchi's gate, the decision to fight had been taken from her. Had her honor been lost that day as well?

All eyes in the assembly rested on her.

Sitting next to her on the tatami, Matsu Yojo whispered, "Tsuko-sama, what shall we do?" In his young eyes, she saw reflections of her own confusion.

Slowly, she rose to her feet and propped her hands on her hips.

"The Lion fight for the emperor, and Rokugan as well," she said, trying to force herself to feel the words. "Our ties to the land are strong, but our ties to the emperor are in our souls. I will not break my word to him." She turned to Tsanuri. "You will carry out our duty to the royal house, as will you, Motso."

Kitsu Motso and Tsanuri bowed, though Tsuko saw a spark of displeasure in Motso's brown eyes.

"You will protect Otosan Uchi—as we have always done—at the emperor's behest. As long as I live, I will not break my vow to the Hantei. Neither shall any of you," Tsuko had said. "The Lion's word is our honor—our soul.

"I cannot ignore the pain of the land, though," she continued. "Together with Matsu Yojo and a portion of our troops, I will seek out the vermin that plague our land. I will join Matsu Gohei at the foot of the mountains, reinforcing our army there. I will guard the west, where the sun sets, as you guard the east where she rises. If we act together, we may yet stem the coming darkness." As Tsuko finished, her knees went weak. She felt wearier than she ever had in her life.

I know what is *right*, she had thought. Why can't I bring myself to do it? If only I could fight this battle with steel!

Only five goblins and the shutendoji remained. The demon kept well out of reach of Tsuko's flashing blade, preferring to toss rocks. The goblins tried not to present a direct target either, stabbing at the samurai maiden with their swords and spears and then dancing back among the stones. They cackled and laughed and continued their taunts.

"Damn you!" Tsuko said. "Fight like men, you cowards!"

"Fight like men and die like samurai," one of the goblins cackled. It picked up a stone and threw it at Tsuko just as she ducked out of the way of a hurtling boulder. The goblin's stone struck her on her diademlike helmet.

Tsuko winced and crouched back.

The other goblins decided this rock-throwing was a good idea. They stooped to get stones of their own and were soon gleefully pelting the Lion. The rocks did little more than sting and distract.

Tsuko maneuvered the fight uphill, to a large standing stone. The boulder was big enough to hide behind, and the samurai maiden hoped to gain a moment's respite from the barrage of rocks.

Just before she got there, one of the goblins tarried too long in picking up a rock. Tsuko dashed forward and chopped off its head. She ducked out of the way of a thrown boulder and scooped up the fallen creature's spear.

Darting around the big stone, she caught her breath. Beyond the boulder lay the ragged edge of a cliff. The drop was only a story and a half, but it prevented the goblins from pelting her from the front as she pressed her back against the standing stone.

Tsuko's protective stone shuddered as a boulder hit it. A goblin popped up nearby, and Tsuko threw her newly acquired spear through its neck. Three remained, and the oni.

Another boulder crashed, this time only a pace beyond her. Tsuko smiled. Her standing stone was doing its job nicely, even if she had no clear avenue of escape.

"Come out, little samurai!" the shutendoji bellowed. "I will give you a quick, honorable death!"

"Come get me!" Tsuko called back. "Your death will be quick, if not honorable."

The oni snarled and called to his three remaining companions. "Get her! Draw her out, or I'll have your guts for supper!"

The goblins squawked. They scrambled forward over the rocks, throwing stones as they came. None of the missiles were large enough to dent the samurai's armor. All three approached from the right, hoping to force Tsuko from her shelter. Two brandished curved swords and the other a rusty spear.

A slashing cut from Tsuko's katana parried the blows of the swordsmen. The spearman thrust at the Lion's ribs. She stepped away and grabbed the haft of the spear with her left hand as it passed by.

Turning quickly, she yanked on the spear. The goblin lost its footing and stumbled toward her. Instead of killing it, Tsuko kicked hard into the creature's backside.

The goblin went sprawling past her and landed a few paces away from Tsuko's boulder. A huge rock fell out of the sky and crushed the creature's head. The oni cursed.

Tsuko beat back the swords of her two opponents. One goblin's steel shattered. Tsuko sliced at the goblin, but it stumbled away.

The other thrust through the Lion's guard. Its sword ran along Tsuko's ribs, but her armor turned the cut harmlessly aside. Tsuko chopped the creature from shoulder to breastbone and it fell, dead.

Weaponless, the remaining goblin backed away from Tsuko's attack. The Lion jumped at it, but the creature stumbled out, into the open—away from the boulder's cover.

The goblin looked up, fearing a boulder would end its life. It seemed surprised when no rock came. Before it could recover, Tsuko ran her sword through its chest.

She darted back behind the standing stone as a rock sailed past. The oni cursed.

Tsuko panted. "Too bad you didn't bring more friends."

"I need no one to squash you, little samurai!" the shutendoji bellowed.

The stone against Tsuko's back suddenly shook. The rock groaned and inched forward. The shutendoji heaved behind it, trying to topple the stone on her.

Tsuko darted out from behind the boulder.

The oni had its shoulder to the stone. It whirled as she dashed out to meet it, but too late. Tsuko's katana flashed. The fanged head fell from the broad shoulders. The oni's body slumped into the dust.

Tsuko stood over the corpse. There was no satisfaction in the kill—no honor, no glory anymore. At least there was solitude, but in the sudden stillness, the clamor in Tsuko's head seemed only louder.

▲▲▲▲▲▲▲▲

"Toturi's army is on the other side of the river," Matsu Gohei said. "They came out of the hills upstream, apparently trying to get past our guard. So far, we've kept them from crossing, though I'm not sure how. They outnumber us badly, even though we've killed many of their samurai. Before nightfall, they retreated to a position several miles away, out of range of easy reconnaissance."

"This 'Black Lion' lacks courage as well as honor," Matsu Yojo added. He folded his arms across his chest and scowled.

Tsuko frowned at both samurai. "Honor, yes, but courage . . . ? Once, I would have said so. Now, though . . . Gohei, why do you think he doesn't cross the river?"

"I don't know, Mistress," the bold general said. Gohei leaned against his yari and thoughtfully stroked his chin. He smiled. "Perhaps he's tired of my killing his samurai."

"Has Toturi sent envoys to parley?" Tsuko asked.

Gohei shook his head. "After all the months I've spent harrying his troops? I'd be surprised if he did."

"Nothing Toturi does surprises me," Tsuko replied. "Perhaps I could surprise him, though."

"How, Mistress?" Yojo asked.

Tsuko ran her fingers through her long, golden hair. "I need to think about it some more. In the morning, we'll form up and march east. As we rode in, I heard reports of Shadowlands marauders nearby. We'll find and slay them."

"That will leave our backs to the Black Lion," Gohei said. "He may cross the river."

"Perhaps, but we'll still stand between him and the capital," Tsuko said. "As Gohei said, he doesn't seem to want a real fight. He's more a wolf than a lion." She turned and gazed into the mountains. Far away, the smoke of Toturi's campfires smudged the darkening sky. "Have our troops prepare to move out come dawn."

Yojo and Gohei nodded. "As you will, Tsuko-sama," Gohei replied.

"Keep a sharp lookout for tricks tonight," Tsuko said. "Toturi may be miles away, but that doesn't mean he won't try something if he can. He's still too clever by half. Even though we're leaving this place, we must still be on our guard. I'll be resting in my tent if you need me."

The other two bowed and returned to their duties. Tsuko crossed to her pavilion and entered it.

Rest did not come easily for her. When she slept, she dreamed of plague and death and the slaughter of her Lion army . . . and Akodo Arasou. She saw his face clearly, as if he were beside her. Then the face changed into that of Toturi, the Black Lion.

Tsuko woke with a start, sweating, her heart pounding. She stood and walked around the tent, taking a drink of sake to calm her nerves. It didn't work.

Perhaps a bath, she thought. The nearby river ran strong and swift. Its waters were swollen with the spring and would be very cold—just what Tsuko needed. The river would be guarded by her men. A late night bath should be safe enough.

Tsuko walked through the flaps of her tent and toward the river. Guards nodded politely at her, but no one questioned where she was going.

Soon, she reached the river, a rushing watercourse ten paces wide in the narrowest spots. Boulders churned the water white and sprayed the banks with a fine mist. The chill droplets felt good on Tsuko's hot forehead.

The new spring moon painted ghostly shadows on the water's surface. The night smelled of pine and newly thawed earth. Spring's warm fingers caressed the dark air. Over the river's laughter drifted the voices of Tsuko's guards. It gave her comfort that her people were so close, though she longed for solitude as well.

She stooped down on the bank, cupped some water in her hands, and splashed it onto her face. She began to strip off her armor, then stopped, thinking.

Only this small ribbon of water and a few miles separated her from the man who had dishonored her clan, the man who had cost her fiancé and all the Akodo people their name. In the dark, swirling waters of the river, Tsuko saw Toturi's proud face. He stared at her, steely-eyed, looking right through her.

Toturi gave up everything, she thought, yet he still fights for the empire. He still fights. Can I do less?

Looking around, she saw no one watching. Carefully, the Lion daimyo darted across the boulders toward the opposite bank. She almost fell in but quickly regained her footing. She bit back a curse and continued on. Soon, the moist earth of the far shore greeted her feet.

Toturi's samurai made no attempt to conceal their camp; the army was far too large for that. Tsuko had little trouble picking out the distant smoke of their fires in the dim moonlight. She dashed through the pines, quickly and quietly.

Her mind whirled with thoughts and possibilities; the miles flew past as she ran. Anger welled in her, then sadness, and then resignation. She nervously fingered the hilt of her lion-headed katana. Her eyes darted through the forest, watching for any sign of sentries.

Well before dawn, she stood at the edge of the woods, only a few paces away from the camp's perimeter. Her own people lay far behind her, sleeping—too far away to help if anything went wrong. She needed to do this one thing right.

The moon edged behind the mountains as Tsuko watched, waiting for her chance.

It never came.

Underbrush rustled nearby. The Lion daimyo whirled, but strong hands seized her from behind.

"Got one!" a gruff voice said. Tsuko cursed herself for being caught unaware.

Someone hit her in the back of the head. Stars burst before her eyes and, for an instant, Tsuko regretted leaving her helmet in her tent. Then the world spun around her, and she fell.

12 THE CRAB

The granite walls of Kyuden Hida pressed in on Hida Yakamo. The air was dank and warm. The Crab Champion's lungs ached from drawing it. Even in the highest tower of the castle, even with the windows open, Yakamo felt smothered.

Outside, the sky hung dark with storm clouds. A wind from the south brought no respite. Rather it filled the air with the stench of the Shadowlands. Neither the proud Twilight Mountains nor the great Kaiu Kabe wall could protect the Crab lands from that vile odor.

This year, there would be no true spring; this year, the turning of the seasons heralded the rebirth of the Evil One, Fu Leng.

Yakamo rose and walked to the window. The steel shutters protecting the room had been thrust wide, but still the atmosphere inside the room oppressed him. The son of the Great Bear looked out, away from the castle and toward the sea.

The Last Stand River flowed through the town outside the castle walls, meandering sluggishly to the Bay of the Earthquake Fish. The bay's green waters shimmered in the red light of the setting sun. The waters looked like a thousand campfires on a verdant plane.

The young Crab samurai sighed deeply. He tried to lean against the windowsill and nearly lost his balance. He had no hand to support him against the rail. Yakamo cursed himself for forgetting. With his father dying, he must be stronger than ever; he must not make such mistakes.

He looked down at the ragged stump of his arm. What he saw there made him shudder. Once, that arm had been joined to the Crab Hand, a powerful artifact. With it, Yakamo had conquered many enemies and become one of the most feared men in the empire. The Crab Hand had also made him a pawn of evil. It had poisoned him with the ambition of Fu Leng, undead master of the Shadowlands. For a time, both Yakamo and his father had thought the darkness to be light.

The Crab had sought the throne. They'd sailed to Otosan Uchi and destroyed the Lion forces protecting the capital. Then they'd faced the corrupt Hantei emperor—and they'd lost. Kisada, the Great Bear, fell to the boy emperor's sword. In that blow, Yakamo saw the hand of Fu Leng himself. No wonder their demon allies hadn't saved them!

Yakamo had cast off the accursed Crab Hand and led the Crab armies back to their own lands. Now the Great Bear lay in his chambers at Kyuden Hida, barely clinging to life. Yakamo cursed them all for being weak fools.

The Crab Champion looked at the festering stump of his arm. Though he had rid himself of the Crab Hand, the battle for his soul was not finished. Oozing disease ran up his arm toward the elbow. It was not the taint of the Shadowlands, but gangrene would kill him nonetheless.

In his mind, the accursed hand still called to him: *I will save you! Reclaim me!*

Storm clouds blotted out the setting sun, and black rain fell. Yakamo shuttered the windows and retreated into the palace.

He wrapped his stump in white silk and left the room. He walked deep into the castle, trying to escape the evil that hung over him.

Without thinking, he made his way to his father's chambers.

The shugenja attending Hida Kisada rose when Yakamo pushed back the fusuma screen and entered the room. They bowed low as the Crab Champion walked to his father's side. Yakamo paid the women no attention.

The room was dark, lit only by a few lanterns and a great brazier, smoldering near the slumbering daimyo. Sweet, incense-laden smoke filled the air. Gray stone walls swallowed the lanterns' light.

The Great Bear lay insensate on his futon, sweat pouring from his brow, his limbs twitching with dark fever. The wound in Kisada's side still bled; it would not heal. The imperial sword had inflicted a fatal wound to one who sought the throne.

Fatal. Hai. That's what it was. Though Kisada might linger for days or even months, in the end, Fu Leng had killed the Great Bear.

Yakamo's heart grew cold. He could hardly imagine life without the stern daimyo.

Am I worthy to lead the clan? I will have to be.

Father, I will avenge you, Yakamo thought. The disease in his stump burned in reply. Kisada's son gritted his teeth against the pain.

He turned to the women, still kneeling on the floor at the daimyo's bedside. "Leave us."

The women rose, bowed again, and quickly exited the chamber, pulling the screen shut behind them.

Yakamo unwrapped the silk from his arm and looked at the stump. The wound festered, oozing yellow pus. The skin flaked off in long, gray-back strips.

The champion looked at his father, back at the stump, and then at the brazier by Kisada's feet. The coals in the iron cauldron burned red; the air above them shimmered with oppressive heat.

"I will burn the disease from my body and my soul," Yakamo said, addressing the Great Bear. Though his father did not reply,

Yakamo thought a grim smile pulled at the daimyo's lips.

Turning to the cauldron, Yakamo thrust his arm into the fire. Pain such as he had never known tore through the champion's body. This was worse than when he'd acquired the Crab Hand, worse than when he'd torn it from his arm. Worse, even, than when he saw Fu Leng's pawn destroy his father.

Flames roared up the champion's arm and into his soul. Agony racked him, and he screamed. Yakamo's cries filled the dark chamber, echoing off the stone walls. His world filled with deafening sound. Still, he kept his arm in the coals.

The Crab Hand howled in his head. Its call was louder than his own screams. He ignored it and pressed the stump farther into the blaze. He held the arm there until the roar of the fire drowned out the wails of the evil hand. Even then, he did not pull his arm out.

Finally, when it felt as though his entire body would be consumed, Yakamo removed the stump from the brazier. He fell onto his backside, sweat pouring from his brow, pain drawing a curtain of red haze over his eyes. He gazed at the charred and blackened stump.

Most of the diseased flesh had been burned away. There, though, near the wrists, small pustules lingered, throbbing red like evil fireflies against the darkness of his arm.

It had not been enough. All the fire in Rokugan would not be enough.

Yakamo's head swam. He blundered to his feet without knowing where he was going. His ears roared with a sound like crashing surf. In the distance, he heard something else: music—the wandering melody of a Shintao flute.

Blindly, he stumbled out the doorway and into the darkened corridors beyond. He didn't bother to open the fusuma screen, but rather crashed through it, leaving an outline of his massive form in the door's painted paper and wood.

The castle walls closed in around him once more. Yakamo wandered, delirious, within the stone hallways. His mind reeled with images of his dying father, the battle before Otosan Uchi, the evil smile on the young Hantei emperor's face, the tainted Crab

Hand, and the leering visage of Yakamo no Oni—the demon to whom he'd given his name.

What a fool he had been! He had even given it mastery in the naming. Had it been Oni no Yakamo, he would have controlled it, but as Yakamo no Oni, it had controlled him.

Yakamo could almost hear the monster laughing at him now. Its image danced before him, leading him ever deeper within the bowels of the castle. The demon faded, and a figure appeared in the corridor ahead of him, a man in a hood, playing a long flute. The figure turned, fading away into the darkness.

"Stop!" Yakamo cried. "Who are you? What are you doing here?"

The champion shambled forward, barely aware as his powerful legs propelled him onward.

The figure stayed in front of him, always just at the edge of his sight. Eerie music drifted back to Yakamo, enticing him. Rage built within the Crab's massive chest.

Who was this invader who walked the hidden corridors of the Crab fortress as if he had been born there?

"I command you to stop," Yakamo said, his voice rasping and weak.

The figure merely kept walking, playing his long flute.

With an incoherent scream, Yakamo rushed forward, lunging at the specter, trying to grasp it. He missed and fell forward. Hard stone rushed up to meet his face.

Darkness swirled around Yakamo in nauseating waves. His lungs ached from pain and exertion. As the blackness clouding his vision faded, he saw a great chamber piled high with treasures beyond imagining. Dim light suffused the room, glinting off the golden surfaces and making them sparkle.

The Hooded Ronin stood on the far side of the chamber, leaning against his flute-staff. Beyond him, half-buried in the hoard, Yakamo glimpsed something green: jade.

"How did we come here?" the Crab Champion gasped. Fighting hard to stay conscious, he struggled to his knees. His head throbbed, and every muscle in his body burned with dark fire.

"I am given to understand the secret ways of the clans," the hooded man said.

"Why?"

"Because you are needed," the ronin replied.

Yakamo held up his stump. "I am . . . diseased." The sickly infection glowed in the dim light. Yakamo's vision swam, and darkness closed around him once more.

The Hooded Ronin reached into the pile of treasure and withdrew the jade object. He walked to where Yakamo knelt.

"Look," the Hooded Ronin said. "*This* is your destiny, Hida Yakamo. You must come when called." The stranger held an articulated hand made entirely of fine jade.

Half-conscious, the Crab extended his mangled arm.

The ronin placed the hand on the stump and bound the wrist with a silk cord inscribed with wards and protections against evil.

Again, Yakamo screamed; again his body burned with fire. This time, though, it was a cleansing flame. The inferno spread up his arm and through his spine. It coursed to every part of his body, driving out the corruption of the Crab Hand.

The image of a starry dragon danced before his eyes—bright, fiery, but somehow comforting. For a moment, Yakamo felt as though his entire being were made of pure, white light.

▲▲▲▲▲▲▲▲

He awoke in his own chamber, with no memory of how he'd gotten there. The first rays of sunlight peeked over the sea and through Yakamo's window. For the first time in many months, the sunlight warmed the paper-walled chamber.

Yakamo sat up and looked around. Nothing seemed amiss; he saw no trace of the Hooded Ronin. He rose and flexed his mighty muscles. At the end of his arm, his new hand flexed as well.

The Crab Champion gazed down at the wonderful artifact. It shone green, reflecting the early morning light in a thousand emerald sparks. Yakamo lifted the Jade Hand up to the level of his eyes.

His arm looked healed; no trace of the diseased Crab Claw remained. With the Jade Hand, Yakamo was whole once more. He was restored, body and soul. He clenched the green fingers into a fist.

The voice of the hooded stranger echoed in the Crab's mind. *You must come when called.*

Hida Yakamo nodded. He knew that he was ready.

13 MEETING OF LIONS

For a few moments, Matsu Tsuko didn't know where she was. Then her years of battle training cleared the clouds from her mind. She stood suddenly and thrust aside the samurai trying to capture her.

A young man in ragtag armor grabbed for her arm. Tsuko punched him squarely in the nose, and he sprawled over backward, landing in a pile of damp leaves.

The Lion daimyo drew her ivory-handled katana and flourished it in a wide circle. The four samurai surrounding her backed out of range and quickly drew their own swords. They formed a wide circle and pointed their blades at her. Tsuko stood in their center, her cold eyes staring at each of them in turn, daring them to attack.

"The next one to lay a hand on me dies," she snarled. "I am Matsu Tsuko of the Lion. I demand the respect my station deserves."

The four samurai looked nervously at each

other. The fifth rose from his bed of leaves, clutching his nose. Blood leaked out between his fingers. "That's a ridiculous story," he said. "Why would the Lion daimyo be sneaking into our camp in the middle of the night?"

"Look at my sword if you don't believe me," Tsuko said.

The young samurai gazed carefully at the carved ivory handle of the katana in her hand. His brown eyes roamed over the snarling lion's head that topped the pommel. He studied Tsuko's stern, battle-worn face and iron-muscled form. He nodded at her and pulled a silk handkerchief out of his kimono.

"Back away," he said, wiping his nose. "Give her some room to breathe." When the guards looked at him questioningly, the youth said, "What are you waiting for? Can't you see she's telling the truth?"

The samurai circling the Lion daimyo nodded to the youth and cautiously edged farther from Tsuko.

"Sheath your weapons," Tsuko said. "If I'd come to kill you, you'd already be dead."

The young leader put his handkerchief away and waved his hand at his comrades. "What are you trying to do, insult her? Put your swords away!"

The four other samurai reluctantly did as the young man bid. The young samurai bowed to Tsuko. "I'm Toku," he said, smiling. "I'm very honored to meet you, Tsuko-sama."

Tsuko's eyes narrowed as she appraised the boy. Neither his armor nor his demeanor was impressive. He seemed more like a farmer than a samurai. His face was unshaven and retained some baby fat. Yet, his muscles looked firm, and his body in good fighting condition. Perhaps . . . yes. She hadn't noticed it before in the dim light, but he wore the emblem of the Emerald Champion upon his shoulder. This child was an Emerald Magistrate, as well as being one of Toturi's soldiers. Clearly, in the Black Lion's camp it was a mistake to judge by first impressions.

"I've come to see Toturi," Tsuko said.

The four other samurai hemmed and hawed, pawing the fresh earth nervously with their straw sandals, but Toku merely bowed and said, "Of course. I'll take you right to him."

Tsuko nodded.

"What are you waiting for?" Toku asked his men. "Form up! Give the lady the escort she deserves."

"No, no," Tsuko said. "I don't want a lot of clamor. This is to be a secret meeting."

Toku's young face scrunched up in thought for a moment. Then he smiled again. "All right," he said. "I'll escort the lady myself. The rest of you, go back to what you were doing. And don't whisper a word of this, or I'll have your heads on pikes before morning."

The other samurai bowed and scurried off into the night, clearly relieved to be free of this tricky, politically charged burden.

"Toturi will be surprised to see you," Toku said as he led the Lion daimyo toward his commander's tent.

"Yes. I'm sure he will."

"Next time you decide to drop by, you really should send an envoy first. We've been having a lot of trouble with your people lately, and you could easily have been killed."

The boy clearly had no idea of the gravity of the situation. Already, his prattle was beginning to tell on Tsuko's frayed nerves. "I think I can find my way on my own."

"Oh, no, I wouldn't hear of it," Toku replied. "Toturi would never forgive me if I allowed you to wander in without an escort."

Tsuko frowned but said nothing more. As they meandered through the vast camp, she found herself impressed. The setup was magnificent, not the makeshift tent city that Tsuko had envisioned. The pavilions were well ordered and clean, arranged in defensive positions in case of sudden attack. Banners festooned the encampment, blowing gently in the night wind, their colorful designs dancing in the firelight.

Confident voices drifted up from between the tents—samurai chatting with their fellows and enjoying the evening air. Several guards stepped from the shadows to challenge them as they walked, but when they saw Toku, they vanished back into the night.

"I really must apologize for the condition of our camp," Toku said buoyantly. "If we had known you were coming, we would have done the place up proud."

"It's fine, really," Tsuko said, trying to keep the admiration out of her voice. Looking around, she could see that what Matsue Gohei had told her was true: Toturi could have easily crushed the small force she had opposing him. Why doesn't he do it? Tsuko wondered. What is he waiting for?

For a moment, fear sprang up within her heart, and she doubted she could go through with her plan. Then she steeled herself. "I'm surprised you could feed yourselves over the winter," she said, taking in the camp with her eyes.

"Oh, the people feed us," Toku said. "They're glad to have Toturi around. Besides, our army wasn't so big during the winter. The spring thaws have brought samurai out of the woodwork like beetles. More join us every day. People are eager to fight for what's right." He smiled, and the firelight gleamed off his bright eyes.

Tsuko nodded grimly. While we have grown weaker, he has grown stronger, she thought, fighting down a feeling of anger mixed with grudging admiration.

They soon reached a large, plain pavilion in the center of camp. No guards stood before the door flaps—a sign of Toturi's confidence. Tsuko glanced from the tent to Toku and then back again. We'll see, soon, if Toturi's confidence is well placed, she mused.

"I'll announce you," Toku said. "Wait here, please." He bowed.

As Toku went inside, Tsuko's eyes strayed around the camp. Admiration burned her gut. Yet for all he'd done, he was ronin—honorless. She had paid a terrible price, but her honor remained intact. In this, at least, she had the upper hand.

Toku poked his head through the flaps. "Come on, please, Tsuko-sama. Toturi's waiting." He held aside the tent flap, and Tsuko entered.

Toturi stood before her in a black sleeping kimono with golden trim. His dark hair hung above his broad shoulders; his scalp had been shaved clean, in the samurai tradition. The Black Lion looked alert, though clearly he'd just been woken up. His daisho swords were already tucked into his belt. He bowed, just slightly. "Tsuko," he said quietly. "To what do I owe this honor?"

She said nothing, but glanced at the boy grinning in the doorway.

Toturi turned to Toku and said, "Leave us."

Toku frowned.

"Don't worry," Toturi said, "everything will be fine."

Toku bowed, first to Toturi and then to Tsuko before backing out of the tent.

The Black Lion looked at the lady daimyo and smiled. "Make yourself comfortable," Toturi said, in a voice that reminded Tsuko very much of her dead fiancé.

"Do you want me to lay my swords aside, as if I were one of your followers?" Her brow furrowed angrily, and she began pacing.

Toturi shook his head. "I'd never dream of asking. I was thinking perhaps you'd like a seat, or some sake."

Tsuko waved him off. "They say you're a coward," she said, not looking at him. "They say you don't fight our army because you're scared."

"Is that what you think, Tsuko?" Toturi asked.

"I've hated you ever since Arasou died in your place."

Toturi nodded, the shadows around his eyes growing dark in the light of the tent's sole lantern.

The Lion daimyo continued to pace. "I've tried to be everything you're not. I've fought our enemies, giving no quarter and asking none. Our people have grown strong under my command."

"You'll get no argument from me," Toturi said.

"I've lived by the emperor's command and been proud to do so." Tsuko stopped her pacing and glared at him. "And I've allowed our people to die because of a boy—a sick boy who no longer knows right from wrong, good from evil, or honor from disgrace."

"I wept when I heard of the battle at Otosan Uchi," Toturi said quietly.

"So many samurai . . ." Tsuko lifted her face toward the tent roof. "Good men and women . . . all dead." She blinked back the moisture welling on the corner of her eyes.

She turned on him so suddenly that Toturi's hand flew to the hilt of his sword.

"Why don't you fight us?" she screamed, shaking her fist at the ronin lord. "Why don't you crush my army honorably, and then march to the capital and slay the oni who drink the blood of Otosan Uchi?"

"Sometimes, the measure of a samurai is knowing when *not* to fight," Toturi said. "I will not battle the Lion when the real enemy sits upon the Emerald Throne."

Tsuko hung her head. Her pale golden hair fell over her cold, brown eyes. "The Lion are bound to me, and I am bound to the emperor. That the Hantei is possessed does not matter. The honor of our clan is at stake. I cannot break my vows."

Toturi nodded. "I understand."

"I'm trapped between my duty and what I know to be right," Tsuko said quietly. "Surely, you felt something similar when you overthrew the Scorpion and took the Emerald Throne."

"Hai," Toturi said. "Sometimes, there are no good choices."

Just then, Toku burst into the pavilion. He bowed hastily. "A thousand pardons, but we've been tricked! The camp is under attack."

Toturi looked from the boy to Tsuko.

"I know nothing of this," she said.

In her guiltless, pleading eyes, the Black Lion must have seen the truth. "Come with me, then. We'll soon get to the bottom of this." He pushed past Toku and out of the tent flaps. Tsuko followed behind him, and Toku trailed them both.

On the far side of camp, a great fire burned. Samurai ran here and there, shouting and waving their swords. Toturi stopped one of the men and asked, "What's going on?"

"One of the supply tents has caught fire, and two of the guards were found unconscious."

Toturi looked from the man to Tsuko, but she merely shook her head. He turned to Toku. "Find Bentai and have him double the watch. Then get every available samurai to join the bucket brigade. I want that fire extinguished quickly. This may just be sabotage, or it may be a distraction from the true attack."

Toku glanced suspiciously at Tsuko. Then he bowed and turned to go, but before he could leave, a sound from the tents behind them froze him in his tracks.

A Lion samurai burst from between the tents and into the

small clearing before Toturi's pavilion. His armor was muddy and covered in pine needles. His face had been deliberately blackened with mud, but his eyes shone brightly in the firelight. He brandished a yari. Its point shone in the light of the setting moon. Seeing Tsuko, he charged.

Toku and three of Toturi's samurai leapt forward to meet the man, cutting the invader off from the Black Lion and his guest. Weapons clashed. One of Toturi's defenders fell—stabbed by the Lion's spear.

"Stop!" Matsu Tsuko's voice bellowed.

"I followed you, Tsuko-sama," the yari wielder said. "From afar, I saw your battle at the edge of camp," the yari-wielder said. "I've come to free you!"

Toku slashed at him, but he fended off the blow easily.

"Gohei—I'm here of my own free will," Tsuko said sternly. She held him with her dark eyes. "Put up your weapon."

The Lion general looked as though he might obey, but Toturi's samurai pressed in around him. More ronin troops rushed out of the night to their master's defense. The Black Lion's guardsman soon had the invader thoroughly surrounded.

"Enough!" Toturi barked. "We will talk now, not fight. Toku, carry out my commands. You three, tend to our wounded comrade. The rest, move back, out of earshot. I want to talk to these two."

Toku said, "But, Master—"

"Now!" Toturi commanded. His samurai bowed and carried their fallen friend away to a healer. Toku left on his errand. Toturi looked from Tsuko to her general.

"His bravery outweighs his good sense, I think," he said.

Tsuko scowled. "Gohei, why are you here?"

"As I said, my lady, I saw you enter the ronin camp," Gohei replied.

"But you followed me." Anger flared in Tsuko's dark eyes.

"I saw you cross the river and became worried," Gohei explained. "I decided to follow, at a discreet distance, in case you needed help. When I saw *his* samurai surround you, I feared for your life. A quick rescue seemed to be in order. Our army was too far away to fetch them in time."

A sly smile parted Matsu Tsuko's lips. "My brave fool," she said. "Such an attack was suicide. Would you go so willingly to your death?"

Gohei bowed low. "For you, Lady, anything."

Toturi chuckled. "His devotion is admirable. I could use him in my army."

Gohei's grip tightened on the shaft of his yari, but a glance from Tsuko stopped him. "Toturi and I are in parley," she said calmly but firmly. "You will withdraw until I have need of you."

Gohei looked around suspiciously. Toturi's troops had stepped back a respectable distance, but he was still very much surrounded.

Toturi motioned one of his samurai forward. "Misae, see that General Gohei is made comfortable. Fetch him sake, and anything he requires."

The former Crab samurai-ko bowed. "As you will." She rose and motioned for Gohei to follow. He did, but not without a final glance back at his mistress.

Toturi and Tsuko walked back into the Black Lion's tent.

"You should be proud of him," Toturi said.

"I am," Tsuko replied. "Even if he is a headstrong fool." She smiled.

"Headstrong is a trait that runs deep in Lions," Toturi said.

"You should know."

He nodded. "Hai. I know it too well."

Tsuko took a deep breath and sighed. "In another lifetime, you and I could have been friends."

Toturi nodded. "Perhaps. We are much alike."

"Not so much as you think," she replied, a spark of anger flickering in her eyes. "Though you are more like your brother Arasou than I realized."

"I've grown up since you last knew me," Toturi replied. "All of us have."

She paused, not looking at him, and held her breath. "You should lead our clan once more."

"I cannot," Toturi replied. "I am no longer daimyo. I am both less and more. My responsibilities are greater than they were, though my honor is less. I sometimes long for the days when I led our clan; those times seem so much simpler. I wish, though, that I had not made so many mistakes."

"I wish that as well," Tsuko said, still looking away. "For myself as well as you. Rectify some of those mistakes now. Take my sword and return to your rightful place."

"The Lion will not follow me now. They may never follow me again. I'm not refusing out of politeness, but out of practical consideration. *You* are the Lion now."

Tsuko spun suddenly and glared into his deep brown eyes. "The emperor is *evil*," she said. "I cannot serve him any longer. *Fu Leng* sits upon the Emerald Throne."

Toturi held her with his gaze. "Then join me."

Tsuko spoke through gritted teeth. "My oath to the emperor cannot be broken. I am not you; I cannot choose to do what you have done. To do so, I would have to destroy both my honor and that of our clan." She paused as the anger seeped out of her, and then added, "I will *not* destroy my soul. So long as I live, my word is my bond."

Toturi nodded his understanding. "Are you saying there is only one course of action open to you?"

She nodded back. "Hai. Only one course."

"You would force my hand in this? You would compel me to take up the gauntlet, though it might mean still more useless deaths?"

"I would," Tsuko said. "Someone must. You've waited too long, as have our people. Soon, nothing will remain of our clan or the empire."

"Surely there is another way," he said.

The Lion daimyo shook her head, and her golden hair shimmered in the light of the tent's sole lantern. "There is no other way."

Toturi sighed. "Then tell me how I can help."

"You cannot help," she replied. "I know what I must do, and it is my honor and duty as a Lion to do it."

14 THE PHOENIX

Fire surrounded Isawa Tadaka. He wiped the sweat from his brow and pulled his black hood up tight over his nose. The smoke stung his eyes, despite the power of the enchantment surrounding him. Kyuden Isawa, the great castle of the Phoenix, was burning—and the Master of Earth could do nothing about it.

He forged ahead through the inferno, into the blazing hulk of the castle, wondering if anything could be salvaged and hoping beyond hope that some of the Phoenix's age-old wisdom might yet be saved. He knew in his heart that his quest was futile.

He and the other Elemental Masters had all been willing to give their lives, to make any sacrifice to prevent Fu Leng's return to Rokugan. Only his sister, Isawa Kaede, had fled rather than participate in their mad scheme. And mad it had been.

In the flaming ruins of the Isawa Palace, Tadaka saw that he and the other Elemental

Masters hadn't stopped the return of Fu Leng; they had hastened it. The moment they opened the Black Scrolls, they had assured their own doom, and that of their people.

Tadaka dodged a fiery timber that fell in his path and continued toward the heart of the citadel.

How long can the castle burn, he wondered, before it consumes itself utterly? He wondered similarly about himself. How long could he withstand the inferno of his taint before he became utterly corrupt? He said a prayer to Amaterasu, the sun goddess, for strength.

As he gazed at the glowing embers of a thousand years of Isawa history, he realized that he was deceiving himself even now. It was not knowledge he sought to save; his motives were not so high-minded. *Revenge* drove him through the castle's blazing skeleton.

Somewhere within the ruin lurked the Oni no Tadaka—the demon with his name. The creature had tricked Tadaka and the others, fed them Fu Leng's lies when they'd sought the truth. The results burned all around him. Now, the oni would pay.

The Elemental Masters had been away when Yogo Junzo set the Phoenix capital ablaze. They had been seeking knowledge, ever more knowledge—but that had been just another part of Fu Leng's plan. Now Tadaka had returned, too late to save the castle, too late to save the precious library, too late to save his own soul.

Too late, even, to destroy Junzo, who had moved on to burn other cities. The oni, though, remained. Tadaka felt it in his bones, in the green veins of Shadowlands taint that ran like a road map across his skin. He would have his revenge.

A fallen wall barred his way, the massive stone blocks towering like broken ribs out of the palace's corpse. Tadaka concentrated and drew on the power of the earth. The stones shuddered and moved aside, vassals making way for their master.

He found the steps leading underground, down into the great Isawa library. Oily, ash-laden smoke belched from the blackened hole, confirming what Tadaka already knew. Nothing remained.

Realization of the loss overcame Tadaka. He leaned against a red-hot stone and wept, the tears drying on his face almost before they left his eyes. Tsuke, the Master of Fire, Tomo—his brother—the Master of Water, Uona, the Mistress of Air . . . how had they all been so blind?

He wondered about Kaede, his sister. Where was she? Gone into the Void, some said. Had she foreseen this terrible conflagration when she fled? Did she know this would happen when he and the others summoned the oni? Tadaka thought that, perhaps, she had. Someday, he hoped to ask her about it.

If he survived. If she did. If the world did.

Taking a deep breath of the scorching air, Tadaka moved on.

Around him, the palace continued to burn, as if both the walls and the magic that sustained them for a thousand years fed the fire. Jagged pieces of the castle still thrust themselves into the afternoon sky, bony fingers reaching for a heaven forever denied them.

Tadaka gazed up at the storied pillars, memories filling in the ruins: bedrooms, council chambers, great dining halls, and atop them all, the great garden of the Elemental Masters—a space both within the palace and separate from all of Rokugan. They'd birthed the monster in that sacred place.

The Master of Earth's mind filled with visions of the hideous creature: slavering jaws, poisonous spines, writhing tentacles. It shared his name and corrupted his soul.

Tadaka felt tendrils of darkness creep into his mind once more. *Join us! We will give you power such as you have never dreamed of.* The Master of Earth banished the voices with a warding spell; the price of what they offered lay all around him.

A shadow moved to his left; it darted quickly through the burning ruins. Tadaka turned and recognized a ghostly, green-white form flitting through the embers.

The Kuni witch hunter was tall and rail thin. She wore a demonic jade mask—cracked across the forehead—and a long white robe. In her bony hands she carried a long, double-forked spear.

Tadaka's heart swirled with emotions at the sight of her. He had befriended her on his last trip into the Shadowlands; later, after he became tainted, they had fought. He had spared her life that day.

"You lied!" the Kuni cried as she leapt at him. A shimmering jade-green aura surrounded her, protecting her slim body from the heat. The glow emanated from a small bronze mirror on a cord at her throat. Next to the mirror hung an arrowhead talisman. Tadaka had given the arrow to her when they parted; it allowed her to find him even here, deep in his own personal Jigoku. The witch hunter thrust her forked spear at Tadaka's chest; he stepped aside only just in time.

"Stop!" he said. He reached out with his mind to the stones under her feet, and they tripped her. "There's no reason we should fight."

The Kuni pitched forward, rolled, and sprang to her feet once more. "You said we would settle our differences when the time came. That time is *now*."

"No!" Tadaka said, drawing his katana and parrying as she jabbed at him once more. "My work is not yet finished."

She laughed a sepulchral laugh. "What work? Summoning more demons? Causing more ruin? Haven't you learned your lesson yet, Master of Earth?" She swung at his belly, hoping to spill his guts.

He drew his sword and barely turned the blow aside. "I've come here to destroy a demon, not to raise one." Despite the wards protecting him from the heat, sweat beaded on his forehead.

"So *you* say! But I can feel the evil here. It tears like talons at my soul, and you're part of it. I'll not let you bring more destruction to the world, Isawa Tadaka. I'll kill you, as I should have when we first fought." She jabbed at him again.

He leapt over the thrust, landed behind her and kicked her in the back. The Kuni fell, but rose again before Tadaka could command the charred flagstones to seize her. The green taint lacing his body tugged at his muscles, trying to make him kill her. His sword swung for her neck of its own accord. Summoning all his will, he turned it aside and brought the blade down on the haft of her forked spear instead.

Her jab sneaked under his guard and traced a long cut across his ribs. He gasped in pain.

Beneath her expressionless jade mask, she said, "Ha!"

The room around them shuddered, and several flaming timbers fell from the ceiling. The Kuni stepped out of the way as one crashed at her feet. The distraction gave Tadaka time to recover his breath.

As he did, the burning pile before him bulged, as though giving birth. Suddenly, the Oni no Tadaka loomed up out of the wreckage before him. It shook hot coals from its immense back the way a dog sheds water. Black blood oozed from wounds the Elemental Masters had inflicted upon it while questing for their dark knowledge. The sharp spines along its back dripped poison. Its huge tentacles lashed out, striking the burning walls and raining timbers down on the Elemental Master and the witch hunter.

Tadaka spoke a word of power to ward himself against the flaming debris.

The Kuni darted out of the way and fended off an oozing tendril with her spear. "You show your true colors! No matter. I'll slay both of you, demon summoner." She leapt high in the air and stabbed at the monster's misshapen face.

The beast brought up three scorched tentacles and turned her thrust aside. The witch hunter twisted in the air and landed on her feet to one side, just out of range of the monster's arms. The aura around her flickered slightly.

"This creature is no friend of mine," Tadaka said. "I've come to destroy it."

The oni laughed, a sound like rocks breaking. "I bear your name, Tadaka," it said. "You cannot kill me! I *am* you!"

"Never!" Tadaka cried, his shout echoing off the burning walls around them. He scooped a handful of red-hot rocks from the ground and hurled them at the demon. As they flew, the coals turned into blazing darts. The fiery shuriken struck the beast's face, piercing its scorched and flabby brain.

The monster screamed. Tadaka saw now that it was more gravely wounded than the Elemental Masters' interrogations could account for. Its neck had been cut nearly through. The flesh had been scorched from the skull, leaving the great head a mass of bone and brain. The brain itself was crushed and deformed.

How the thing still lived, the Master of Earth could not fathom.

The Kuni sprinted beneath the oni's flailing tendrils and thrust her spear up through the bottom of the monster's sagging jaw. The forked tines of the weapon pierced the skull and burst through the brain, sending a spray of black liquid and mottled purple flesh into the scorching air.

Again, the aura around her dimmed; patches of sweat formed on the chest of the witch hunter's white robe.

Her magic is failing, Tadaka thought. She needs to get out of this inferno.

He shouted over the roar of the fire, summoning the life force of the earth to himself. Jagged spikes of rock thrust up from the floor and in from the remaining walls. They pierced the oni's flayed body in a hundred places.

The Kuni rolled out of the way, avoiding both Tadaka's deadly rock spines and the monster's flailing tentacles.

At a word from their master, the stones erupted from the oni's body, splattering its innards over the flaming ruins. The huge monster squealed in agony, fell into the coals and ashes, and lay there twitching while its black lifeblood ran out.

"... betrayed ... betrayed!" the oni burbled.

"Junzo betrayed you?" Tadaka asked. "He did this to you?"

Hideous laughter racked the oni's immense, tortured body. Then, with a bubbling hiss, its breath ran out and it died.

Tadaka gazed at the charred and bloody form. He could see the mark of dark sorcery upon the carcass. Why would Junzo do this? Tadaka wondered. Did the oni really tell us so much? The Master of Earth shook his head. Whatever the reason Junzo had done this, the dark sorcerer had unwittingly helped Tadaka.

"Now ... face me!" the witch hunter hissed from behind him.

Tadaka turned as she walked forward, her steps labored and uncertain. Sweat drenched her white robe, making it cling to her thin frame. The aura protecting her flickered and dimmed.

"I'm *not* your enemy," Tadaka said.

"So ... you ... say," the Kuni gasped. She pointed her forked spear at his chest. Her legs gave way. She toppled forward, and Tadaka caught her in his arms. The magic protecting her dimmed and went out. Her bronze amulet blackened and turned to ashes.

Tadaka chanted a sutra to Amaterasu and extended his protection around the Kuni's prostrate form. He lifted her sweat-slick body and carried her out of the burning castle. Even unconscious, she clutched her spear tightly in her fist.

The sun sat on the shoulders of Mori Isawa, the great wood of the Phoenix, when Tadaka finally reached the edge of the ruins. Amaterasu shone the pale, crimson rays of her waning light over the denuded trees and red-needled pines. Spring had not brought renewal this year; it only reminded the people of the evil walking the land.

The Master of Earth's human burden weighed heavily in his arms. The wound in his side ached and burned. He paused next to a remnant of fallen wall and laid the Kuni witch hunter down on the cool sand.

Kneeling beside her, he took a flask of pure water from his belt. Lifting her mask slightly—not enough to reveal her face—he put the vial to her cracked and bloody lips. Gently, he poured the liquid into her mouth.

The eyes behind her jade mask flickered open.

"Perhaps . . . some spark of humanity . . . remains within you yet," she said weakly. She took the flask from him and continued drinking.

Tadaka sat down on the sand next to her. "Hai, perhaps."

"It makes no difference, though," the Kuni said. She sat up slowly and stretched her lithe form. "We must still have our reckoning."

"Saving your life makes no difference?"

She shook her head, and her eyes gleamed. "It was pursuing you that endangered my life in the first place. I am pledged to fight evil; you are tainted. Saving me has won you only a temporary respite." She pulled the arrowhead from the cord around her neck and held it out to him in her pale hand. "You gave this to me to find you when the time came—so that we could finish our battle. Your people have been destroyed because of your corruption. As soon as I've recovered fully, it's time to settle old debts."

The Master of Earth peered into the dark eyes behind the jade mask. "The time is close now, but my obligations here are not yet finished."

"Would you do more damage? This could have been prevented if I had killed you." Her grip tightened on her forked spear. She rose and pointed the weapon at his breast.

Tadaka sat calmly on the sand. "Perhaps, but perhaps our fortunes are stronger than our will. My fate will not be complete until I have rectified the damage I have caused."

"You cling to life like a frightened child," the witch hunter said, lowering her spear.

"No," he said. "I merely wait to fulfill my destiny. Before I met you, on my mission into the Shadowlands, I met another man. He warned me against the journey and said it would be my doom."

The witch hunter nodded and her dark hair danced around her lithe form. "He was right."

"Hai. I see that now. He said something else, though, that we would meet again when the end of the world was nigh. That time is fast approaching. I feel it in the earth. I feel it in my bones. My mission is not yet complete. I ask you to wait. When my task is finished, then you can do with me what you will." He held her with his dark eyes until she finally nodded.

"Very well," the witch hunter said. "I'll wait. But I'll also watch. I won't let you make the same mistakes again, Isawa Tadaka."

Still sitting, he bowed to her. "I'm glad to hear it. Domo arigato gozaimasu."

Tadaka couldn't tell if she frowned behind her mask or not. She bowed curtly to him and then walked quickly away. "Remember," she called back, "I will be watching." She vanished into the descending night like a black-maned specter.

As she disappeared from sight, Tadaka suddenly felt tired. The elemental master rose from the sand and seated himself on a fallen stone at the edge of the ruins. He pulled the round-brimmed hat from his head and wiped his brow. "How much longer, Amaterasu?"

He sat on the beach beside the castle until well after sunset, meditating and carefully binding his wounded side. He took his supper in solitude, eating dried fruits and seaweed and drinking from a jade flask. The green stone burned his palms where it touched, a legacy of the Shadowlands curse that afflicted the Master of Earth. Still, he fought the pain and refused to give in.

The fires behind him beat back the night, casting their orange glow over the wide beach around the castle. Out to sea, the first stars flickered to life. The cascade of the surf and snap of the fire combined to form a strange, rhythmic music. Far off, he thought he heard the sound of a flute.

He wondered where his brother, Tomo, and the other Elemental Masters were. Did they even know that the Phoenix palace had fallen? Was Tomo sitting beneath the waves somewhere, talking with the dolphins? Was Uona flying naked above the clouds, gazing down on the mountaintops? Was Tsuke toiling beneath his fortress, forging enchanted weapons to fight the enemy?

Tadaka shook his head. *They* had become the enemy—all of them. In their zest to defeat Fu Leng, he and the other Elemental Masters had used the Evil One's methods, employed his servants. The burning of the great library was just a down payment against the debt on their souls. Tadaka silently vowed to balance the accounts.

The veins of taint scarring the back of his hands itched, and he scratched them. So much to make amends for, and very little time left. He felt it in his weary bones.

"Is there nothing left?" a deep voice beside him asked.

Tadaka looked up to find Isawa Tsuke, the Master of Fire, standing near his elbow. Light from the castle's fires played across Tsuke's harsh face and made his eyes glow red.

The Master of Earth shook his head. "Nothing."

The crystal jewelry decorating Tsuke's orange and red kimono rattled and sparked in the darkness. He looked around suspiciously and rubbed his shaved head. "What about . . . it?"

"The oni?"

Tsuke nodded. "Hai."

"Dead," Tadaka replied. "Junzo left it behind when he burned the castle. It was crippled and weak. I still had to slay its body, though."

"You had no trouble doing so?" Tsuke asked.

"None," Tadaka said. In his mind, he saw the witch hunter's spear flashing toward his side. He put his hand on his bandaged ribs and rubbed the indigo silk covering them.

"Too bad the beast didn't serve us better," Tsuke said grimly. "Still, we found what we summoned it for—power and knowledge to rival Fu Leng's own. When the time is right, we'll strike."

Tadaka pulled his round-brimmed straw hat low over his face. His eyes blazed green in the darkness. "Yes," he said. "Very soon, now."

15 HONOR

Warm winds blew from the south over the Spine of the World Mountains. The breeze was wholesome, untainted by Shadowlands stench, and spoke of spring and new life. It rattled the prickly needles of the tall cryptomeria and made the cherry blossoms shake. Birds chirped happily in the boughs, and new shoots of green sprouted up through the damp ground.

Spring is very late, Toturi thought, but it has finally come. He strode purposefully through the silent encampment. He'd ordered the campfires extinguished this morning, so that no smoke would stain today's air.

Overhead, the weather seemed to be cooperating as well. Only a single, high cloud hung in the silvery predawn sky. It will be a glorious day, Toturi thought—as it should be. He turned and gazed back down toward the river valley below. The mountains behind them, the river before them. They were caught in the midst of two worlds. It was only fitting.

The Black Lion exhaled slowly, and the cloud of his breath drifted up to heaven. Winter had not yet completely released its grip. Perhaps, today, though . . .

He made his way through the tents to Tsuko's pavilion. He'd given her his own tent, as there was no time to prepare one suitable for her. Toturi bowed slightly to Bentai and Gohei, standing guard on either side of the door. They bowed low to him in return and stepped aside to let him enter.

Inside, Matsu Tsuko sat quietly on a pillow in the center of the floor. Her eyes were closed in meditation, but she opened them when Toturi entered. He bowed to her; she stood.

Tsuko walked to the stand holding her daisho. She picked up the wakizashi—her soul—and tucked it into her belt. Then she turned and held out her lion-headed sword to Toturi. "Here," she said, "take this."

"I couldn't," the Black Lion replied.

"You must," she said, her dark eyes full of fire.

"It would not be right."

She insisted. "It is your duty."

"I am not worthy of this gift," he said, finishing the ancient formula of polite refusal.

"I will have it no other way," she replied. "Take this, for the sake of the empire." Their eyes locked for a few moments. "And for my sake, as well," she added. "If ever you loved your brother, take it."

Toturi bowed once. He held out his hands and took the katana from her. He tucked it into his broad obi. She handed him a sheet of perfect white rice paper, folded once. He tucked that into his belt as well. "Are you ready?" he asked.

Tsuko nodded. "I am ready."

She looked magnificent in her pure white robes. Toturi admired her grace and perfect tranquility. *She truly is the Lion*, he thought. They turned and left the pavilion together.

The paths between the tents stood deserted. All of Toturi's samurai had retired inside, as Tsuko desired. As Tsuko and Toturi passed through the tent city only the spring breeze and the chirping of birds disturbed the silence.

At the edge of the camp, an old monk greeted them. His name was Kazuo, and he had once been a tutor to the Matsu. His features were wizened with the passage of many summers, and his limbs shook as he leaned against a tall pole blazoned with the Lion mon. He had joined Toturi's army after Junzo's forces destroyed his monastery.

Kazuo bowed very low as Tsuko and Toturi approached. They bowed in return. Tsuko stepped forward, and Kazuo fell in behind her, proudly carrying the Lion standard. Toturi solemnly brought up the rear.

They walked uphill to a jutting rock far above the encampment. A small wooden scaffold had been set atop the rock, forming a kind of natural stage. A smooth curtain of white silk encircled the platform, blocking out the trees behind and leaving the front open to the landscape and the sky.

Kazuo planted the golden mon of the Lion in a small flower-dappled clearing in front of the platform. The standard flapped in the breeze, its silk whispering of power and grace and honor.

As the three of them approached the platform, Toturi looked downhill. The tall pines of the forest hid all of the encampment, except the very top of his own tent. Far beyond that, the river stretched out silver in the predawn light.

Somewhere on the other side, Tsuko's Lion army searched for their mistress. They would not find her. Before long, Matsu Gohei would ride into their camp and have them march east—turning over command of the troops to Matsu Yojo. Then Gohei would return to Toturi's camp and wait for word from his mistress.

If Tsuko looked for her encampment or her samurai friend, Toturi did not notice.

Kazuo mounted the platform before them, chanting a Shintao prayer of purification. Finishing, he turned and bowed to the waiting lords. Tsuko walked up the short steps to the top of the platform. Toturi came behind Tsuko, taking his place on her right. The priest stood silently on Tsuko's left.

Matsu Tsuko bowed to Toturi, then toward Otosan Uchi—hidden in the fog and darkness beyond the valley and far to the northeast. She knelt on the platform and spread out a roll of pristine white rice paper. She took the wakizashi from her belt and placed it carefully on the paper's surface.

She bowed low to the east, where the sun still loomed below the horizon, and said a quiet prayer. Then she stood and stepped carefully onto the middle of the paper. Folding her legs under her, she knelt down and sat on her heels in the traditional seiza position.

Tsuko picked up the wakizashi and unsheathed the blade. Kazuo stepped forward with a bucket of clear water. Tsuko held the sword out to the side, and he ladled the water down the blade, purifying the steel.

The Lion daimyo nodded a bow to the monk. He bowed in return and stepped back. He walked to Toturi, who had unsheathed Tsuko's lion-headed katana, and purified the blade in the same manner. Toturi raised the blade high in salute and readiness. Kazuo stepped back into his place. Tsuko picked up a small piece of white rice paper and folded it around the blade.

She gripped the sword in both hands and positioned it over her belly, below her navel and to the left. Calmly, she gazed out over the forest and mouthed a final, silent prayer.

Steeling her jaw, Tsuko plunged the blade of the wakizashi into her body.

The wind sighed and rustled through the trees. White cherry blossoms sailed off their branches and danced through the air. They surrounded Tsuko and caressed her, but she took no notice.

Slowly and carefully, she cut her belly from left to right. Her face remained calm; she did not cry out. Warm blood stained the front of her white kimono, but the fabric held her guts inside her. When she had finished the left-to-right incision, she moved the blade upward, toward her heart.

At that moment, the sun rose. The light of the goddess shone in Matsu Tsuko's dark eyes. "Arasou," she gasped, "I come!" Tears welled up at the corners of her eyes. Her hands hesitated, as if her strength might fail.

Toturi stepped forward and, with one swift stroke, severed her neck. Tsuko's face flopped onto her breast, a thin flap of skin holding her head to her body. Kazuo nodded grimly; the cut had been perfect—Tsuko's head would not be dishonored by touching the ground.

Toturi stepped back, and the priest washed Tsuko's blood from the Lion-headed sword. The Black Lion wiped the blade dry with white rice paper and then resheathed it. His jaw trembled, and tears welled at the corner of his deep brown eyes. White cherry petals fluttered around him like butterflies.

Toturi walked to the front of the platform and removed the paper from his belt. He unfolded it and, tears streaming down his face, read Matsu Tsuko's death poem. The Black Lion's deep voice rolled across the hillside like the surf on the shore.

> "In winter's sorrow
> Despairing shadows grow long
> In my eyes, spring dawns"

At the final word, a small white cloud in the sky opened up, showering gentle snow upon Toturi, Kazuo, and the wildflowers in the tiny meadow below the platform. The flakes danced with the cherry petals before settling to earth. The delicate crystals lingered a moment before evaporating into the late spring air.

"Amaterasu weeps as well," Kazuo said quietly from behind Toturi.

The Black Lion stepped back and bowed his head. For a long moment, silence reigned over the hillside, and in the valley below. Then Toturi walked quietly off the stage.

Kazuo stepped forward and laid the Lion daimyo's body flat across the platform. He gently replaced Tsuko's head atop her shoulders and said a prayer to the sun goddess for her soul. He backed to the edge of the stage, and Toturi handed him a blazing torch.

"I have served Matsu Tsuko's family long and well, yet I wish that I could do more for her," the monk said quietly.

"It was her wish that I alone witness her seppuku," Toturi replied. "You have done well. No samurai could give more." He bowed. "Domo arigato gozaimasu, Kazuo-sama."

The monk bowed as well. "Domo arigato gozaimasu, Toturi-sama. I will prepare the way for her passage and feast with her tonight in paradise." Kazuo walked to the center of the stage, sat down, and lit the platform ablaze.

Tsuko's pyre ignited swiftly, and white smoke quickly carried her body up to the heavens. Kazuo sat silently and ascended with her. In front of the blaze, the golden mon of the Lion flapped quietly in the wind.

Toturi turned and walked down the hill to the waiting encampment. He wiped the moisture from his eyes, but he did not look back.

16 THE MESSAGE

"Matsu Tsuko has carried her clan's bond with the emperor into heaven with her," Toturi said, his voice booming across the hills and through the tents of his army. "She sits beside Amaterasu now, the bravest, most honorable Lion who ever lived. Know that she watches over us, and expects us to live—and die—as bravely as she.

"Our task on Rokugan is not yet finished. To me, she left her sword as well as our common mission: To root out the Evil One wherever he may hide. To fight our way across the land, slaying his minions wherever we find them. We will never stop. We will never slacken. Even if our quest takes us to the gates of Otosan Uchi itself, we will fight on! Are you with me?"

As one, the assembly rose and thrust their fists into the air. "Hai!" they thundered in unison.

The Black Lion turned to Gohei, who—having returned from his mission—stood beside him. "Matsu Gohei," Toturi said, "will you fight at my side?"

Gohei bowed and said. "Until darkness covers all the world. No longer will I serve a corrupt emperor. I now serve the empire itself. I will do whatever it takes to destroy this evil."

Toturi nodded at the Lion general and then turned his gaze out over his own troops, assembled amid their tents. "What of you, my samurai? Ronin, Dragon, Scorpion, Crab—peasants and lords alike—will you cast aside your bickering and join with me to wipe corruption from the face of the empire?"

"Hai!" Toturi's samurai thundered.

"Let us shake the pillars of heaven with our war cry!" Toturi said. "Let Fu Leng hear our words and know fear in his evil heart!"

The entire army thrust their fists to the sky once more and shouted, "Banzai! Banzai! Banzai!"

"Gambatte!" Toturi cried. "Fight on! Fight until not one of Fu Leng's minions remains!" He raised Tsuko's sword over his head, and the steel shone white in the morning sun.

As the ovations died away, the Black Lion turned to Gohei. "Take the news of Tsuko's sacrifice to the Lion armies. Tell them we welcome their strength in the battle to come." He handed Tsuko's death poem to the general.

Gohei took it and bowed. "Hai, Toturi-sama."

Toturi bowed in acknowledgment. Turning, Gohei mounted a swift charger that had been tethered at the edge of the camp.

Toku and Ikoma Bentai stepped to the Black Lion's side. "Until this moment," Bentai said, "I never believed we truly could win."

Toku frowned at the old general. "You didn't? Well, you sure fooled me."

Bentai smiled. "Age and guile always outstrip youth and enthusiasm. Tsuko watches over us. Her armies will join ours against Fu Leng. The Lion will be one again. We cannot lose."

"Hai, but the worst is still ahead of us," Toturi said grimly.

"We're not afraid," Toku said.

Toturi smiled and nodded at his young commander. "Hai. With all my soul, I vow that we will free the land from the Evil One's grip. The emperor's madness *will* end."

▲▲▲▲▲▲▲▲

Matsu Gohei's mighty charger thundered down the hills and across the plains into the core of the Lion lands. Next to his heart, he carried Tsuko's death poem.

The Lion general rode grimly, determined to see Tsuko's last wishes carried out—resolved that the clan should unite under Toturi and battle Fu Leng and the possessed emperor. Hearing that Tsuko's mountain army, now led by Matsu Yojo, had returned to the capital, he rode directly for Shiro no Yojin.

He wasted little time, stopping only when his horse needed water, food, or rest. He ate in the saddle and slept there as well. Blight-stricken land flew by under the charger's hooves.

From the Lion capital, Gohei could search out Ikoma Tsanuri, Kitsu Motso, and the other Lion generals. Likely, he would find some of them at the castle already. Shiro no Yojin was close to Otosan Uchi, a natural place from which to enforce the emperor's will.

The emperor! Gohei's soul burned at the thought of how he'd dishonored the Lion. At Hantei's order, many of their best samurai lay dead on the beach before Otosan Uchi. For all Gohei knew, their bodies reposed there still, left to rot by the boy emperor and his terrible allies. The evil Shining Prince had forced Matsu Tsuko to take her own life to preserve the Lion's honor.

With her sacrifice, the remaining Lion were free. Tsuko was bound to the emperor; her armies, though, were bound to her. Her death released the Lion from her oath. Now, Gohei and his kinsman could fight for the empire itself, and the emperor be damned. He hoped the others would see that as clearly as he did.

Gohei rounded a bend in the muddy road and topped a small rise. The scene that greeted him caused him to rein in his charger. The awful spectacle froze his bones.

A short distance down the road lay the remains of a country teahouse. It was a place Gohei had visited several times during his travels to and from the Matsu palace. Once, delicate painted lanterns had hung from the bamboo rafters below the green tile roof. Now the roof lay in pieces on the ground, the rafters were burning, and the lanterns had been trampled into the mud. A band of Shadowlands raiders stood amid the ruins, slaughtering the shop's owners and patrons.

A white-skinned shugenja in black robes crouched above the shop's tea servers. She cackled with delight at the terror of the three young ladies. The women shivered and tried to crawl away from the sorceress but had nowhere to escape. The shugenja pulled one of the women to her feet and gazed into her eyes. The woman screamed, and her skin shriveled up like dry leaves.

Nearby, a teenage boy and a doughty field worker brawled with a huge, bone-faced samurai. A circle of other Shadowlands forces, at least a dozen strong, surrounded the lopsided melee. Some of the evil samurai rode onikage—demon horses. Most, though, padded across the moist earth on their rotting feet. They cheered and laughed as the big samurai toyed with the courageous men.

In the center of the carnage stood a tall skeletal creature with long fangs and immense bat wings—an oni. The pupils of the demon's black eyes blazed red with hate. The teahouse's owner, a gentleman named Tahei, lay in a puddle of his own blood at the monster's feet. Tahei's wife and young son knelt at his side, weeping piteously. Several dead patrons lay next to the proprietor, looks of terror etched indelibly on their peasant faces.

In the moment it took Gohei to drink in the awful scene, the oni seized the owner's wife by the hair and lifted her off her feet. The child with her screamed, and clutched frantically at the mother's ankles. The oni sank its fangs into the mother's neck and ripped her throat out. Blood fell like red rain.

With a cry of fury, Gohei spurred his steed and charged down the hill.

The Shadowlands forces looked up in surprise at his approach. He struck like thunder, smashing into the samurai circling the teahouse. The charger's hooves crushed one man, while Gohei's yari skewered another. The Lion general kicked the bandit's body off his spear.

A black-armored samurai-ko charged him. He smashed her

face with the yari's haft and kept riding. An onikage horseman rode forward to meet him. Green fire blazed in the raider's eyes. He aimed a wooden lance at Gohei's heart.

Gohei caught the long spear on the head of his weapon. Wrenching his wrist, he drove the rider from his saddle. The man fell under the hooves of his own demon steed and perished.

By this time, the rest of the Shadowlands brigands appreciated the threat Gohei posed. The bone-faced man dropped the teenager he'd been strangling and drew his swords. When the doughty farmer made an attempt to stop him, the huge back samurai lopped his head off. The farmer's surprised face landed in a puddle at the raver's feet.

The second of the serving women crumbled into a pile of ashes at the hem of the white-skinned shugenja's kimono. Though the third woman lay helpless before her, the black-robed maho witch turned from her prey toward Gohei.

Gohei charged directly for the huge oni. The creature brushed aside the child pounding on its bony shins and turned on the Lion samurai. The boy fell to the mud, wailing piteously.

The general bore down on the monster. The oni slashed at Gohei with its long, clawlike fingers. Gohei thrust at the demon's ribcage. The creature leapt into the air, and Gohei's yari passed harmlessly beneath its wings.

Gohei ducked, trying to avoid the demon's sharp-taloned feet, but the bony nails raked across his face, spraying his own blood into his eyes. The demon swooped down on the blinded samurai.

The Lion swung his yari in a defensive maneuver, twirling it over his head like a bo staff. The weapon's haft hit the creature's bony skull. The demon hissed and arced up into the air, green spittle flying from its mouth.

Gohei blinked the blood out of his eyes. He wheeled and threw his yari with all his might at the airborne monster.

The spear struck deep into the oni's chest. Crimson fire leaked out of its skeletal body. The creature faltered in air, a surprised look washing over its emaciated face. It fastened its bony talons around the yari's haft and pulled.

The spear's point ripped out of the oni's body, pulling a huge chunk of purple-gray flesh with it. The demon shrieked in agony. Scarlet flame shot out of its gaping wound. The monster tumbled awkwardly toward the earth. As it fell, the Lion drew his sword.

Gohei met the monster before it struck ground. His keen-bladed katana flashed; the oni's head flew from its shoulders. The decapitated creature fell dead in the mud, red fire blazing from its writhing body. Its head crashed into the ruins of the teahouse and exploded.

"Kill him!" the maho witch screamed in fury to the remaining Shadowlands ravers.

The huge, bone faced samurai nodded and loped toward Gohei. "Gom kill!"

The others shouted, "Hai, Kurioshi-sama!" and closed in.

Ignoring a half-dozen raiders, Gohei wheeled his charger toward the maho witch.

The black-robed shugenja whispered an evil spell, gathering deadly red energies between her pale hands. One remaining serving girl clawed at the shugenja's ankle, trying desperately to help Gohei. The evil sorceress turned, and red energy cascaded from her fingertips. The girl's head burst, splattering the witch's robe. The white-skinned shugenja smiled, and her long black hair danced in an unfelt wind.

Her pleasure was short lived. Gohei reached her. She tried to duck, but his blade traced a long gash from her chin to her scalp. The wound wasn't fatal, but she fell to earth, stunned and bleeding.

Gohei reined his horse quickly and turned it to finish her. He spurred his steed toward the fallen witch, his eyes narrow with concentration and fury. He didn't notice the big man sprinting toward him until it was almost too late.

Gom, the bone faced samurai, swung his tetsubo, wielding the great iron-studded club with one hand. The Lion ducked under the weapon just in time. The big man followed the swing with a quick, left-handed punch. His armored fist slammed into Gohei's midsection.

Air rushed out of the general's lungs, and he fell from his

saddle, landing hard in the mud. He scrambled to his feet as Gom came in for a finishing strike. Gohei rolled under the blow and slashed his sword across the samurai's gut. The man's dark mail turned the blow aside.

The samurai counterattacked. His swing clipped Gohei's face, and the Lion general staggered back. He nearly toppled into the demon's burning body.

The other raiders surged toward the disoriented Lion, but Gom called, "Give room!" He smashed one of his fellows with his club and the others moved back.

Gom swung again.

Gohei dropped to all fours. He wheeled, lashing out at the larger man with his leg. The spin kick caught the big samurai in the shins.

Gom gasped and toppled forward, falling onto the demon's burning corpse. He screamed and staggered to his feet, his flesh and clothing aflame. Gohei's blade passed under Gom's helmet, through his mouth, and out the back of his head.

Gohei yanked the katana back, and the burning man fell over, dead.

Gom's comrades angrily closed in on Gohei, cautious lest he escape their deadly circle.

Someone screamed. Gohei turned to see the maho witch standing over the body of the shop owner's son, the child's blood staining her pale hands. She smiled; her facial wound began to heal.

Gohei's spirit fell. Many raiders remained. His favored weapon, the yari, had been destroyed in the demon fire. He'd lost his horse, and no one remained to be saved. In this battle, the Shadowlands had triumphed.

Cold reason replaced anger. His mission was not to die here. Perhaps he could defeat all the remaining ravers. If he did not, Matsu Tsuko's final message would never reach her people. He cursed himself for being a fool.

A soft whinny drew Gohei's attention outside the enemy circle. His charger stomped on the earth beyond the ravers. A smile drew across Matsu Gohei's bruised and bloody face. Sparing one last glance toward the shugenja, he picked his spot in the enemy line and charged.

"Matsu Tsuko!" he screamed.

The samurai facing Gohei slashed with her katana.

Gohei met the sword with his own and then counterattacked. The samurai-ko fell dead. Gohei sprinted through the line and leapt onto the back of his charger. He spurred the horse hard, and it shot down the muddy road.

One of the undead riders followed him. Her skeletal steed glowed with unnatural energy; it hadn't ridden for many days like Gohei's charger. She drew her bow and fired. The arrow hit Gohei's left shoulder and stuck. The impact jarred his body, but he ignored the pain. The evil samurai-ko drew her sword and rode up next to the wounded Lion.

The Lion turned and chopped with his katana, severing the onikage's spine. As the undead horse pitched forward, its rider leapt from her mount. She landed on the charger's back behind Gohei and tried to pull him from the saddle.

He spun on her and thrust the point of his sword into her throat, just below her helmet. The woman clutched at the katana, yanking it from Gohei's hands. She fell backward off the horse, spraying black blood. Gohei kept riding as she landed, twitching. The Lion smiled. Another weapon lost, but the battle won.

As he turned to face the road once more, he heard the shugenja shriek with rage. He laughed and kept riding.

Suddenly, he felt fire burning across his chest. Gohei looked down to see the silk of his kimono blazing with crimson flame. Though he had escaped the samurai, clearly he was still within range of the maho witch's power.

The paper! he thought. Tsuko's poem! He tried to pat out the flames with his gloves, but the magical blaze would not extinguish. It clung to him like a living thing.

Gohei remembered a stream running near the road ahead. Gritting his teeth, he spurred his animal on. Fire burned over nearly all of his armor by the time he splashed his charger into the water.

He dived from the saddle, landing hard and accidentally rolling onto the arrow embedded in his shoulder. White-hot pain shot through his body. Gohei struggled to remain conscious. He submerged in the cold water of the stream, diving under for as long as he could.

Finally, the arcane fires went out. Gohei rose from the water scorched, sodden, bleeding, and barely conscious. He whistled gently to his steed, and the horse came to him. Every bone in his body ached as he climbed onto the noble animal's back.

Stars flashed before his tired eyes; his ears rang with the sound of huge temple bells. Wearily, he urged his mount forward.

They may still follow! his mind screamed. You may not have lost them yet. You're too weary to fight again. Clinging desperately to his saddle, he nodded to himself and spurred the horse to a gallop once more.

17 ANCIENT POWERS

The summer stars shone brightly in the sky above the great Dragon fortress of Kyuden Togashi. They arced across the heavens in slow, graceful patterns that remained unchanged since the beginning of the world.

Nearly as old were the white stone battlements of the Dragon's fortress. They thrust themselves up out of the living rock, like graceful fingers reaching to touch the Sun Goddess, Amaterasu. Burnished gold decorations adorned the castle's cornices; the roof tiles were gold as well. The entire palace shimmered under the dim starlight, like a dream come to earth.

Proud Dragon samurai guarded the castle's gates, their many tattoos serving in place of armor. With keen, unwavering eyes, they watched the frontiers below their lord's mountain kingdom; their bodies never tired. Such was the gift of their great lord, Togashi Yokuni.

For many long years, the Dragon had stood

apart from the rest of the empire. Their lord did not deign to involve his people in the affairs of lesser men. It was whispered that Yokuni feared no living man, not even the Hantei emperor.

The great lord himself never spoke of such things. In fact, he was seldom seen by his people. Day-to-day administration of the castle fell to his servants and courtiers. Sometimes, the Dragon's son, Hoshi—a great tattooed warrior—would tend to his father's business. Often, though, he roamed the land in disguise, gathering knowledge or tending to his own secret concerns.

Despite their long isolation, the Dragon had of late sent their troops abroad in Rokugan. At Togashi Yokuni's order, a force of Dragon samurai had recently joined Toturi's march toward the City of the Shining Prince. Soon, they would have more allies.

The huge ivory gates of the Dragon palace swung open. Great hordes of samurai and tattooed men streamed down the marble steps and into golden-scaled dragon boats waiting in the lagoon. Silently, they took their places beneath the oars as their lord and his companions watched from the head of the stairway.

Togashi Yokuni was the very essence of power. His armor, covered in fine inlaid scales of gold and jade, shone in the darkness. The daimyo's golden eyes gleamed from beneath his horned helmet. He looked taller, larger, prouder than any man could be—though his stature was not much greater than those who stood next to him.

On his right stood Reiko, the captain of the lord's dragon ship. Her daisho swords were tucked into the belt of her sea-green kimono. An exquisite dragon tattoo wound up her neck and curled over her left eye. A wry smile played across her pretty face.

To the great lord's left stood the Hooded Ronin. He leaned against his flute-topped staff and watched the preparations below. The green of his cloak matched that of Yokuni's armor.

As the final samurai settled into their positions, Reiko turned to her master, bowed, and said, "All is in readiness, great lord."

Togashi Yokuni nodded to his samurai-ko. *Prepare to leave.* Though his lips never moved, his deep voice rumbled like thunder in their minds.

Reiko bowed again and hurried down the steps. The Dragon lord turned to his companion. *Now,* his mind spoke for the

Hooded Ronin alone. *Tell me, my friend, do we come too late?*

The Hooded Ronin shook his head. "I know no more than you. To see the future is to change it, Shinsei tells us."

Hai, said Yokuni. *I know it well.* He turned his head to survey his palace and the mountains surrounding it. *This place is like paradise to me. I hate to leave it.*

"The battle to come will shake the pillars of heaven," the Hooded Ronin replied. "Perhaps, once the final echoes of conflict die away, you will need never leave your home again."

Togashi Yokuni nodded grimly. *Hai. This will be my final journey. I both dread and welcome it. My eyes gaze far, ronin, but beyond this I see only the Void.*" He took a deep breath of the cool mountain air. The palace seemed to shake as he exhaled. *Have you spoken to the others?*

"All except one."

Yes, and I, too.

"We have done what we could, you and I. You have summoned the souls of the Seven Thunders even as I have gathered their bodies. Soon, body and spirit will be one. Even now, they come."

The Seven Thunders, Yokuni rumbled, *together again for the first time in a thousand years.*

"They are not the same men and women, great lord," the ronin said gently.

Their spirits are the same, Yokuni replied. *That is what matters. The strength of their souls will allow us to defeat Fu Leng once more.*

"The Fortunes willing," the hooded man added.

Hai, the Fortunes willing. The Dragon's thoughts echoed into silence. *But we have one more straggler, you and I. . . .*

"Your 'daughter,' Mirumoto Hitomi," the ronin said.

Togashi Yokuni nodded. *A difficult one, she. Though not of my blood, our fortunes are deeply intertwined.*

"She burns with the fires of hate," the Hooded Ronin replied.

But she is destined for great things, said Yokuni. His voice echoed in the ronin's head. *I drew the tattoos upon her body with my own hands. I have seen her future. I'm sure she'll do the job fated for her.* The lord of the Dragon gazed out over his kingdom once again, and his eyes took on an otherworldly gleam.

The Hooded Ronin regarded his old friend respectfully, waiting for the lord to speak again.

I have seen her. I will speak to her now, for both of us.

With that, he faded into starlight. The ronin leaned against his staff and waited. He felt the eyes of the Dragon troops on him, but he paid no attention. The samurai had seldom seen their great lord; they were not used to the miracles he could perform. In the days to come, the ronin knew, they would see many more.

The stars turned slowly but inexorably. Finally Yokuni reappeared as silently as he had gone.

"Did you find her?" the ronin asked.

Hai. His voice rumbled like a volcano in the traveler's mind. *I have set her feet upon the correct path.*

"Then the Day of Thunder is at hand."

Hai—after all these countless years. Let us depart.

Yokuni walked down the long, white steps toward Reiko's dragon boat. His armor made no more noise than the scales of a serpent plying the Sea of the Sun Goddess. The Hooded Ronin followed, his footsteps echoing off the gold and marble walls.

They boarded the golden craft and took their positions at the bow.

"Open the gates!" Reiko called to her samurai on shore. The warrior men and women worked the huge winches that opened the gigantic doors of the Dragon's secret lagoon.

The colossal boat swept forward as a hundred samurai pulled on the mighty oars. Water surged before the ship's bow, creating great white waves to herald the Dragon lord's coming. The other ships in the armada formed up behind their daimyo, trailing close in his powerful wake.

The dragon ship passed through the gold and ivory gates of the lagoon and into the rapids beyond. The mighty vessel seemed almost to fly through the water.

The Hooded Ronin picked up his staff and blew a somber tune across the flute end.

The storm is coming. Yokuni's unheard voice shook the ship's timbers. *Soon, there will be thunder.*

18 CITY OF EVIL

A pestilent summer wind scorched the great city of Otosan Uchi. In the emperor's gardens, flowers thrust themselves from the earth only to perish in withering heat. The great waterfall, Fudotaki, ran slowly, its river polluted with debris, plague-stricken bodies, and things far worse. The castle walls shone green with mildew and sickly moss. Ashes and dark lichens clung to the high, red-tiled roofs. In the Forbidden City, the silence was broken only by scurrying rats and screams from the city beyond.

In the city, chaos reigned. People built piles of their plague dead and burned the bodies in the streets. Temples blazed with orange fires. Worship of Amaterasu and her kami had been replaced by supplications to just one god: the living god Hantei the 39th. The people built new altars and sacrificed their neighbors, even their children, to one they hoped would save them from the plague.

High in the palace towers, Empress Kachiko gazed out over the city, watching greasy black smoke roll into the gray summer sky. Thunderclouds boiled constantly overhead, mingling with the smoke. From the clouds fell ebony rain. People who drank it died.

On a distant rooftop, Kachiko noticed the sacrifice of a teenage girl. The murderers wrote the characters of the emperor's name in their victim's blood and flew it on a banner above the house.

The fools, Kachiko thought. The blind fools. The emperor will not save you; he wants you all dead.

She pulled her kimono tighter around her supple body, despite the warmth of the summer day. Bone-chilling cold permeated the great castle, no matter how hot it grew outside. Darkness closed in on Kachiko. She clenched her fist so tightly that her fingernails bit into her soft palms.

Patience, she told herself. You must be patient and survive. Salvation is at hand.

Already, the combined armies of the Great Clans massed outside the city walls. Skirmishers hemmed in the tainted city, permitting no Shadowlands sympathizers to enter Otosan Uchi. Evil men and creatures that tried to leave were killed.

Still, the battle for the city had not yet been joined. Hantei the 39th kept his troops at the ready. Shadowlands monsters, corrupted Crab, and loyalist Lion massed within the city walls. These last, Kachiko did not understand at all.

Tsanuri led the Lion. Kachiko knew they were loyal, but she couldn't believe that their loyalty to the Hantei outweighed their good sense. The half of the Lion led by Kitsu Motso milled outside the walls by themselves. They had not joined Toturi, and so they stood on their own, proud and defiant, but still opposed to Fu Leng.

So far, the divided Lion forces had not fought each other. So far, Lion had not spilled Lion blood. When they finally did, all of Rokugan would be awash in crimson. The empress cursed Toturi for not bringing the divided clan together.

Toturi.

His name still burned in Kachiko's brain. He had slain her husband, Bayushi Shoju. She hated him for that. Yet, now her salvation depended on him—on many people she hated. A cold hand clenched around Kachiko's heart.

Her anger, once her strength, had now become poison. Enemies surrounded her, within the castle and without. Her husband, the dark kami's pawn, could slay her at any moment. Those outside the walls could kill her just as easily. Amaterasu knew she had given many of them cause to want her dead. Yet, in those same people lay her only hope, perhaps the hope of all Rokugan.

Kachiko's heart faltered. In her mind, the path to the outside world blazed brightly. She knew the secret ways of the palace; no one would stop her. No one would even know she was gone before it was too late.

She started walking, leaving the pale light from the window behind, ignoring cries of death from outside the palace. She strode confidently beneath tall-timbered halls. Droplets of brown, sticky moisture fell from the high ceilings around her. The air smelled dank—like a grave. Strange, soft music drifted to her ears.

Music. It called to mind her words with Togashi Yokuni. The Great Dragon had come to her the last time she contemplated leaving the palace to flee Fu Leng's impending wrath. Yokuni had turned her aside from her intended course. He had spoken to Kachiko of her hatred, and abandoning it to fulfill her true mission. The Mother of Scorpions bridled at the thought. She knew Yokuni as well as anyone in Rokugan. She fathomed secrets about him that only the Dragon lord—and the Scorpion—knew. This should have given her power during their meetings.

Yet, in his presence she still felt like a child. He told her that her fate was to stay in the palace, that here she must fulfill her destiny. Though every fiber of her being told her she should flee, Kachiko had turned back.

The Mother of Scorpions cursed her own weakness. She wished that she had ignored the Great Dragon's advice and fled the castle when she had the chance.

Her feet slowed to a halt. Reaching into her kimono, Kachiko pulled out a small, blue crystal vial. She held it up to the window to catch the light. Little of the dark fluid remained within.

This poison, subtly administered to the Hantei, had kept the boy emperor near death for many months. Now, though, he grew stronger, even as she increased the dosage. Kachiko feared that soon the poison would have no effect at all. She feared what would happen then, both to herself and to the world. She could not stop now; she could not flee. She was caught in a trap of her own making.

Tears welled up in the corners of her eyes, and she longed for the advice of her slain husband, Bayushi Shoju. At night, even as she lay with the boy emperor, Kachiko sometimes felt Shoju beside her. She heard his melodious voice drifting in the sea breeze. In her mind, she saw Shoju dancing his catlike kata of destruction—the practice and exercises that had made him the greatest swordsman in Rokugan. Her body longed for his touch. Her heart ached at his absence. He was the best man she had ever known, the only man worthy of her love.

"Bayushi Kachiko," a voice rasped from behind her, "it has been a long time."

Kachiko's heart froze, and she spun on the balls of her feet. In the corridor behind her stood Junzo, the dark sorcerer. Once, he had been the most prominent shugenja in her clan; once, he had been her friend. Now, though, he was death incarnate, Fu Leng's herald upon the tainted soil of Rokugan.

The empress had known Junzo was within the city walls. She had heard tales of his dark deeds. Until this moment, she had managed to avoid him. Now she stood alone with him, trapped in the middle of a decaying hallway. Kachiko's mind quickly calculated the distance to the nearest secret panel. She could not reach it before Junzo would catch her.

Fu Leng's herald was an awful sight. Moldering crimson robes hung from his skeletal frame. Long, talonlike fingernails curved from the ends of his hands. His stringy white hair hung over his bony shoulders in long clumps. His eyes blazed with unholy green fire. He licked parchmentlike lips with a slimy, purplish tongue.

"Yogo Junzo," Kachiko said calmly, using his "forbidden" family name as he had used hers—all Scorpions had lost their names by the emperor's decree. "I heard you were in the city. Have you slain everyone outside the walls then?"

"Not yet," he said, his voice like steel against slate. "Soon, though." He smiled, the skin near his mouth crinkling like leather to reveal his yellow teeth. "I was hoping you and I might have a chance to . . . talk." He slowly walked forward until only a few paces separated him from the empress.

Every fiber of Kachiko's being screamed at her to flee, but she stood her ground, regarding the shugenja calmly with her black eyes. The green flecks within her dark orbs sparked with anger. "There is little we have to say to each other."

"There is much," Junzo said, inching closer. "We are much alike, you and I." His blazing eyes ran up and down Kachiko's magnificent form.

She suppressed a shudder. "We are nothing alike."

"But we are," he said, licking his pale lips. "Both of us are driven by revenge—the desire to right wrongs done to us by others. And we have much to seek redress for, many who must pay for crossing us, am I not right?" He was close enough now that she could feel his fetid breath on her smooth, white neck.

"You are wrong."

"I think not," he said leaning so close that he could have licked her face with his diseased tongue. "No matter how much you may deny it, we are *soul mates,* you and I."

Kachiko held her breath. She forced her gaze away from his burning eyes and looked past him. She felt the sallow warmth of his body. He will embrace me, and I will die, she thought. Then, her eyes caught sight of something that made her heart sing. Bayushi Aramoro, her brother-in-law and most faithful servant, stepped silently from a secret passage at the end of the corridor.

Aramoro was a tall, lithe figure—strong but supple, much like her late husband. He had a rugged, handsome face and black eyes that sparkled in the corridor's dim light. His midnight blue kimono made no noise as he walked, nor did his footsteps make a sound on the wooden floorboards. Seeing the confrontation between Kachiko and Junzo, his hand stole to the hilt of his katana.

Kill him! Kachiko thought, urging her brother-in-law forward. Kill him! She kept her eyes from focusing on her friend, but Junzo felt his presence nonetheless.

"I sense that we are no longer alone," the dark shugenja said, turning to look at Aramoro. "Bayushi Aramoro, it has been a long time."

"Much has changed since we last met, Junzo," Aramoro said in his pleasant, deep voice.

"Still a lapdog, I see," Junzo said.

"And you as well," Aramoro replied.

Junzo's ashen face flushed red with anger. His blazing eyes gazed from Kachiko to Aramoro, and then back again.

He is judging whether he can kill Aramoro and then do what he wants with me, Kachiko thought. Or whether he may have to kill us both. The Mother of Scorpions felt none too sure of the odds. She had never met anyone, save her late husband, that Aramoro could not kill—but she had never met anyone like Junzo, either. The empress held her lips tight, lest they should quiver.

"Isn't it time you checked on the emperor?" she asked.

Junzo looked around nervously and listened. "Perhaps you are right, Lady Kachiko," he finally said. Bowing curtly, he turned and glided away, his bony feet floating lightly above the polished wooden floor.

Aramoro walked quickly to Kachiko's side. "Did he harm you?"

Kachiko shook her head. "He might have if you had not arrived when you did. Thank you."

"I could still slay him if you like," Aramoro said, gazing down the hall in the direction Junzo left.

"Don't be so sure," Kachiko replied. She reached up and brushed a damp lock of hair from her forehead. Until that moment, she hadn't realized how much she had been sweating.

Aramoro nodded to her. "You should let me take you out of here."

Images flashed before Kachiko's mind: the Spine of the World Mountains; the great sea Umi Amaterasu, so close to the walls, yet forbidden to her; the River of Gold, flowing through lands once controlled by the Scorpion; Kyuden Bayushi, now lying in ruins. Ruins.

"I can't," she said. "Though it tears my heart to do so, I must stay. The Hantei must be stopped."

"I understand. What do you want me to do?"

Kachiko took a deep breath. "You must be my link to Toturi and the others."

"Toturi . . ." Aramoro said softly, venom in his voice.

The empress continued as if she had not heard him. "My husband has cut me off from the rest of my servants, and there is no one else I would trust with the job anyway. You alone can escape the emperor's gaze. Only you can pass in and out of the castle and live. You must be my eyes and ears in the outside world."

Aramoro bowed slightly. "I understand."

"Go now. Bring me news as soon as you are able. Tell Toturi . . ." she paused and looked around nervously, ". . . tell Toturi I am with him. I wait only for the proper moment."

"I still think you should leave."

Kachiko shook her head and her raven locks danced around her perfect shoulders.

"Then I go." Aramoro bowed once more, moved swiftly down the corridor, opened a secret panel, and slipped inside.

Only after he had left did Kachiko let her control slip. Her body shook, and her knees went weak. Cold sweat beaded on her skin. She stepped through another secret panel, exited to an exterior corridor, and threw the window open to get some fresh air.

Hot, smoke-filled wind from the city flooded into the hallway. Kachiko coughed and backed away, a wave of nausea sweeping over her. She slumped to her knees, and her eyes stung with tears.

Thunder shook the castle's foundations, and Kachiko tightly clenched her fists. Small rivulets of blood trickled down her palms and spattered gently on the floor.

Soon, the storm would break.

19 THE THUNDERS ASSEMBLE

Toturi stood on a hill outside Otosan Uchi and watched clouds of smoke roil into the morning sky. His gaze took in the great city, the imperial precincts, the palace, and the sea beyond. What he saw tugged at his heartstrings.

The City of the Shining Prince had fallen into chaos and insanity. The great walls hemmed that madness in, and Ikoma Tsanuri's Lions manned those walls. Even from this distance Toturi recognized her, walking energetically among her troops, cajoling and encouraging her grim-faced samurai.

Occasionally, a Lion war cry would drift over the parapets and out to where Toturi and his troops stood, waiting for the battle. Kitsu Motso's Lions, separate from Toturi's troops, shouted back defiantly at their former comrades.

Toturi frowned. The Black Lion's army had grown great—but the Lions had not joined it. Dragon, Unicorn, Phoenix, and Crane were among his troops. Even the Crab general Hida Yakamo had rallied his forces to Toturi's side.

Scorpions came with the Black Lion's troops, too. Shoju's people had been stripped of their names but not their willingness to fight. The Dragons also brought Naga, the strange serpent people from the deep wilderness. Nezumi, the ratlings, sent envoys as well; they were a brave, feral people, ready to fight the dark lord.

The minor clans—Fox, Hare, Dragonfly, and others—supplied samurai where they could, and support elsewhere. Each stood united in the allies' cause—to free Rokugan from the Evil One's grip, or perish trying.

The absent Lion, though, played on Toturi's mind. Thoughts of his former people kept him from calling the attack. He hoped Tsanuri—hidden behind the emperor's walls—might change her mind; he hoped that Motso's people might yet rally to his side. He hoped that his troops would not have to spill Lion blood.

Toturi sighed and gazed toward the great pavilion in the center of his camp. Soon, the allied powers would gather—the greatest generals, the clan champions, the Elemental Masters, the Hooded Ronin, and even Togashi Yokuni himself. Thought of the Great Dragon filled Toturi's breast with awe and hope.

When he was younger, the Black Lion had seen visions of dragons. The mighty creatures had appeared to him in moments of trouble or need. Time froze when they spoke to him, always guiding him toward the path of right—even when Toturi did not heed their words. No one else ever saw the dragons that spoke to him, and the Black Lion never knew whether the beasts were real or some amazing figment of his imagination. They'd ceased appearing to him after Hantei the 39th stripped Toturi of his land and titles. Perhaps the dragons were tired of his failures. Or, perhaps, they merely had nothing more to teach him.

Togashi Yokuni reminded Toturi of those dreamlike beings. The Dragon daimyo had a presence unmatched by any other person in Rokugan. The way the late Bayushi Shoju had inspired awe and fear, Yokuni inspired respect and admiration. Toturi doubted that the world would see the like of either man, ever again.

As Toturi stood atop the ridge, lost in thought, Toku came

scurrying up the hill to the Black Lion. "Bentai's coming back!" the boy gasped. "And Gohei's with him!"

"What?" Toturi asked. "Are you sure?" Bentai had been sent to parley with Kitsu Motso. Toturi had not seen nor heard from Gohei since the Lion general left his camp following Tsuko's seppuku.

Toku scratched his shaggy head. "I saw them. Do you think it means the Lion will join us?"

"We'll know soon enough," Toturi replied.

General Ikoma Bentai, his horse breathing hard, thundered up the hill after the boy. Gohei sat in the saddle behind him.

"Well?" Toturi asked.

Bentai and Gohei dismounted and bowed low.

"I have failed, Toturi-sama," Bentai said. "Motso refuses to join us."

"It is my fault, Toturi-sama. Forgive me," Gohei said.

The Black Lion noticed that Gohei's skin looked sallow, unhealthy. A large bandage wound around the Lion general's left shoulder.

Gohei knelt and pressed his head to the earth. "I was not worthy of the task you set me. I fought Shadowlands forces that I should have avoided. I . . . I lost Matsu Tsuko's poem. It was destroyed in the combat."

"Did you not deliver her message, then?" Toturi asked sternly.

"I did, Lord," Gohei said. "Even without the paper, I conveyed Tsuko-sama's words to the rest of the Lion."

"Motso said as much," Bentai added, "but he still wasn't swayed. Tsuko's loss has been a heavy blow to our former clan. Motso and Tsanuri are as divided and stubborn as ever."

"But will Motso attack when our army does?"

"Hai," Gohei said. "I think so. Even though he will not ride with you, he has no love for the emperor. If I had only been able to show him the poem . . ."

"I doubt the actual paper would have made any difference," Toturi said quietly. He gazed at the city walls and saw that Tsanuri's forces moved when Motso's did—each echoing the other in a deadly dance. The possessed emperor was making sure the two Lion armies would clash.

"I will walk into the jaws of death to atone for my failure," said Gohei, still prostrate in front of Toturi.

"Rise, Matsu Gohei," Toturi said.

Reluctantly, the Lion general stood.

The Black Lion gazed into Gohei's face. "You have fought the enemy well," Toturi said. "No man could do more. That the hearts of Motso and Tsanuri are hardened against us is not your fault. In the days ahead, I will need men such as you. Return to your troops and see that they are ready for battle."

Gohei bowed low. "I will, Toturi-sama." He rose and walked downhill.

Toturi turned to Toku. "Are the clan leaders ready?" he asked.

Toku nodded. "Hai, Master. They're assembling in the great pavilion even now."

"Good," Toturi said. "Let's go. Bentai, see that our troops are ready."

The old general bowed again, mounted his horse, and rode into the sea of tents. Toturi and Toku walked quickly downhill after him.

Soldiers shouted encouragement to the Black Lion as he and Toku walked through the vast encampment. Many of the samurai had waited a long time for this battle, and their spirits soared at the prospect. Toturi acknowledged their cries, nodding to the troops and occasionally stopping to speak with a samurai he'd known a long time.

The ronin lord's heart swelled with the enthusiasm of his army. The battle ahead of them would be terrible, but they were ready.

It took him only a short while to reach the great pavilion. It was not a tent, but an immense space ringed with silken fabric wound around stout support poles. The interior of the pavilion lay open to the sky. Toturi's battle standard, a red wolf in a circle, blazed on the outside of the silk. Hot wind tugged at the fabric, making the bracing timbers groan and shudder.

Toturi's shugenja chanted outside the pavilion's silken walls, shielding the meeting from spies and enemy magic. Two dozen of Toturi's best samurai surrounded the enclosure. As

Toturi approached, Toku took his place among the other guards.

Doji Hoturi stood by the flaps, waiting for his ronin friend. He and Toturi nodded and smiled to each other. They walked past the guards and through the pavilion's sole opening. Two samurai stepped forward and closed the fabric behind the Black Lion, making an unbroken circle. Once inside, Toturi allowed a confident smile to creep over his lips.

Before him stood the greatest assemblage of power seen on Rokugan since the original Seven Thunders slew Fu Leng; Doji Hoturi of the Crane, Hida Yakamo of the untainted Crab, Utaku Kamoko of the Unicorn, and Aramoro, formerly of the Scorpion. The ronin lord's eyes lingered for a moment on the Scorpion's so called "Master of Assassins." Toturi moved on.

Every clan must contribute, the Black Lion reminded himself, or all will fail.

Commanders and generals were there as well: sour-faced Mirumoto Yukihera of the Dragon, lovely Shiba Tsukune of the Phoenix, and the Emerald Champion Kakita Toshimoko. Four of the five Elemental Masters of the Phoenix had come: Tadaka, Tomo, Uona, and Tsuke, all from the Isawa family. Only Kaede, Toturi's former fiancée, remained missing. The great Phoenix shugenja stood to one side of the enclosure, talking quietly to one another.

And, at the back of the forum, the Hooded Ronin and Togashi Yokuni, the Great Dragon, stood side by side. If they spoke, Toturi did not hear them.

The other people in the pavilion nodded polite bows to Toturi as he entered. Some bowed lower than others, but many of the samurai here considered themselves the Black Lion's equals, or perhaps—since ronin were held in very low regard—even his superiors.

Toturi bowed curtly in reply. Politeness demanded that he mingle amid the august company before calling the proceedings to order. Hoturi left the Black Lion's side and walked over to the Unicorn Kamoko, smiling. Toturi crossed to where the Elemental Masters stood, cloistered by themselves.

Approaching, he noticed that the Phoenix shugenja did not look nearly so vital as they once had. Isawa Tadaka, the Master of

Earth, glanced around nervously. His round-brimmed straw hat and black hood hid most of his face from view. Only his eyes shone out from beneath the shadows. Tadaka's brother, Isawa Tomo, the gentle Master of Water, rubbed his hands together as if he were cold. His body looked hunched and slightly twisted. Isawa Uona the Mistress of Air held herself stiffly erect. Her pretty face had a new harshness, and she fidgeted restlessly with the hem of her gold and red kimono. Stern-faced Isawa Tsuke, the Master of Fire, paced back and forth as if anxious for something—anything—to happen.

The alteration in the powerful shugenja disquieted Toturi. He pushed the feelings down. Bowing slightly to the Master of Earth, he said, "Tadaka-san. Your sister, Kaede—is there any word from her?" His heart fluttered at the thought of his former fiancée and the wrong he'd done her.

"Not since she left Kyuden Isawa with Seppun Ishikawa and Shiba Ujimitsu, the Phoenix Champion," Tadaka replied. His voice sounded hoarse and weak. He coughed and wiped his lips with the back of his sleeve.

"Ishikawa has returned," Toturi said. "He's joined my army, along with his brother, Kiaku. Kaede forced Ishikawa to leave her as she entered the deep mountains."

"Oh?" Tadaka said, arching one black eyebrow. "Did Ujimitsu return with him?" The Master of Earth's quiet voice sounded hopeful.

Toturi shook his head. "Not so far as I know," the Black Lion replied. "I wish that your champion were fighting at our side. He's one of the finest blades in the empire. He'll be missed."

"Ujimitsu goes where he is required most," Isawa Tomo said softly, running his long fingers over his shaved scalp.

"I'm sure that, when the time comes, he will be here," Uona added, her black hair fluttering in an unfelt wind.

Toturi nodded.

Tsuke, the Master of Fire, frowned. "In any case, you'll find the four of us at your side when you assault the city." He folded his muscle-knotted arms across his broad chest.

"Good," Toturi said. "I'm counting on every one of you."

"As I am counting upon you, Toturi," said a deep, pleasant voice.

Toturi and the Elemental Masters turned to see the Hooded Ronin standing next to them.

"You, and many others as well," the ronin finished. He leaned against his long staff and smiled. "May I speak with you, Toturi-sama?"

Toturi nodded. With polite bows to the Elemental Masters, he and the ronin walked to a more private section of the pavilion.

"We are as ready as we shall ever be," the Hooded Ronin said.

"What about Hitomi of the Dragon, and Kachiko?" Toturi asked. "Are we to be five Thunders rather than seven?"

The ronin shook his head. "Yokuni and I have everything prepared. Kachiko is where she needs to be. Aramoro can speak for her at this assembly."

Toturi glanced from the ronin to the former Scorpion. Aramoro stood watchfully, talking to few, but taking in everything. "My gut tells me not to trust him," the Black Lion said.

"Are there no Scorpions in your army then?" the ronin asked.

"Yes," Toturi said, "but . . ."

"And is one of them not the cousin of Bayushi Shoju, the usurper you killed?"

"Hai, he is, but . . ."

"Then why should you doubt the Scorpion's brother more than his cousin?" the ronin asked. "Every person has his place upon Rokugan, his own karma, his own unique destiny to fulfill. In carrying out his mistress's will, Aramoro is completely trustworthy. Besides, if Kachiko fails us, we are lost anyway."

Toturi nodded slowly. "You speak with Shinsei's wisdom."

"At times," the ronin replied, smiling, "I have that gift. Call the others together. The moment has arrived."

The Black Lion nodded. He strode to the center of the assembly and said, "Friends, comrades, allies—long have we felt the heel of Fu Leng upon our necks. His minions have ravaged our lands. His plague has slain our people. Clan has battled against clan while the Evil One grew strong.

"In the beginning, Hantei the 39th was just a boy orphaned by terrible circumstance. In the past two years, though, he has become more than that. No longer is he a callow youth whose foibles can be dismissed as the actions of a naive foundling. Make no mistake about it, now he is our enemy."

The last word brought a grumbling of assent from those within the pavilion.

"Evil itself dwells in the palace walls," Doji Hoturi said.

Toturi continued. "The emperor has allied himself with the armies of the Evil One. More than that, he commands those terrible forces himself. The Emerald Throne has been corrupted, and he who sits on it has become the pawn of evil. He is possessed by the spirit of Fu Leng." He turned in a slow circle, gazing at each of the attending samurai in turn.

"I speak not for myself," Toturi said, "not for the Lion and the countless others the Hantei has betrayed. Rather, I speak for Rokugan. Will we allow this blight upon our land to grow?"

"No!" the others in the circle shouted.

"Will we allow evil to hide and fester within the great city itself?"

"No!"

"Will we pay whatever price, take whatever risks necessary, to free the land from this evil?"

"Yes!" thundered the others.

Toturi nodded, and his eyes grew grim. "Yosh. We will take the palace and destroy the evil that waits there. The Seven Thunders will assemble once more.

"Before the Thunders can do their job, destroying Fu Leng for all time, all must do their duties. Many will die, and not all those who lose their lives will be evil."

Togashi Yokuni stepped forward, next to Toturi. *Such is the price of freedom*, the Great Dragon said, his voice booming in the minds of all those present. The silk curtains billowed and shuddered as though buffeted by a thunderstorm. *We are ready to sacrifice all for this cause.*

Toturi nodded again. He turned to all those present. "Prepare your troops. We attack at sunrise."

▲▲▲▲▲▲▲▲

The goddess wore red when she rose from the sea the next morning. Peering out beneath storm clouds, Amaterasu cast her vermilion light over the choppy waves and across the ravaged land. Her bright fingers crept up the shoreline, painting everything scarlet—first the beach, then the houses, then the moldering palace of the Hantei, and finally the hills beyond Otosan Uchi. The advancing dawn made the vast sea, the poisoned river, and the choked waterfall dance with heavenly fire.

Toturi sat astride his charger amid an ocean of samurai. Ronin, Dragon, Crab, Unicorn, Crane, Scorpion, and the rest stood ready, waiting for his command. The Black Lion gazed downhill at the pestilent city, anger and pity filling his heart. In the hills nearby, Kitsu Motso's Lions rumbled like a thunderstorm about to break.

As sunlight touched the top of his army's banner, Toturi raised the standard high and gave the order to charge.

Motso's Lions charged of their own accord.

With a thundering cry, Toturi's combined army swept forward across the hills toward the outer walls of the city of the Shining Prince. The gates of Otosan Uchi opened wide, and Hantei's forces surged out: goblins and demons from the Shadowlands, undead foot soldiers and horsemen, tainted Crab troops, and honor-bound Lions led by Ikoma Tsanuri.

Toturi's jaw grew tight as he saw his old friends take the field. This day, the Lion would slay their kin. His soul wept, but his resolve stayed firm. In his mind, he heard the words of Matsu Tsuko: "There is no other way."

Lion met Lion first. Motso's people crashed into Tsanuri's with flailing swords and shouts of "For the empire!" Tsanuri's troops cried out, "For honor!" The two Lion generals commanded their samurai vigorously; blood soon drenched the armor of both leaders. Overhead, lightning flashed and thunder rumbled, though no rain fell.

Toturi's army crashed against the legions of evil like a huge wave breaking against the rocky shore. Flights of bat-winged oni arced through the cloud-darkened sky. "Fire!" Toturi cried, and the air grew black with the shafts of his army's arrows.

Some demons died and fell like fireballs to the earth. Others dived on the front lines of Toturi's force, tearing with iron talons and using dark magics to slay the vanguard of allied foot soldiers.

Fu Leng's army fired arrows of their own. Black shafts screamed as though possessed by evil spirits. Several samurai next to Toturi fell under the barrage, but the Black Lion's armor turned aside the only arrow that struck him.

Nearby, Doji Hoturi pulled a black fletched shaft out of the shoulder of his kimono. Hoturi smiled, indicating that the arrow had not found flesh.

As more arrows flew, Toturi called, "Tsukune, do something about those oni!"

The Phoenix general nodded. She directed her shugenja to bolster the vanguard against the demons' attacks. Soon crimson and jade fires burst up from the front lines as Tsukune's people confronted the oni and fought the dark magic of Junzo.

Toturi rode with Hoturi, Kamoko, and many other allied generals straight into the heart of the enemy formation. The Shadowlands forces surged around them like a black tide. The bodies of the fighting and dying looked like great mounds of insects squirming before the city gates.

The Black Lion peered to where his kinsmen fought. The Lion partisans attacked their brethren viscously, neither asking quarter nor giving any. As the sun slipped behind the looming thunderheads, a final ray of light struck Kitsu Motso's mon. The golden lion emblazoned on the banner turned the color of blood.

Though it may mean my death, Toturi thought, I cannot let this fratricide go on!

Turning his horse, the Black Lion spurred it through the body of his troops, toward the clashing columns of Lion.

"My lord! Where are you going?" Toku cried as Toturi charged. For a moment, the young samurai looked around, confused.

"Follow me, boy," commanded Ikoma Bentai, Toturi's old friend. "Wherever he's bound, we must protect him!" Bentai turned his horse as well and dashed after the Black Lion.

"Amaterasu protect us!" Toku cried. He dug his spurs into his shaggy mount and plunged into the teeming horde.

Toturi drove toward the Lion. A wall of enemy spears appeared before him—goblins and undead samurai trying to end his life. Matsu Tsuko's sword hummed in the Black Lion's hands. He smashed the spears and swept through Fu Leng's forces like the wind through sharp reeds.

An oni rose and barred his way. It was a hideous black gelatinous thing, like a monstrous jellyfish. Its many tendrils lashed at him, only to be turned aside by Toturi's armor. The allied general clicked a command and spurred his warhorse. The steed shot forward, trampling the oni into the dust. It squealed and writhed in its death throes as Toturi galloped on.

He burst through the advancing lines and rode up onto a rocky prominence. Once, this long flat boulder had been part of a natural shrine outside the city. Peasants often came to it with offerings for the local kami, hoping to win favor for themselves or their families. With the coming of Fu Leng's minions, though, the simple temple had been burned, and its ashes scattered to the four winds.

Now the site stood at the center of the clashing Lion armies. Swords flashed like lightning around him as Toturi rode between the opposing sides. Tsuko's sword cleared his way through the melee, turning aside blows aimed at him, but never shedding any Lion blood.

Toturi reined his horse atop the rocky platform. The animal reared and neighed. Toturi rose in the saddle, and a flash of lightning silhouetted him against the dark sky.

"Lions!" Toturi shouted. "Slay your kinsmen no more! Despite our differences, we must be *one* against our common enemy! If you want my blood, if you want my *head*, you can have it—*after* we have pulled Fu Leng from his corrupt throne and destroyed him!"

For a moment, the tide of Lion forces swirling around him paused. Toturi turned in the saddle, gazing out over the sea of combatants. Kitsu Motso hesitated nearby, his armor red with the blood of his own clan.

Ikoma Tsanuri, though, turned and spurred her horse forward. She lowered her spear and aimed it directly at the Black Lion's breast.

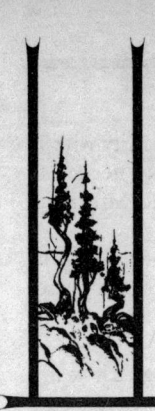

20 THE DRAGON

Mirumoto Hitomi pressed her back against the short stone escarpment and held her breath. A contingent of undead samurai, goblins, and demons marched past her, close enough that she could have spat on them.

Sweat poured down the Dragon lady's brow, and the tattoo on her back burned. She shivered, though the day was smotheringly hot after the cool of the Dragon mountains. Hitomi had returned to the great capital, only to be caught among the ranks of her foes. It had been difficult to sneak this far through enemy territory, but Hitomi was determined to reach her troops. Part of her longed to lay into the Shadowlands patrol and slay them all. That was not her mission, though. Not now. Not yet.

The battlefield roared hellishly. Hitomi peeked around the corner. The Shadowlands contingent had passed by, though another would come soon. Her samurai heart burned at the thought of skulking in the shadows like some nameless Scorpion.

She glanced toward the city and the Forbidden City within, and wondered if Kachiko remained alive. Kachiko needed to live to fulfill the Great Dragon's plans—just as she, Mirumoto Hitomi, did.

Hitomi raced across open ground to a tree to shelter her. The stench of death permeated the fields. Smoke and storm clouds hung overhead like crows waiting to pick clean the bones of the dead.

Hitomi darted down a trench and slipped through a hole in a barricade. Sounds of demon footsteps caused her to press back against the stones. She couldn't fight them. Not yet.

She gazed down her arm to the Obsidian Hand, clenched at the end of her wrist. The cold, black thing shone darkly, even against the shadows. Hitomi flexed stony fingers and smiled. This gave her all the power she would need to wreak her revenge.

She would find the Crab Champion Hida Yakamo and kill him. First the Crab had slain Hitomi's brother. Then he had taken her true hand at the battle of Beiden Pass. That combat had cost Hitomi dearly. She had lost not only her hand, but also her army—and perhaps her destiny as well.

In her mind's eye, the Dragon saw Yakamo's death, over and over again. She savored each time his head burst, relished the snap of his spine, gloried in the warmth of his blood as it flowed over her skin.

A sound snapped her back to reality: strange flute music, drifting over the fields to her ears. Hitomi reached up with her human hand and wiped the sweat from her shaved head.

Hitomi had heard such music often, in her master's court. The man she'd last heard playing such a tune was a ronin. Hitomi didn't know much about him, save that he was a friend of the Great Dragon.

An image of her master, Togashi Yokuni, formed unbidden in her mind. She saw the Great Dragon standing before her, his golden mail shifting silently, like the skin of an immense lizard. His golden eyes blazed out from beneath his horned helmet. His deep voice shook Hitomi to her bones.

To kill Yakamo is not your destiny, he had said. *If you do so, the Seven Thunders will never assemble, and the world will die.*

The words echoed in Hitomi's mind, and she knew the truth of them. Yet, the fire in her belly burned nearly as brightly. How could she give up something she'd sought so long? How could she forsake it, even if the empire would fall?

The Dragon lady clasped her hands over her ears to shut out the noise, but the words echoed in her skull. The eerie music filled her, winding around her soul. Hitomi wanted to cry out, but she kept her mouth clamped shut.

A goblin straggler walked by her hiding place, chewing on an arm. Hitomi's eyes ran over the tattoo on the arm's sallow flesh. The owner had been a Dragon.

Hitomi leapt from the shadows. She bounded over the mud. Fire and death flared in her eyes.

The goblin whirled to face her. It dropped its snack and drew its sword. The katana swung at Hitomi's head.

She reached up and caught the blade in her stone hand. The Dragon twisted her wrist, and the goblin's steel shattered into a dozen pieces. Hitomi grabbed the goblin by the throat. Anger coursed through her body as the Obsidian Hand squeezed.

The goblin gurgled. Its eyes bulged out of its head. Black blood leaked from its misshapen mouth. Hitomi felt its neck break under her grip. She let go, and the creature fell to the mud. Thunder boomed in the sky above.

Hitomi's eyes strayed to the severed arm lying in the mud. Her people. These evil monsters were killing *her* people.

Heedless of the danger, Hitomi sprinted across the fields outside Otosan Uchi. She dodged between piles of the dead and leapt over barricades.

Two undead samurai sprang up before Hitomi. She shattered their skulls without even breaking stride. Their bodies fell twitching to the mud. A few quick leaps took the Mirumoto daimyo to the top of an embankment.

A skeletal defender rushed to confront her. It swung a metal-studded tetsubo club at Hitomi's head.

She ducked under the blow and seized the undead thing by its tattered kimono. Hauling the monster overhead, Hitomi cast it over the bank. The creature hit the hillside and smashed to pieces. It fell onto one of Fu Leng's unwary defenders, destroying it. Hitomi smiled.

Thunder cracked. Clouds burst, pelting her scalp with oily rain. Hitomi wiped the stinging black water out of her eyes and peered over the field of battle.

In the distance, great armies clashed. Hitomi recognized two different Lion flags, as well as the mons of Crane and Unicorn and the ronin Toturi. The minions of the Evil One also carried their own standards, terrible banners made from still-living flesh.

Thunder rattled, and a bolt of lightning drew Hitomi's gaze to a different part of the fray. There, the banner of the Dragon waved bravely in the downpour.

The Mirumoto daimyo felt a pang of regret. She should be with her clan, fighting—and if need be, dying—beside them. Something else caught her keen eyes: the banner of her old rival, Mirumoto Yukihera. In her mind's eye, she saw the green-armored samurai sneer at her. The dragon tattoo on his shaved head seemed to writhe as he wrinkled his brow. He laughed a ruthless, condescending laugh.

Hitomi's old foe led the Dragon troops into a bad position. Shadowlands forces leapt on the tattooed warriors, rending and slaying, causing terrible bloodshed. The Dragon army fell back, but the enemy dogged them. Yukihera called to his samurai, and they rallied bravely, though their position left them vulnerable.

"Pull back!" Hitomi screamed, well aware that her people could not hear her. "Use your shugenja to delay the enemy so you can strike their flank!" Her shouts did no good.

Thoughts of slaying Hida Yakamo fled from the Dragon's mind. Yokuni was right; killing Yakamo could wait. First, she needed to wrest control of her army from the madman Yukihera. Once she had regained her birthright, she could think about revenge against the Crab.

Again, images of gruesome deaths for Hida Yakamo played through her brain. The tattoo hidden on her back burned anew, and strange flute music drifted to her ears.

Yes. First things first.

She scrambled over the hill and clambered quickly down. Wind blew from the north, and the smell of smoke and carnage drifted to her nostrils. Thunder crashed overhead.

Her people were waiting.

Hitomi strode across the devastated field toward the site of the battle.

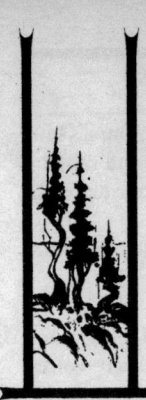

21 THE LION

Tsanuri charged her old teacher, death dancing in her dark eyes. Lightning clashed, and her spear point gleamed in the afterglow. She aimed her weapon at the Black Lion's throat.

Toturi's hand tightened on the carved ivory handle of his katana. With one swift motion, he raised the sword high over his head. The clouds above him parted slightly, and the morning sun peeked through. The light caught the sword's blade and shone off it, like the goddess herself come to earth.

The Black Lion's voice boomed like thunder, echoing off Otosan Uchi's walls and rebounding from the hills:

"For Matsu Tsuko!"

Ikoma Tsanuri reined to an abrupt halt, her spear point stopping a mere hand's breath from Toturi's flesh. Her eyes darted to the Black Lion's katana, shimmering like fire in the morning light. She glimpsed the lion-headed hilt, and recognition dawned in her deep brown eyes.

Toturi gazed at her, his eyes burning into his former pupil's soul.

Tsanuri dropped her spear. She drew her katana and raised it high next to Toturi's. "For Matsu Tsuko!" Her voice caught the dying echo of Toturi's own words.

Kitsu Motso pushed through the crowd and raised his sword as well. "Matsu Tsuko!"

All at once, the embattled Lion troops stopped fighting. Silence fell as they looked to their leaders. As one, the Lion samurai raised their swords and roared, "Matsu Tsuko!" Their voices, thousands strong, shook the nearby hills and rattled the plague-infested walls of Otosan Uchi.

"For Rokugan!" Toturi, Tsanuri, and Motso cried together. They wheeled in perfect unison and galloped through the troops toward the flank of Fu Leng's army.

The Lion samurai turned with them, charging the enemy together, the soul of Matsu Tsuko alive in their Lion hearts.

An ogre rose before Toturi. The lion katana flashed. The top of the monster's head fell to the ground, its brains spilling out. Toturi rode on as the huge body crashed to the muddy ground.

Behind him came the massed troops of the Lion, as powerful an army as Rokugan had ever known. Their cries echoed in Toturi's ears, but his head reverberated with the sound of Matsu Tsuko's strong voice. His heart filled with pride, remembering her sacrifice. She, not he, had made this day possible. Toturi wished he could thank her.

Tsanuri and Motso's horses fell into step with the ronin general's. Behind them came Bentai, Toku, Motso, Gohei, Yojo, and the body of the united Lion army.

Overhead, the storm broke. Clouds rolled low over the hills, as if the very elements might join the battle. Torrents of rain fell, dividing the bloodstained earth with sticky red-black streams.

Lions crashed upon their enemy's flanks, breaking the Shadowlands line. Fu Leng's undead dropped back toward the city walls. They screamed and cursed. Maho shugenja rose from their midst, aiming deadly spells at the allied forces. A hail of arrows rained from Toturi's army, silencing the magic on the shugenja's lips.

Suddenly, a mass of demons, led by the Yakamo no Oni surged from a side gate. They sprang among the allied forces, slaying heroic samurai with frightening efficiency. The hideous, demonic mockery of Hida Yakamo snapped ashigaru in half and drank their blood. He laughed at his foes' misery.

Mirumoto Yukihera's Dragon troops charged the demons, failing to see the trap the monsters had set. Fu Leng's forces scrambled over the walls in huge, black swarms, surrounding the hapless Dragon.

Toturi turned to Matsu Yojo. "Summon the Elemental Masters!" he said, shouting to be heard above the battle. "We need help now, or Yukihera is lost."

Yojo nodded to the Black Lion and spurred his steed to where the Phoenix sorcerers battled enemy shugenja.

Yukihera's troops fell back as far as they could.

Toturi crashed his armies into the mass of the Shadowlands forces. The evil warriors turned and fought the newcomers, but the Dragons remained trapped within the enemy forces.

Toturi's jaw clenched. *They will be slain if we don't get to them soon!* he thought. His concern for the Dragon distracted him, and he didn't notice the pikeman bearing in on his back until it was too late. The Black Lion turned, staring down the point of an enemy spear.

Ikoma Bentai shot forward, using his own body to push the shaft of the weapon aside. His horse stumbled, but the wily Lion general kept his seat. The pikeman turned toward him, lifting his spear. Bentai's sword flashed, and the pikeman's head fell into the mud.

"Thank you," Toturi said.

The Ikoma ronin nodded and laughed. "I think you'll breathe more easily without that pike in your lungs."

"I expect so." Toturi turned and felled a skeletal warrior trying to drag him from the saddle. He and his allies spurred forward again, aiming to break the back of the enemy troops. The Shadowlands forces turned to meet them, howling with pestilent voices. Hordes of bats and black flies filled the air over Fu Leng's armies.

As the Black Lion cut down another foe, he saw Toku disappear into a crowd of warriors. Toturi said a quick prayer to Amaterasu for Toku's safety and then shattered another skeleton with his lion-headed katana.

The army's charge soon turned into a bloody push. Horses and onikage fell, and samurai struggled in the mud against their undead foes. In the midst of it all, the Dragon troops fought in an ever-tightening circle of enemies.

Will even the Elemental Masters be enough? Toturi wondered.

Just then, a cry went up from the Black Lion's samurai. "Yoritomo! Yoritomo!" the ashigaru cried. Toturi turned and saw the green-armored troops of the Mantis lord swarming up the beaches behind Fu Leng's army. A smile drew over Toturi's lips.

Riding beside the ronin lord, Ikoma Bentai asked, "You knew they were coming?"

Toturi shook his head. "I did not know, but I *hoped*." He turned back to the fighting in time to see Isawa Uona arcing high in the air over the battle. The Mistress of Air flew gracefully through the storm, her winds turning arrows aside before they ever reached her. In her slender arms, she held Isawa Tomo, the Master of Water.

Uona circled over the Shadowlands forces that hemmed in the Dragon. As she did, Tomo's body began to elongate, like honey dripping from a honeycomb. His gentle features blurred, and he dissolved into a torrent of rain.

Tomo's rain fell like iron spears among the enemy. His watery figure pierced armor and the flesh beneath. Demons and their undead allies screamed and slashed with their swords at the Master of Water, but Isawa Tomo merely seeped into the ground.

Moments later, the earth erupted in a great muddy wave. The swell surrounded the embattled Dragon forces. Tomo pushed their enemies away. Fu Leng's minions fell back in disarray.

Thunder cracked overhead, and Uona laughed. The clouds opened up, and a whirlwind twisted down into the midst of the enemy. The small tornado cut a swath through the Shadowlands line, smashing evil samurai against the city walls or sucking them up into the clouds.

Tomo smothered the enemy under his fluid body, crushing the air from the lungs of some and drowning others. A huge gap opened in the enemy line, and the Shadowlands troops fell back. The Dragon forces surged forward, killing any goblins too slow to get out of the way.

For long minutes, the evil cries of dying monsters filled the air. Then the black army moved away, retreating to the safety of the city walls.

As they departed, they splashed through a great crimson and brown puddle. Occasionally, the puddle would reach up and unhorse a retreating samurai. Soon, though, no enemies remained within reach. Gradually, the great puddle resumed its human form. Tomo walked over to Toturi and gazed up at the ronin lord.

"I think the Dragon can fend for themselves now," he said, a crooked smile creasing his boyish face.

Isawa Uona hovered in the air above them, her long black hair tossing in the windstorm. Rain streamed down her body, making her gold and red kimono cling to her lithe form. This was not the black rain that assaulted the rest of the allied troops, but a clean, clear liquid that seemed reserved for her and the Master of Water alone.

Despite the ease of their victory, the two Elemental Masters looked tired.

Toturi bowed to the Isawa samurai. "Domo arigato. You have done us a great service. But why didn't all of you come?"

"With the Mantis on the way, two were enough," Uona said flatly.

"Would you have Tsuke and my brother abandon their tasks when they were not needed?" Tomo asked. He smiled again, but the smile seemed to pain him slightly.

As the Master of Water spoke, the earth shook, and a great gout of flame shot up near the main gate to the city.

Toturi nodded. "Tadaka and Tsuke are about their business, it seems."

"They've breached the gates," Uona called from above. "The Shadowlands troops are falling back inside. We can press them farther if we hurry!"

"Do so," Toturi called up to her.

Uona swooped down and seized Tomo in her slim arms. Together, they flitted over the battling armies toward the great gate to the city.

As they disappeared from sight, Toku staggered forward, his wiry form covered head-to-toe in blood. He looked like a crimson fountain.

"Are you all right?" Toturi asked, worry crossing his face.

Toku smiled at the Black Lion. "None of the blood is mine. Some is my horse's, but most belongs to our enemies. I'd say a horse is a good trade for an oni and five undead samurai, wouldn't you?"

Toturi couldn't help smiling.

Yukihera, the Dragon general, rode up to Toturi. He spat blood from his mouth and said, "This diversion of forces wasn't necessary, Toturi-san. I had everything under control. Rest assured that the Dragon can do their part in this." Turning, he galloped off into the retreating enemy line, taking his battered people with him.

"Well, the Lion may be united again," Toku said, "but that doesn't mean everyone's on the same side—even if we are all fighting Fu Leng."

"Never mind Yukihera," Bentai said gruffly. "No great loss if his recklessness gets him killed."

Toturi frowned and shook his head. "In the end, the actions of one man may turn the course of the war."

"I still say we're better off without him," Bentai replied. He turned to rejoin his samurai, but a black-barbed arrow flew across the enemy lines and found the joint in his armor, between his right arm and his breast.

The old general looked at the shaft, pain and surprise playing equally across his grizzled face. Then the arrowhead exploded. The force of the blow knocked Bentai from the saddle. He landed hard in the mud next to Toturi's steed.

The Black Lion slid from his saddle. Another black arrow arced toward him. Toturi acted instinctively. The lion blade flashed from its sheath, destroying the deadly missile before it could strike.

With a cry of rage, Toku ran toward the retreating army and threw himself into the milling crowd. He cut down two black samurai and reached the maho bowman who'd felled Bentai. The evil sorcerer pointed his bow at the boy, but Toku severed the string with his first slice. His second cut spilled the magician's guts. The shugenja fell dead.

Toku ran back to Toturi's side.

The Black Lion knelt beside his old comrade.

Bentai lay in the mud, his right arm gone, his blood spurting onto the dark earth. Toturi cradled the general's neck in his hand. He looked at the wound, and then at his friend's face. There was no hope.

Bentai's breath rattled in his throat. "Take my helmet," he said to Toturi, "and place it on the highest tower of the castle. Turn it to the east, so that I may see the sun rise over a free Rokugan."

"I will," Toturi said, removing the helmet from Bentai's head.

A smile crept over the general's craggy face. Then his breath leaked out, and he was gone.

"I—I will miss him," Toku said, wiping tears from his eyes.

"All of Rokugan will miss him," Toturi replied. He removed his cloak and laid it over his friend's body. The rain pressed the silk down around the slain general, outlining his body.

The Black Lion stood, anger burning in his breast. He mounted his steed and pulled Toku into the saddle behind him. They galloped off into the fray and slew many enemies in Bentai's name.

▲▲▲▲▲▲▲▲

The allied armies quickly forced the enemy back within the city's outer wall. Toturi's samurai swept into Otosan Uchi, driving the Shadowlands troops before them. Fu Leng's minions set fire to the few standing buildings as they fled. The city filled with choking black smoke.

Uona used her powers to dissipate the evil vapors, and Tsuke quelled the flames where he could. The fighting within the walls, though, was brutal. Many brave samurai died within Otosan Uchi before Amaterasu dipped her golden head below the mountains.

As night fell, both armies pulled back, though bloody skirmishes still raged before the walls of the Forbidden City. Toturi's men set up his headquarters inside Otosan Uchi's tall gates. The Black Lion called his generals and the great lords to meet with him. One by one, they straggled in, as their duties permitted.

"I haven't seen Ikoma Ujiaki," Toturi said, glancing around among his own people. "Where is he? Was he slain in the battle?"

Tsanuri shook her head, and her black hair fell limply over her shoulders. "No. Though my heart fills with shame to tell you, he has taken his troops from the field."

"What?" Toturi asked, fire burning in his eyes.

"They say he would not desert the emperor, so he has marched away. Where he has gone, I do not know."

"I know," said Tetsuo, stepping from the crowd. "There's little that a Scorpion's ears do not hear. Ujiaki has gone south, to the lands of the Evil One, to do the Hantei emperor's bidding. I doubt he will return, Lord."

The Black Lion silently cursed Tetsuo's subtlety. He seemed to know more than he was telling. "Make sure our troops are prepared," Toturi said to Yojo, Motso, Tsanuri, Toku, and the others. "The enemy must gain no ground tonight. Tomorrow, we will storm the Forbidden City and take the palace, or die trying."

The Lion and ronin generals bowed and left Toturi alone with his other guests. Toturi scanned the assembly.

The Elemental Masters looked tired, but grimly determined to carry on. Near the end of the day, Junzo had sallied out of the Forbidden City and caused them some difficulty. Still, the combined might of Tadaka, Uona, and Tomo had been enough to drive away the evil shugenja; Tsuke had been busy suppressing fires at the time.

The Great Dragon and the Hooded Ronin looked little the worse for wear, though both had fought hard. Toturi admired their cool serenity, even in the midst of chaos.

Aramoro, Kachiko's envoy, seemed—if possible—even more unruffled. He stood near the tent flaps, his muscular arms folded across his chest, his black eyes drinking in every nuance of the scene. In tribute to his dead lord, he once again wore his Scorpion mask.

Kakita Toshimoko, the Emerald Champion, stood near the tent flaps, rubbing salve into an arrow wound in his arm.

Utaku Kamoko sat on a low stool near the center of the pavilion, having a long cut on her arm bandaged by her lieutenant Tetsuko. Many Unicorn forces still fought, trying to save the citizens of Otosan Uchi from their demonic oppressors. Toturi admired the Unicorn's courage, and their devotion to peoples often ignored by the other clans.

Hida Yakamo grumbled some final orders to his Crab generals and sent them back to the fray. They bowed low to the other lords as they left the tent. Yakamo lifted his gaze and stiffened.

Mirumoto Hitomi had just emerged through the flaps of the pavilion. She folded her arms over her chest, and the Obsidian Hand gleamed in the dim light cast by the paper lanterns scattered around the room's perimeter.

"Hitomi," Toturi said cordially, nodding a quick bow. "Good to see you. Where's Mirumoto Yukihera?"

A wry smile drew across Hitomi's lips. She bowed in return. "Yukihera had an urgent appointment with his ancestors. The Dragon army is under *my* control once more."

Toturi and the other members of the council looked grimly at the Mirumoto daimyo, then nodded their understanding. The Black Lion glanced from Hitomi to Yakamo and then back again. The two stared daggers at each other and clenched their stony fists.

Doji Hoturi walked to Toturi's side and whispered, "Can we trust them not to kill each other?"

"I don't think we have much choice," Toturi answered.

The evening wore on as they discussed plans for the next day's battle. The hour grew late, and many of the daimyo drifted off to their clans to relay information, shore up battle lines, and get what little rest they could. Toturi felt some relief when Hitomi returned to her own tents. Yakamo also relaxed after his old enemy left. As midnight approached, only the Black Lion and a handful of lords remained in the pavilion.

Suddenly, the tent flaps opened, and Yoritomo, the Mantis leader, strode into their midst. He was a tall, muscular man wearing green armor. From one side of his wide obi hung the familiar daisho swords. From the other hung a pair of matched scythes with short handles. In battle, Yoritomo wielded the scythes like the claws of the Mantis from which his clan derived its name. Two green-armored lieutenants flanked their leader as he entered.

"Welcome, Yoritomo," Toturi said. "Your aid today is greatly appreciated."

All eyes turned to the Mantis. Instead of kneeling before the general of the combined armies, Yoritomo merely bowed cordially.

The hands of several lords strayed to the hilts of their swords at the perceived insult. Toturi, though, merely stood quietly in the center of the tent.

"You say you appreciate my help," Yoritomo said, his rough voice booming. "I'm here to tell you that it is the last help you'll receive from my army. I will not fight beside you again, unless I fight as an equal.

"Even now, my troops hold the beaches below the castle. Make the Mantis one of the Great Clans, or we will board our ships and sail home this very night."

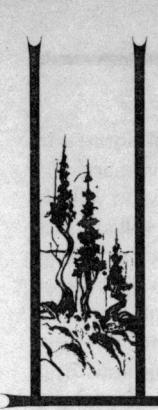

22 THE MANTIS

"You dare to speak to us this way?" Doji Hoturi said, stepping forward. His bright eyes flashed, and he tightened his grip on the sword. "You have not earned the right to be a Great Clan. In a thousand years, no minor clan has risen to that prominence."

"I have earned that right today," Yoritomo insisted. "My people have won this prize with their blood. Without me, the Dragon would have been crushed. Without my troops, you would never have gained entry to the walls of the city. If we leave—as we will, I assure you— you will not be able to hold what you have taken. Your strength is nothing without mine. We deserve to be treated as equals."

"You would leave the battlefield even though it means the empire might fall?" Toturi asked.

"What care I for the empire if it cares nothing for me?" Yoritomo replied. "I repeat: the Mantis have won this right with their blood. We will die before we relinquish that right."

"You cannot force us to elevate your station," Doji Hoturi said sternly, "though we can force you to obey Toturi's commands."

"You can try," Yoritomo admitted, "but many of you will die in the attempt. We are committed to this cause and will sacrifice our lives if need be—just as we are willing to sacrifice our lives to your cause, *if* we may do so as equals." He folded his arms across his muscular chest and stood silently amid the assembly.

Deep laughter broke the quiet. All eyes turned to Hida Yakamo. The Crab Thunder chuckled and folded his arms over his chest as well. "A bold move," he said. "So bold, in fact, that I must support it."

Others in the pavilion nodded and grunted agreeably.

The Emerald Champion edged close to Toturi. "We will need the strength of every samurai if we are to succeed."

Toturi nodded. "Hai," he said quietly. "I know it." Raising his voice, he said, "Yoritomo, no one can doubt your valor upon the battlefield today, nor the boldness of your request." The Black Lion turned to the others in the room. "I suggest we grant his clan the status he desires—and that they deserve."

One by one, the others present nodded their approval.

"We're agreed, then?" Toturi asked.

"Hai," the others said as one.

"Then may Amaterasu bless our decision," the ronin lord said. "With her grace, the Mantis are now a Great House and Yoritomo their daimyo."

Yoritomo bowed curtly to the others and they bowed in return.

Toturi turned to the Mantis and said, "If we fail to destroy Fu Leng, though, your clan, Lord Yoritomo, will be very short lived."

The Mantis puffed out his wide chest. "Then we shall not fail."

▲▲▲▲▲▲▲▲

Morning dawned darkly. Battles raged within the once-proud city. Thunderclouds hung low in the heavens, and lightning struck the earth with frightening regularity.

Toturi slept little, directing the movements of the troops

throughout the night, making sure that the enemy gained no advantage during the darkness.

Yoritomo's forces fought with renewed fury after the meeting of the lords. Many Shadowlands creatures died upon the blood-soaked beaches of Otosan Uchi.

After dawn, Toturi moved through the lines, speaking with each of the five other Thunders present: Hitomi, Yakamo, Tadaka, Kamoko, and Hoturi. Each was confident, eager for the final confrontation. The previous day's success filled the Thunders' troops with inspiration.

Toturi's heart felt uneasy, though. Before the day's initiative, he talked to his old friend, the Crane daimyo, under the boughs of a withered cherry orchard. The leaves on the trees were small, brown, and brittle. Long cuts in the trees' bark bled oily sap. Toturi picked one of the leaves and crushed it in his hand. He frowned.

"It seems more like late fall than summer," he said. "The Evil One sucks the life out of the land itself."

"Save the people, and you save the land as well," Doji Hoturi said.

"Do we?" Toturi asked. "I hope so. We've yet to reckon with Junzo. He's barely been visible in the fray, and we know he can bring considerable force to bear."

"We have the Elemental Masters, though," the Crane said. "That must frighten even a shugenja of Junzo's power. Besides, raising the dead to fight on their side must occupy much of Junzo's time."

Toturi nodded. "Hai. It must." He thought of their former comrades, returned from the dead to battle for the dark lord.

Hoturi gazed toward the distant towers of the moldering palace. "The sooner we confront the emperor, the sooner this will be over."

"Let's seize the day, then," Toturi said. "I'll see you at the palace." He mounted his warhorse.

"Hai." Hoturi smiled. "And I'll get there first."

"Only if you grow wings," Toturi replied. He shook the reins and spurred his mount toward the battlefront.

The Black Lion soon rode past a pile of bodies as deep as his horse's flanks—remnants of the previous day's fighting. Most of the dead belonged to the Shadowlands forces. Too many, though, were brave ronin and samurai from Toturi's army. Some still gasped out their last breaths. Priests and healers tended those they could, but few of these victims would live to see the day's end.

Up ahead, Toku darted in and out of the lines, joyously slaying his foes. Each time Toturi saw him, the young Emerald Magistrate was covered with more blood. Fortunately, very little of the blood belonged to Toku.

"They're not so tough," Toku said to Toturi during one of his forays near the ronin lord.

"Keep your helmet on," Toturi replied, "or someone may hand your head to you."

"I know that," Toku said, slightly annoyed. "You think I don't know that?"

At that moment, thunder cracked, and the earth shook beneath them.

Tetsuo, the former Scorpion, emerged from the battle to report. "Junzo has ridden out of the Forbidden City. He's cut deeply into the Unicorn line, but the Elemental Masters are moving to help."

Toturi nodded. "We'll take our forces there as well. We need to take the inner gates and force them open so that we can carry the fight to the Evil One. This may be a fatal mistake on Junzo's part."

"Or it could be a trap," Tetsuo said.

Toku frowned. "Leave it to a Scorpion to think of such things."

"I'd thought of it as well," Toturi replied, smiling. He turned to Ikoma Tsanuri, riding nearby. "Rally our forces to me. We'll catch Junzo in the open and crush him."

"Hai, Toturi-san," Tsanuri replied. She rode into the troops, commanding them to form up behind their leader.

Toturi spurred his horse toward the gates of the Forbidden City. Toku ran beside him, felling Shadowlands samurai as he went.

Junzo wasn't hard to find. A black cloud of biting flies hovered around the evil shugenja and his dark troops.

Toku swatted a fly on his cheek. "Ouch!" he said. "I guess bugs don't bother dead samurai."

"If these bites are the worst you get," Doji Hoturi called, "you'll be a very lucky young man."

The Crane's troops had rallied to Toturi's call as well. Hoturi split the skull of an undead samurai and trampled the creature's body beneath the hooves of his horse.

Thunder clapped, and Isawa Uona flew low over their heads. The Phoenix Mistress of Air's face was set in a grim mask. She gestured toward the cloud of flies, and they parted before her winds.

Junzo shot a bolt of red fire toward her, but Isawa Tomo rose up from the melee like a great wave and swallowed the evil magic. He belched boiling steam, scalding the flesh from a number of Junzo's retainers.

Tadaka stepped forward, and the ground shook. The earth opened up at his command, swallowing the right side of Junzo's bodyguard. The evil magician shot pale lightning toward his enemy. Tadaka reached into his kimono and drew out his jade fan. He flicked it open just as the magic struck.

The bolt rebounded off the enchanted jade and felled a dozen of Junzo's own troops. Cursing, Fu Leng's lieutenant retreated toward the Forbidden City. The massive gates creaked open as the shugenja approached.

Toturi's voice boomed over the clamor of the melee, calling to the only Elemental Master not otherwise occupied. "Tsuke! Stop him!"

The Master of Fire glanced at the Black Lion, his eyes burning. Then he turned toward Junzo and unleashed a firestorm. Many allied samurai had to dive for cover as the hellish conflagration roared past.

It was no use. Before the flames reached the evil sorcerer, the enchanted gates of the Forbidden City slammed shut. Tsuke's magic broke against the walls like the surf against a mountain, and with as little effect.

Toturi cursed.

He and Hoturi rode forward as their troops mopped up the few Shadowlands forces remaining outside the gates.

"Get those gates open," Hoturi cried. "We need to press our advantage against Junzo while he is weakened."

Samurai rushed forward at the Crane lord's command and threw themselves against the immense doors.

"Stand back!" boomed a deep voice. Samurai turned and saw Isawa Tadaka approach. The Master of Earth's eyes glowed green beneath his wide-brimmed straw hat. "The Elemental Masters will handle this."

The troops parted before Tadaka. He, Tomo, and Tsuke strode up to the gate. Uona circled overhead. All four of them studied the enchanted barrier.

On her tall steed, Kamoko rode up to Toturi and the others. She wiped the blood from her face and frowned. "Well? Every moment we stand here is another moment they recover."

Tadaka turned and walked to where Toturi, Hoturi, and Kamoko sat astride their mounts. "The enchantments on the walls are strong. All of you learned that during the Scorpion Coup."

Toturi and the others nodded.

"I sense a weakness in the spells, though," Tadaka said. "It may be that Fu Leng's presence within the city has eroded the magic."

Though no one could see Tadaka's face beneath his hood, the others present sensed that the Master of Earth smiled. "If the Fortunes are with us, we should have the gates open quickly."

As Tadaka spoke, Isawa Tomo transformed himself into a great wall of water. He crashed against the gates and seeped between the cracks in the enchanted timbers.

"Use caution," Toturi said. The battlefield had grown far too quiet. "All may not be as it seems."

"So right, traitorous ronin," a voice called from the top of the wall. Junzo stood atop the parapet, his stringy white hair blowing in the wind.

Uona arced high over the battlefield, toward the evil shugenja. She dived on him, a powerful death spell forming on her lips.

Junzo merely raised his hand, and the Forbidden City's enchantments rose to protect him.

The Mistress of Air crashed headfirst into the unseen barrier. Bright sparks flew, and lightning flashed from the clouds, striking her supple form. Uona fell from the sky like a wounded bird and fluttered toward her kinsmen below.

"My master will not be confined within these walls for long," Junzo cackled. "His reach extends into the land itself, into the sky above, even into the ranks of our enemies." The evil shugenja's eyes blazed red, and thunder crashed over the castle.

Uona landed beside Tsuke. Her legs shook, and she almost collapsed. She lowered her head and concentrated, calling upon her elemental powers to replenish herself.

Isawa Tsuke spun toward her; his eyes blazed orange with preternatural fury.

Uona looked up, her beautiful face registering the danger a moment too late.

White-hot flames erupted from Tsuke's fingertips. He laughed, his voice cold and cruel.

The wounded Mistress of Air screamed as her flesh sizzled and her hair caught fire. Uona's skin flaked off in long black strips, and her eyes exploded. She fell to the earth, a trembling charcoal heap.

Tomo tore himself away from the gate, his body regaining solidity as he ran toward Tsuke, a cry forming on his watery lips. "Noooo!"

Tsuke turned on the Master of Water and vaporized him. Tomo's cry lingered in the air as his body dissipated into oily white mist.

The laughter of Yogo Junzo and the Master of Fire echoed off the enchanted gates, booming over the blood-strewn battlefield.

Tsuke whirled and pointed his blazing fingertips toward Toturi.

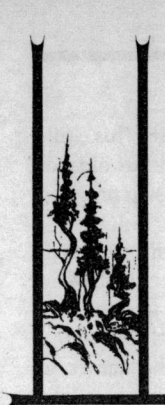

23 THE FIRE INSIDE

Time slowed to a crawl for the Black Lion. The entirety of the situation seemed unreal. One moment, the Elemental Masters had been assaulting the gates of the Forbidden City. The next, Tsuke had turned on his fellows and slain two of them. All that remained of Uona and Tomo was ashes and steam.

As the Master of Fire whirled toward him, Toturi instinctively drew his sword. Tsuke was too far away to strike down, so Toturi flicked his wrist and threw. The lion-headed katana spun end-over-end toward the renegade Elemental Master.

Tsuke jumped aside, deadly flames flickering on his fingertips. The Master of Fire's attack faltered for a mere moment, but it was time enough for Isawa Tadaka to act.

The Master of Earth stepped between Tsuke and his intended prey. Tadaka called on the power of stone. He grew taller, and his skin turned rocky. The Master of Fire blasted forth his lethal energies once more.

The firestorm broke against Tadaka, scorching his still-transforming flesh. The Master of Earth screamed but did not relent. He fought through the molten assault, each step bringing new agony. "Traitor!" Tadaka's rocky lips hissed.

"Fool!" Tsuke replied. "Fu Leng offers so much more than your pitiful allies ever could. He showed me the power I'll have in the eons to come. He sacrificed the Isawa Library to feed the fires of my soul. He'll give me even more once I've burned your pitiful bones to dust." His words sounded brave, but the flames in Tsuke's eyes flickered with uncertainty.

Toturi turned to a band of archers nearby. "Fire!" he commanded, pointing toward Tsuke.

The archers loosed a deadly volley.

Many shafts bounced harmlessly off Tadaka's rocky skin. Others incinerated before they reached Tsuke. One, though, penetrated the Master of Fire's left shoulder.

Tsuke staggered back toward the gates of the Forbidden City. Tarlike blood leaked from the wound. The blood turned to fire, and the injury quickly mended. Before Tsuke could recover, though, Tadaka came at him again.

The Master of Earth's great, stony fist hammered into Tsuke's chest. The Master of Fire gasped and flew backward through the air, landing just outside the enchanted gates.

Suddenly, those gates opened, and a great Shadowlands horde poured out. They would have trampled the Master of Earth to death, but Tadaka called a stony barrier up around himself. The evil troops thundered around Tadaka's rock-encased form and crashed into the front of Toturi's army.

Fighting for his life against undead samurai, Toturi saw Tsuke slip inside the gates and disappear into the mob. The Black Lion's chest ached as he watched the traitor's escape.

In the midst of the enemy rode Junzo, crimson death flashing from his gnarled fingers.

Toturi's shugenja rose up to meet him. Among them marched Yogo Miyuki, handmaiden to the empress and Junzo's former pupil. Lightning flashed from Miyuki's hands, and several of Junzo's ogres fell dead.

Junzo shrugged off his kinswoman's assault. He summoned a whirlwind of hornets and sent them streaming into the allied shugenja's ranks.

Toturi's sorcerers screamed, frantically forming spells to counter the stinging insects' attack. Junzo laughed.

Hida Yakamo slew two skeletons with one swing of his tetsubo and thrust himself through the chaos of battle. As always, he fought on foot.

An undead samurai swung a long no-dachi at Yakamo's head. The Crab general grabbed the sword with his Jade Hand and broke it in two. He spun, striking with the tetsubo in his right hand. The iron-studded club dashed out the samurai's greenish brains, and the monster fell dead at the Crab's feet.

In the space before Yakamo, a swarm of goblins dragged Doji Hoturi from the saddle. The Crane fought them off with a few deft cuts of his katana. Yakamo smiled appreciatively and waded back into battle.

Nearby, Toturi jumped from the back of his horse to the ground. He kicked a goblin standing in his way, crushing its head with his foot. Another goblin ran at him with a long spear. Toturi stepped aside, seized the shaft, and yanked hard. The goblin lost its grip and sailed through the air, landing on the spears of its companions.

Ten human-faced oni swooped in on the Black Lion. They were little more than rotting heads with bat wings, but their long tongues ended in poisonous barbs.

Toturi spun his newly acquired spear over his head, keeping the bobbing monsters at bay.

Seeing Toturi's predicament, Doji Hoturi appeared at his friend's side. The Crane sliced two of the small oni out of the air before they even realized he was among them. The bat-winged creatures swarmed around Hoturi, lashing out with poisonous tongues.

"They remind me of some courtiers I've known," Hoturi said glibly.

Toturi nodded. "Hai. And some courtesans as well."

Hoturi laughed. "What brings you into the middle of these beasts?"

"I need to retrieve my sword," Toturi replied. "I threw it at Tsuke, but it didn't strike home."

"Curse his eyes," Hoturi said, spitting.

"When next we meet, I'll put my sword through those eyes," Toturi said grimly.

"The loss of Tomo and Uona will not be easy to recover from."

Toturi nodded. His spear point found the mouth of one of the demons, and he thrust it through, smashing out the back of the monster's skull. The spear stuck, and Hoturi had to slice another monster's tongue off in midair to keep the Black Lion from being hit. Much to the Crane's dismay, the tongue re-grew instantly.

"These oni may be tiny," Hoturi said, "but they're highly annoying."

"And agile," Toturi replied. "They dart around like flies!" He swung his spear, and the head impaled on it flew off and crashed into another flying monster.

Before the stunned oni could recover, Hoturi spitted it on the end of his sword. "We work well together," Hoturi said to his friend. The rest of the battle swirled around them, surging and retreating with the rhythm of their blows.

"We'll die together if we're not careful," Toturi said. "Watch your back!"

Hoturi turned in time to see three new bat-winged oni swooping down on him. Before he could react, two figures stepped from the fighting to protect him. Both, Hoturi realized with some surprise, had once been Scorpions.

Tetsuo sliced the first oni cleanly in half before it could strike its prey. A flash of black fire from Miyuki's fingertips felled the second. The shugenja's face and hands were swollen from hornet stings, but she seemed otherwise little the worse for wear.

The third oni darted aside, avoiding both Tetsuo's cut and another blast from Miyuki. The creature's barbed tongue flashed out toward the Crane daimyo, but Tetsuo stepped in between them.

The young Scorpion gasped as the monster's stung his neck. He pitched forward into the mud. Hoturi quickly ran the monster through.

Enraged, the other oni dived on the group, but Miyuki was ready for them. As Toturi and Hoturi cut the monsters from the air, the shugenja uttered a terrible word of power. The remaining onis' bones turned to dust, and they fell to the ground, flapping like squid out of water.

Hoturi and the Black Lion quickly finished them. No other foes remained close enough to strike Tetsuo. Miyuki knelt at her fallen comrade's side. Toturi and his friend came and stood beside the wounded Scorpion.

Tetsuo's dark eyes darted from one man to the other. "Who'd have thought that I would save your lives?" he asked through gritted teeth.

"I had thought it," Toturi said, "or I would never have let you join my army."

"You're a better judge of character than I," Tetsuo said, sweat pouring down his pale brow. His limbs began to shake uncontrollably.

"Perhaps," Toturi replied, "but not a better man. Domo arigato, Tetsuo-san." He bowed slightly.

Hoturi did the same. "Domo arigato."

Tetsuo smiled weakly. He seemed about to speak, but his strength failed. The poison from the sting was rapidly turning the skin of his neck black.

"If I am to save this man," Miyuki said sharply, "I need him to be quiet."

Toturi nodded grimly. "Do whatever you need. Take him to my pavilion if it will help. You should be safe there from enemy reprisals."

The lady shugenja scowled, the expression making her exotic face seem feral. "Nowhere is safe from Fu Leng." Commandeering several ashigaru to carry her clansman, Miyuki quickly moved Tetsuo to the rear of the battle.

Toturi walked to where the sword of Matsu Tsuko lay and retrieved it. He whistled for his horse, and the animal came, crushing enemies beneath its hooves. In one smooth movement, the Lion remounted his steed.

Hida Yakamo emerged from the crowd. "We're wasting time.

The gates of the Forbidden City are open. We should enter them before the enemy thinks to bar the portal once more."

"Hai," Toturi agreed. "Summon your troops and lead the charge. Take Shiba Tsukune and the Phoenix with you. I'm sure they want revenge against the Master of Fire. They'll fight doubly hard."

Yakamo nodded. "Hai. My evil double is somewhere in the Forbidden City as well. Many scores shall be settled before this day is out."

"Don't forget our true goal, though," Toturi said. "We must reach the throne room and confront the Evil One."

"Plenty of time for that," Yakamo said, turning to go. Calling his troops to his side, he made a push toward the open gates.

Shadowlands warriors still streamed from that maw: undead samurai, goblins, and oni. A few tainted Crab were among them as well.

Reflections of burning buildings flashed in Yakamo's eyes as he gazed at the traitors. He surged forward, killing all who stood in his way.

Shiba Tsukune, the Phoenix general, rode beside him, her katana dealing death on all sides.

Toturi and the Crane daimyo rallied their samurai as well. They pushed the evil forces back to the wall, and then across the threshold of the gates themselves.

Suddenly, the Master of Fire appeared atop the parapet. His deep voice boomed with the power of ancient, evil spells. Fire fell from the heavens and rained down on the allied troops. Tsuke laughed as brave men and women died in his inferno.

"We must kill him!" Hoturi called over the screams of the dying.

"Hai," Toturi said. "I'll climb the wall and take him."

Hoturi shook his head. "No, you're too valuable to our cause. I'll do it."

Suddenly, the ground before them rumbled and split open. Isawa Tadaka rose from the sodden earth like a specter from the grave. Though Shadowlands troops had overrun him, he bore no marks from hooves or claws. His skin was charred and blackened from his fight with Tsuke. The Master of Earth's clothes hung in tatters from his wiry form. He looked frail and worn out. Yet, beneath his ragged hood, his eyes blazed with green fire.

"Neither of you will kill him," Tadaka said. "Leave Tsuke to me. He has much to answer for."

Toturi and Hoturi glanced skeptically at each other. "Go, then," Toturi said. "May Amaterasu guide you."

Tadaka bowed and shambled toward the great wall. Though the Master of Earth looked haggard, he drew new strength from the stones in the wall. He set his hands to the rocks and climbed up the enchanted surface as easily as if he were a spider.

The Lion and the Crane turned and charged into the fray once more.

24 BATTLE OF THE ELEMENTS

Atop the wall, Tsuke rained fiery death down upon the allies. It was all Toturi's shugenja could do to keep the blaze from spreading. The Master of Fire laughed with sadistic delight. The goblins and undead samurai on the wall laughed with him.

Their laughter turned to screams of terror, though, as the parapet suddenly shook. Tsuke stopped his assault against the allied samurai and fought hard to keep his feet. His evil companions fell from the battlement to their deaths.

Over the wall rose a dark, earthy form.

"Tadaka!" Tsuke hissed. "I thought I had slain you."

"Slain the man, perhaps," Tadaka said, setting foot on the wall, "but not the mission. The souls of Tomo and Uona cry out to me for vengeance!" He cast his hands forward, and the parapet shook like a great rug.

Tsuke toppled toward the edge. He summoned the power of his element. Flames sprang up around him and kept Tsuke from falling. They lifted him lightly and held him up. His feet did not touch the ground. Tsuke hovered in the air just above the wall, a deadly, living embodiment of the fiery Phoenix itself.

"You are weak, Tadaka," Tsuke said, "as were Tomo and Uona."

"Better to be weak of body than weak of mind," Tadaka said, spitting the blood from his mouth.

Tsuke lashed out with a burst of flame. Tadaka gestured, and a stone wall rose from the parapet to defend him. The Master of Fire's assault broke against the rocky barricade.

Tadaka's blazing green eyes narrowed. "Attack!"

The wall exploded into a thousand tiny stone projectiles. Many melted into nothing as they met the fiery aura surrounding Tsuke. Some few, though, penetrated the Master of Fire's defense, tearing his skin and ripping holes in his clothing and flesh. Tar-like blood leaked from Tsuke's wounds.

Eyes burning, Tsuke spoke words of power, summoning a blazing whirlwind. He hurled it against the Master of Earth.

The fiery cyclone buffeted Tadaka. He chanted spells of protection and drew strength from the stones beneath his feet. The Master of Earth fell to his knees as the conflagration sucked the air from his lungs. His skin blistered and peeled.

Summoning all his strength, Tadaka used a powerful counterspell to shunt Tsuke's firestorm up into the clouds. The Master of Earth leaned on his hands and knees, his face hanging limply over the edge of the parapet. Blood dripped from his mouth and nose. He tried to raise his eyes to face his enemy, but weakness overcame him. Tsuke's mocking laughter echoed in his ears. The sights of the battle far below burned in Tadaka's eyes.

At the gates, intense fighting raged. Tadaka saw his friends struggling mightily against the Shadowlands troops. Toturi, Hoturi, and the others fought bravely against incredible odds. Sprays of blood and gore filled the air with red mist. As the Master of Earth's sight dimmed, a bright flame darted among the allied troops.

Tadaka's heart fell. *I have failed them! Tsuke knows I am no threat, so he has turned his attention back to my allies. He will burn them all!*

Sweet blackness threatened to engulf the Phoenix Master of Earth. Then Tadaka realized that it was *not* Tsuke's magical flames amid his embattled friends; it was a man—a samurai in gold and red. Tadaka smiled, and hope bloomed in his heart. He staggered to his feet.

Tsuke landed atop the wall and bore in, a human torch holding a blade of deadly steel.

The Master of Earth drew his own katana and turned Tsuke's weapon aside, barely.

"Give it up, Tadaka," Tsuke hissed. "You know you were never my match with a sword. I will make your death quick and painless."

"I prefer that *you* die suffering," Tadaka said through gritted teeth. He beat off another blow and aimed a cut at Tsuke's chest. His katana slipped inside Tsuke's guard and sliced a long gash across the Master of Fire's breast.

Tsuke screamed in outrage as black blood leaked out of his wound. He aimed a quick succession of blows at Tadaka's head, his shoulder, his midsection.

The Master of Earth beat the attacks away. He retreated, almost stumbling. "Not so proficient as you thought, are you?" Tadaka gasped, a smile forming on his parched lips.

The Master of Fire's red eyes narrowed. Rather than reply, he blasted his foe with all the blazing hatred he possessed.

Tadaka staggered and fell before the fiery assault. He tried to rise but couldn't muster the strength. Every part of his body was scorched. He blinked blood out of his eyes. Through charred ears, he heard Tsuke's deep voice.

"It's not too late for you to join our side. In Fu Leng's care, you would grow strong once more—just as I have grown strong. The taint is powerful in your body. Your reward will be great."

The green striations lacing Tadaka's form tingled. He heard the seductive whispers of the Evil One. He saw himself leading a huge army of Shadowlands undead, fighting at the side of Tsuke and Junzo. Men and women died before him like rats. He tasted their blood in his mouth.

Thunder cracked overhead. The fires burning on Tadaka's skin guttered low, and cool rain fell on his back. Moisture dripped down his head and under his charred hood. He tasted the water on his lips: sweet, salty. How simple to let his suffering end.

"Join us!" Tsuke hissed.

Slowly, painfully, Tadaka raised his head. Tsuke towered over him, hovering a hand's breadth off the parapet. His fiery katana hovered high for the kill.

"Never!" Tadaka whispered.

Tsuke struck.

Before his blade split Tadaka's skull, another sword rose and met the Master of Fire's weapon. The gleaming katana beat Tsuke's sword aside. Lightning flashed in the heavens, and the new steel struck just as quickly.

Tsuke's right hand flew through the air, still clutching the fiery katana. The hand, though, was no longer attached to Tsuke's arm.

The Master of Fire screamed and reeled back, his flames barely keeping him aloft. His sticky black blood spurted from his wrist and burst into fire. He turned and gazed at his unexpected opponent.

Shiba Ujimitsu, the Phoenix Champion, smiled grimly. "Not so confident now, are you, master of evil?" he said. He held his sword parallel to his right ear and advanced on the wounded Master of Fire.

"You—you fled with Kaede!" Tsuke said, unbelieving.

"I was needed, so I returned," Ujimitsu said. He dashed forward and sliced at the Master of Fire.

Tsuke darted out the way, barely. He kept retreating, clutching his wrist to stop the blood flow, but Ujimitsu would not let him escape.

The champion aimed cuts at his foe's chest, hips, and thighs. Twice, the gleaming blade connected. Black blood gushed from Tsuke's wounds, and he screamed with impotent rage.

"You will never take me, Phoenix!" Tsuke threw a burst of fire at his foe, but a whirlwind of stones sprang up between them. The flames broke against the magical barrier. Tsuke turned and glared at the cause: Tadaka leaning on his hands and knees, barely conscious, chanting the spell to protect his old friend.

Ujimitsu thrust at Tsuke's midsection. His sword penetrated the flesh just below the Master of Fire's ribs. Tsuke gasped and lost his grip on his wound. Black blood spurted from the Master of Fire's wrist, covering the Phoenix Champion and igniting.

Tsuke laughed and danced back, over the edge of the parapet, his flames keeping him from falling.

Ujimitsu stood engulfed in flames. Skin cracked and peeled, silk melted, hair sizzled and fell off in clumps, but the champion did not cry out.

Tsuke laughed, hovering in the air just out of reach of Ujimitsu's blade.

Tadaka crumpled to the stones, unable to do anything more.

The Phoenix Champion stood atop the wall, a living embodiment of his clan archetype. The Master of Fire hung in the air before him, a burning avatar of corruption. Shiba Ujimitsu fixed his gaze upon his floating enemy.

"You are not Uona," Ujimitsu said, a smile cracking his burnt lips. "You cannot fly with the weight of two." His eyes gleamed with the fire of his Phoenix ancestors. He leapt, wrapping his strong arms around the Master of Fire.

Tsuke screamed and struggled, but the champion held him tightly. The two of them plummeted from the parapet to the earth far below.

▲▲▲▲▲▲▲▲

Shiba Tsukune looked up from her battles and saw a bright comet fall from atop the wall surrounding the Forbidden City.

Ujimitsu!

The blazing fireball struck the ground and exploded, not far from the Phoenix general's position. Tsukune cut down the goblin standing before her and ran.

She forced her way through opposing troops and allies alike, knowing she hadn't a moment to waste. She found Shiba Ujimitsu lying on his back, alone in a wide, scorched area at the base of the wall.

Tsukune sprinted to her friend and knelt at his side. Gently, she put her hand under his head and lifted his blackened face.

Ujimitsu seemed not to see her at first, but then his scorched eyes focused on her pretty face. "Tsukune," he said, "I am so glad it's you."

"Don't talk," she said quietly, tears streaming down her cheeks. "I'll get our shugenja. They can save you!"

He shook his head weakly. "The damage is . . . too great . . . for even a Phoenix to mend," he gasped. "I gladly join my wife and daughter. . . . Sending Tsuke to Jigoku was worth it."

She held his broken hand and pressed it gently to her face. "Please," she said, "don't go!"

He leaned forward and whispered seven words into her ear. For a moment, he held her with his deep brown eyes as the breath rattled out of his charred lungs.

Tsukune saw the fire die within her old sensei's orbs. His hand grew cold. Tsukune's body tingled with a new flame. As the fire grew, Shiba Ujimitsu quietly slipped away.

Tsukune rose, leaving the broken body of her mentor where it lay. The voices of her warrior ancestors echoed in her head, offering comfort and advice. Foremost among them was her friend Shiba Ujimitsu. He chuckled and spoke in a quiet, gentle voice, just as he had in the prime of his life.

Tsukune smiled, and the fire of the Phoenix Champion danced in her eyes. "Yes, I understand." A smile drew across her pretty face. It all seemed so easy now: the fighting, the strategy, the weakness of the enemy, all burned into her brain with amazing clarity. This battle was but another test among many—one she could effortlessly pass. With a thousand years of experience, how could she lose?

Turning, she sprinted back into the fray, her gold and red kimono fluttering in the breeze like a living flame.

▲▲▲▲▲▲▲▲

Toturi scowled and hacked away the arms of the goblin clinging to his saddle. The creature fell to the muddy ground, its body joining a growing carpet of the dead and dying. Gray rain washed the blood from the ronin lord's body. Doji Hoturi rode beside him, hacking and slaying in tandem with his old friend.

Toku pushed through the frenzied crowd. "Did you see the falling star?"

The Black Lion shook his head. "Where?"

"I spotted it near the top of the wall, and it landed somewhere near the base," the boy said.

Hoturi added, "I think it came from where Tadaka and the traitor were fighting." He kicked the face of a skeleton trying to pull him off his horse. The monster's skull stove in, and it toppled into the mud.

"Tsuke's fires have died away," Toturi said. "Probably the star means Tadaka has defeated him."

"You think the fireball was Tsuke's body?" Hoturi asked.

"I hope so," said Toku.

"As do I," said Toturi. "I also hope that Tadaka survived."

"I'll go see," said Toku. He vanished into the vast melee.

"One day he'll get killed rushing off that way," Hoturi said.

"We need to gather our forces, not dissipate them," Toturi replied. "The Shadowlands army is splitting us apart."

"The clans aren't used to working together," Hoturi said. "We still have a natural distrust of each other."

"If we can't overcome that, we're doomed," Toturi said, his face stern. "Gather your forces. We have to reinforce the Crab as they push inside the gate."

"What about the Unicorn?"

"They can hold the outer city with the Mantis," Toturi said.

"But *Junzo* is there," Hoturi said gravely.

The Black Lion frowned, and the muscles in his jaw tightened. "We'll have to trust Kamoko and her Battle Maidens to handle him."

"But if she should be killed . . ."

"Hoturi, my friend, there are no good choices today," Toturi said. "Until we can breach the castle's inner walls, every battle we fight is just a holding action." He whistled for his commanders, and Matsu Yojo rode to his side. "Form up! We'll push inside the gates and take the battle to the palace."

Yojo nodded his understanding and rode off, barking orders as he went. Hoturi did the same, and soon he and the Black Lion rode at the head of a mighty column of samurai. They pushed through the Shadowlands troops, killing and maiming as they went.

Just beyond the gate, Toturi spotted Yakamo's embattled Crabs. The army of evil swarmed around them like a black tide. Yakamo's tetsubo smashed the head of many an evil samurai. Blood streamed down the Crab lord's massive body. A thundering call to arms boomed from his huge chest.

Yakamo's scattered troops formed up once more, pressing ever deeper into the enemy's sanctuary. Toturi's combined forces of ronin, Lion, Crane, and Dragon fought their way to the Crab's flanks.

The melee intensified. Samurai and ronin battled undead warriors, skeletons, goblins, and minor oni. The tide of the fighting pushed Toturi away from Hoturi and the other commanders.

His steed fell out from under him, pulled down by the claws of his enemies. The ronin lord found himself surrounded by green-skinned goblins intent on his death. Toturi whirled in a wide circle, chopping at shoulder and thigh in a classic Lion sword tactic. Some of the goblins fell, hamstrung. Others dropped their weapons from their disabled arms.

Toturi beheaded the two goblins left uninjured and stepped past the others, sparing only a brief glance for his fallen horse.

Togashi Yokuni appeared suddenly beside him. Gore dripped from the Great Dragon's golden armor, but the daimyo seemed unharmed.

"Hida Yakamo's wisdom has deserted him," Togashi said. "He has left his troops to chase the Yakamo no Oni. Even now, the Crab is surrounded by his enemies, though he does not know it. His desire for revenge may be his undoing."

The Black Lion nodded grimly. "I'll order the troops to press on. We'll take the battle to him, bring him back into the fold."

"It is too late," Yokuni said. "He is too far away."

"Is there no one who can arrive in time to help?"

"My daughter Hitomi pursues Yakamo, though the desire for revenge burns brightly in her as well," the Great Dragon said.

Toturi looked at him darkly, "If Yakamo falls or if they slay each other, Fu Leng will triumph."

Doji Hoturi, blood dripping from his armor, rode through the bodies to his friends' side. "Hitomi must choose mercy over revenge? Then everything we've done, all we've sacrificed, is lost!"

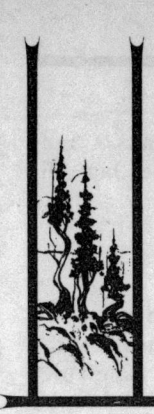

25 TRAPPED

Junzo cackled with delight. Flesh sloughed from the bones of a Unicorn Battle Maiden. The samurai-ko didn't even have time to scream before she died.

Nearby, his lieutenant Yakushi set a home ablaze. Folk ran from the burning doorway into the street. Yakushi fired flaming arrows into the backs of each family member in turn. They died pleading for mercy. Yakushi got off his steed and kicked their bones from the ashes of their bodies.

"Stop wasting time," Junzo growled.

The charred samurai bowed and remounted his onikage. Junzo pointed toward a square where Utaku Kamoko fought alongside her daimyo, Shinjo Yokatsu, and many other Unicorn samurai.

Yakushi nodded and led a contingent of Junzo's undead troops to crush the embattled Unicorns.

Behind them came Junzo himself, lording

over the carnage and drinking the deaths of his enemies. A crimson aura, brighter than the setting sun, surrounded him. His laughter shook the burning buildings nearby.

▲▲▲▲▲▲▲▲

Shinjo Yokatsu, Master of the Four Winds, looked up as a new Shadowlands contingent joined the fray. A frown tugged at the corners of his mustache, and a look of deep concern washed over his handsome face. Utaku Kamoko's eyes followed her daimyo's gaze and mirrored his concern.

The odds against them had been perilous; now they were overwhelming. Still, the Unicorn fought. Despite the plague, despite the long occupation by Fu Leng's minions, Otosan Uchi was home for many untainted, innocent people.

The Unicorn fought for these oppressed and forgotten peasants. Even Utaku Kamoko, though she'd heard the call of the Thunders, could not ignore people in need. All her Battle Maidens felt the same. Kamoko gazed over her troops and wondered if any of them would survive the day.

Utaku Tetsuko fought close beside her general. Dirt smudged the young Battle Maiden's face. Her mouth was set in a grim line. She charged an ogre and impaled the beast on the horn of her horse's armor. The dying monster tried to grab at her, but Tetsuko cut off its hands.

Kamoko smiled; she had trained her samurai well. If they could not live through the day, at least they would make brave deaths for themselves.

A howling wind rose on the battlefield, whipping hot ashes into Kamoko's eyes and blinding her. The Unicorn general reined her horse and blinked, trying to clear her vision. When the gray haze lifted, she saw Yakushi charging toward her.

A halo of fire surrounded his evil face. Flames burned brightly up the length of his katana. He clutched the weapon in his bony hand and aimed at the Unicorn's neck.

Kamoko brought her sword up just in time. Yakushi's fiery weapon skidded past, scorching her cheek. She spun and slashed at his back as he rode by. Her katana cut through the burning man's armor and into the skin beneath. Fire leaked from the wound.

Yakushi laughed. He wheeled his onikage to charge Kamoko again. Black smoke blew from the smoldering buildings, obscuring the distance between the foes.

A white Unicorn charger burst from the sooty cloud. The animal lowered its head and rammed its armored horn into the side of Yakushi's demon steed.

The burning samurai looked up, surprise registering in his blazing eyes.

Utaku Tetsuko, mounted on the charger's back, swung her sword toward Yakushi's neck.

The evil samurai brought up his sword, parrying the blow.

Tetsuko spurred her horse hard, nearly pushing her enemy's steed off its feet. The warrior maiden swung again, but Junzo's lieutenant ducked out of the way.

Yakushi tugged on the onikage's reins, trying to regain his momentum, but the living horse crashed into them again. The onikage lost its footing. The evil samurai toppled sideways, crashing into a supporting timber in the front of a burning building. Under the onikage's weight, the charred log gave way. Junzo's lieutenant howled as the building fell on him. Tons of burning rubble buried Yakushi, silencing his cries.

Tetsuko reined in her horse before it skidded into the flaming ruins. She glanced at her general and smiled.

Kamoko wiped the remaining soot from her eyes, bowed slightly, and said, "Domo arigato." Tetsuko bowed in return.

Junzo screamed his displeasure. He spread his arms wide, and a black wind billowed forth, blistering the skin of every untainted person it touched. The evil shugenja's troops surged forward, pulling down many confused and injured Unicorn riders.

"Form a circle," Shinjo Yokatsu shouted, his deep voice booming over the howl of the wind. The others turned to obey, quickly riding to their master's side. At the tail end of the group rode Kamoko and Tetsuko. Their foray had cut them off from their fellows, and the evil horde was fast closing around them.

Yokatsu's shugenja worked furiously to counter the black gale. They clasped hands and chanted, summoning the east wind to beat back the scalding cloud. Kamoko and Tetsuko rode into the shugenja's protective circle just as the evil wind began to dissipate. They turned to reinforce the line.

Wave after wave of undead crashed against them.

Tetsuko jerked suddenly upright in her saddle. Red lightning coursed through her body. The Battle Maiden fell from the back of her horse and lay twitching in the mud.

Kamoko gasped but didn't dare dismount to help her friend; the undead army was just too close.

Junzo laughed and rode toward his trapped prey. He turned his attention to the Unicorn shugenja. The crimson lightning struck again, felling the allied sorcerers.

The Shadowlands horde encircled the embattled Unicorn, hemming them in the small plaza. Devastated homes and piles of rubble surrounded Shinjo Yokatsu's samurai, cutting off the horsemen's avenues of escape. The Unicorn tried to push through the enemy line, but goblins and undead held them back. Slain Unicorns rose to join Junzo's unholy army.

Fu Leng's general loomed over the battle, sitting astride his onikage, savoring the victory to come. His minions hung on his every word, waiting for orders.

A frightful smile parted Junzo's red lips. "Slay them all!"

▲▲▲▲▲▲▲▲▲

Kachiko ran, her heart pounding. Her feet fumbled across the floorboards, nearly tripping on her ornate robes. A lock of her long hair came undone and trailed across her face like a black ribbon. Sheer terror marred her beautiful countenance.

Behind her came her husband, the Hantei Emperor, his pace slow and methodical. No longer was he a callow, sickly youth. Now the fires of hatred burned bright within his eyes. Supernatural power suffused his gangly limbs. His long toenails scraped the floorboards as he scampered after his wife. An evil smile creased his boyish face.

Kachiko darted through a secret panel and pulled it shut behind her. She thrust one of her sandals into the door's base, jamming it closed. Quickly, she turned and ran to the other end of the hidden corridor. She opened the panel at the far end and closed it behind her, jamming her remaining sandal in the exit to keep it shut.

She turned to run again, but as she did so, she tripped on the hem of her robe. The Mother of Scorpions landed hard on the moist wooden floor. Before she could rise, the panel behind her shuddered and erupted into a shower of splinters, paper, and stone.

Hantei the 39th stood in the sundered portal, his eyes blazing with eerie green light. "Hello, my *loving* wife," he purred, stepping through the opening. "I've been looking and looking for you. But you kept running away. Why is that?" Not waiting for an answer, he reached down and seized her by the neck of her kimono. "You've caused ever so much trouble for me. Ever so much. In fact, I think you're the cause of all my problems. Perhaps I should end those problems . . . right now."

He twisted the silk of her robe and lifted her effortlessly into the air.

"Y-you can't kill me yet," Kachiko gasped.

"Oh, can't I?" the evil emperor replied.

Kachiko's voice remained firm and confident, but sweat poured from her brow. "Every creature in Rokugan obeys its fate. Even you are no exception. The Fortunes have decreed that only after the Thunders are assembled can you kill any of us. It is written in the stars."

A wicked smile crept across the boy emperor's sallow face. "Is that so? Perhaps I should rewrite what the stars say then, just as I will leave my mark on the face of Rokugan itself. Rules and prophecy mean nothing to me!" He tightened his grip on her robe, and Kachiko watched in terror as he raised his long, sharp fingernails toward her eyes.

A surprised squeak from the other end of the corridor startled the possessed emperor. Both Hantei and Kachiko turned and saw that Seppun Bake had just entered the corridor through a fusuma panel at the far end. The aging courtier's face went completely white.

"E-excuse, me," he said sheepishly. "I did not mean to intrude. Please, go about your business, Highnesses." He nodded a polite bow, and his carefully cut kimono rustled quietly, like the feathers of a frightened bird.

The emperor's grip relaxed only a moment, but long enough for Kachiko to wriggled free. She sprawled to the floor. "Bake! Help me!"

"Em . . . How should I help you, Empress?" Bake asked, twisting his fingers nervously.

Hantei laughed—a cold, wicked laugh that filled the hallway.

Kachiko scrambled to her feet and sped away from her husband. "Idiot!" she shouted angrily at Bake.

Bake looked from the possessed boy to the running woman. Kachiko was coming straight at him. He seemed unable to move. "I-I'd be happy to help, Empress," he stammered. "Just tell me what you need."

"Get out of my way, you fool!" Kachiko snapped.

"W-with pleasure, Empress," Bake said, bowing nervously and stepping aside. "Please, excuse my clumsiness."

Kachiko streaked past him and down the hall. Bake's eyes darted back and forth between the emperor and his wife, his head bobbing like a chicken's. He stroked his balding pate with thin fingers.

The emperor's face grew stern as he turned his burning gaze on the well-dressed toady.

"Sh-should I not have let her pass, Highness?" Bake asked. He bowed very low, trying not to notice the bloodstains on the boy emperor's bony hands.

". . . Not have let her pass . . ." the evil boy said hollowly. His voice sent a shiver down Bake's spine.

"W-well, she can't have gone far," Bake said. "I'm sure you can catch her. Or *I* could catch her if you like, Highness." He bowed again. When the emperor didn't respond, he added, "Are you f-feeling well, Otennoo-sama?"

"Very well indeed," the boy said, striding nearer. "I've been . . .

speaking with some of my advisors. The . . . *conversations* have made me feel vastly better."

"Gl-glad to hear it, Highness," Bake said. Not knowing what else to do, he bowed once more. As he rose, Hantei seized him by the throat and lifted him off his feet. The demonic boy's fingers dug into the well-dressed courtier's throat. Bake struggled in the emperor's steely grip.

"You know what, Bake?" Hantei the 39th asked casually.

"Wh-what, Highness?" Bake gasped.

"I never liked you," the emperor said. He squeezed and crushed the squirming courtier's neck. Then he tossed Bake's body to the floor.

Lurking in a secret passage nearby, Kachiko heard Seppun Bake's grizzly death. She had doubled back in a parallel hallway, trusting that the emperor would not think her so bold. She held her breath and hoped he wouldn't smell her fear.

She waited a moment until Hantei's scraping footsteps headed down the corridor in the opposite direction. When the noise of his passage had echoed to nothingness, she opened the secret exit and stepped out. She walked quickly past Bake's body, sparing only a brief glance to make sure he was dead. Despite her peril, she took some small pleasure at the toady's demise.

As she opened a new panel in the opposite wall, a faint sound behind her froze her in her tracks. "Kaaaa-chi-ko-o-o-o . . . Where aaaare youuuu?"

The emperor's voice dripped with honeyed poison. He was seeking her within the mazelike secret passages lacing the castle walls.

"I only want to give you a kiiisssssss!"

For a moment, terror gripped the empress's soul. Her bare feet felt as though they had been nailed to the wooden floorboards. Fear clutched at her heart. Despite the prophecies, her husband hadn't given up on killing her yet.

He will find me, and I will die.

Standing so near Bake, her mind flashed back to another body she'd found in a palace corridor. It was near the end of the Scorpion Coup, when all their plans were falling apart. The body she'd discovered then had been that of Dairu, her son.

The thought of the boy, barely in his manhood, brought tears to the empress' eyes. She heard her son's gentle voice, felt the soft touch of his hand on hers. Then, another sound arose—a deep, melodious voice—drowning out the eerie calls of the corrupt emperor.

You are the soul of my strength. In the utter darkness, you are my light. I shall never leave you. We will be together until the end of the world.

The voice belonged to her dead husband, Bayushi Shoju. He had spoken the words to her a long time ago, in the silence of their bedchamber at Kyuden Bayushi. Now the castle was gone, and Shoju was gone as well. The end of the world was coming.

Kachiko felt the strength of the Scorpion flow into her weary body. Her resolve firmed, and her feet unstuck themselves from the floor. She darted into the panel and drew it shut behind her. She knew these hidden corridors better than anyone living.

The emperor would not find her, not until she had accomplished what she'd set out to do. After that, he would have to deal with not *one* Thunder, but *seven*.

▲▲▲▲▲▲▲▲

Junzo's unholy army surged forward. The Unicorn stood their ground, slaying the monsters that tried to break their defensive circle. Kamoko rode with Yokatsu's other bold horsemen, swiftly patrolling the edges of the line. She spared only a quick glance for her friend Tetsuko, who lay insensate amid the Unicorn formation.

Many of Junzo's troops died, but Unicorns began to fall as well. The undead had been weakened, but there were just too many. Kamoko knew her people could hold the pestilent army back for a while but sooner or later, they would succumb.

Crimson fire burned in Junzo's yellow eyes. He laughed madly, and his stringy white hair blew in the rain-swept wind. He pointed at Shinjo Yokatsu and muttered a spell of destruction.

26 THUNDER STRIKES

Yokatsu drew his bow to shoot the evil shugenja, knowing he would never have time to fire before Junzo completed his awful spell.

A cry arose from the edges of the undead army. Junzo's troops whirled at the sound. Bands of shabby-looking peasants, thousands strong, surged from the crumbling buildings at the plaza's edge. They carried clubs and pitchforks, timbers and rocks, anything that could be used as a weapon. The unruly rebels crashed into the rear of Junzo's troops, breaking the Shadowlands line.

Junzo, stunned by the sudden attack, paused in his spell.

Yokatsu fired.

The Unicorn daimyo's arrow struck Junzo just as the Unicorn army surged into Junzo's surprised troops. The well-aimed barb entered the evil shugenja's throat just above the collarbone. The arrowhead smashed Junzo's voice box and spine, but it did not kill him. His head lolled sickeningly, but the sorcerer's magic kept him alive.

Junzo gasped, and his yellow eyes grew wide with fear. He tried to finish his incantation, but all that came from his mouth were croaking gasps. Black blood and crimson fire leaked from his wounded neck. He grabbed the reins of his onikage and wheeled the demon steed away from the battle.

Utaku Kamoko thundered through the enemy, slaying dozens with her katana and crushing more under the hooves of her mighty steed.

Yokatsu pulled his bowstring to his ear and fired twice in rapid succession. His first arrow struck Junzo's demon-horse as it turned away from the fight. The creature staggered, and Yokatsu put his second arrow through the onikage's eye.

The demon steed's head exploded as Yokatsu's bolt smashed out the other side of its skull. The skeletal horse staggered and went down, taking its evil master with it.

Junzo's left leg snapped when the onikage fell on him. His travel bags split open, spilling the sorcerer's evil scrolls into the mud. Junzo pulled himself out from under the beast. His bony hands quickly wove a spell of binding to shore up his wounds. His leg knitted, and his neck set itself to right once more; his shattered throat began to heal. He rose just as the melee parted behind him.

Through the opening in Junzo's diseased troops thundered Kamoko. Her powerful horse galloped across the muddy earth, its breath heaving from its nostrils in great white puffs. The Battle Maiden held her katana high. Lightning flashed overhead, and the blade gleamed white, like the sun come down to earth.

Junzo's eyes blazed red with hatred; he turned to run.

Kamoko spurred her steed and trampled him into the ground. The horse's iron-shod hooves smashed the magician's hips, his ribs, and his skull.

The body of the most powerful shugenja in Rokugan quivered and shook, flopping in the mud like a beached fish. It refused to give up its unholy animation. Junzo's crushed fingers reached toward the powerful scrolls lying scattered nearby. As his black brains oozed out of his broken head, the sorcerer's whispering voice beseeched Fu Leng for one final boon. He stretched out his bloody hand toward the scrolls. His fingertips brushed their evil, wizened surfaces.

The gnarled fingers stiffened. The shattered body shuddered once and then lay still. Junzo's corrupt form quickly melted into putrid slime. What little remained, the rain dissolved into nothingness.

Kamoko let out a joyous cry. She killed the goblin closest to her and wheeled to look at her clanmates. With the peasants' help, they were already driving the remnants of the Shadowlands army away from the plaza.

The peasants saved us, Kamoko thought. We fought for them during the dark times, and when we needed them, they rallied to our cause. She pulled on the reins, and her horse reared. She raised her sword in salute to Shinjo Yokatsu and cried, "Rokugan!"

Yokatsu and the other Unicorn raised their swords in unison and took up the call. "Rokugan!"

Tetsuko and the wounded Unicorn shugenja rose slowly to their feet. With Junzo dead, the effects of the spell that incapacitated them faded quickly. They, too, shouted. "Rokugan!"

Enmeshed in terrible battle, the peasants also echoed the Unicorn's cry.

Utaku Kamoko smiled.

▲▲▲▲▲▲▲▲

Doji Hoturi rode through the melee to Toturi's side. The Black Lion stood amid half a dozen foes, hacking them with Matsu Tsuko's blood-encrusted katana. Hoturi killed the lone samurai separating him from his friend. A smile broke across the Crane's handsome face. "Junzo has fallen, and the Shadowlands forces are breaking," he said. "We can *win* here!"

"We win *nothing* unless Fu Leng is destroyed, "Toturi replied. Thunder cracked overhead. "Where are the others?"

Hoturi shrugged and wiped the sweat from his brow. "My scouts report Kamoko and the Unicorn are fighting their way back to us. I haven't seen Tadaka since he battled the Master of

Fire atop the wall. Perhaps he, too, perished in that awful conflagration. As to Hida Yakamo and Mirumoto Hitomi . . . who knows?"

Toturi cursed. His dark eyes scanned the battlefield and soon found the person he sought. "Bring me the Hooded Ronin." Toturi pointed toward the cloaked samurai. "The time has come for us to stand or fall together."

Hoturi bowed slightly. "Hai, Toturi-sama." The Crane's eyes sparkled, and a wry smile curled the corner of his mouth. Hoturi spurred his horse and dived once more into the frenzied mob.

The Hooded Ronin stood amid allied troops, Lions, snakelike Naga, and even a ratling or two. All battled fiercely against Shadowlands undead.

The ronin stove in heads with his long, flute-topped staff. Mud and gore caked his green cloak. Long scratches traced his masculine face, but he paid them no heed.

The Crane daimyo joined the fray, and with his help, the ronin and his allies quickly cleared an area around the hooded wanderer.

"Come with me," Hoturi said. "Toturi thinks the time is now."

The Hooded Ronin smiled grimly. "He is right." He pulled himself into the saddle behind the handsome Crane.

As Hoturi fetched the ronin, Toturi and his samurai pushed the battlefront past a ruined Shintao complex. The temple had been burned and desecrated. The bones of monks littered the courtyard. Only the great torii arch had resisted efforts to destroy it. Its tall, red columns showed burn marks and scars from swords and axes, but they still stood proudly, defiant of Fu Leng's reign.

Toturi met the Crane daimyo and the Hooded Ronin below the torii's lintel. Thunder struck, and the courtyard reverberated with the sound.

"The time has come," Toturi said.

The ronin nodded. "Even now I can feel Fu Leng in my bones. I will summon the Thunders. Help me climb to the top of this torii."

Using Hoturi's horse, all three of them scrambled to the top of the sacred wooden arch. They stood together, side by side as the black rain pelted them.

Poised between the Crane and the Lion, the Hooded Ronin lifted his staff high. The wind made the flute on the end of the walking stick howl like a legion of demons. "To me, Thunders!" the Hooded Ronin cried. His voice boomed over the city, louder than the peals of thunder that accompanied his words. "Shinsei's descendant summons you now! Your time has come! The battle will not be won within this devastated city, but at the Emerald Throne itself!"

The ronin's summons still echoed as he, Toturi, and Doji Hoturi climbed down from the torii. They took position beneath the great arch to await the others.

Instantly, Togashi Yokuni appeared beside them. All traces of blood and grime were gone from him. His golden armor gleamed in the dim light of the cloud-shrouded afternoon. The black rain seemed not to touch him. *Though I am not a Thunder, I still have unfinished business with Fu Leng.*

Toturi nodded. "Have you seen Hitomi, Great One?"

She is approaching even now. And she does not come alone. He turned his golden eyes toward the battlefront.

Mirumoto Hitomi emerged from the crowd. Her golden armor gleamed, though not so brightly as that of her lord; black blood covered her from head to toe. Her face was set in a stern mask.

Beside her walked Hida Yakamo. He, too, was battered, bloody, and out of breath. Like Hitomi, he looked ready to fight one last battle.

"It seems they decided not to kill each other after all," Hoturi whispered to Toturi.

The Lion nodded. As Yakamo joined them beneath the massive Shintao gate, Toturi asked, "Did you slay the demon with your name?"

"It is dead," Yakamo replied.

"*I* killed it," Hitomi said proudly.

The Lion and the Crane glanced at each other, but neither said anything further.

Kamoko rode up, the hooves of her horse shaking the muddy ground. She dismounted and bowed slightly to the others. They did the same.

"Utaku Kamoko of the Unicorn stands with you," she said. Glancing at the Hooded Ronin, she added, "You called, and I came."

The ronin bowed to her. "I knew you would," he said good-naturedly.

"I would expect nothing less from Shinsei's descendant," Kamoko said, smiling.

"How do your troops fare?" Toturi asked.

"Junzo lies dead, crushed beneath the hooves of my steed," she replied. "Without him, his army is like a headless snake; their thrashing may be dangerous, but they will not live for long. Shinjo Yokatsu will make sure of that."

Toturi folded his arms over his broad chest. "Good."

"I see only five of us," Hitomi said impatiently. "With the one inside the palace, that only makes six. Where is Tadaka?"

"I am here," said a weak, gravelly voice.

All eyes turned to see Isawa Tadaka shamble up the temple's steps. He looked thin and frail, and Toku supported his left elbow as he walked. The Master of Earth leaned heavily against his young companion. His clothes hung in charred tatters. Only the swords at his hip and the bow slung on his back seemed untouched by the inferno. Terrible green scars, like an evil road map, ran across Tadaka's scorched body. His skin was covered with open sores. He coughed, and his lungs rattled.

"He'll be no use to us like this," Yakamo said.

"Don't be too sure," Tadaka hissed. "I have enough magic left in me for one final task. Perhaps, two—if I must fight you, Crab." He glanced back the way he had come and saw a fleeting white shadow dash across the parapets. "Then," he said, sighing, "I can rest."

The Hooded Ronin stepped forward and gave his flute-topped staff to the Master of Earth.

Tadaka accepted it gratefully, not bothering with the formality of refusing a gift three times. "I am ready."

"Me, too," piped Toku.

The Lion turned his dark eyes on the young samurai. "This is not for you," Toturi said quietly to his friend. "Your destiny lies elsewhere. You cannot come with us."

Toku hung his head a moment and looked at his sandals. Then he lifted his face, and his eyes brightened. "I'll free the city for you before you return," he said enthusiastically.

Hitomi and Yakamo laughed, but the Lion merely nodded. "Yosh. See that you do."

Drawing his sword, Toku bowed low, and then scurried off to the battlefront. "For Tsuko! For Toturi! For Rokugan!"

At a command from Toturi, the allied forces pushed forward, clearing the way to the walls of the imperial palace.

Yokuni, the Hooded Ronin, and the six Thunders walked grimly between the battle lines. As they did, the rear gate to the castle swung silently open. Inside stood Empress Kachiko.

She looked resplendent and powerful in her long ivory kimono, her hair wrapped in an elegant bun atop her head. Two black hairpins embossed with crimson scorpions held the hair in place. Her full red lips glistened, and her eyes flashed with the lightning. "Quickly. We do not have much time."

They followed her through a blighted garden to a nondescript section of palace wall. Kachiko moved one stone, pulled back another, and pressed a hidden stud. A section of the wall slid away, revealing a long, dark passage leading toward the castle's interior.

She stepped into the darkness, and the others followed swiftly behind. The passage closed behind them, leaving only the dim light from Kachiko's red-paned lantern to lead them on.

"Now, we are seven," Kamoko said quietly.

The others rumbled their agreement.

As they entered, Togashi Yokuni spoke, his words echoing in their minds. *Even though you are powerful, even though the spirits of the original Seven Thunders live within you, Fu Leng is more powerful still. In his current state, you cannot harm him. His soul is split between Jigoku and Rokugan. While he is not fully of this world, he is immortal. If you fight him then, he will surely slay every one of you.*

The others nodded their understanding.

I must battle him first. If my plan succeeds, he will lose his advantage. Then you will be able to destroy him.

"What if your plan fails?" Tadaka asked.

Then the world will die.

"The Great Dragon's plan will not fail," Hitomi said, scowling.

"How will we know if your plan has succeeded?" Doji Hoturi asked.

A faraway look crossed the Dragon lord's brilliant green eyes. *If my plan succeeds, Hitomi will kneel beside me and then rise again. When she does, you will know the time has come for battle.*

"Yosh," said Toturi. "Let's find Fu Leng so we can slay him. Kachiko-san, lead the way."

Kachiko moved cautiously down the secret hallway toward the heart of the castle. Toturi and the others followed.

As they walked ever deeper into the palace, the Great Dragon slowed his pace and quickly fell to the rear of the group. Mirumoto Hitomi hung back as well and stopped altogether when her lord came to a halt.

"What is wrong, Great One?" she asked, glancing from the Dragon daimyo to her rapidly disappearing allies.

I have things to tell you that are for no other ears.

Hitomi merely nodded.

▲▲▲▲▲▲▲▲

"Hitomi's gone," Yakamo said, glancing back the way they'd come. He peered suspiciously into the darkness.

"Yokuni is with her," the Hooded Ronin replied. "She will return to us when the time comes. Have no fear. Hitomi will fulfill her destiny."

"As will we all," Hoturi said.

Kachiko opened another panel, and the six Thunders stepped into a hall deep within the palace. "Though there are hidden places within the chamber itself, there is no secret access to the throne room. We must walk these last steps in the open."

"As it should be," Yakamo said, puffing out his chest. "We are not all Scorpions to be hiding in the shadows."

Kachiko's beautiful face grew stern, and the green specks in her black eyes flashed brightly. "The emperor is not to be trifled with. He is not the sick, weak boy you all knew."

"Truer words have seldom been spoken by my wife," a low, sweet voice said.

Out of the antechamber at the far end of the hall came Hantei the 39th. He was taller and more muscular than when last they'd seen him, and his eyes blazed with unholy light. His hands and toes ended in long, ragged nails, and his stringy black hair trailed down over his shoulders. Blood stained the front of his white kimono a bright crimson.

Toturi and Kamoko stepped in front of Kachiko and drew their swords. Hoturi and Yakamo drew their weapons as well. Kachiko studied her husband, seeking signs of weakness. Tadaka began to chant softly.

"You expect to harm me with those?" Hantei asked sweetly. "I assure you, it's far too late for that."

He roared, and the hallway filled with his pestilent breath. Hot wind coursed through the corridor, blasting the Thunders and stinging their eyes. Kachiko pressed herself against the wall; Tadaka staggered and fell to his knees.

Thunder echoed in Toturi's ears and he thought he heard Matsu Tsuko's voice crying, "Kill him, you fool!" Despite the Great Dragon's warning, he would have tried to attack then, but the noxious wind held him back.

Toturi watched in horror as the boy's skin began to split open. Spines and black scales shone through the cracks in Hantei's pale flesh. His face grew long and narrow; his ears turned into horns. The thing that had been the emperor grew rapidly, like a bellows filling with air. Soon, the corridor was too narrow to contain his huge form.

The creature shook his scaly body, and his long tail shattered the fusuma panels on either side of the hall. He rose up and leered down at the six Thunders, no longer a boy, but an immense, black dragon.

"I am not the weak and callow Hantei you knew," the dragon hissed. "I am Fu Leng!"

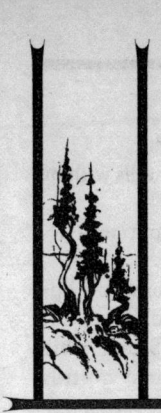

27 THE GREAT DRAGON

As the evil dragon spoke, the stifling wind died away. Fu Leng lunged at the assembled Thunders. Iron talons shredded the oak floor as Toturi rolled away. A huge barbed tail swished just over Hoturi's ducking head.

Tadaka began to mutter a spell, but a fit of coughing caused the incantation to die on his blistered lips. Kachiko helped the disfigured Master of Earth to his feet. "I am weak," he muttered. "These paper walls and wooden floors vex me. I need *stone* to replenish my strength."

"The walls of the throne room are stone," Kachiko said, "if only we can get there." Her black eyes searched the corridor for some way past the monster.

"I fear," Tadaka said, "we may not survive that long. As Yokuni said, Fu Leng is all but indestructible in this form."

"Where is Yokuni?" Kachiko hissed. "We need his power!"

Lion, Crab, Unicorn, and Crane scrambled

out of the monster's way, retreating down the corridor.

Fu Leng pursued, destroying the castle's ancient walls with his iron scales as he sought to kill the six Thunders

Hoturi ducked under another blow. "We can't wait for Yokuni!"

Fu Leng reared back, and a smile parted his monstrous lips, showing row upon row of daggerlike teeth. "You needn't wait. You may die—now!" The monstrous body took a deep breath. Wafts of smoke billowed from his gaping jaws and flared nostrils. Within the awesome mouth, obscene fires glowed.

The Hooded Ronin stepped forth, his katana held before him like a torch. The weapon shimmered in the corridor's dim light. "Back, creature of the pit!"

"Shinsei!" Fu Leng hissed. "I have been looking for you!"

"You have found me or, rather, I have found you," the ronin said. "I am not Shinsei, though his blood flows in my veins. As he and his allies defeated you a thousand years ago, so shall I defeat you now. Begone, I say! Return to your dark realm and trouble us no more!"

"You have no power over me, little man," the Evil One said. "I, however, have the power to make you die!" At the last word, the black dragon exhaled a huge burst of fire.

Togashi Yokuni suddenly appeared between the Evil One and his intended prey. The fire smashed into Yokuni's golden armor like waves against a breakwater.

The Thunders shielded their eyes. The heat from the blast scorched their lungs. Yet, the Dragon lord did not perish. When the flames had passed, he stood proud and unharmed.

The dragon that was Fu Leng cocked his immense head. "Brother!" he purred. "I wondered where you were hiding."

"Not hiding, Fu Leng," Yokuni said. "Waiting for the proper moment. That moment is now!" Casting aside his swords, he began to change. His arms and legs grew longer and more powerful. His body became sinuous and serpentine. His golden armor transformed into titanic scales.

The dragon that had been Togashi Yokuni was as awe-inspiring as Fu Leng was terrible. Togashi flexed his immense body, and the castle shook. The two creatures, one as bright as the sun and the other as black as midnight, stared at each other across the devastated corridor.

"He's a dragon, too?" Kamoko asked.

"He is *the* dragon." Kachiko replied. "He is Togashi, the kami who fell from the sky a thousand years ago."

"Surely he's the kami's great great grandchild," said Hoturi, "a descendant of Togashi. Becoming a dragon is some kind of magic he's using."

"No," Tadaka said, leaning against his borrowed staff. "Can't you feel it? He's the original. For all these years, he's led his clan in secret—pretending to be human. That is why he can fight the immortal Fu Leng; he is immortal himself. Togashi reveals himself to battle his dark brother."

"The Master of Earth is correct," said a firm voice behind them. Mirumoto Hitomi stepped out of the shadows and joined the other six Thunders. "We should keep out of his way, so that he can do what must be done."

The dragons lunged at each other, talons flashing, bodies coiling. They effortlessly smashed a pillar wider than two men. The ceiling above caved in, raining timbers and tiles down on both titans. Neither one even noticed.

"Give them room," the Hooded Ronin said, backing away. "There is nothing we can do to help. This battle is for the kami alone."

Fu Leng raked his iron claws toward his brother's golden eyes. Togashi ducked, and the evil kami's talons stove in a huge section of wall. The golden dragon fastened his daggerlike teeth on Fu Leng's arm. Fu Leng howled and sprayed fire from his mouth. Togashi blinked, but did not let go.

The Evil One swung his whiplike tail and coiled it around Togashi's long neck. The good kami responded by twining his brother's ebony body with his own. Together, they rolled across the corridor, knotted in a deadly dance. The palace shook to its foundations as they writhed in mortal combat. Smashing the wall of the throne room antechamber, they tumbled inside.

The Seven Thunders stayed well back, knowing the dragons could crush them and never even notice.

Tadaka drew his bow and several jade-tipped arrows from his back. The wood of the weapons had been blackened by his fight with the Master of Fire, but he chanted strength into them as he fitted an arrow to silken string. He aimed at the dragons, his limbs trembling from exertion.

"You know that you can't harm him; he's a kami—an immortal," Utaku Kamoko said to the Master of Earth. "Why even try?"

Tadaka glanced briefly at the Unicorn and gritted his teeth. "What harm in the testing, then?" He almost faltered, but the empress kept him from falling.

"Take care," Kachiko said, black eyes flashing with worry. "If you should hit Togashi by mistake . . ."

Hitomi stepped up behind the two of them. "If he harms my master, I'll gut him before Fu Leng has a chance to," she said, placing her hand on the hilt of her katana.

Tadaka ignored her and let fly. The arrow sailed through the air and struck one of the bony ridges above Fu Leng's eye. The shaft exploded in bright green sparks. The evil dragon hissed and spat fire, scorching the mighty timbers supporting what was left of the anteroom's ceiling.

"You're right," the Master of Earth said quietly to the women. "My aim is not what it should be."

"We must bide our time," Toturi said, "and save our strength, should Togashi fail. Pray the Dragon lord can sunder Fu Leng's magical protection."

"He will *not* fail," Hitomi said angrily. "See? Even now he gains the upper hand."

As Fu Leng blinked away the jade arrow's embers, Togashi seized the Dark One's tail in his powerful talons. He unwrapped Fu Leng's coils from around his neck and snapped at the ebony dragon's throat. The Evil One darted back too slowly.

Togashi fastened his jaws around his enemy's neck. Fu Leng bellowed in pain, but the good dragon's teeth did not penetrate his iron-scaled throat. Fu Leng slashed his deadly talons across Togashi's eyes, and blood ran down the good kami's face.

The golden dragon winced and lost his grip on his enemy. Fu

Leng's hind claws raked up, leaving long wounds on Togashi's belly. Togashi hissed and smashed his barbed tail into his evil brother's face.

Fu Leng reeled back, blinking away black tears. Togashi leapt on him, claws flailing, teeth snapping. The force of the blow carried them both through the antechamber wall and into the throne room itself; the floor quaked with the impact.

Fighting to keep their feet, the Thunders followed the battling kami.

The black dragon lashed his head forward and snapped his chin up. Fu Leng's horns caught under the good kami's jaw and pierced his throat. Still, Togashi did not cry out. Rather, he wriggled free and smashed the side of his head into Fu Leng's face. Fu Leng reeled back, and Togashi coiled his serpentlike body around the dark lord once more.

Together, they writhed in a conflagration of fire, talons, and blood. The golden dragon's claws struck hard, but they seemed to leave little more than scratches on Fu Leng's ebony scales.

The Evil One's talons opened up great gashes on Togashi's belly, breast, and back.

"You cannot best me, Brother, anymore than your pitiful Thunders can!" the black dragon hissed. "I am of the underworld, not Rokugan. While you have linked your form and power to this pitiful world, my power comes from the bottomless pits of Jigoku!"

"Your time is finished, Evil One," Togashi bellowed. "Never again will your vile form pollute Rokugan." His immense golden body surged up, propelling both of them into the great ironbound doors of the throne room. The doors smashed into a thousand splinters, and the room's stone walls crumbled where the kami hit them. Rocks the size of boulders rained down on the combatants.

The falling stones seemed to daze Togashi. Before he could recover, Fu Leng thrust them both into the antechamber once more. The golden dragon's neck snapped back, and his head crashed against the oak flooring. The floorboards shattered under his weight, but the impact stunned the Great Dragon.

Fu Leng lunged. His fangs tore a huge chunk out of the golden kami's breast. Togashi gasped and smashed his talons into the side of Fu Leng's head. The blow merely scratched the Evil One's scaly hide. Fu Leng laughed and spit his brother's blood from his mouth.

"It seems it is *your* time that has passed, Brother," the black dragon said.

The wounded Togashi tried to get to his feet.

Before he could, Fu Leng seized Togashi's bleeding body in his dark coils. White steam spurted from the golden dragon's mouth as his evil brother squeezed.

The Seven Thunders stood stock still, rapt in fascinated horror.

Togashi never cried out, though the light in his golden eyes began to dim. He breathed flames, but they shot harmlessly to the ceiling. He tried to cut himself free, but his claws slid off Fu Leng's black scales. He snapped at his brother's face. Fu Leng opened his wide jaws and caught Togashi's snout between them.

The castle quaked with their titanic struggle. A thunderous sound shook the palace to its foundations.

"He's broken Togashi's back!" Kamoko gasped.

The Great Dragon fell limp in his brother's coils, his body shrinking even as it slumped to the floor. Fu Leng raked his iron claws across Togashi's belly, and the Great Dragon's guts spilled out. White steam leaked up from the golden body and through the shattered ceiling, into the storm outside.

Fu Leng laughed, and the sound was more terrible than the winds of a cyclone. The undamaged rafters swayed, and pestilent yellow dust, a mixture of plaster and evil mold, drifted down from the ceiling and settled on the dying kami's body.

Horrified, Hitomi knelt beside her master's bleeding form.

"My brother can no longer protect you," Fu Leng hissed, his voice shaking the pillars of the castle. "Prepare to die!"

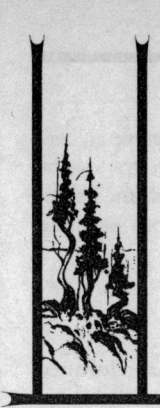

28 THE HEART OF THE DRAGON

Hitomi, my daughter, a pain-racked voice whispered.

"You still live!" The Dragon Thunder gasped. She gazed into her dying lord's golden eyes as she knelt beside him.

Togashi Yokuni nodded his huge head. *The time . . . we spoke of . . . has come. Do what . . . you must.*

Hitomi's Obsidian Hand tingled and glowed with arcane power. She plunged her fist into Yokuni's chest and pulled out the Great Dragon's still-beating heart. She gazed at it only a moment before crushing it in her ebony fingers.

The heart caught fire, burning so hotly that Hitomi felt the blaze through her stony skin. When the flames died away, only a long, dark object remained—the final Black Scroll.

The wizened silk was as dark as midnight and wrinkled like ancient leather. The air hissed with evil whispers as Hitomi held the cursed artifact in her fist. The fingertips of her

Obsidian Hand throbbed with the scroll's obscene power.

You must open it, but do not read!

Hitomi broke the seal and slowly rolled the unholy artifact open. As she did, she squeezed her eyes shut, turned her head away, and rose to her feet once more.

▲▲▲▲▲▲▲▲

The room went cold, and the howling of a thousand tortured souls filled the air.

Fu Leng's glowing eyes grew wide and a wicked smile drew across his monstrous face. His laughter shook the castle to its rotten core. "Do you know what you've done? The original Seven Thunders died to trap my spirit in those damnable scrolls. Since you opened the final one, my power is complete!"

"Now!" Toturi yelled. While Hitomi had knelt at her master's side, the Lion had organized the remaining Thunders in an attack plan. Now, the six advanced as a fighting unit.

Tadaka fired jade arrows at the dark kami's eyes. Kachiko supported the Master of Earth's ravaged body and poured poison onto each arrowhead as Tadaka shot. Kamoko, Toturi, the Hooded Ronin, and Hoturi ran forward brandishing their katana. Yakamo charged beside them, swinging his iron-studded tetsubo toward the evil dragon's belly.

Fu Leng hissed and blinked when Tadaka's arrows struck the horns above his eyes. His arms lashed out to ward off the weapons that slashed at his chest and belly. Metal clanged and slid off iron-like scales. The Evil One swung his huge talons at the Thunders, but they darted nimbly aside. He struck Yakamo with his barbed tail, but the Crab dropped his tetsubo and seized the black armor with his jade hand. Where Yakamo's fingers touched, Fu Leng's scales burned. The Evil One howled with rage. He shrugged his massive form and shook the Thunders from his body.

The champions landed hard. Most quickly scrambled to their feet. Yakamo, though, fell through a destroyed section of floor. He caught the edge with his fingers and clung precariously for a few moments before pulling himself back through.

"Fools!" Fu Leng bellowed. "My power is increased a thousandfold since the opening of the scroll! You are no more than gnats to me!"

"A gnat is difficult to slay with a katana," Toturi noted.

"Not so difficult with fire," the Evil One replied. He smiled and filled his immense lungs with hot, damp air.

Chanting, Tadaka withdrew a small pouch from his ragged sleeve and threw it toward the dragon. As it arced over the other champions' heads, Tadaka spoke a word, and the pouch exploded into a cloud of green dust.

Fu Leng roared fire at his enemies. The flames shot from his mouth in a great ball. When the burning sphere struck Tadaka's jade cloud, it turned and rebounded against its maker.

The fire danced around the evil dragon's head, green sparks stinging his iron-scaled skin. Fu Leng screamed with pain and rage. He reeled back against the crumbling throne room wall. His great horned head smashed another hole in the ceiling. Black rain poured into the room from the sky outside.

"I hope you have more tricks like that up your sleeve," Hoturi said.

"Not nearly enough, I fear," Tadaka replied.

"Don't let up!" Toturi cried. "We have to keep at him!" He rushed forward again as the jade cloud dissipated.

Kamoko and the others followed close on his heels.

Before they reached Fu Leng, though, the black dragon dwindled. "Perhaps you are right," the Evil One hissed. "My true form is too large to combat such as you in this confined space. As a man, though, I can crush you easily."

The evil kami fell back into the demolished throne room, his size diminishing by the moment. As he crossed the threshold, he transformed into a huge, black-armored samurai. His scaly face looked like that of the Hantei emperor, though infinitely more corrupt and evil.

As the Thunders followed their ancient enemy, Hitomi lingered behind, staying next to the body of her dead lord. She had rolled the last Black Scroll closed once more but still held it in her bloody hands. She looked from the scroll to her master's body and then back again. A glazed, faraway look stole over her golden eyes.

Fu Leng's wicked orbs blazed green as he peered into the rain-spattered darkness. Ethereal red energies swirled through the shattered throne room as the dark lord drew energy from the carnage in the city outside. The spines on his armor bristled, and the air crackled with power. An awful smile broke over his blackened, pustulant lips. He threw back his raven-haired head and laughed. "How fitting that I should destroy all of you here, in the very heart of the empire!"

Kamoko charged. "How fitting that in this room we should cleanse the world of your filth forever!" She swung her katana toward the dark lord's neck.

He batted the blade aside with the back of his hand and then smashed his huge fist into the side of her head.

Kamoko sailed across the room and landed hard against the wall near the shattered doorway. She crashed to the floor but then rose and charged once more.

Toturi slashed his blade across Fu Leng's shoulder, but the demon's black-scaled armor turned the blow aside. Hoturi thrust his katana at the Evil One's throat, but Fu Leng ducked away.

The master of demons twirled, kicking out with his right leg. The black-taloned foot struck the Lion and the Crane hard and sent them toppling back. Yakamo and Kamoko rushed forward to take their place.

Blood streamed down the side of Kamoko's head where Fu Leng had hit her. It leaked into her eyes, and she blinked back the pain as she ran.

"Little fool!" Fu Leng hissed at her. "Don't you have the sense to die?" Pestilent green energy blasted from his fingertips toward the Unicorn's slender body. At the last second, Hida Yakamo's tetsubo smashed Fu Leng's arm aside, deflecting the evil spell.

The deadly magic only clipped Kamoko's side, but the blast still spun the Unicorn around and threw her back across the chamber. She landed in a pile of stony rubble. Her head snapped backward onto the rocks, and she lay still.

The Hooded Ronin ran to her side and knelt to tend her wounds.

Fu Leng raked his long talons across Yakamo's chest. The Crab Thunder reeled back, bleeding profusely. The dark lord didn't finish him, though. Rather, Fu Leng turned and breathed fire toward Shinsei's descendant.

The ronin jumped away, leading Fu Leng's aim from the body of the fallen Unicorn. The evil flames burst against the wall behind Shinsei's descendant. His cloak singed with the heat of the conflagration, but the fireball missed Kamoko's prostrate form.

Tadaka stepped away from Kachiko, who had been supporting him. With each step he took into the stone-walled room, more strength flowed into his frame. The rocks whispered to him, restoring a measure of his vast power. He threw his borrowed staff to the Hooded Ronin, saying, "Take this. I don't need it any longer."

The Master of Earth drew a jade tipped arrow from his quiver and chanted power into it as he strung it to his bow. He took aim at Fu Leng's head and fired. The arrow shot straight and true.

At the last second, Fu Leng sensed the danger. He turned his demonic head, and the shaft exploded against the horns of his helmet. The horns shattered, and the evil kami roared with rage. Fu Leng spun, batting aside the Lion, the Crane, and the Crab.

"So, Tadaka," he said. "You would seek to slay me? Don't you realize that you could never harm your master?" Even as the dark lord spoke, the destroyed portion of his helmet regrew.

"You are not my master," Tadaka replied, fitting another arrow to his bow.

"Your body is racked with taint," Fu Leng said. "Thus, you are mine!" He reached out his clawed hand and twisted it into a fist.

Tadaka's body jerked, and he gasped as though his skin were on fire. His limbs stiffened and refused to obey his mind's commands. His bow slipped from his hand, and his jade arrows clattered uselessly to the floor. He fell to his knees and sank to the ground, his charred body racked with pain. The green veins of taint on his skin glowed with unholy light.

"So, 'Master of Stone,'" Fu Leng said, "how does it feel to have met your match?" As he gloated, the other three Thunders recovered and sprang to the attack once more.

Yakamo and Hoturi struck simultaneously, katana and tetsubo pounding into the evil kami's ribs.

Fu Leng shrugged off the attacks and flung his massive arms to either side, smashing his fists into his opponents. The blows sent the Crab and the Crane sprawling backward, their heads reeling.

Toturi gripped the sword of Matsu Tsuko with both hands and brought it down, intending to split Fu Leng's rotting skull.

The dark lord's hands flashed up, and he caught the blade of the katana between his palms. "This is a good blade, a powerful blade, filled with anger and pride. Perhaps it might even cause me harm." Fu Leng laughed and, twisting, wrenched the sword from Toturi's hands. The Lion's katana sailed through the air and landed near the Hooded Ronin, who was tending Kamoko's wounds once again.

As quick as lightning, Fu Leng grabbed Toturi by the chest and lifted him up off the floor.

The Lion felt the heat of the dark lord's grip, smelled the foulness of his breath. He reached for his wakizashi, but the dark lord scratched his hand with stinging talons.

"You are the leader of this annoying rebellion," Fu Leng said. "Thus, it will be my pleasure to kill you first."

Kachiko ran forward. She threw her body against the massive form of the man who had been her imperial husband and clawed at his eyes with her sharp fingernails.

The dark lord threw Toturi against the far wall of the chamber and turned to his lovely wife. "So, Kachiko, you finally show your true colors. I always knew you were weak inside. You could have sat at my feet, ruling over this miserable world. Instead, you'll die like the others. In fact, I've changed my mind about killing Toturi first. I think I'll kill *you* first."

Kachiko opened her mouth to reply, but the dark lord's gaze froze her where she stood. She watched in horror as Fu Leng's taloned hand reached for her white throat.

He grasped her gently, almost lovingly, and slowly lifted her from the floor. Kachiko choked as the monster who had been her husband applied pressure to her long, slender neck. The dark lord raised her face to his and licked her cheek with his rotten tongue.

"Now, my loving wife," Fu Leng hissed, "a final kiss before you die."

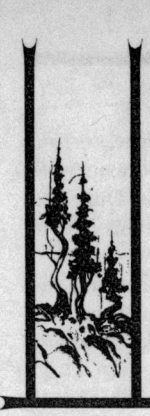

29   THE POWER OF FU LENG

Mirumoto Hitomi watched her daimyo's blood leaking out between her fingers. The deep, red liquid ran in fiery rivers down Hitomi's arm and dripped onto the splintered floor. The blood of her lord became her blood as well, and Hitomi felt the Dragon's soul burning within her chest.

The sights of a thousand years stretched out before her. She saw the world through her dead lord's eyes: clans rising and falling, forests and cities growing and then burning and returning to dust, the never-changing arcs of the sun, the stars, and the moon. She witnessed herself being born, growing to womanhood, becoming samurai.

She saw the world as a kami saw it—small, temporary, impermanent, easily damaged. She understood, then, why Togashi had acted in such subtle, cautious ways. To do otherwise was to risk destroying everything. It was a risk she now shared.

Hitomi felt her emotions burning away. Love, hate, sorrow, fear, it all meant nothing. Such feelings were as impermanent as the leaves on the trees, and of similar consequence. Duty and honor mattered, nothing else. Togashi had completed his duty to the world of Rokugan. Now, that duty was hers.

Beyond the shattered entrance to the throne room, the Dragon saw the other Thunders battling the hideous kami. She watched calmly as Fu Leng beat her comrades back, wounding and perhaps killing them.

Was this what it felt like to be Togashi? Was the whole world just a play unfolding before his timeless eyes? Was there no love, no hate, no emotion at all?

There is another way! something hissed.

She looked at the Black Scroll in her hands. Even in her transcendent state, she could feel the power in the wizened silk.

Read me! the scroll murmured. *Use me as you will! The world is within your grasp if you will take it! Use the power as a kami is meant to!*

In her mind's eye, Hitomi saw fire and battle and blood running in the streets. Lightning flashed overhead, and black rain fell. People bowed down, pressing their faces in the mud, and prayed—prayed to their new lord, prayed to Hitomi. Her benign and twisted countenance hung in the clouds, overseeing all that she had wrought. The whole rotten world belonged to her alone.

Then, the words of Togashi echoed in her skull. *Do not read it!*

Your power will be great! the scroll whispered.

"Yes," Hitomi said slowly. "But I would be truly *damned*." She smiled, "My brothers, I've passed the kami's test."

She stuffed the black silk inside her armor, next to her ribs. The scroll felt both hot and cold against her skin. The feeling didn't matter. It was transient, inconsequential.

Though she was beyond such mortal concerns, she wondered how the battle against her brother, Fu Leng, would turn out. Surely there could be no harm in seeing. Hitomi took a deep breath and walked calmly toward the shattered throne room.

▲▲▲▲▲▲▲▲

Fu Leng pressed his decaying muzzle closer to Kachiko's lovely face. She felt the dark warmth of his lips so close to hers. Her body trembled as he slowly sucked the breath out of her. She struggled, to no avail.

"What's the matter, Empress?" Fu Leng asked. "Are you so terrified of dying?" His rasplike tongue darted out and licked her soft cheek. Savoring the taste of her flesh, the monster relaxed his grip on the Mother of Scorpions ever so slightly.

With a last surge of strength, Kachiko reached up and withdrew the long daggers concealed in her hairpins.

In a flash, she plunged the hairpins into Fu Leng's face. Her left blade punctured one of his glowing eyes. The right traced a long, black scar down his rotting cheek.

Fu Leng screamed and tossed Kachiko against the far wall of the room. Light exploded within her head as her body struck the moldering whitewashed stone.

▲▲▲▲▲▲▲▲

Black ichor and green fire spurted from Fu Leng's wounds. Uncomprehending, he clutched his gore-covered face, pulled his hands away, and gazed at bloodstained palms. "How? She does not have the power! None of you do! I am a god!"

The Hooded Ronin laughed. "You've forgotten something, master of demons. Though your power is complete, it is not the body of an immortal kami that you inhabit. It is the body of the Hantei Emperor."

As the ronin spoke, Hitomi appeared in the shattered doorway. Her hands were dark with her lord's blood. "The boy was *mortal*," she said, her golden eyes blazing, "and now, so are *you*."

"And you face Seven Thunders once again," Doji Hoturi added. "Just as you did the first time you were slain!" The Crane was only a few steps away from the shocked dark lord. He closed the distance in an instant. He slashed his katana at the Evil One's chest.

Fu Leng turned aside, and Hoturi's katana merely shattered a rib plate of the dark lord's black armor. The Crane's blade traced a long gash down the monster's festering side. The wound glowed with sickly green fire.

The evil kami spun and smashed his huge hand into Doji Hoturi's chest. The demon's iron-thewed fingers crushed ribs and sinews. His long claws ripped gaping holes through the Crane's guts. Fu Leng's talons emerged from Hoturi's back, spraying the room with blood. The dark lord yanked his hand back out of the Crane's chest.

Hoturi gasped.

The evil kami brought his fingers to his festering lips and licked them clean.

The Crane daimyo staggered back, his face pale with shock and horror. Blood gushed from the huge wound below his breastbone. His sword slipped from his hand and dropped slowly to the floor. A hollow clatter rang in Hoturi's ears as the blade slid across the charred and splintered wood. The katana spun three times and came to rest near the rubble-strewn entry.

Hoturi reeled away from the dark lord, pressing his hand to his wounded chest. He tried to stanch the flow of blood, but it seeped between his fingers and poured onto the floorboards.

The Crane stumbled toward the doorway. He tripped over some fallen stones and collapsed next to Kachiko's dazed and bloody form. He looked up at the Mother of Scorpions, fear and longing in his brown eyes. She raised her bruised face, and her eyes met his. Hoturi saw green flecks dance in Kachiko's black orbs. Then his world went dark.

▲▲▲▲▲▲▲▲▲

Even as Hoturi fell, Toturi and Yakamo charged Fu Leng. The Hooded Ronin retrieved Matsu Tsuko's blade and tossed it to the Lion. Toturi caught the sword on the run. A curse on his lips, he swung the lion-headed katana at Fu Leng's scaly neck. The dark lord opened his mouth and threw his arms wide.

Black, pestilent wind blasted from the dark lord's maw. The evil gale assaulted Lion and Crab, lifting them off their feet and tossing them across the room.

Toturi landed atop the Hooded Ronin, and both fell hard to the floor. They lay there, stunned. Nearby, Yakamo rolled to his feet and charged once more.

Fu Leng spoke a word of power, and iron chains sprang up through the floor in front of the Crab Thunder. Yakamo smashed the chains with his tetsubo, but the enchanted shackles danced around him like metal serpents. They bobbed and struck, avoiding his blows but bruising the Crab's mighty body.

"Curse you!" Yakamo cried to Fu Leng. "Fight like a man!"

"But I am *not* a man," Fu Leng hissed. "I am a *god!*"

A thick link smashed into Yakamo's jaw, and he reeled back. He regained his senses, but too late. The iron chains wrapped around his muscular frame like snakes around an infant. He fought their power, but they wrestled him to the floor. The Crab Thunder lay there, struggling futilely as the enchanted bonds wound ever tighter around him. Iron entwined Yakamo's entire body, smothering his cries for vengeance.

Fu Leng laughed and turned back to the Lion. Toturi lay insensate atop a pile of rubble. Beside the Lion, the Hooded Ronin rose. Leaning heavily on his staff, Shinsei's descendant struggled to his feet.

"You will not take him," the ronin said, stepping unsteadily toward the dark lord. "Not while I live."

"Then die, both of you!" Fu Leng growled. He spread out his hands, and red lightning blasted forth from his fingertips.

The Hooded Ronin twirled his staff in the air, whispering a prayer to Amaterasu. The long wooden stick blurred into a circle, like a transparent shield. The flute carved into the weapon howled, filling the air with a mournful wail. Fu Leng's evil spell crashed against the whirling staff. Crimson lightning rebounded, shot high into the air, and struck the throne room's ceiling. Beams shuddered and then cracked.

The Hooded Ronin looked up as tons of debris fell on him. When the dust cleared, all that remained of him was a corner of his long green cloak, poking out from beneath the rubble.

Fu Leng laughed and turned toward the only Thunder still standing. The kami's remaining eye blazed with malevolent power, but Hitomi, standing in the doorway, did not shrink from his gaze.

"Will you not fight me, little Dragon?" Fu Leng hissed sweetly.

Hitomi shook her head. "To what end? You have already defeated the dragon within me. I see no point in battling further."

"Are you afraid to die?" Fu Leng asked.

Again, Hitomi shook her head. "I have seen death, and I do not fear it. Nor do I seek it. My duty is to my clan. My duty is to survive. This is a battle for mortals; I have done my part."

"What's to keep me from simply killing you, then?"

A wry smile crept over Hitomi's hard face. "I'm not what I was earlier. Now, I am far more. If you seek to kill me, you will pay a terrible price." She gazed into his blazing eye, showing neither weakness nor fear.

Fu Leng blinked.

Hitomi nodded, turned, and walked away.

The dark lord's rotting face drew into a hideous mask of hatred. Flames licked from the corners of his mouth, and his remaining eye blazed with green fire. He pressed his sharp talons into the palm of his right hand. Black blood leaked forth. The demon ichor burned as it hit the air. Fu Leng chanted power into the blood, and it turned into a flaming sword.

Without warning, he sprang at the Dragon Thunder's back. "I killed my brother today," Fu Leng hissed. "Surely I can kill my sister as well!"

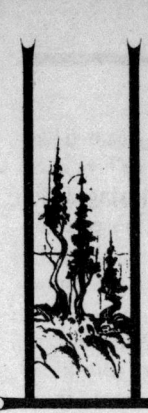

30 THE DAY OF THUNDER

Toturi roused himself, and the dust of battle parted before him. Rubble fallen from the ceiling obscured his view of the room, but he heard Fu Leng bellowing from beyond the heap.

He tried to rise, but his limbs felt like wood. His body ached from combat. He fixed his gaze on the shattered debris and saw the corner of the Hooded Ronin's green cloak peeking out from underneath.

He gave his life to save me, Toturi thought. He vaguely remembered the ronin's twirling staff deflecting Fu Leng's crimson lightning.

A comforting warmth drew over Toturi's body, and he slumped to the floor. It would be so easy to lie down here. So easy to sleep. The sounds of battle were far away, and he was weary to the bone.

Get up, fool! a sharp voice said from somewhere near his shoulder.

Toturi raised his head and peered at the armored form of Matsu Tsuko, standing before him. She looked proud and angry. Her golden armor gleamed like the noonday sun. *I didn't give up my life to have you lie here until you're slaughtered.* Her form shimmered in the gathering darkness, and the rain falling through the shattered roof passed right through her.

The ronin lord opened his mouth to speak, but no sound came out.

Tsuko snarled at him. *You call yourself a Lion? Don't lie there like a mouse! Get up! Fight! Buy back your honor with your life if you must! Fight like a man! Fight like a Lion!* Slowly, the vision of Matsu Tsuko faded. *Fight like Tadaka....*

Through a crimson haze, Toturi saw Tadaka struggling nearby. Fu Leng's horrible taint riddled the Master of Earth's charred body, but he fought it for control. He closed his eyes and chanted a sutra of power. His blistered hand clutched a huge stone. Slowly, the green striations webbing his body faded. The stone crumbled beneath Tadaka's touch as he drew power from it.

Tadaka rose silently, dust falling from his scorched and bloody form. He continued his chant, drawing strength from the room's walls and the untainted earth far beneath his feet. Power surged into the Master of Earth's crippled and decrepit form.

▲▲▲▲▲▲▲▲

The dark lord leapt at Hitomi's unprotected back and swung his flaming sword. It struck true, though the Dragon daimyo was no longer there.

She stood calmly, a few paces to one side, gazing at him.

Fu Leng roared his displeasure. He closed the distance between them and thrust the ebony weapon through her breast. The sword never hit its mark.

Instead, Hitomi now stood behind the lord of the oni. Fu Leng spun on her, opened his mouth, and roared. Black wind spouted forth, tearing through the Dragon's insubstantial form.

Hitomi merely laughed.

"Curse you!" Fu Leng bellowed. "Are you dead already?"

"I told you," she replied, "I am far more than I was before.

I have become the riddle of the ages. I am beyond such petty squabbles now. You cannot harm me."

An evil smile crept across Fu Leng's scaly face. "You have made a mistake, Dragon. For if I cannot harm you, you cannot harm me, either."

"Cannot and will not are separate things," Hitomi replied.

"Then," snarled Fu Leng, "you will not save your friends when I kill them."

"Perhaps I have already saved them. Good-bye, Brother." She turned and walked away. The darkness in the corridor beyond soon swallowed her lithe form.

▲▲▲▲▲▲▲▲

A tornado of rocks and small stones sprang up around the dark lord. The pebbles tore at his undead flesh, ripping it away from his iron bones.

Fu Leng howled and summoned evil energies to disperse the spell. Enmeshed in the whirlwind, he turned and spotted Tadaka near the sundered throne of the Hantei.

The Master of Earth crouched beside the Emerald Throne. Its back and seat had been damaged during the Scorpion Coup, but the stone chair remained solid enough. Tadaka clasped his blistered hands around the throne and sang to it, lifting it lightly in his arms.

The Phoenix changed his chant, funneling the power of his own soul into the throne. As he sang, the green stones changed. They became opaque and shone with the purity of the sun, the blessing of "Amaterasu's Tears"—the power of *jade*.

As Fu Leng dispelled Tadaka's whirlwind, the Master of Earth hefted the throne over his head and threw it at the dark lord.

The jade throne shattered against Fu Leng's iron-scaled body. The room exploded with sound and thunder. Green fire shot up to the heavens. The dark lord howled in pain. Flames sprang up around Fu Leng, clinging to his pestilent skin.

Shards of jade rained back on Tadaka, but he turned them aside with a word.

Burning, the dark lord pointed his flaming sword at the Master of Earth. Crimson fire shot from the tip of the evil blade.

Tadaka drew his jade fan from his tattered sleeve and flicked the artifact open. The fan shattered under Fu Leng's magic, but it turned the evil fire bolt aside. Tadaka dropped the remains of his shield and focused his power once more.

Sharp pillars of stone shot up through the wooden floor. They closed around the burning dark lord like the fingers of a great rocky hand.

Fu Leng swung his blazing sword and cut the stone fingers in half. He strode through the gaps toward the Master of Earth, his eye burning.

Tadaka's eyes blazed as well, but with the purity of jade and the strength of Amaterasu.

The dark lord blasted red lightning at the Master of Earth, but rock rose up and protected Tadaka. Still, the Phoenix master's power waned as he drew upon the last of the castle's pure stone. The throne room walls crumbled.

Slowly, inexorably, Fu Leng strode forward to snuff out Tadaka's life. Crimson bolts lashed the Master of Earth. They flayed the charred skin from the Phoenix's trembling form.

Tadaka thrust his hands forward, pouring every last bit of energy into a final, desperate spell. Jade winds burst from the Master of Earth's emaciated body and crashed against Fu Leng's corrupt form.

The dark lord reeled back, screaming in agony as his skin slowly turned to jade. Deadly blasts of red energy poured from the Evil One's remaining eye, only to be turned aside by the power of Tadaka's spell. For long moments the elemental forces of earth battled the powers of corruption.

Thunder boomed, and black rain fell. Timbers already weakened by the battle cracked and toppled to the floor of the throne room.

Tadaka screamed his agony, his power crashing like waves over the evil kami. In his mind, the Phoenix lord saw the faces of his brother Tomo, of fair Uona, of brash Tsuke—corrupted by Fu Leng's evil—and finally the placid face of his half-sister, Isawa

Kaede. The visions sustained the Master of Earth, driving him beyond the breaking point.

Fu Leng reeled, buffeted by the Phoenix's power. The dark lord's skin burned and blistered. His limbs grew stiff like stone. He called to his minions to draw upon their lives. Beyond the castle walls, they crumbled into dust to feed him.

Finally, the Master of Earth's battered frame could give no more. Tadaka collapsed like a paper lantern folding into itself. The Phoenix fell to the floor, his body little more than a charred husk.

Fu Leng gazed down at Tadaka's pitiful form and laughed.

▲▲▲▲▲▲▲▲

Fight like Tadaka. . . .
Bloody and dazed, Toturi rose to his feet.

31

THE FINAL BATTLE

Her face contorted with pain, Kachiko crawled to where Doji Hoturi lay bleeding. She tore a long strip of silk from her kimono and pressed it into the wound in her former lover's chest, saying a prayer to Amaterasu for the Crane's soul. She held his hand, and tears welled up on her bruised and bloody face.

At the touch of her fingers, Hoturi's eyes flickered open. "Am I in paradise, then?"

"No, damn you!" she hissed. "You're not dead yet! You must fight! Toturi will be killed if you don't. My hip is broken; I cannot stand. I cannot help him. You *must!*"

Hoturi raised his aching head and gazed across the room. Toturi stood toe to toe with the evil kami, his lion-headed blade flashing against the dark lord's fiery katana. Strength ebbed out of the Crane, and he collapsed once more, resting his head in Kachiko's lap.

She looked down at his dazed, confused

eyes. Her tears fell on his cheeks. "Hoturi! Get up! If you don't, Fu Leng will win!"

▲▲▲▲▲▲▲▲▲▲

Toturi brought his sword up just in time to parry a blow that would have split his skull. Fu Leng's blazing katana slid off the Lion's blade, scorching Toturi's shoulder as it passed. The Lion stepped back, but the evil kami bore into him.

A hideous smile wrinkled Fu Leng's scaly, half-human face. "The boy whose form I've taken admired you, once—until you let his father die, that is. He watched you when you came to court, studied accounts of your battles. He memorized every tactic of your swordsmanship." Fu Leng struck high, then low, then to Toturi's gut.

Toturi beat the fiery blade away twice, but the third cut traced a long gash across his ribs. He fell back farther, gasping for breath.

The dark lord laughed. "I know everything that foolish boy knew. I know where you will strike before you do!"

Toturi frowned and spat the blood from his lips. His keen mind flashed back to his previous battle in this same throne room—the battle he'd fought against Bayushi Shoju, the Scorpion usurper.

Shoju had beaten him, then—beaten him soundly. It was the only duel Toturi had lost since coming of age. The Scorpion's graceful movements danced before the Lion's mind; he saw them in perfect clarity, their every detail etched upon his brain. A wry smile drew across Toturi's battered features.

Fu Leng came in, aiming a deadly cut at Toturi's neck. Toturi parried the blow, but instead of aiming a counterthrust at the dark lord's neck, he spun aside, as Shoju would have done.

The demon cut low, but Toturi wasn't where he had expected. Instead, the Lion whirled at the dark lord's side. His katana flashed and bit deeply through Fu Leng's armor and into his ribs.

Fu Leng staggered, blood and fire spurting from the wound. He barely ducked under the Lion's follow-up blow.

Rather than pressing in, Toturi danced away, studying his foe closely.

The monster roared and charged, his blazing sword raised high overhead.

Toturi moved lightly on the balls of his feet, his arms held wide in a welcoming gesture. When Fu Leng swung at his head, Toturi dived under the blow and rolled to his feet behind the monster. He chopped again at Fu Leng's ribs, opening up a gash opposite the one he'd made earlier. As the demon lord whirled, trying to take his head off, Toturi danced away.

The dark lord pointed with his left hand, and razorlike fingernails shot out like darts.

Toturi stepped aside, realizing almost too late that the deadly volley had been only a ploy. He swung his blade around just in time to avoid having his skull crushed. The power of Fu Leng's blow traveled down the parrying blade and shook the Lion to his bones. As Fu Leng reared back and sliced at Toturi's neck, the Lion dropped and with all his might kicked his enemy in the chest. Fu Leng staggered, and Toturi danced back, breathing hard.

Fighting like Shoju may save my life for a while, Toturi thought, but I will tire long before this monster does!

▲▲▲▲▲▲▲▲

"Do you want your friend to perish, and the empire with him?" Kachiko whispered into Hoturi's ear, piercing the red haze that filled his consciousness. Her once-lovely voice, now clipped and filled of pain, echoed inside the Crane's head.

Hoturi felt her tears running down the side of his face. In his mind, the Crane daimyo saw the capital burning. He heard the cries of the dead and the damned as the fire spread from Otosan Uchi over the whole of Rokugan. The Great Clans withered and died, friend and foe alike. The land turned black and evil. Demons roamed the countryside, torturing those unfortunate enough to have survived.

"Save him!" Kachiko whispered. "Please! Do what I cannot!"

Blood leaked from Hoturi's nose, and he tasted the sweet bitterness on his lips. Soon, the whole world would know this taste, this pain. He could not let it happen.

Slowly, the Crane daimyo rose to his feet. He felt his lifeblood oozing out past the bandage that Kachiko had shoved into his riven gut. His breath wheezed out of his lungs in ragged gasps. He retrieved his katana, gripping it so tightly that his knuckles turned white.

Before him, Fu Leng and Toturi stood, locked in deadly battle. The dark lord bore in on the Lion, but Toturi danced away, cutting beneath Fu Leng's guard. The evil kami bled from nearly a dozen wounds, while Toturi seemed little the worse for wear. Still, the Lion gasped for air as the monstrous emperor bore relentlessly down on him.

Toturi tripped over an unseen stone and stumbled backward, recovering only just in time. Fu Leng pressed the Lion back toward a rubble-strewn corner of the devastated throne room.

He will trap Toturi there and finish him, the Crane daimyo thought.

Hoturi willed his battered legs to run. Step by painful step, they responded. The Crane's speed built as he charged across the room. Anger and pride welled up within his shattered breast. He screamed, bellowing his fury against the dark lord.

▲▲▲▲▲▲▲▲

Fu Leng spun toward Hoturi. Surprise flashed across the demon's hideous visage. He retreated a step to face both Lion and Crane at the same time. The evil kami's sword flashed toward Toturi's neck.

The Lion spun away from the blazing katana. Hoturi ducked under the evil kami's guard. He thrust his sword at Fu Leng's chest, putting all his weight behind the blow.

Toturi whirled lightly, his lion-headed blade describing a graceful arc in the air.

Hoturi's katana plunged through the dark lord's black heart.

In the same instant, Toturi's blade found Fu Leng's neck. The Lion's katana bit through the corrupt flesh, shattering the demon's spine and carrying through to the other side.

A look of utter disbelief marked Fu Leng's horrible countenance. His immense body tottered a moment as his head fell to the rubble-strewn floor. Hoturi withdrew his sword from the evil kami's chest, and the huge, scaly carcass toppled. It landed atop the demonic skull, crushing it to a bloody pulp.

Thunder shook the palace, and rain cascaded through the huge openings in the roof. Not the black, pestilent rain of the evil lord, but good, pure rain once more.

Fu Leng's gruesome corpse burned where the rain hit it, dissolving quickly into a puddle of black slime. In moments, nothing remained of the evil kami.

A cry of victory burst from Toturi's lungs. He thrust his lion-headed katana into the air and cried "We've won!"

Doji Hoturi nodded weakly. "Hai," he said. "We've won." Then his knees gave way, and he crumpled to the floor.

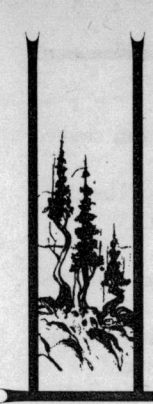

32 GOOD-BYES

Toturi knelt by the fallen body of his friend. Blood oozed past the bandage and out of the gaping wound in Hoturi's front.

With Fu Leng dead, the evil kami's magic also faded quickly. Shaking off his chains, Hida Yakamo rose and walked to the Crane's side. He looked down at Toturi. "Is he . . . ?"

Toturi rose and nodded. "There's nothing more we can do."

"Nothing more . . . *you* . . . can do, you mean," said a pained voice from nearby.

The Crab and the Lion watched as Empress Kachiko dragged herself toward them. A horrid clicking sound came from her broken hip. Despite the pain, she labored across the floor to the Crane's side.

"Can you heal . . . ?" Toturi started to ask.

She shook her head, tears streaming from her black eyes. "Leave us!" she commanded.

Toturi and Yakamo turned away and went to check on the other Thunders.

Kachiko rose painfully into a sitting position and cradled Hoturi's head on her lap.

The Crane's eyes flickered open. "Paradise, again?" he asked weakly, blood leaking from the corners of his mouth.

"No," she replied, sobbing. "Not yet."

He took her pale hand in his and gazed into her tear-filled black eyes. "Forgive me."

Kachiko choked back her tears. "For my son and my husband . . . ? Yes," she said. "And for loving me too much."

Hoturi nodded weakly. "I forgive you as well. I know that everything you did, you did for love."

He squeezed her hand one last time. Then he closed his eyes and died.

Kachiko buried her head against the Crane's shattered breast, her long, black hair covering the terrible wound that had killed him. Rain fell through the broken roof and washed away her tears, mingling with them and Hoturi's blood. For a long time, the sound of her weeping filled the vast chamber.

Finally, Utaku Kamoko came and knelt at the empress's side. "We need to tend your wounds."

Kachiko looked up. "Kamoko," she said, surprised, "you survived."

The Unicorn general nodded. "Hai. All the rest of us live, though there is not much left of Tadaka, I fear."

Toturi and Yakamo were helping the Master of Earth to his feet. Burns covered much of Tadaka's body. Only small patches of ashen, dead-looking skin remained. The Phoenix's face looked haggard and skeletal. No trace of the evil green taint marred his form, though. The battle with Fu Leng had freed him, though it had also exhausted his magic. A fit of coughing shook Tadaka's frail body.

"The ronin?" Tadaka gasped. "Where is he?"

Toturi shook his head. "We don't know."

"All we found under the rubble was his cloak . . . and this," Yakamo said. He held out the ronin's flute-topped staff.

Tadaka took it gratefully and clung to the stout wood. He gestured for the Lion and the Crab to step away from him, and they did. "We've won, then?" Tadaka asked.

Toturi surveyed the rubble-strewn throne room and the scarred and bloody bodies of his friends. Every one of them looked exhausted beyond imagination. His eyes settled on the corpse of Doji Hoturi and lingered there. "Hai," he said finally. "We've won."

Yakamo looked around the ruins. "Where's Hitomi?"

"She left," said Toturi.

The Crab nodded. "Perhaps its just as well. I've no desire to fight any more today."

"We've spilled enough blood here to end all feuds forever," said Kamoko.

"Hai," Yakamo replied. He turned and walked out the ruined back wall of the throne room and into the palace courtyard. The rain and the descending darkness quickly swallowed him.

Toturi nodded and turned reflexively toward his friend Hitomi. The Lion's face fell. He would never again hear the Crane's pleasant voice. "Let's leave this accursed place. We'll send someone back to attend to Hoturi."

One by one, the remaining Thunders nodded, even Kachiko. Toturi and Kamoko joined together to lift her. They carried her out the doorway and made their way through the ruins to the courtyard.

Tadaka clung to his borrowed staff, refusing any help. He staggered out past burning buildings. Bursts of lightning lit the ruins of the palace. A flash of white atop the castle wall caught his eye. He stopped and concentrated, peering through the gloom and rain.

Lightning crashed, and in the pale illumination he saw the Kuni witch hunter standing on the parapet. Her long, black hair waved silently in the wind, and her eyes flashed behind her jade mask. In her gaunt hand she held her forked spear.

"What is it?" Kamoko asked. She followed Tadaka's gaze but saw only the storm.

"Nothing," Tadaka replied. "Just an old debt that needs paying." He turned to the others and said, "I go to fulfill my destiny."

Toturi nodded in understanding. "What shall we tell your clan?"

Tadaka paused and took a long, ragged breath. "Tell them I died from the wounds Fu Leng gave me. After all . . . it's the truth." His black and bloody face broke into an ironic smile.

Toturi bowed to him; the others did the same.

Tadaka bowed back weakly. Then he turned and wandered into the storm.

In a flash of lightning, Toturi imagined he saw the Master of Earth standing atop a ruined wall, side by side with a pale ghost of a woman. When lightning struck in the next instant, both figures had vanished.

Toturi and Kamoko carried Kachiko out of the courtyard and into the ruins of the Forbidden City. Together, they climbed to the top of the battlement and gazed down on the wreckage below.

With their master's death, Fu Leng's troops had fallen quickly. Only a few escaped. Most died before the swords of the allied samurai.

Kamoko's keen eyes gazed over the burning ruins of Otosan Uchi. "There's still life here," she said. "The darkness has ended, and tomorrow brings a new dawn. We can start rebuilding then."

"Hai," Toturi replied. "There is much to rebuild."

Kachiko said nothing, but her dark eyes strayed back to the palace once more. A single tear rolled down her pale cheek.

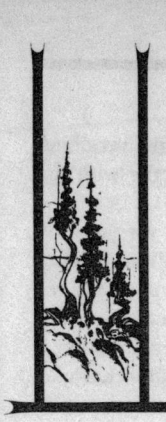

Epilogue:
THE LION EMPEROR

Toku pulled at the bandage on his chest and scratched underneath the silk. "All in all, things could be worse," he said jovially.

"I suppose," Toturi replied. He matched the young samurai stride for stride as the two of them walked through the ruins of the capital.

Toku frowned at his friend. "You should cheer up, Master. Rokugan's free and it's a lovely fall morning; General Bentai's helmet must be pretty pleased with the view from the castle's highest tower. The Unicorn are working with the peasants to rebuild the outer city, and I'm very glad that you and the other Thunders weren't killed battling Fu Leng. Losing only two of you was pretty lucky."

"If you call it luck," Toturi said. His mind flashed back to Hoturi, Bentai, and all his other fallen comrades.

"Well, I suppose you'd feel happier if *you* had died and Hoturi and Tadaka were alive," Toku said peevishly.

Toturi stopped walking and shook his head. "No. Everything turned out the way fate decreed. Who am I to argue with the Fortunes?"

"You said it," Toku replied. "If it hadn't been for you, the whole world might have died. Now we've got the Unicorn helping the peasants, and your friend Tsanuri coordinating the clans' recovery. Things are better now than they've been in years. Even the plague is gone. We'll have this place put back together in no time."

"Maybe. I doubt, though, that anyone will submit to Kachiko as empress. Perhaps she was just another of Fu Leng's victims, but many still distrust her."

"Who can blame them? I don't trust her either," Toku replied. "Once a Scorpion, always a Scorpion, as Bentai would have said."

Toturi sighed heavily at the mention of his old friend. "Let's check in on Tsanuri."

Together, the two of them went to the encampment outside the main walls of the city. They found Ikoma Tsanuri bustling about, shuttling between the Lion troops and the tents of their allies. She bowed low at Toturi's approach.

"It's a difficult job you've set me," she said, sighing. "In the end, you'll probably wish you'd chosen a diplomat rather than a warrior."

Toturi smiled at her. "I'm sure you're doing fine. You fought hard in the battles outside the castle. All the others respect you."

"Respect, hai," she said, tossing her black hair over her shoulder, "but they won't follow me much longer. What we really need is a new emperor."

"Perhaps," Toturi said, scratching his chin. "When the time comes, I'm sure we'll find someone to pull things together—a person both the peasants and the clans look up to, and who can manage the affairs of the empire."

Tsanuri smiled at him. "I think we already *have* a leader like that. I've spoken to the other clans, and they all agree."

"Really?" Toturi said, arching one eyebrow. "Who have they chosen?"

"Some tall, handsome, stubborn fool who's too blind to see that the job's already fallen to him," Tsanuri replied.

A smile broke over Toku's young face. "Oh! I get it."

"So do I," Toturi replied. "Though I'm not sure I like it."

"It's not up to you," Tsanuri said, mock-gravely. "I've told you, all the other clans agree. Whether you like it or not." She winked at the ronin lord and smiled once more.

Slowly, he smiled back.

▲▲▲▲▲▲▲▲

Toku poked his head out of the door and peered into the starlit night. He gazed out over the castle walls and spotted a tall, dark figure silhouetted beneath the autumn sky and looking up at the stars.

The young Emerald Magistrate stepped out onto the parapet and pulled the shoji panel closed behind him. He ducked under the bamboo scaffolding along the walls and, quickly and quietly, walked to the new emperor's side.

The Lion Emperor glanced at his young commander. Then he turned away, and gazed over the city stretching out below the castle. The sound of carpentry drifted up to them through the cool autumn air.

Toku stood silently at his master's side for a moment. Then he asked, "What are you thinking, Toturi-sama?"

"I was thinking that fall is a time when things wither and die. Yet, here we are, rebuilding, bringing new life into the world."

"Hai," Toku agreed. "That's odd, I'll admit. Still, we couldn't have waited for spring to start, could we?"

Toturi turned toward him and chuckled. "No, we couldn't."

"Do you like being emperor so far, Master?"

"I don't feel much like the emperor—so far," Toturi said wryly. "My ascension was only this morning."

"I was just curious, because I think people are asking after you already," Toku said. "In the great hall below, I mean. Wondering where you've gone."

Toturi nodded. "They'll find me soon enough, I expect. It didn't take *you* long to find me." He paused and smiled at his friend. "I wouldn't let anyone else hear you talking to me so informally, though. My advisors would probably insist I have you executed for insolence."

"My etiquette may need polish, but my wits are sharp, and I know you pretty well," Toku said. "That's how I found you so quickly. It'll take the rest of the empire a while to catch on, probably. You'll have to come up with some new ways of avoiding people."

Turning his face up to Toturi's he asked, "Have you heard anything of Kaede, um, Toturi-sama? I meant to ask earlier, but I forgot. Do you think she'll become your fiancée again, now that you're emperor?"

Toturi shook his head. "No, no further word," he replied. "Even the Phoenix—what's left of them—don't know when she'll return." He folded his arms and sighed. "As to whether she'll marry me, the stars only know." He turned his gaze toward the heavens once more.

Overhead, the constellations whirled slowly, imperceptibly, in their preordained paths. Scorpion, Unicorn, Crane, Phoenix, Crab, Dragon, and Lion—all had their place within the heavens and on Rokugan.

"Is there a Mantis constellation, Master?" Toku asked. "I'm only wondering, because if there isn't, Yoritomo will probably want one."

Toturi folded his arms across his broad chest and chuckled. "Yoritomo will have to wait. I think he's garnered enough favors for the moment and shouldn't press his luck. Besides, I've another heavenly matter I want to attend to first."

"Like what?"

Toturi pointed toward the stars. "Do you see the Lion constellation, dancing there next to the Scorpion?"

Toku nodded.

"I want to rename it . . . for Matsu Tsuko."

The young samurai smiled. "I think she'd like that, Master," he said. Then his face fell, "I'm not sure the other lords will go for it, though. I don't think they like change very much."

"No one does," Toturi said, "except maybe the Scorpion."

"I think those guys have probably had enough change to last them for several generations. Kachiko especially."

"Let's hope," Toturi replied. He took a deep breath of the cool evening air. "Anyway, no matter what anyone else says, from now on, those stars will always be Matsu Tsuko to me."

"To me as well, then," Toku said. "Look! She's winking at us!"

Toturi laughed again, his deep, warm voice filling the autumn night. He shook his head and sighed. "From ascetic, to daimyo, to ronin outcast, to emperor. I wonder if this is what the Fortunes had planned for me all along."

Toku shrugged. "I never try to outguess fate. I have enough trouble trying to guess what's for dinner." He paused and looked hopefully at the new emperor. "By the way, Master, what *is* for dinner?"

Toturi chuckled and turned back toward the castle. "Let's find out together."

The Lion Emperor and his young commander walked together to the Palace of the Shining Prince. They slid back the many-paneled paper screen and stepped into the brightly lit room beyond the veranda. Then they pulled the shoji closed behind them, shutting out the darkness.

THE END

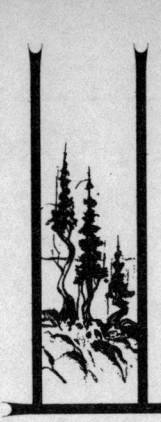

Afterword

And so the Clan War saga comes to an end. I hope you've enjoyed the time you've spent with it. I know that I have.

I've also enjoyed meeting the many wonderful people who—for brief moments of their lives—have chosen to call Rokugan home. If the tales I've related differ somewhat from those you've heard over gaming tables and by the light of paper lanterns, I trust that you will write it off to this author's desire to tell the best stories he could. If my interpretation left out or mistreated your favorite character or offended you in any way—I hope you will forgive me.

I also hope we'll all be able to meet again in Rokugan sometime soon. Keep the lanterns burning.

Thank you Ree, thank you Rob, thank you John Wick, thank you . . . everyone.

Domo arigato gozaimasu.

Sayonara.

—S.D.S.

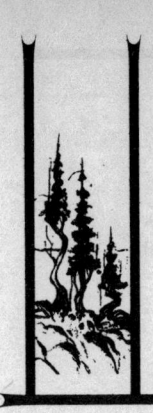

Glossary

Amaterasu—the Sun Goddess
ashigaru—foot soldier
bokken—wooden practice sword
bu—a coin, money
bushi—warrior
bushido—the code of a warrior
-chan—suffix: young one—an endearing term for a child or lover
chi—the seat of the soul, the power of a samurai
chui—lieutenant
daisho—the katana and wakizashi sword combination worn by samurai
dai-kyu—long bow
die tsuchi—war hammer
doji—castle
domo arigato—thank you very much
domo arigato gozaimasu—thank you very, very much
engawa—roofed veranda
eta—the unclean, the lowest caste who do the dirtiest jobs, such as burying the dead
fundoshi—loincloth

fusuma—an interior paper wall (see *shoji*)
gambatte—fight on
ganbari masu—don't give up
gempuku—coming of age ceremony
gunso—a sergeant in charge of a small troop of bushi
hai—yes
hakama—wide trousers
hanko—"chop mark," signature
haramaki-do—heavy lacquered armor
heimin—the peasant caste
iaijutsu—fast-draw sword technique
iie—no
ishii—a game played with stones on a board
jakla—a naga shugenja
Jigoku—the underworld, the afterlife, or hell
jigokuni ochimuratachi—"the lost," warriors fallen into hell
Kabuki—melodramatic theater
kami—the ancient children of Lady Sun and Lord Moon; also, a nature spirit or a god
kanji—characters, letters, runes
katana—the samurai long sword, part of the daisho
kata—a series of exercise or martial arts forms
konbanwa—good evening
kon-nichiwa—good day
kosode—narrow-sleeved kimono (undergarment)
-kun—suffix: old friend
kusazuri—metal skirt, a form of armor
kyuden—palace
matte—halt
mempo—armored face mask
maho—dark, blood magic
naga—creatures with human heads and torsos and snake tails
nage-yari—short javelin
naginata—polearm topped by a sword blade
natto—sweet bean paste
nezumi—ratlings, a race of human-sized rats
ninjato—ninja short sword

ninjitsu—the art of ninja
no-dachi—two-handed sword, taller than a samurai
Noh—minimalist theater
obi—a belt of folded silk
on—emblem or symbol
oni—demon
onikage—demon steed
Onnotangu—the Moon God, husband of Amaterasu
ono—battle axe
otennoo-sama—great lord, highness, exalted one
ratling—nezumi, a human-sized rat creature indigenous to the Shadowlands
ronin—samurai without a master
sake—rice wine
-sama—suffix: most esteemed, lord, master, highness
-san—suffix: honored, sir
seiza—a kneeling position for prayer
seppuku—ritual suicide
shamisen—guitar played with pick
shiburi—flicking technique used to clean blood from a sword
shiro—castle
shiruken—throwing star
shoji—paper walls, exterior (see *fusuma*)
shugenja—a wielder of magic
shuriken—throwing stars or darts
soba shop—a shop offering food and drink
sochu—strong sake
sode—shoulder guard
sumimasen—sorry for causing you trouble
suneate—shin guard
sutra—a meditation or precept
taiko—large drum
taisa—captain of a small unit of bushi
tanto—dagger or knife
tatami—mat for sitting upon the floor
torii—wooden archway with two pillars and a crosspiece
tetsubo—wooden clublike staff with iron studs

tono—lord
tsuba—hand guard on a sword
udon—soup with flour noodles
wakizashi—samurai short sword, part of the daisho; the "soul" of the samurai, used in seppuku
yari—a six-foot-long spear with a straight blade
yojimbo—bodyguard
yosh—"good," an assenting grunt
yumi—a type of bow, fairly short, can be fired by a standing man
zeni—a copper coin
zori—straw sandals